"*Duplicity* is a hall-of-mirrors metafictional masterpiece in which everything has its equal opposite and nothing is quite what it seems. Peter Selgin has found the perfect narrator for his fratricidal-suicidal romp: the dark, mordant, too envious, too inventive, Stewart Detweiler, who lurks in the black, jealous heart of every writer whose cloistered brilliance remains unseen and rebuffed by the world. Here is Stewart's brief moment in the sun, his chops and voice unfettered at last, and to the end—and we are dazzled."
    —Peter Nichols, bestselling author of *The Rocks* and *A Voyage for Madmen*

"*Duplicity* is an entertaining ouroboros of a book—a cleverly collated confession that takes its rightful place in a tradition of doppelgänger-haunted novels that reflect on the instability of identity and the inadequacy of language. While poking gentle fun at plot, clichés, and other elements of conventional mainstream fiction, Selgin harnesses those same workhorses to his suspenseful tale. Smart, funny, satirical, and yet heartfelt, *Duplicity* is a book worth reading twice: once as a metafictional page-turner about twins, accidental criminality, and mid-life malaise, again as an instructive treatise on writing itself."
    —Andromeda Romano-Lax, author of *Annie and the Wolves* and *Behave*

"How to write a blurb for such a stunning novel? *Duplicity* is dauntingly brilliant. Twins may be at the novel's center—equal and opposite twins colliding—but *Duplicity* is utterly, deliciously, singular. It should be taught in both literature and creative writing classes in perpetuity!"
    —Gayle Brandeis, author of *The Art of Misdiagnosis*

"*Duplicity* explodes every rule of the novel, written and unwritten, through sins of omission and commission. It makes a cat's toy of clichés and inflates conceits expressly to puncture them. It breaks the spell of its creation, only to take up the strands and weave them into a more complex enchantment. This is no accident. Peter Selgin is a master who engages the possibilities of the novel from the inside out. *Duplicity* is for anyone who has seen through a novel, and for anyone who has found a world in one."
    —Vincent Stanley, author of *The Responsible Company*

"Stewart Detweiler dreams of writing a book that 'no matter how many times you open it, or what page you open it to, it feels like you've never read it before.' In *Duplicity* he lives the dream. Selgin/Detweiler promises you, Dear Reader, 'the single most unreliable narrative ever composed,' and assures you that he is not to be trusted. He is a man of his word. Book A does indeed falsify Book B. And Book B verifies Book A. Their name is Duplicity, for they are one. Each is absorbed by its equal opposite. And so will you be."
    —H. L. Hix, author of *Demonstrategy*

"Darkly exuberant and completely riveting, *Duplicity* breaks through the metaphorical fourth wall, wrestling with the boundaries of identity, the precariousness of reinvention, and the nature of fiction itself. Peter Selgin's storytelling mastery is on full display in this provocative meditation on the writing life."
    —Amy Gottlieb, author of *The Beautiful Possible*

DUPLICITY

DUPLICITY

a novel

~~STUART DETWEILER~~
PETER SELGIN

with an afterword by
Professor Gayton Sinclair, PhD

SERVING
HOUSE
BOOKS

Published by Serving House Books
Copenhagen, Denmark and South Orange, NJ
www.servinghousebooks.com

ISBN: 978-1-947175-43-3

Library of Congress Control Number: 2020947174

Member of The Independent Book Publishers Association

First Serving House Books Edition 2020

Cover design by the author

Set in Sabon type

Serving House Books Logo: Barry Lereng Wilmont

10 9 8 7 6 5 4 3 2 1

for George

"The water so clear & pale that you are seeing into it at the same time you are looking at its surface. A <u>duplicity</u>—all the way through."
—Elizabeth Bishop in correspondence

"...a great book is a great mischief."
—Robert Burton

To the Reader:

The document that you hold originally took the form of six marbled composition notebooks of the kind still sold today in office supply, grocery, convenience, and so-called "dollar" stores. The notebooks were bound with rubber bands and labeled, on half a sheet of loose paper, in large capitalized letters, "DUPLICITY." The handwriting in the notebooks is of different colored inks—red, blue, black—and increasingly stingy, so small that at first it was mistaken for code.

How the notebooks came to be published is explained in the afterword. For now, suffice it to say that they have been published as discovered, with only obvious spelling and punctuation errors corrected. Since there were so few of them (impressive, given the swiftness of composition), struck-out words, phrases, and sentences have been eliminated. Otherwise, apart from having been set in type with standard conventions of book design brought to bear, the result, down to the pen sketches that are the author's own, faithfully duplicates the contents of the six notebooks.

As to the provenance of the notebooks, who wrote them and how they were discovered and came to my attention, all this is explained in the afterword.

However it is strongly suggested that you read what follows first.

— G. S.

[the notebooks begin here]

"Book B is false."
　　　　—Book A

"Book A is true."
　　　　—Book B

book **A**

I. ARRIVALS

HOW WOULD YOU FEEL IF YOU FOUND YOURSELF DEAD?

How would you feel, seeing yourself hanging naked from an oak ceiling beam, held there by a length of blue nylon rigging rope looped around your neck? How would you feel, seeing the same brown eyes, the same thinning hair, the same hairless pale legs with the same knobby knees, the same size ten-and-a-half feet with the same splayed toes featuring the same ingrown toenails, the same long arms and bony wrists, the same small hands with identical stubby fingers and twin pasty palms held out at the hips as if answering the question *("Why???")* with a shrug?

I might have been looking in a mirror save for:

1. that blue rope around my neck
2. the red-purple blotches at the body's lower extremities
3. and the fact that, unlike me, my doppelgänger was thoroughly, utterly, categorically dead.

That's the vision that greeted me on my arrival here seven or eight weeks ago, on a day as windswept and stormy as the one that finds me here, now, writing these words for you in a black marble composition notebook, Dear Reader, whoever you are.

That's one beginning. Beginning A, let's call it. As beginnings go you can do worse than start with a dead body, *in medias res*—as I teach, or taught, my students at the Metropolitan Writing Institute.

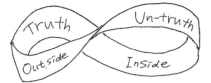

At their extremes all opposites meet. Travel far enough East and you end up in the West. Love and hate are inseparable. In their absolutely pure states, black and white are both impossible and therefore identical. Being born is the first step toward dying. Beginnings and endings depend on each other.

Every story has a beginning, a middle, and an end. This one has two beginnings. It has two endings, too. Like Noah's Ark, it has two of everything. It is, after all, a tale in twos.

A Tale of Two Twins.

• •

It was our mother who launched me on my journey, who phoned me at one a.m. (normally she's asleep by eight-thirty) to say she was worried about my brother. Correction: she wasn't worried, she was hysterical, beside herself. Her voice quivered with consternation. She could hardly get the words out, she was shaking so badly.

"Mother, what is it?" I said. "What's the matter?"

I'd answered the phone in the hallway next to my kitchen. My Bronx apartment was the kind called a "railroad flat," a series of rooms arranged in a straight line running the length of my building, a tenement. In the kitchen, at the center of its brown linoleum floor, a lion-clawed bathtub squatted. As my mother quivered and gasped, I sat in the gloomy kitchen on the lip of that tub, trying to unravel the phone cord (I still had a landline; I owned no cellphone), which, as always, had become hopelessly tangled. It soon became clear to me, through the twisted phone line and my mother's quivering voice, that my brother Greg—or "Brock Jones, PhD," as he was known then—hadn't been in any kind of accident, not as far as anyone, including my mother, knew. As far as my mother knew nothing had happened to him.

Her hysteria was the result of dream.

She dreamed that my brother was a child again, five or six or seven years old, that he was swimming somewhere, and that something—a rope, some weed, a fishing line (a tangled phone cord?) had snagged his foot and was holding him under. She saw it all clearly—as clearly, she said, as though she were watching a movie. There was Greg under water, struggling, cheeks puffed, eyes bulging, face contorted and turning blue. In the film's final frames he opened his mouth to gaping and gasped. That's when my mother woke up.

And that's when she phoned me.

"I didn't know what else to do," she said.

• •

Mother is eighty-four years old. Despite being diabetic, nearly blind, and confined to an assisted living facility in North Carolina, she is in full command of her senses. She's also an inveterate worrier. Not that our mother doesn't have things to worry about; she does. Her kidneys are failing, for one thing. Her ankles are swollen. Her blood pressure is high. She's anemic. She's lost—or is losing—her appetite. She is legally blind. Does she worry about these things? No. She finds other things to worry about, things far less pressing, things that aren't even real. Most of her worries are pure products of her fancy, to where I have to wonder if worrying isn't a passion with her, if she doesn't thrive on the possibility of things going wrong, if anticipating negative outcomes doesn't in some way fulfill her spiritually and possibly even erotically. Not just knowing that things may go wrong, but imagining the very worst possible ways in which they might do so. When it comes to worrying, my mother is possessed of an Olympian resourcefulness.

And though it may seem to upset her terribly, apart from the fact that it distracts her from what should be her real concerns, her worrying does my mother no real harm. On the contrary, it invigorates her. It keeps her circulation, her digestive, her respiratory, her nervous, endocrine, and other systems operating at an enterprise scale. Worrying brightens Mother's legally blind eyes; it gives her something to chew on—the way Taiwanese people chew on betel nuts and Bolivians chew on coca leaves. She tends to her worries like a master gardener tending her tea roses and gardenias, giving rise to splendiferous, fulsomely-scented blooms.

I shrugged Mother's nightmare off. True, neither of us had heard from Greg/Brock for some time. Except for one very brief encounter, five years had passed since I had last spoken with him, but then I hadn't wanted to speak with him. Our last talk ended with me telling Greg (or Brock, though I refused to use that other name) I'd see him in hell before I engaged him further on the mortal sphere. That's just what I said to him. I'll even put quotation marks around it: "…" With that self-consciously literary utterance I'd sent my twin brother packing. Since then I'd had no communication with him.

That was five years ago.

Back to my mother and our conversation. Despite repeated phone messages left by her on my brother's cellphone and with his assistant and other people in his circle, she hadn't heard back from him, not a word in more than three weeks. Suddenly her worries had this enormous new object at their center, this boulder to build a monstrous pearl of anxiety around. Did I share her concerns? Not a bit. My twin had doubtlessly gone off somewhere to "reinvent" himself again, as he was wont to do, as he was famous for doing; he'd made a career out of it, not to mention a fortune. It was probably some sort of publicity stunt. Whatever my brother was up to, for sure he wasn't thinking about me or of our mother. I knew all too well from firsthand experience his capacity to completely forget his family—to forget that he had a family, a twin brother, especially. As far as my brother was concerned, if he considered it at all, to him my existence was at best an inconvenience, at worst an embarrassment.

Anyway that's how I suspected he felt. And who knew him better? We are—or were, after all—twins.

"Will you please go?" my mother said.

"Go where?"

"To find Greg. To see if he's all right."

"Where am I supposed to find him? He could be anywhere."

"I know where he is," Mother said cryptically.

"Where?"

"Your father's house."

"What makes you think he's there?"

"The lake—the one in my dream? It was your father's lake. He's there—at your father's house. I'm sure of it."

"You've never even been to that house!"

"It doesn't matter. I *know*."

"Mother—"

"Please: go there for me. Won't you please?"

Was she kidding? Drive sixteen hours to Georgia on the remote possibility that my brother was staying at our dead father's former lake house—a house that, as far as any of us knew, hadn't been occupied in years, one that should have been sold ages ago, that was no doubt besieged with mice, spiders, ants, termites, mildew, mold, and whatever else flourishes in houses neglected too long? For all we knew the place had burned to the ground or been leveled by a tornado. Besides, my mother knew my feelings toward my brother, they weren't exactly a secret. She also knew I wasn't inclined to take her lurid worries that seriously.

"Mother, it's an sixteen-hour drive!"

"Take a plane."

"I hate flying. Besides, by the time I get to LaGuardia, fly to Atlanta, rent a car, drive two hours to the lake, it'll take as long. Even assuming he's there, which you have to admit is a huge assumption, and assuming that something bad has happened to him (which I doubt), there's no chance I'd get there in time to prevent—"

"But at least then I'll know."

"Look, I'll call the County Sheriff for you, if you like," I offered. "If you're really that worried—"

"I don't want you to call the sheriff!"

"Why not? At least then you won't have to worry."

"I already called them."

"You did? When?"

"Yesterday."

"So—what did they say?"

"They went there."

"And?"

"They said the house is completely abandoned. The lawn is overgrown and the mailbox is falling down, they said. There were no cars in the driveway."

"Did they go in?"

"They didn't need to, they said. No one could possibly have been living there."

"There," I said. "See?"

"I still think he's there."

"Why would you—?"

"It's the third time I've had the dream. I had it last night, and the night before that. Please, Stewart—"

"Mother, if you could just—"

"Please!"

"—calm down and be reasonable. Asking me to drive all that—"

"All right! Fine! Forget it. Never mind."—said in that tone blending disgust and resignation that never failed to inject its subject with the maximum dosage of venomous guilt.

"Fine," I said, trying to match my mother's martyrdom with my own, failing. "I'll leave first thing in the morning. After all," I couldn't help adding, "it's not like I have anything better to do."

"Go now."

"What? Mother, it's one-thirty in the morning!"

"I'll pay for the gas," my mother said.

• •

The fact is I had nothing better to do. For the past few months, when not at work at a meaningless menial job, I had spent most of my time either in my tenement apartment or aimlessly walking the streets, but always alone. I'd grown disgusted with life—not just my life, but life in general. My state of disgust was categorical and comprehensive. The rich disgusted me. The poor disgusted me. The middle class, what little was left of it, disgusted me. Cities disgusted me. Small towns disgusted me (and forget the country; the mere thought of a barn induced in me a state of nausea). People who took advantage of other people disgusted me, but then so did those who let themselves be taken advantage of. Meat eaters disgusted me. So did vegetarians. Vegans were ridiculous and disgusting. Music disgusted me. Books disgusted me. Newspapers disgusted me. Magazines were especially disgusting. Most art was bad. Those who appreciated it had little if any taste, ergo they disgusted me, too. Cats were less disgusting than dogs but disgusting all the same. All modes of transportation disgusted me. Young people were an endless source of revulsion, ditto the old, the ugly, and the infirm. Liberals and conservatives alike made me want to throw up. Religions of all sorts were a source of contempt. The concept of heaven I found abhorrent, though less so than the concept of hell. Computers, cellphones, the Internet, TV, movies, sports, weddings, funerals, bars, nightclubs, restaurants, parties, misogynists, misandrists, fascists, fundamentalists, postmodernists, Communists, Marxists, straights, gays, transsexuals, asexuals, pansexuals, sapiosexuals, sex in general, chewing, digesting, pissing, shitting, farting, shaving, flossing... all, to various degrees, disgusted me. But none of those things disgusted me as much as I disgusted myself.

I was, in a word, depressed.

• •

The drive took twenty-two hours. I drove and drove, mostly through freezing rain, in a twenty-four-year-old Mazda RX-7 convertible with a blown-out muffler, a faulty defroster, a permanently retracted left pop-up headlight, and a cracked windshield. I could afford no motels, so I drove and drove, mostly below the speed-limit, the windshield wipers (which needed new blades) slapping relentlessly, the faulty defroster blowing useless air, the constellations of headlights and taillights blurring in front of me, the pale/ruddy orbs contorted into diamonds and lozenges by a blend of gelid rain, nearsightedness (I was due for a new prescription), exhaustion, and preoccupation.

I was preoccupied—by the journey and what instigated it, but by other things, too, chief among them the fact that my life had fallen apart. My life! As I write those two little words a smile creeps over my face—or I feel it creeping over my face, since without looking in a mirror I can't very well see it. It's an ironic smile, though eight weeks ago I wouldn't have seen the irony; eight weeks ago there wouldn't have been any irony. Eight weeks ago it would never have occurred to me that this thing known as "my life" was negotiable, that it could be traded in for another, like a lousy poker hand or a used Mazda RX-7.

I'm getting ahead of myself. I need to slow down. The point of this confession, if it has one, is to put matters into perspective, not to excuse my actions, but to explain them, to make you understand that what I did wasn't the ghoulish, greedy, selfish act it may look like superficially, to the uninitiated. On the contrary, it was a selfless, noble act, an act of redemption, an act of love.

Ergo I need to ease off the gas. That's right: I'm in a car. We're in a car, Dear Reader: a twenty-four-year-old Mazda RX-7, headed south on Interstate 95 toward a lakeside dwelling that for twenty-eight years belonged to my Comparative Religion and Philosophy professor father, but that has since — along with a half-dozen other dwellings here and abroad — become the property of Brock Jones, PhD, née Gregory Detweiler, my rich and famous bestselling twin.

I say we're in this car, though I'm the only corporeal entity. You are here with me in spirit only — just as well, for your sake, with the heater not working. That sensational opening you read a few pages back? It has yet to happen. We're in the past perfect of that event, that inciting incident, headed toward it.

As I've said, the weather was terrible. It started out that way, with the first drops of frozen rain striking the cracked windshield halfway across the George Washington Bridge, and persisting thereafter, coming down so hard at times I had to pull over, I couldn't see a thing, not with a bad defroster and worn wiper blades, me leaning forward, peering through the napkin-sized patch of windshield that the wipers had some effect on, wiping the condensate away with a wad of paper towel.

I was no fan of driving in any kind of weather, let alone at night in the freezing rain. I had been a New Yorker for thirty-four years, most of my adult life. It was only five years ago that I "bought" the Mazda from a friend of mine whose job had posted her overseas and who offered it to me for 500 dollars. I demurred. What do I, a dyed-in-the-wool New Yorker, need a car for? "I'll have to move it twice a week," I protested. "That or pay through the nose to garage it. I rarely leave the city, and when I do there's always Hertz or Avis."

My friend—Julie's her name—was having none of it. "Why rent a car for forty five dollars a day," she argued, "when you can own one for a few hundred? Besides," Julie added, "once you own a car, you'll leave the city more often."

"And go where?" I was curious to know.

"You'll visit your mother in North Carolina."

"I do that once a year—which, trust me, is more than enough."

"You'll drive to the beach," Julie informed me.

"No I won't," I told her.

"You'll drive to Vermont in October," Julie maintained.

"Why would I want to do that?"

"To watch the leaves turn."

"They can turn without me."

"Really, Stewart."

"Well, they can."

"Don't you ever want to get out of this place?"

"Not especially," I lied.

"Who knows," Julie said, "you may decide to leave the city altogether, once you discover that it's not actually surrounded by a dragon-filled mote."

Julie smiled; I smirked. We were seated at one of the few remaining authentic New York cafés that have all since been displaced by Starbucks. Like most New Yorkers I was defensive of my cosmopolitan provincialism. Julie was all too eager to point this out to me—she who, having recently won both a National Magazine Award and a Pulitzer Prize ("The gift that keeps on giving."—Julie) for her journalism, had been offered a job with the Paris bureau of *The New York Times,* and would soon be relocating to a city twice as cosmopolitan as New York, with more parks, better food, and sexier people. She no longer needed her car.

In the end, Julie didn't want the 500 dollars. When she handed me its keys, the Mazda was in decent condition, the paint job faded, but no dents or scratches. Within three months all four fenders bore the fruits of my inability to parallel-park. A Pepsi bottle fell from the back of a sanitation truck, cracking the windshield. I'd put less than two hundred miles on it when the clutch went; three months later the muffler followed suit. The driver's seat upholstery tore, the dashboard split, the rocker panels rusted, the crack in the windshield grew from a little white worm into a jagged parabola leaping across my view. The retractable right headlight wouldn't retract; the left one wouldn't pop out. The once sexy vehicle's dissolute past had finally caught up with it. It looked like a drunk in the late stages of syphilis following a series of encounters with lampposts. Still, it ran. It delivered me here, to my fate.

• •

That has yet to happen. We're still in the Mazda, still on the road, still heading toward that gruesome opening scene.

If one is inclined to brood, the driver's seat of a freezing, passengerless car on the interstate is a perfect place to do so. Mixed with the rain, memories splattered the cracked windshield: of me and Greg when we still got along, of us riding our bicycles, playing catch, digging a snow fort, hiking in the woods behind our Connecticut home. The memories coalesced into one of those corny seventies montages set to music by Burt Bacharach. There was that rock we used to climb, the one the neighbors found us crouched behind, holding each other and crying when we were three years old. When our mother wasn't looking, we'd wandered into the woods. After searching for over an hour our mother called the police. Soon the whole town was out searching for us, combing the forest. Come dusk they were still at it, flashlights and lanterns lighting up the woods. All the while we crouched there behind that rock, huddled together, shivering and crying a few hundred yards from the house. Much time we spent in those woods, Greg and I. We'd hike to the crest of the hill, to a copse of pine trees there. We would sweep the pine needles into an enormous mound and take turns jumping into it, until our hands and clothes stank of pine resin. We played war games up there. The pinecones made good hand grenades. One of us would throw a grenade and the other would die in a flurry of pine needles. Then we'd race down the hill together, side-by-side, holding hands, leaping gazelle-like over fallen tree trunks and rocks. These and other memories the wiper blades beat back and forth like a team of inquisitors beating a confession out of a subject. Confess! (slap); Confess! (slap). Admit that you once loved each other, you and Gregory, your twin brother. Admit that you loved each other more than you loved anyone else in the world. Admit it! Admit that in becoming estranged from your twin you suffered a terrible, an irrevocable, loss. Though you can't be blamed for that, on the whole you've made a botch of things, Stewart Detweiler. You had it all—looks (slap!), youth (slap!), talent (slap!), charm (slap!), health (slap!), a good start to a promising career (slap, slap!). And you blew it. Admit it! Confess! *Slap! Slap! Slap!*

• •

I'm getting ahead of myself again. Or behind, I'm not sure. My present state negates perspective. There is no longer the sense of life as a journey toward that elusive dot on the horizon known as the future. You're probably too young to remember Jon Gnagy, the goateed, flannel-shirted host of the Saturday morning TV show called "Learn to Draw." It was Gnagy who taught me and a million other baby boomers perspective with his charcoal rendering of train tracks diminishing into the distance, the telegraph poles knitting closer together in their march toward infinity. Those railroad tracks were life. That vanishing point: it held all the hopes and possibilities of the future.

Now here I am at the vanishing point, that tantalizing dot on the horizon.

The rain falls harder, striking the overhead skylight. I'm sitting here with my back to the balcony railing, the one overlooking the main room, with its fieldstone fireplace, its cathedral ceiling, its pair of enormous triangular windows that by day expose a panoramic view of the lake but at this moment frame only watery gloom.

Behind me a rope dangles, the same blue rope that my brother used. One end is tied around the oak beam, the other is braided into a loop just large enough to fit over my head. I've followed a "recipe" I found online. The Internet: so informative. How to make devilled eggs; how to get rid of sugar ants; how to hang yourself.

• •

It was still raining when I got here. And foggy. And dark. I'd travelled a series of increasingly narrow winding roads, each smaller than the last. There was a full moon, or I wouldn't have been able to see at all. The radio was on. NPR reporting the latest calamities. Russian troops in Crimea. Eventually the signal faded. By then I was on an unpaved, one-lane road. No lights, no signs of dwellings. I wondered if I'd taken a wrong turn. Then again it had been at least thirty years since I'd last been to what I still thought of as my father's house.

67 Turtle Cove Drive.

I was about to give up when a strange thing happened. Out of the fog that had settled in, three pairs of red rubies hung suspended in the middle of the road, one pair lower and centered between the two other pairs. I stopped the car. The rubies remained, scintillating, motionless, hovering there in the dark foggy air. They weren't rubies. They were eyes. The two higher pairs belonged to a deer (to the left) and a doe (to the right); the lower pair to a fox. They stood there staring at me, or at my car, a tableau out of an Edward Hicks painting. The Peaceable Kingdom.

I sat there with the Mazda's Wankel engine idling.

Then the deer walked off. The doe soon followed. Only the fox remained. It stood there for another minute or so. Then the fox walked away.

More fog rolled in.

Soon there was nothing but fog. Fog and wind and more rain.

Tentatively, I rolled the car forward. I'd rolled a dozen feet when the Mazda's one working headlight struck a rusted falling-down mailbox with the number 67 on it.

67 Turtle Cove Drive.

I'd arrived.

We—you and I, Dear Reader—have arrived.

2. TWIN HOUSES (THE PAINTER OF GROUNDS)

I ONCE TRIED TO WRITE A STORY ABOUT TWINS—NOT THIS STORY, the one you're reading, but with much in common with it: its twin, you might say. The plot was based on a game Greg and I used to play. In the game one of us would pretend to be a millionaire, and the other a pauper. The game figured into the plot as one that the twins played when they were kids. In my story, the Millionaire (Twin A) is an enormously successful motivational speaker and bestselling author. Twin B, the Pauper, is a failed novelist.

I'd divide the book into two sections or parts, each self-contained—Book A and Book B—and have them printed dos-à-dos or *tête-bêche* like the old Ace Doubles science fiction paperbacks, the kind with titles like *The Sword of Rhiannon* and *Stepsons of Terra*. You would read Book A, then turn the thing over and upside-down, and read Book B—or vice-versa, since it wouldn't matter which of the two books you read first. Each of the books would end where the other began and begin where the other ended, so in theory anyway one would never have to stop reading. The book—or books—would go on and on forever, sustaining and prolonging itself. A literary perpetual motion machine.

The novel's two books would also contradict each other so thoroughly that as a whole it would self-destruct interminably, a chain reaction of equally opposite forces bound together in a ceaseless cycle of mutual obliteration, with everything becoming nothing and nothing becoming everything, on and on forever ad infinitum (as happens, or supposedly happens, when matter and anti-matter collide).

In the aggregate, my twin novel would constitute the single most unreliable narrative ever composed. For this and other reasons I would call it "Duplicity."

To break all the rules of novel writing—that was my intention. And not just to break them, but to break them *hard*. That's what you have to do. First learn the rules, then break them with conviction and without mercy so they stay broken.

So I taught my students at the Metropolitan Writing Institute.

• •

I digress, something else I'd take my Metropolitan students to task for. I should be writing about the rainy foggy March morning I arrived here at what had been my father's lakeside cottage, and where, our mother believed, my twin brother was hiding out.

There I am—there we are—freshly arrived in my beleaguered Mazda. According to the dashboard clock it's just past six-thirty in the morning. Dawn is just breaking. A dense fog has rolled in from the lake that I can't see because it's behind the house—or in front of it, since the house was built facing the water. I haven't been here in thirty-five years. Except for one or two weekend visits by my brother and his wife, no one has been here, as far as I know.

The house looks smaller than in memory. A "modified" A-frame. Even through the fog I can see the yard is overgrown, the garden turned into a jungle, with weeds rising almost as high as the gutter. Where not overgrown the lawn is covered with dead leaves. To the far left of the house: a pile of rotted firewood. To the right a sagging carport with a tarpaulin-covered vehicle hunkered under it. Next to it, an overturned plastic trash container with a fallen sweetgum tree lying nearby. No lights burn inside the house. The place looks dead, haunted, the lake just visible behind it now through the already dissipating fog.

All I've just described is as seen through the Mazda's cracked windshield. The engine still rumbles, the impotent defroster still blows, the wipers still wipe. Except where I've rubbed it with the wad of paper towel, the windshield is as opaque as the fog outdoors. The radio exudes a blend of static and bad news. I'm biding my time, not wanting to leave the car that suddenly feels like a warm, comfortable womb, afraid of what awaits me inside that house—despite that, apart from my mother's dream-born hysteria, there's no reason behind my fear. Why should anything bad have happened to my brother? He's lying low, doing his Thomas Pynchon/J. D. Salinger recluse act, playing hard-to-get with the media and his fans. His last book didn't sell that well. The ratings on his latest PBS fundraiser special disappointed. Or maybe he just needed a break from it all.

So I tell myself as I sit with the staticky radio telling me more about Russia and Crimea ("Dispensing with legal deliberations, despite U.S. and European pressure, a defiant Vladimir Putin announced a swift annexation of the Ukranian peninsula") and daylight seeping into the surroundings. Why should I give a damn, anyway? Since when has my brother given a damn about *me*? Not since his fucking epiphany, his metamorphosis. Since he reinvented himself, becoming rich and famous beyond anyone's dreams. Meanwhile I, his twin, fell to pieces and went to seed. Like this house I'm looking at.

• •

As for the house, like the man who once occupied it, it was once proud and happy. I recall the first summer I spent here with him, with my father. I'd just turned seven. Greg and I used to take turns, alternating summers. Dad would drive all the way up to Connecticut, then drive us all the way back down, the same journey I just took, more or less. It was cheaper than him flying, renting a car, and so on. Or maybe he felt it would be more fun. Apart from stopping at a few roadside attractions (one of which featured a scaled-down Eiffel Tower), all I remember about that first trip here with him is me saying, "Are we almost there yet, Daddy?" pestering my poor father the way kids do. "Not yet, Stewie." I kept having to pee. *You peed ten miles ago! / I need to again. / Can't you hold it, Stewie? /*

No! Instead of pulling into a gas station, my father quoted philosophers on the subject of patience. ("He who seeks the truth must have infinite patience." — Socrates; Nietzsche: "Patience is so very hard that the greatest poets did not disdain to make its antithesis the theme of their poetry.") I peed in my pants. By the time we got here, my father's car reeked and we were both miserable.

Still, as soon as I saw the place, I fell in love with my father's house, and by extension with my father. We hardly knew each other. Greg and I were only four when he and our mother split up. I knew he was a professor and that he lived on a lake. That's all I knew. I'd seen him two or three times, at one or another holiday gathering. He'd arrive smelling of books and pipe tobacco, bearing gifts. Then he'd be gone again until next year. He existed in our lives like a tweedy, pipe-smoking Santa Claus (minus the white beard). It was only after I'd seen his house for the very first time that my father became real to me.

The house was magical. So it seemed to me. Though no larger than the one before me now, it seemed bigger. I remember, entering it for the first time, how the cathedral ceiling lived up to its grandiose name, with its wooden beams and ceiling fans, and the huge triangular windows through which thick rays of sunlight speared the cavernous space at 45-degree angles. Below the windows were two sets of French doors, their venetian blinds raised, letting in more sunlight. Through them I had my first glimpse of the lake, glittering through the slats of the deck railing beyond a phalanx of potted geraniums: this vast, wide, glimmering lake, with a dock jutting into it, and two wooden chairs on the dock, and the lawn sloping down. My Daddy's house! Over each set of French doors he had mounted a wooden oar. At one end of the cathedral ceiling, suspended by a pulley system, hung what I soon learned was my father's pride and joy, his Adirondack guide boat, complete with folding caned seats. Between the sets of French doors was a fireplace, its mantle formed of rugged fieldstones. But I couldn't stop looking at that boat. I was entranced by it. I'd never seen anything more beautiful, its smooth hull a deep ultramarine, its varnished gunwales gleaming gold.

"Daddy, Daddy, can we take the boat out? Please, Daddy?"

"Tell you what," my father said. "We're both sweaty and stinky from all that driving. What do you say we go jump right in the lake?"

To which I responded: *"Yipppeeeee!"* (If that "Yipppeeeee!" didn't represent the happiest moment my father and I ever shared together, it came close.)

We had a good time on that first visit. We did indeed take out his boat, which I kept calling a "canoe" ("It's not a canoe, Stewie; it's an Adirondack guide boat"). Almost every day we took it out, in the mornings before breakfast and evenings at twilight. We swam, fished off of the end of the dock, did jigsaw puzzles, cooked pancakes and French toast, went for walks, barbecued on the deck, watched TV. All very father-son, straight out of the *Andy Griffith* show. He introduced me to his colleagues at the university, those who hadn't left for the summer. My father seemed happy, fulfilled. I had no idea how depressed he was. I didn't know that word, let alone what it meant. My father didn't strike me as sad, let alone as someone who, thirty-one years later, a few weeks shy of his twin sons' 36th birthdays—six months after his 67th—would, as they say, "take his own life."

How? you ask.

He hanged himself. From the oak beam of his modified A-frame. As my brother would. As I myself will soon do. While I still have the chance.

Before they come for me.

• •

That can wait. Right now I'm still remembering—we're still remembering—that happy moment with Dad the first time we visited him here. He was a kind man, an intelligent man, a gentle man. A philosopher, a scholar, a professor. We recall our last summer here with him. We were sixteen. Impatient, impetuous, rebellious, obsessed with girls and sex. The novelty of our father's house, the lake, the rowboat, the hammock, barbecues and puzzles and card games, had long since worn off. We would have rather been back in Connecticut with our friends. We grew increasingly surly, petulant, unpleasant. For the rest of the summer we wore a perpetual scowl.

We treated our father like shit. (Was it really *that* bad? Maybe not, but guilt makes us remember it that way.)

Something peculiar happened during that last visit with my father here, an episode eerily relevant to this confession's overarching theme.

My father and I had had a quarrel. I'm calling it a quarrel, though what really happened was that I abused him and he stood there taking it. It happened during the third week of my five-week visit. I'd been complaining about everything. The lack of young people for me to interact with, my father's cooking (good at barbecues and breakfast, hopeless otherwise; we ate pancakes, bacon and eggs, or hot dogs for every meal), and mainly the fact that, despite the learner's permit in my pocket, my father refused to let me borrow his vermilion 1963 Alfa Romeo Giulietta Spider convertible roadster, the one he used only in perfect weather and otherwise kept tarped under the now tottering carport (his regular car was a 1974 Ford Pinto).

"What for?" he asked me.

"So I can drive into town," I answered.

"Drive into town for *what?*"

I shrugged. "To see what's there," I said.

"I'll tell you what's there, Stewie. Nothing. That's what's there."

You can imagine how pleased I was with this response. Of course, he was right; there was nothing to the town, a sprinkling of seedy antique shops and tattoo parlors, a few hamburger and pizza joints, the usual soporific student dives and strip malls. Apart from the college, the town's only points of interest were the coal-fired power plant at the other end of the lake, with its three-hundred foot tall smokestack, and the grounds of the formerly bustling state mental asylum, now deserted, its brick buildings spangled with kudzu and NO TRESPASSING signs, and which my father and I had already explored several times.

"Besides," my father added, "if there's something you really want to see, I'll happily take you. There's no reason for you to drive alone."

Oh, but there were reasons, two of them. First: to drive my father's spiffy car with him not in it, so I could go fast, as fast as I wanted to go, which was very fast; second: to get away from him, from my father. How I longed to escape him and his bacon and eggs and rounds of Parcheesi and gin rummy and aimless walks along the course of which he would regale me with Spinoza and Erasmus and Plutarch and Plato and Descartes and all the rest of his dull fucking philosophers. It's all coming back to me, this event tinged with shame and remorse. Hey, I was sixteen. Not a prime audience for Spinoza. What I wanted were girls, *a* girl, any girl. To be seen by said hypothetical girl in my father's non-hypothetical Alfa, tooling around in aviator sunglasses with the top down, one hand barely steering, my opposite elbow slung loosely over the driver's side door. In search of this conjectural encounter, I'd have driven all the way back to Connecticut, siphoning gas all the way, on the off chance that said girl would bear witness to this cameo starring yours truly and an Italian sports car.

My father refused to hand over the keys, denying me my fantasy, igniting the fuse of the outburst that would occur a short while later during one of our post-breakfast rambles.

Dad wore his tweed eight-panel newsboy cap—his "thinking cap," he called it. He wore it always on his walks, even in hot weather, and it got, gets, very hot down here. He claimed it made him think better. His "negative capability cap." He had his whatchamacallit, his shillelagh, too, that also apparently helped get his philosophical neurons firing. Anyway, we were walking. Along these lake access roads there's little to see but acres of scruffy loblolly pine, good for paper pulp, but not much to look at. The subject that morning: dualism, the role of opposing equal forces in philosophy, science, politics, and religion—good and evil, darkness and light, mind and body, yin-yang, particle and wave, socialism vs. capitalism. As always my father did all the talking. If memory serves me, he was going on about Plato's first argument in the *Phaedo*, the Argument of Opposites, how whatever has an opposite must come from or be a product of that opposite. For instance, if we consider some entity to be tall, or taller, that entity can only have arrived at its tallness from having been shorter. If something is "darker," it obtained its darkness from a state of being less dark, or lighter. The process works in both directions:

that is, things can become taller, but they also can become shorter; things can become sweeter, but they can also become more bitter. We awaken from the state of sleep and go to sleep from having been awake. Each state depends on the other. Similarly, since dying comes from living, living must come from dying. Life depends on death and vice-versa. According to Socrates, as recorded by Plato in the *Phaedo,* it is only during the very fleeting interim between death and rebirth that the soul exists apart from the body and thus has the chance to glimpse the Forms unmingled with matter in their pure, undiluted fullness. Death liberates the soul, increasing by an order of magnitude its apprehension of The Truth. This, according to Socrates by way of Plato, is why the philosophical soul isn't afraid of death and actually looks forward to death as a form of liberation, as a release from the isolating, insular, soul-crushing solitary confinement of the body.

This—or something along its lines—is what my philosopher father went on and on about that morning during our after-breakfast stroll, with me walking a dozen sullen steps behind him, hearing but only half listening to him, still enormously pissed off that he wouldn't hand over the keys to his snazzy Alfa. How far we had walked, how long my father had gone on about dualities and opposites, I'm not sure. At some point I blurted: "Jesus, Dad, do we have to *always* talk about this stuff? Can't we for once talk about something else for a change?"

My father stopped, turned, looked at me, his eyes wet with dismayed confusion.

"I mean," I went on, "can't we have a goddamn *normal* conversation? Do you always have to *lecture* me like I'm one of your goddamn students?"

My father smiled. It wasn't a real smile but an expression of discomfort and anxiety that tightened his lips so they curved upward at the edges, the same look I'd seen on his face a day or two before when I put a gouge into the hull of his boat, having failed to prevent it from colliding with the dock. I knew then that I had injured him no less than I'd injured that boat, which made me feel awful. Which made me angry—at myself. Which anger caused me to lash out again.

"Jesus," I snapped, "how do you *live like this?*"

"Like what?" My father tucked his chin in wonderment. "How is it that I live, Stewie, in your enlightened objective view?"—asked in the same soft, placating voice he must have used with his students, though I could see he was rattled.

"Questioning everything! Mulling, probing, brooding, analyzing, vivisecting—as if life's some pickled frog your biology teacher made you dissect. Christ, how the fuck can you *stand* it?"

Instead of waiting for an answer, which would only have resulted in another interminable philosophical disquisition, I took off. Not running, exactly, but at a very fast walk, as fast as my two feet could carry me without leaving the ground simultaneously.

I returned to the house. Where else could I go? Except for those acres of loblolly pine there was nowhere to escape to. And I wanted—I needed—to escape. So I went back to the house, which had the advantage of being on water. Dad's house, this one, features what realtors call "big water"—a grand, open view of the lake. It truly is a fantastic view, the sort of view that expands the mind while fostering the impression that all sorts of things—things that bounded by dry land would seem impractical if not altogether impossible—fall within the realm of possibility. It was this view, united with my need to escape, that beckoned me back to my father's house that morning.

The keys to Dad's Alfa being unavailable, I availed myself of the next best, in fact the only other, means of conveyance: my father's beloved Adirondack guideboat, the one I had dented, and that hung by a pulley system from his cathedral ceiling. I had only to undo the (blue, 5/8", nylon) rope from its cleat, lower the boat, open one set of French doors, put the boat on its dolly, grab the two wooden oars from the wall hooks they clung to, and roll the thing out onto the deck and down the ramp my father had built for that purpose, then on down the sloped lawn to the strip of beach a few yards from the dock, where I'd give it a shove and—as it gained buoyancy—jump in. Having maneuvered myself inelegantly into the central folding caned seat, with some initial awkwardness, I'd start rowing. No keys or permission required.

I'd rowed my father's boat often enough with him in the other seat to know the procedure. I'd even taken it for a brief solo run, under my father's solicitous dockside gaze, the voyage that culminated in my dinging the hull into the dock. Now, though, I was on my own, the whole lake mine. It was my enraged, remorse-driven intention to row across it, all 15,000 flooded acres. Or until it got dark, whichever came first.

• •

Though with her stiff prissy Queen Anne-style caned seats she didn't look it, my father's boat—which he'd named after my brother *and* me, with *Stewart* on the port bow, and *Gregory* on the starboard—was an impressively fast rowboat, as fast as a man-powered vessel built for purposes other than racing could be. Even propelled by my less-than-coordinated strokes, she sliced through that morning's glassy water such that within a few strokes all that remained of my father's A-frame was a gray dot on the shore. Except for one flat-bottomed fishing boat there were no other vessels on the lake. It was too early in the day for pontoon boats, jet skis, wake boats, and other pleasure craft. A faint, ghostly mist danced on the water.

A few more strokes carried me out into wide-open water; a few more had me within sight of the dam to which the lake owed its existence. Seeing it, alone out there with all that fresh water separating me from the rest of the world, for the first time since my father had picked me up at the airport (once I grew old enough to fly on my own we'd abandoned the long-distance drive), I felt something close to freedom. Anyway it would have to do.

I rowed hard, eager to be anywhere and nowhere, each stroke carrying me further not only from my father but from myself. I'm not sure how long I rowed—long enough to raise twin blood blisters on each of my palms—when I found myself at the mouth of a cove. By then I'd passed a dozen coves like it, yet for some reason this one enticed me, I can't say why. I steered my father's boat into it. Like most cynics—I was as cynical then as I am now, if not more so—buried alive under my cynicism was an optimist begging to be exhumed. What is cynicism if not a method of pre-empting disappointment?

As the boat rounded the bend and four Detweilers—myself,

my father (as represented by his boat), and his twin boys (ditto)—entered that cove, though the pessimist in me would have denied the existence of any such entity, I couldn't help feeling the hand of God or Fate or Destiny or What-have-you upon that rowboat, guiding it and us: father, sons, and Holy Ghost (me). With each stroke more and more I felt something extraordinary was about to manifest itself. It would appear around that bend, in that cove.

So it did. From behind a stand of pine trees, the same unprepossessing loblolly pines that surrounded the lake, it came into view: an A-frame like my father's in every respect, almost: a modified A-frame with a pitched roof, gray siding and slate-blue shutters, with an identical deck, an identical dock, an identical sloped lawn sprouting identical sweetgum trees. If all that wasn't weird enough, between the two sweetgum trees closest to the dock a striped hammock had been strung, identical to my father's striped hammock, but with different-colored stripes. Otherwise, everything was the same, so much so that for a moment I felt that without realizing it I'd rowed the boat in an enormous circle back to where I'd started.

But this was a different house, in a different cove, one with a less grandiose view, and that, furthermore, faced east, into the rising sun, the glare from which blinded me as I kept rowing, my back to the house that was my object, sighting it from time to time over my shoulder, whereas my father's house faced west, away from the rising sun, toward those sunsets, that were—still are—spectacular.

So this had to be a different house. Still, everything about it, aside from its location, was identical. It had to have been built by the same contractor. For all I knew there were dozens like it dotting the lake's shores, making my remarkable discovery not-so-remarkable. Still, it struck me then as freakish, an episode straight out of *The Twilight Zone*. It wouldn't have surprised me to see my father's snazzy Alfa parked under an aluminum carport in the driveway, or my father himself waving at me from the dock of that alternative, quantumly entangled universe.

I know, I know, Dear Reader. You're thinking: this isn't what you bargained for. At best we've wandered into metaphysical territory, at worst into science fiction—or, even worse, some form of domestic magic realism, which is no better than domestic Parmesan cheese. I can't help it. It's what happened. I'm merely the messenger here.

Determined to have a closer look, I rowed up to the dock. There, with my shadow looming over its boards, I noticed more differences. The dock's boards were warped, splintered, and rotted (to keep them from rotting, you had to seal them once every two or three years). They obviously hadn't been treated in decades. The dock ladder was coated with rust, so were all the cleats and the nails poking up out of the warped decking. Other nails were broken or missing. From frayed ropes three plastic dock bumpers hung, waterlogged and black with lake algae. Like my father's dock, it had a pair of cleats on it.

I secured the boat to the cleats. Then I climbed up on and walked the dock's length to the shore, noting, as I did so, how in need of repair the seawall was, with boards missing and weeds sprouting through the gaps, with some areas entirely breached and sink holes yawning behind the breaches. The hammock was heavy with stagnant green water and rotting leaves. As for the lawn, it hadn't been mowed in a long time. Dirt, weeds, leaves, and fallen branches replaced grass. The house itself, I saw as I drew nearer to it, was in disrepair, the siding cracked, a few shutters gone. Two of the French doors were covered with plywood. A carpet of mulch covered the deck, from which a section of railing was missing. Needless to say the place was abandoned. It looked, come to think of it, like this house when I arrived here eight weeks or so ago, but worse.

A chill passed through me, as if I'd stepped, rowed, into the future, one I'd arrive at again thirty-seven years later in a Mazda with a blown muffler, the one confronting me now, parked in that vehicle in this driveway looking at my father's former house in which I'll discover—

But that hasn't happened, not yet. Well, it has yet to happen for *you*, Dear Reader. As with anything that has yet to happen, there is always the possibility, however slim, that it *will not* happen, that somehow the tragedy will be averted. Think positive.

• •

Like the front door of my father's house, the door to this one had been painted red, though now it looked pink, it was so badly faded. Why was I not surprised when it opened? Inside, darkness and must. I half-expected to encounter not only my father's living room, but Dad himself sitting there on his wicker chair, reading a philosophical tract, smoking one of his plethora of pipes. Instead I found the cathedral-ceilinged space empty, save for a big plastic blue marlin over the mantle, the irons in the fireplace, and a few furnishings.

The furnishings: an artist's taboret, a worktable, and a pair of wooden H-frame easels, all thickly encrusted with paint. Both easels had paintings on them. Whoever lived there was obviously an artist. I examined the works-in-progress. I guessed they were works-in-progress, since they held no discernable subjects, only solid fields of pale color, the canvas on the easel to the right a wan ochre, the one to the left a grayish pastel pink. Leaning against both easels, piled and staggered on the taboret and across the worktable, were other paintings or would-be paintings, on canvases and tablets and other surfaces, all different muted shades: sand, smoke, butter, paste, powder—plowed fields ready to be seeded, cloudless skies yearning for a kite or a dirigible. From a rack on the wall I pulled down one painting after another, eager for a subject, *any* subject. They were all the same, or rather they were all different except for their subjects, which were identical, which were *nothing*.

As I stood holding a canvas, gawking at it, I was overcome by a sense of—I was going to say emptiness, but that's not right. It wasn't emptiness I felt, but something closer to what you feel when you gaze at the stars and try to wrap your mind around infinity. I was reminded of those conversations I'd had with my father, if they counted as conversations with one of us doing all the talking, when he'd try to engage me on some philosophical issue, monologues that went on until at last my silence got the last word. Now that same silence shut me out. It was like flipping through the pages of a blank notebook. Yet in their silences somehow those empty paintings spoke to me, whispering softly—so softly I couldn't hear them, let alone make out what they were saying, or trying to say. I picked up another, and another, always with the same result: more muted whispers. Each blank canvas added to the chorus, until that cathedral-ceilinged space throbbed and echoed with its mute requiem mass of sublime nothingness.

My head ached. I'd seen, or heard, enough. I put the last painting back where I'd found it and went out the way I had come.

•   •

The air had turned dark. I'd lost all track of time. Before leaving, I walked to the side of the house facing the road. Sure enough, there was a realtor's sign there, overgrown with weeds. As I stood looking at that weed-covered sign, shivering, I realized my shivering wasn't just out of fear, but that it had gotten cold. I looked up and saw the clouds closing in overhead, dark ones, and heard the wind rustling the leaves of a nearby sweetgum tree. A storm was coming. I hurried to the dock, untied the boat. By the time I started rowing, the sky was black, the wind kicked whitecaps across the lake. I felt a drop of rain and heard thunder. It started pouring. I rowed like mad.

I thought I'd die out there.

By the time I got back I was soaked. My father's boat was half-swamped. There, standing in the pouring rain at the edge of his dock in his sopping cap with his shillelagh, in a picture that would etch itself permanently into my brain, stood my philosophy professor father, his rain-drenched face contorted with tears, regret, relief. He stood there waiting for me, his son.

3. QUANTUM ENTANGLEMENT

A GIFTED STUDENT OF MINE ONCE BEGAN A STORY WITH THE FOL-
lowing eloquent and, in their way, prophetic words: "Dear Reader,
Fuck You." A fine opening, I thought, as good in its way as *Call me
Ishmael* or *They threw me off the hay truck about noon.*

"Dear Reader, Fuck You." Was ever an opening more piquant
or to the point?

• •

The news report ended. The next program featured classical music,
Von Suppé's *Poet and Peasant* overture mixed with more static. I
switched the radio off. And the headlights. I took the keys from
the ignition. Then I sat there, holding the keys, still unwilling to
enter the house.

I've switched back to the first-person singular. Sorry to exclude
you, Dear Reader, but this story must be told that way. It's a confession, after all, as all first-person narratives are confessions.
We're getting something off our chests, unburdening ourselves of
an experience or experiences that have moved us to where we can
no longer bear to keep them to ourselves. We must share them,
and in sharing them we hope to make you, our reader, understand

what we've been through, and in the process make you complicit in our actions.

To make you my twin: that's the point of this and all confessions. No longer will you be able to say, "Under the same circumstances, I'd have done differently." On the contrary. Under the same circumstances, you would have done exactly as I did *since you would have been me.*

Then again, it's all a conceit. Having read the first paragraph of this testimony, you know perfectly well that I'm not really sitting in a car in front of my former father's former lake house at six thirty (6:45 now) a.m. Furthermore you know—or anyway you suspect—that this chapter will end with my seeing my twin hanging from a ceiling beam.

Still, you're in suspense, as if you hadn't read that first paragraph, or you've conveniently forgotten it. Coleridge calls it *the willful suspension of disbelief.* Maybe that opening was just a dream, like the nightmare my mother had about Greg drowning. These days especially, given all the postmodern shenanigans, with respect to narratives, anything's possible, including my being simultaneously in this car hesitating to enter my former father's former lake house, and—having already entered and seen the awful thing inside it—sitting with my back to the loft railing writing these words in one of a series of black marbled composition notebooks.

There's a scientific term for it. *Quantum Entanglement* ("Spooky Action," Einstein called it), the theory that two objects existing in completely different places may be "entangled," so that whatever happens to one happens to the other. Apart from being in different places they are, for all intents and purposes, identical. The term applies to atoms. But—theoretically, as I see it—what's true of atoms must also be true of things that are made of atoms. Of everything, in other words.

Is it not the case that I, your narrator, sitting in this parked car avoiding what awaits me in that house, am *quantumly entangled* with the narrator who wrote that opening paragraph, while he in turn is—or was—quantumly entangled with the owner of the corpse who is its object? As I will soon be, though presumably I don't yet know it?

If that's not complicated enough, there's also this entity known as "the author" who isn't any of those narrators, but who is, nonetheless, quantumly entangled with each of them—as you, Dear Reader, are quantumly entangled with me.

Notwithstanding which I'm still sitting here, in my car, in the driveway of the lakeside A-frame to which, according to our mother, my twin has retreated: a claim backed by the late-model BMW R1200C Phoenix Cruiser motorcycle parked under the same declining carport under which my father kept the Alfa Romeo. The Alfa is still there. My eyes trace its contours underneath the tarp that, along with the carport's metal roof, is covered with leathery brown magnolia leaves, like a mantle of discarded wallets.

With a deep breath I got out of the car (note sly switch to past tense). Having grabbed my gym bag from the rear seat (I hadn't packed much), I made my way to the front door, on the right side of the house. I knocked. Seconds later I knocked again, louder. I tried the door. It was locked. I circumnavigated the deck to the first set of French doors to find them likewise locked. I tried the second set. Though it stuck hard to the frame, the door opened.

A smell that I'll try but fail to describe greeted me: a blend of ashes, mildew, mold, damp carpet, and something else, ripe and repugnant in equal measure. A repulsive, awful, abominable...*Adjectives aren't descriptions, they're opinions.* I'd never smelled anything so hideous.

"Greg?" I spoke to the darkness. "Greg?"

Then, realizing my mistake:

"Brock?"

Though by then the sun had come up, inside the house was still in darkness. The blinds and curtains were drawn. I found a light switch and switched it on. Nothing. I tried more switches with the same result. Had Greg—I'm sorry—had Brock been living there with no electricity? Without lights, heat, or ventilation? In a house that stank of, among other things, a history that included our father's gristly suicide? If so, he really had gone over some sort of edge.

I remembered that my father kept a box of matches on the mantelpiece. I groped for and found them. By the light of a burning match I searched in drawers for a flashlight or a candle. In a lower drawer I found a flashlight, but the battery was dead. I found some candles. I lit three and positioned them at points along the kitchen counter. Their light revealed to me the inside of my father's house much as I recalled it from thirty-seven years before. A bookshelf moved, an unfamiliar sofa, a different-colored oil cloth on the dining table. Otherwise apart from the smell and the spider-webs that I kept wiping off my face it was just as I had last seen it.

I called my brother's name again, his new name. I shouted it. I opened the basement door and shouted again. Taking one of the candles, I walked to the end of the short corridor leading to the downstairs bedroom, where my father had slept during my visits, and shouted it into there. The bed was made. A colorful spread covered it. If Brock had slept there, he left no sign. He must be sleeping upstairs, I thought, in the loft. Or maybe that's not his motorcycle out there. Maybe my father had taken up motorcycling near the end of his life, unbeknownst to me.

I was about to make my way up the stairs when I saw something else, something I hadn't seen before, a dark oblong shape hanging there, above me, a few feet from the balcony railing. My father's boat, I thought. Yes, that must be what I'm seeing.

But it wasn't a boat. It was too small to be a boat, too small, and—unless the hoisting rope had come off one of its pulleys —oblong in the wrong direction. The oblong boat hypothesis made no sense, but neither did an obscure, human-shaped chandelier. Or was it just a shadow? I thought of Plato's Allegory of the Cave as relayed to me by my father, wherein a group of POWs chained inside a cave imagine the fire-cast shadows on the wall to be men, women, horses... The point, my father explained, lecturing me as usual, is that human beings tend to mistake the conclusions offered to them by their limited perspectives for reality. Plato's Cave had become my father's A-frame, and I its solitary prisoner watching the shadow-play performed by the sepulchral light that had just started seeping in from outdoors, the oblong shadow becoming increasingly human.

Oh God, I thought, *Oh dear God...please...please...no...*

Then I did what I had resisted doing until then. I pulled aside the curtains over the French doors. I opened the blinds on the triangular windows.

The fog had lifted; the skies were a dim, pale, cloudless, colorless color. Shadowy light streamed in. With the house flooded with daylight, I turned around and looked up. And saw.

And screamed my twin brother's name.

4. COFFEE, BLACK

"*In shaping our personalities, which plays the more deci-
sive role: our innate qualities, the ones we were born with
("nature"), or environmental factors, including our experiences ("nurture")? Nature or Nurture? But supposing there
were a third choice? What if the third choice were: Neither!*"
— from *Coffee, Black*, by Brock Jones, PhD

IF I SAY, "DEAR READER, FUCK YOU," IT'S NEITHER AN IMPERATIVE
nor an insult. It's a plea. I'm asking you for what every human being
secretly wants: to be loved unconditionally. Behind this desire to be
loved unconditionally lies something deeper still: the wish for me to
accept my own imperfect self, to embrace my limitations, however
severe and disconcerting those limitations may be.

Having applied all the wisdom of my years of teaching — albeit
at an unaccredited, private learning establishment operating out
of the basement of a Quaker school in Gramercy Park (when
not being used for A.A. meetings) ... having spent all those years
teaching plot and point-of-view, scene and summary, action and
description, analepsis and prolepsis, tone and diction, structure
and style ... having assimilated my teachings as best I could into
my own creative efforts and met with only the most modest success, in these pages I foreswear trying at all.

I give up; I surrender. Dear Reader, Fuck You. That's my new credo, my slogan, the motto inscribed in Latin *("futete, cara lectorem")* on the heraldic banner I unfurl into the gunpowder-and-blood scented breeze.

• •

He had everything to live for. That's what I told myself as I sat with my back to the loft railing, my brother's naked body dangling by a blue rope several feet behind me. *He had everything to live for.* Whereas I, his twin—comparatively speaking—had nothing to live for.

How, you wonder, did it come to pass that my twin brother and I, once so close in spirit, had grown so far apart?

There's a simple answer, one that can be stated in two words. The first word is "coffee"; the second is "black."

Coffee, black. Those two words form the title of my brother's book, his first, a runaway success, twenty-nine weeks on or near the top of *The New York Times* nonfiction bestseller list.

This was six years ago, in the summer of 2008.

No one expected it. I certainly didn't.

Even when it happened, I didn't realize it, at first. Sure, I'd heard of the book. You couldn't help hearing about it. There were ads for it everywhere, in every major newspaper, including full-page ones in the *Times. Coffee, Black* was the biggest bestseller since *Dianetics.* Like that book, the modestly sized volume (185 pages) promised to change your life.

I knew about the book, but had no idea my brother had written it since his name wasn't on it. As far as I and everyone else knew, the book's author was someone named Brock Jones, PhD.

By the time I discovered that "Brock Jones, PhD" was Gregory Detweiler, *Coffee, Black* had been riding the bestseller list for weeks. Even after seeing the author's grinning photo in one of those ads, I still had no idea he was my brother. The salt-and-pepper goatee and Philip Johnson glasses didn't help, nor did the bone-white Panama fedora and the surplus peacoat with the collar flipped up to his ears. Least helpful of all was the fact that my brother and I both shared the same not-unpleasant face with the same ho-hum features: insipid nose, indistinct lips, bland jaw, mundane forehead, irresolute brows…As faces go it was impossible to caricature having no distinct features. Like Quebec or Catalonia, it held territory without sovereignty. Stare at it for as long as you like. Five minutes later, you'd forget it.

Those things alone couldn't account entirely for my inability to recognize my brother's—my own—face. "Prosopagnosia" is the neurological term for it, or "face blindness," the inability to recognize faces, even those of close friends and family members. In my case, though, what I suffered from was more like "contextual face blindness," the inability to recognize familiar faces when presented in unfamiliar, unexpected, and, in this case, inexplicable contexts. "Inattentional blindness" is another term for the phenomenon.

A test was done a few years ago to demonstrate it, what became known as "The Gorilla Test." Subjects were shown a video of two groups of people tossing a basketball back and forth. One group wore black T-shirts, the other wore white T-shirts. The viewers were asked to count how many times the people in white T-shirts tossed the basketball to each other. About halfway through the video, someone wearing a gorilla costume crosses the screen directly in front of the camera. Mid-frame the gorilla stops, waves at the camera, then keeps on walking out of frame. After watching the video, the subjects were asked two questions:

1) How often did the people in white shirts pass the basketball?

2) Did you see the gorilla?

Of a dozen test subjects, fewer than half saw the gorilla. The others were too busy counting basketball tosses. Each time I chanced upon my twin brother's goateed, bespectacled face grinning at me from one of those ads for his book, something like the gorilla test phenomenon must have accounted for my failure to recognize it. I must have been intent on something else, on finishing that article I'd started on page one, or daydreaming about my novel-in-progress. Anyway, I failed to take note of the bestselling gorilla who happened to be my twin.

It took the downtown No. 6 local subway to cure me of my prosopagnosia/inattentional blindness. Mid-November, 2009, early evening, rush hour. I was headed downtown to teach a class. I held in my hand a chapter of a memoir by a troublesome student, the sort I'd get periodically and who tries to take over the class. Janice Hauptmann: such a pleasant name for so huge a pain in the ass. Her memoir was about her "torrid" romance with an older man, a supposedly famous Brazilian flamenco dancer whom neither Janice's classmates nor I had heard of, and who'd been old enough to be her grandfather. Had it been modestly well-written, Janice's memoir would merely have been embarrassing. As it stood, it was egregious. To make things worse, Janice was constantly disrupting the class with lengthy authorial exegeses, elucidating her intentions as if they weren't all too plain. When not defending her own work, she attacked everyone else's, decrying their lack of "literary ambition," a pet phrase of hers. She loved the word "literary," which, according to my dictionary, means "valued for quality of form and linguistic distinction"—qualities absent in her view from her classmate's efforts, but that, again, according to her, her own output demonstrated amply. Needless to say she went after me, calling my critiques "reductive" and "artistically reactionary," meaning, I guess, that I'd failed to recognize, was *inattentionally blind* to, her lofty ambitions and trailblazing innovations. So disruptive was Janice that, one evening after our class, with my blessing, her peers confronted her, insisting that she cease and desist. Since then she had been quiet—too quiet, I felt, ticking away silently like a bomb at her one-armed grade-school desk while other people's works were under discussion.

With the latest installment of Janice's memoir in hand, on that crowded No. 6 downtown local, I carefully weighed my response to her work, wanting it to be succinct, generous, open-minded, neither patronizing nor condescending. I wanted to give her nothing to argue or complain to me about, to throw her no bait, to keep her quiet. Another part of me felt sorry for her and hoped to forestall any discussion that might inspire the others to attack her, as they were willing and eager to do. I wanted to rescue Janice Hauptmann from her masochistic self.

While weighing my words, forced against the wall of that rattling subway train by a crush of evening commuters, my eyes met with those of the author of *Coffee, Black*. Subtitle: "Epiphany at

30,000 Feet." Sub-subtitle: "How Small Decisions Can Change
Your Life Radically and for the Better Forever." This time, rather
than skimming over my vision as it had dozens of times before,
the image in the poster advertisement caught me in its grip. At last
I beheld the gorilla waving at me. Forget the goatee! Forget the
glasses! Forget the Panama fedora worn at a raffish tilt! Forget the
leather jacket! All I saw were eyes, my brother's eyes, unmistak-
ably, staring at me alone of all the people in that crowded subway
car, knowing me as perfectly well as I knew them.

It can't be, I thought; it's *impossible*!

But there was no denying the waving gorilla: not once I *saw*
him. To have questioned it beyond that point would have been like
questioning my reflection in a mirror.

• •

We hadn't seen each other in years. The last time we had gotten
together had been over one of the holidays — Thanksgiving, I think
it was — at our mother's house. It was the last holiday she would
spend in the big white house in West Redding, Connecticut. Not
long after that, Greg and I fell out of touch. I remember phoning
him several times. He seemed distracted. Or impatient. In any event,
he hadn't wanted to chat. I remembered that. I recall asking him
if something was wrong. "No," he said. "Things are fine" — or
something like that. But the way he said it failed to convince me.
"Are you sure?" I asked. Yes, yes, he was sure. Things are great.
Everything's great. "How's Sheila?" I asked. Sheila was my brother's
wife. They'd been married seventeen years. "Fine, fine …" That's all
I got out of him. Then: "Sorry, but I really can't talk right now."

"Okay." I nodded to myself. "Well, I guess we'll talk some
other time."

"Yeah," said Greg. "Some other time. Sounds good."

"Fine," I said and hung up.

But it wasn't fine. A sense of disquiet overtook me. I knew
something was wrong. Was my brother depressed? Had something
gone wrong at work, at the university? He was tenured, so even
were that the case how bad could it have been? Maybe he and
Sheila had had a fight. But it didn't sound like it. Maybe he was

upset with me. When the time had come for our mother to move to North Carolina, I hadn't been very much help. I had no money to contribute, first of all. Greg paid for everything. He arranged an estate sale, hired movers, made all the arrangements. I should have made more of an effort, I suppose. But I was busy with the latest revision of my novel, determined to finish it for my agent. Anyway, I wouldn't have been much help.

Maybe Greg was still sore at me for that.

But it didn't sound like he was sore or upset or worried. It sounded like he didn't want to talk to me, like he couldn't be bothered.

Whatever Greg's reason[s] might have been, why couldn't he *tell me?*

• •

We had always been open and honest with each other, Gregory and I. It wasn't like either of us to keep things from each other. I knew my brother suffered bouts of depression. I knew he had been unhappy with his university job and with other aspects of his life. I knew because he had told me so. When not living close to each other, we would phone each other regularly—to catch up, to commiserate, to share news good or bad, to spur each other on and buck each other up. When I felt down, I'd phone him and he'd cheer me up, or try to, and I'd do the same for Greg. We were like a seesaw. When he was down, I'd be up, and vice-versa. That way we could always depend on each other. Whoever was miserable that month would run down the list of causes for his misery, which list the other would meet with an as long or longer list of reasons why the other's lot in life wasn't so bad after all. "Get a grip on yourself, Stew," Greg would say. "You've lost perspective; you're seeing the glass half-empty." Then he'd run down the list. A few weeks later I'd do the same for him. Granted, when it came to uplifting my spirits, Greg could be insistent, something of a bully even, a pugnacious prosecutor making his case to the jury, badgering and browbeating the witness (me), until finally I'd break down and confess to my crime: not having as awful a life as I claimed. So effective were Greg's prosecutorial methods, I'd hang up the phone sometimes feeling more beaten than cheered up. If only to escape my brother's haranguing, I'd cry "Uncle!" and plead happiness. Still, it worked: I would no longer be depressed.

A week or two later, the same scene would play out in reverse: though my methods were less prosecutorial, more compassionate; less prescriptive, more philosophical.

The point is we loved each other, Greg and I. We were *there* for each other, always. If I've made us sound like the Bobbsey Twins, or like the twins in matching sweaters riding a bicycle built for two in those old *Doublemint* gum commercials, I don't mean to. We were nothing like that, Greg and I. We didn't dress alike, or share dates, or speak to each other in a private language that we'd invented and that no one else understood, or do any of the other creepy things identical twins are known to do. Unlike most identical twins, especially when we were younger, we fought—a lot, gruesomely at times. We wrestled, punched, kicked, bit, and threw things at each other. One time I threw a dirt-bomb at Greg. It hit him in the head and drew blood. Had I known there was a rock in it? Possibly. Another time Greg threw a bookend at me, a wooden bookend shaped like choo-choo train, with a similar result. We were lying in our beds when he threw it. We slept in (fittingly) twin beds. The walls of our bedroom were sky blue with tromp-l'oeil clouds. Our mother painted them. The curtains were blue, too, nautical curtains with lighthouses, bell buoys, clipper ships, lifesavers, and anchors. Greg's bed was by the window; mine was closer to the door and the bathroom. We used to torment each other by farting on each other's pillows or claiming to have done so. Greg would go to the bathroom. When he returned and put his face in the pillow, I'd snicker softly. Greg knew what that meant. He'd sniff his pillow and—whether I'd really farted on it or not—be outraged, hurling his pillow and other things at me, including the bookend, a sharp corner of which caught me on the forehead an inch over my left eye. It must have cut a vein, there was so much blood. What inspired me I'm not sure, but as I stood in front of the medicine cabinet mirror with my brother behind me, my hands covering my face and blood dribbling between my fingers, I cried, "*My eye! My eye!*" Automatically, without thinking. Through a gap between my fingers, with the same bloody but otherwise uninjured eye my brother had supposedly blinded, I took in the horrified expression on his face. Only when our mother entered the scene did I abandon the charade, but not before Greg said to her, his voice quivering, "It's his *eye*, Mommy. I—I think I blinded him!" By then my face was a mask of blood. It dripped on to the sink and the bathroom floor. Our normally worrisome mother became hysterical. It took some doing to convince her that my eye was fine. Had I not still been bleeding profusely, she would probably have slapped me. Instead she got me into my clothes and, in the passenger seat next to her in her boat-like black Mercury, with Greg riding behind us in the back seat, drove me to the emergency room. How many such trips my mother made to the hospital for stitches I lost count.

No, we weren't the Bobbsey Twins or Hayley Mills playing two versions of herself in *The Parent Trap*. We were more like Tweedledee and Tweedledum. *Tweedledum and Tweedledee / Agreed to have a battle; / For Tweedledum said Tweedledee / Had spoiled his nice new rattle.* We cursed. We raised welts. We drew blood. As we grew, the fights got worse, until we risked serious injury to each other as well as to property—not to mention embarrassment, with others bearing witness to our battles, forming enthusiastic circles around us, egging us on, shouting for blood like spectators at a cock fight or a gladiatorial contest. We fought on lawns, in parking lots, on baseball fields, on the float at the town park at Candlewood Lake, in school hallways, in the cafeteria and in study hall. Even in Phys Ed class, where we might have looked forward to the novelty of fighting other people, Coach Myers made us wrestle each other, slapping the mat alongside our identical heads, critiquing our form as we went at it with red faces and veins popping and tears in our eyes.

I remember one of our worst fights. It was over Betsy Butterworth, the first girl that either of us kissed, Greg in this instance, thanks to a lucky turn in a game of spin-the-bottle. That was in fifth grade; the fight was a year later. Meanwhile I harbored a huge unrequited crush on Betsy, one that had me walking six miles through a raging blizzard to her home in the development where she lived, on the off-chance that she would see me passing in front of her house and invite me in for a mug of hot chocolate. By then Betsy had emerged as one of the most popular girls in school. She had that discreet cunning coolness, that knowingness that made people want to be close to her, as if she'd licked the problem of life, as though she held the keys to it all.

The fight occurred at a backyard party to which Greg and I were both invited and at which Betsy was one of the guests. Exactly what set us fighting I don't recall, but in a vortex of grass and dust Greg and I rolled down an embankment into a copse of pine trees, where we wrestled on until a pine needle found its way up my left nostril, causing it to spew blood all over both of us. Through a veil of tears, blood, mucus, and pine needles I looked up to see, among a circle of avid spectators, Betsy Butterworth looking down with a self-satisfied grin, aware, as she surely must have been, that she was the root cause of our shameful display.

When not fighting, though, Greg and I got along well. We laughed a lot. Each of us had a "wicked" sense of humor. We loved poking fun at each other, which is to say we liked to laugh at ourselves, since that's what we were doing. There was that game that I mentioned earlier, the one we used to play all the time, the Pauper & The Millionaire. The scenario went something like this. While a storm rages outside, the Millionaire sits in the lounge of his (cozy) mansion—no, in the smoking room, wearing his (cozy) velvet burgundy lounge jacket and carpet slippers, in front of a fireplace in which a (cozy) fire burns, reading a book of (cozy) poems, listening to (cozy) classical music, sipping port, no, not port: cognac, swirling a…a snifter…yes…a snifter of cognac. Everything cozy, calm, luxurious, dignified. Meanwhile (cue Rossini's William Tell Overture Part II: *Tormenta*, "The Storm," familiar to us from Warner Bros. cartoons, hummed by one or both of us) outdoors the storm grows increasingly violent. In rage, on his hands and knees, the freezing pauper makes his way to the front door of the millionaire's mansion. As the tempest rages, he bangs, scratches, and claws at the door, begging, pleading to be let in. "Please, oh, please, Mr. Millionaire, kind sir, I beg of you; I *beseech* you! I'll do anything, anything—anything. Please!" Meanwhile (cue William Tell Overture Part I: *Ranz des Vaches,* dawn; "Pastoral") the Millionaire clips the tip of a Cohiba Corona Especial Laguito No. 2, lights it, takes an appreciative puff, rolls it admiringly between manicured fingers ... all to the whimpers of his counterpart crying: "Oh, please, please, Mr. Millionaire! I'm so cold! I'll do anything, anything! Please, *please...*!"

Irrespective of our roles in this Sadomasochistic tango, by then both of us would be rolling on the floor with laughter. I know, it sounds terrible. How can two brothers who love each other play such a cruel, malicious game? Answer: *out of love,* with affection. Though we played opposed roles, we were joined in spirit.

The Millionaire and the Pauper: they were one, bound together in each of us. One couldn't exist without the other. Those equal opposite clichés, they represented the antipodal natures existing in each of us: rich and poor; good and evil; dark and light; needy and greedy; raging and calm; winner and loser; weak and strong; triumph and tragedy; love and hate. Each of us is two people. Metaphorically, everyone is a twin. My other self just happened to come with its own body.

• •

We played other games, too, Greg and I, by ourselves, mostly, though occasionally our games involved other people. In case you're wondering if we ever pulled the old "switcheroo," trading places to see if anyone would notice, the answer is: yes, a few times. I'd sit in his teacher's class and he'd sit in mine. The problem was we looked so much alike no one would ever figure it out. We'd have to reveal the deception ourselves, which took the fun out of it.

But then — one day — the ideal situation presented itself.

My sixth-grade classroom was in a portable building. When the elementary school became overcrowded, instead of building a costly addition, the Board of Ed. built a dozen small, shoddily constructed, one-story, barracks-like classrooms in a section of the parking lot. The portables had supply closets in them. One day, before my teacher arrived, I hid in the supply closet. Meanwhile Gregory, who'd dressed the same as me that morning, sat down at my desk. Neither of us knew it, but it turned out that my regular teacher, Mrs. Fisk, was sick that day, so we had a substitute. I can't remember her name. A small, mousy young woman, obviously inexperienced. It may have been her very first day as a substitute, poor thing; it wouldn't surprise me at all to learn that it was her last day, too. Anyway, she arrived, explained that Mrs. Fisk was sick, introduced herself, and started taking role.

The substitute teacher was halfway through roll call when suddenly my brother stood up, walked over to the window, opened it, and—against the substitute teacher's alarmed protests—jumped out and ran off. Through a crack in the supply closet door I saw it all. Needless to say the substitute was unnerved. Still, she finished taking role and started teaching the lesson Mrs. Fisk had prepared for her, about the digestive system (we'd been learning all about the human body), specifically the gastrointestinal tract. She had her back to the classroom and was painstakingly reproducing a drawing of a cross-section of villi, those microscopic, finger-like projections that increase the surface area of the intestinal wall to make for greater absorption of nutrients into the bloodstream, on the chalkboard. While she did, I began knocking on the closet door from inside—a slow, subtle, monotonous rapping such as Edgar Allen Poe would have approved. The substitute looked around, befuddled, wondering where the sound was coming from. As she did, by carefully calibrated increments I started knocking again, slowly at first, increasing the rate, volume, and urgency of the knocks until at last she realized they were coming from the supply closet. She put down her chalk, and, after a moment's hesitation, rushed to the supply closet and flung open its doors. Wearing the same clothes as my brother wore that day, I emerged and walked calmly past her to my desk. To the howls of my classmates I sat down as if nothing out of the ordinary were happening. As the laughter swelled the substitute teacher gathered her belongings and rushed out the classroom, never to be seen again

Oh, it was a terrible thing we did to that poor substitute. Terrible but irresistible, and, you have to admit, immaculately executed. We were given a week's detention, my brother and I, and only because our mother convinced the school authorities not to suspend us.

Thereafter, for a while, the Detweiler Twins were mythic out-laws on the order of the James Brothers or *Butch Cassidy and the Sundance Kid,* a movie that happened to be showing in theaters at the time. It brought us even closer together, which is the point I'm trying to make: how close we were, how much we loved and needed each other.

• •

We used to dream about each other, we were so close. One of us would have a dream in which the other would say something funny, and we'd wake up with identical tears of laughter in our eyes. It happened all the time. Sometimes it happened to both of us on the same night. We'd both have the same or a similar dream. The next day we'd call each other.

"Did you dream about me last night, Greg?"

"Did you dream about me last night, Stew?"

I would never be able to recall what my brother had said in the dream that was so funny. He wouldn't remember either. Maybe we both said the same thing; maybe it was the same dream, an identical dream. (Please forgive these tautologies. Then again, you have to admit they're germane.)

I've never been a believer in paranormal phenomena, in men-tal telepathy or extrasensory perception. But for sure there was some kind of dream telepathy going on between Greg and me.

We were as close as two people could be.

• •

That all changed when my brother wrote that damned book. True, in some ways we had already drifted apart. While I banged away at the door marked "artistic fortune," my brother became a tenured academic married to an attractive, intelligent woman who was likewise professionally accomplished. They lived in a quaint Vermont town in a Queen Anne Victorian with a mansard roof and wraparound porch and a white picket fence, the house butter yellow with cantaloupe and cinnabar trim. Pachysandra swooped up the front lawn, stopping just short of the house like well-trained dogs. Speaking of well-trained dogs, my brother and Sheila, his wife, had a cocker Spaniel, Kiki (a name that, among other things, means "beginning, new life"), her flaxen curls professionally groomed. The porch featured a swing, wicker furniture, and a red, old-fashioned, metal postal box. Its ceiling was painted a pale blue-green that, Greg explained, was used traditionally on Southern porches.

"'Haint blue,' it's called," Greg explained. "It's meant to drive away ghosts and witches."

On my last visit there, as we crept up the driveway in his Subaru, my brother filled me in on the latest improvements to their neighborhood, the new cupula on the Episcopal Church (the old one having succumbed to lightning), the new Starbucks downtown, and how, after years of hounding the zoning board with petitions and letters to the editor, he and his neighbors had succeeded in shutting down a local Salvation Army shelter.

"When you buy a house, you buy the neighborhood," Greg informed me.

Inside, my brother showed me around. Each room was a museum display with the velvet ropes down. Tiffany lamps, Newcomb College pottery, Ernest Gimson cabinets, van der Waals bedroom set, Betchelder ceramics, Liberty & Co. Fabrics, Macintosh wallpapers, beaded curtains strung with tourmaline, amber, rosewood, and hornblende (the replacement white woolen threads stained with used tea bags to match the antique originals); mosaic tables, tapestries and stenciling everywhere. Greg's home was a study in meticulously calculated Victorian clutter, no displaced books or strewn magazines or empty coffee cups or other signs of human habitation. The wicker wastepaper baskets were all empty. A cozy coffin, I thought to myself, with coffered ceilings and central air-conditioning.

"Nice," I said.

"And how's your place?" Greg asked, knowing full well that I still lived in my Bronx tenement next door to a crazy lady who kept a legion of cats, and—judging by the smells that drifted out into the hall—rarely changed their litter boxes.

"Fine," I answered.

• •

But that book was the bitter end. In case by some miracle you don't know about or haven't read it, I'll sum it up for you. *Think positive.* That's my summary. It happens to be the summary of every self-help book ever written, by the way, incidentally. And yes, I admit a certain prejudice toward that genre, an understandable one, considering what's happened to me thanks to it. Still, whether meant to help one reinvent oneself or lose weight or cure cancer or think and grow rich or win friends and influence enemies, such books can all—all—be distilled down to those two words: *think positive.* It was something our mother used to say to us, to Greg and me, all the time, when we faced some difficult situation the outcome of which was at best uncertain, *think positive*: she who herself was among the world's least positive thinkers, a prodigious worrier, a maestro of negativity, a high priestess of speculative anxiety. But when it came to other people's doubts and fears, the solution was simple: *Think positive.*

The key of course is to package that stale tidbit of bromidic wisdom in a fetchingly unique container, to couch it in a beguilingly simple yet novel analogy or metaphor. Do that, Dear Reader, and you, too, may have a runaway bestseller on your hands.

So—how did my twin brother do this? What unique container did he arrive at and fill to brimming with platitudinous positive thinking? His book's title tells the story, one he fleshes out in its introduction and that—again, for the elucidation of those who don't already know—I'll paraphrase here. Some time in the early spring of 2007, my twin brother, Gregory Detweiler, as he was still known to himself and others then, boarded a flight from Burlington International Airport, the closest major airport to the small liberal arts college in Vermont where for fifteen years he had, like his father before him, been a professor of philosophy and religious studies, off to deliver a seminar at a conference somewhere—I forget where, it doesn't matter, one of those achingly dull academic conferences that take place in indistinguishable hotel ballrooms and convention centers in cities across the country. The subject of my brother's seminar presentation was a book originally published in 1908 that was said to contain the essential teachings of one Hermes Trismegistus, who was supposedly a combination of the Greek god Hermes and the Egyptian god Thoth. Titled *The Kybalion: Hermetic Philosophy*, the book is divided into seven chapters or "Principles." The fifth of these Principles (and here you'll see why I'm bringing this up), known as "The Principle of Polarity," holds that all things have a dual nature, that everything has two sides, two aspects, two poles: they contain their equal opposite. By extension, there are no truths, only half-truths, since everything is both true and false at the same time. All opposites being united, there can be no such thing as a paradox—which, of course, is the greatest paradox of all.

That's the gist of the seminar my brother was to deliver at the conference he was bound for when he boarded that flight in Burlington. Greg was ensconced in his cabin class aisle seat when the flight attendant arrived with a female passenger, an Indian or Pakistani woman, by the looks of it. "Excuse me," the flight attendant said to him. "But would you mind terribly much letting this passenger have your seat so she can sit with her husband?" Indeed, the man in the center seat was Indian or Pakistani. At first my brother was annoyed, but when the flight attendant explained that the other seat was in First Class, well, that was another story. Soon he found himself stretched out in a roomy aisle seat in First Class, a mimosa on the folding tray table in front of him, his hands scented and tingling from the warm moist towelette dispensed with stainless-steel tongs. The passenger seated next to him was a burly businessman in a rumpled suit. That, too, is an extraneous detail, the rumpled suit, that is (rule of realism: random details confer authenticity). But he was a burly fellow, the type who, back in cabin class, would have taken up both armrests. As the burly businessman put his headphones on and got out his computer and my brother retrieved the draft of his seminar paper from his carry-on, the same flight attendant who had delivered the mimosa and the moist towelette arrived with the hot beverage cart. "Coffee or tea?" she said, leaning over Greg slightly, addressing the burly businessman, who, with his earphones on, intent on his computer, didn't hear her. She reached over and tapped his shoulder. "I'm sorry?" he said, pulling one of the earplugs out. She repeated her question, or a variation of it. "Would you care for some coffee or tea?" It was then that the burly businessman in the undistinguished suit uttered the two words that would change my brother's life forever, that would make him rich and famous while tearing us, Gregory and I, permanently and inexorably asunder. "Coffee, black," said the burly businessman.

Until then, Gregory, who, like me, drank coffee, had always taken his with cream and two sugars. Like me, Gregory had a sweet tooth. The thought of drinking black coffee repulsed him, as it did me. Now, my brother understood—as do I—that there are indeed those who prefer their coffee black, for whom drinking coffee with cream (or milk) and sugar is anathema, who consider it to be no less repugnant than Gregory and I considered the idea of drinking pure, harsh, black, bitter coffee, coffee unsoftened by milk, unsweetened by sugar: repugnant. To such people, drinking coffee with milk and sugar is (here I'm guessing) tantamount to drinking hot melted coffee ice cream. Now, I don't know about you, Dear Reader, but I happen to like coffee ice cream. Should the coffee ice cream be melted, though I might not prefer or go out of my way to encounter it in such a state, I would not necessarily consider that to be a reason to not eat—or rather, to not drink—it. After all, the flavor's the same, as are the ingredients. The same is no less true of *warm* melted coffee ice cream—and, by logical extension, of hot melted coffee ice cream, which, for all intents and purposes, except for the richer texture, is identical to—*is*, in point of fact—coffee with milk and sugar. But not everyone likes coffee ice cream, therefore not everyone likes melted coffee ice cream, hence not everyone likes warm melted coffee ice cream, consequently not everyone likes hot melted coffee ice cream, ergo not everyone likes coffee with milk and sugar. Be all that as it may, still, all the same, notwithstanding which, my brother Gregory found it difficult, as do I, to grasp how anyone could actually enjoy drinking black coffee. Given no choice but to drink either coffee with milk and or cream and sugar, and not drinking coffee at all, not drinking coffee at all would make sense. But drinking *black coffee*? Bitter, foreboding, gloomy, sepulchral, dreary, cheerless, Stygian—those are the terms, the adjectives, that come to my mind, and that came to my brother's mind, whenever he found himself confronted by or contemplating "black coffee." As for people who took their coffee black, there was something sinisterly austere about them, an extreme willingness if not an eagerness to endure deprivation, a quality shared by priests, monks, hermits, and other ascetics, who, when not flagellating or immolating themselves for the sakes of their souls, fasted, abstained from sex, slept on hard floors, wore hair-shirts, ate grass, and tied themselves to rocks. He felt similarly, my brother did, toward those who took their whisky neat (like me, Greg didn't care for whisky at all, but if forced to drink it he'd order it with a splash of soda), who ate their toast without butter, who refused air-conditioning on sweltering days and slept with no pillow under their heads, who eschewed the aspirin, the Percodan, the Vicodin, the epidural, the morphine drip, who had their teeth drilled without nitrous oxide or Novocain. On one hand, he couldn't help admiring such people and envying them their self-discipline. On the other, he found them deeply, deeply disturbing. Why do without such things when you could do with them? Why deny yourself a little kindness, a little softness, a little sweetness, a little relief from the hardships and cruelties of life? Why deprive yourself of such trivial, token gestures of self-love, things that, while hurting no one, gave such comfort? Why? my brother asked himself. Why? Why? *Why*???

This entire inquisition, by the way, this protracted rant, squeezed itself into the sliver of space between the burly passenger's response to the flight attendant's beverage query and the moment when, armed with the same routine and rudimentary question, the same flight attendant turned to my brother and said:

"And for you, sir?"

"Coffee, black," my brother responded.

There, in that moment, with that response, my brother's future and mine were sealed. The moment in which I write these words, the conditions under which I write them, were not only decided then, but engineered down to the smallest detail: this loft, this rainy day, this marbled composition notebook, this pen, the length of 5/8-inch blue marine rope dangling from a ceiling beam behind me. From the moment when my brother uttered those two

fateful words aboard that flight bound from Burlington to wherever, a straight line can be drawn through his ear-popping ascent
to fame and fortune to me, here, in his place—in his shoes, as it
were—penning this, my confession, to you, Dear Reader.

From those two words came the NY Times nonfiction bestseller titled Coffee, Black. From those words came my brother's
discovery that at any given moment we can reinvent ourselves:
we can choose to be someone other than who we've been. Not
only can we make that choice, we can make it spontaneously, with
little or no forethought or pre-planning; and do so easily, effort-
lessly, in a flash, on the fly. Contrary to common wisdom, and
in particular to the two prevalent theories as to when, how, on
what basis, and by what forces human personalities are formed
(innately or natively, based on genetic composition; or empirically
and behaviorally, based on environmental and experiential factors such as parenting and education)...my brother posited—no,
he did more than posit; he demonstrated—that our personalities
can be thoroughly reconfigured by ourselves alone and at will. To
the five-centuries-old Nature vs. Nurture debate my twin brother
added a bold, third option, namely: Neither.

• •

In fact "Nature, Nurture, or Neither?" is the title of Coffee, Black's
second chapter, which sets forth its premise. From there its author
goes on to explain (the present tense is indicated, the book having
remained, since it was first published, not only in print but on
bestseller lists) how his sudden, airborne change of coffee-drinking
preferences opened the way to a series of pattern-altering changes,
starting with other modest modifications: showering at night instead
of in the morning (then switching to baths); wearing pajamas to
bed; subscribing to a different newspaper; installing the toilet paper
the other way; wearing shirts with button-down collars; changing
the style of knot in his ties; trading Bach first for Beethoven then
for Bono, gin for scotch, wingtips for penny loafers...that sort of
thing. From there the changes grew larger: the now six-year-old
beige Subaru became a new, firecracker red Jeep Wrangler Rubicon;
the style of furnishings in his home went from Orientalist Victorian

clutter to mid-century modern.

But Greg's changes went far beyond mere habits and superficial styles; they extended to entire value systems. His politics grew more liberal; his spiritual outlook less pessimistic. Where before he had been a staunch atheist, now he not only accepted the possibility of a personal God, he embraced it wholeheartedly. He even went to church, the Episcopal Church down the street from his home (the one with the new steeple), something that, apart from the occasional wedding or funeral, neither of us had done since we were children.

As described in his book, along with these changes, in conjunction with them, his outlook on life changed noticeably. He felt (he writes) like a different man; indeed, he *was* a different man. There could be no question about it. He felt different in his gestures, different in his bones and in his blood. His skin felt different on his face. When he smiled, he felt the difference in the tension of his muscles and nerves, and he smiled more often, much more often than he'd smiled before. He felt it in the peristaltic movements of his bowels and in the spasms, flow, and contractions of his bladder. His erections felt different; it might have been the power of suggestion, or a placebo effect of all the other changes, but it seemed to him that they were stronger and lasted longer, and that, furthermore, his sexual organ, by what might be called immaculate enhancement, had grown markedly larger in all three of its primary states: erect, tumescent, and flaccid (all this as reported in his book; is it any wonder it sold three million copies in its first year?). His breath was sweeter; his teeth whiter; his hair thicker; his hairline, which for years had been receding, seemed no longer to be doing so. He had much more energy and enthusiasm. He took up cross-country skiing, racketball, even basketball—a sport that, once upon a time, like me, having had neither the height nor the aptitude for it, he'd detested. He installed a basketball hoop in his driveway. There, evenings at dusk, he practiced with such fervor his wife literally had to beg him to come in for supper.

Each of these facts, these observations about himself, made their way into a small spiral notebook my brother started carrying and that formed the basis of what became *Coffee, Black*. For he knew, he understood, that something extraordinary was happening, that he was undergoing a total reconfiguration, a metamorphosis as comprehensive as the one that transforms poor Gregor Samsa into a giant beetle in his bed, but of a more positive nature, and by his own choosing. Each morning Greg exercised: at first a winded, ruddy-faced, one-mile jog. Then two miles, then three, then five. His standing pulse went from eighty-five to forty-eight, Olympic athlete range. Incongruously and against Sheila's protests, he took up smoking, something else he'd never done before: not cigarettes: a pipe, like our father: a long-stemmed Churchwarden of burnished rosewood, also the occasional cigar, as in the Pauper & the Millionaire skit he and I performed together (did he sip cognac from a snifter and wear a velvet smoking jacket? His book doesn't say.). He dyed his hair and wore it long and parted down the middle, donned the Philip Johnson spectacles and white fedora, traded in his button-down Oxfords for chenille jerseys and designer t-shirts, grew the goatee...

So complete was my brother's transformation, his metamorphosis, that—as he writes in *Coffee, Black*—"Whenever I'd chance upon a snapshot or photograph of my 'old self,' though I would recognize him, it was as if I were seeing not myself or even an earlier incarnation of myself, but an entirely different person, my doppelgänger, or maybe my twin, someone who happened to share my DNA and many of my physical characteristics, but who was decidedly, unquestionably, not—and had never been—me." (The author failed to note that he had an *actual* identical twin brother: yours truly. He failed to mention it anywhere in the body of his 185-page book. Nor did any mention of this trivial fact appear anywhere within the book's front or back matter.)

Meanwhile my brother had already started work on what would be his book. At first he had intended only a short paper of some kind. The paper's working title was "Nature, Nurture, Neither: A Personal Experience of Behavior Modification as Related to Nietzsche's *Will to Power* and its Implications for Social Philosophy." The paper has more to do with psychology than philosophy or religion. At any rate—and as its overstuffed title suggests—it quickly burst its boundaries, swelling to fifty, seventy-five, one-hundred, two-hundred pages ... till, at two-hundred and sixty five pages, he had the manuscript of a full-length book, one he retitled "Coffee, Black."

He also changed the author's name. Thenceforth, on the printed page and elsewhere, he would be "Brock Jones, PhD."

From the time my brother uttered those two fateful words aboard that flight to wherever he'd been going to deliver that seminar on *The Kybalion*, to the official launch date for *Coffee, Black*, exactly one year—three-hundred and sixty-five days—had elapsed: an item of trivia that, having made it into the book's preface, was not lost on its fervid readers.

• •

All this time my brother was still living in Vermont, still working at the small liberal arts college where for twenty-five years he'd been a professor in the Department of Philosophy and Religious Studies. For the last seventeen of those twenty-five years he'd been married to Sheila. A lovely woman. Kind, attractive, practical ... self-effacing ... shy, I guess you would say. Petite, brunette, freckled. Not my type (we had different tastes in women), but unquestionably attractive. She too was employed by the small liberal arts college, not as a professor, but by Campus Counseling as a Licensed Clinical Social Worker, a vocation that she practiced on a freelance basis as well.

The same week my brother completed his book, he and Sheila celebrated their eighteenth wedding anniversary. But their marriage, along with my brother's employment status and everything else in his life that hadn't already been changed, was about to. *Coffee, Black* would change it. Rather, the changes that my brother had already made to his life, changes that were both the subject of his book and its cause, set off an unstoppable sequence of deviations, a chain reaction or "snowball effect," so named for its similarity to a snowball rolling down a snow-covered hillside, picking up more and more mass (snow) and momentum (speed) as it rolls along. From an initial state of relatively small significance (ordering a cup of coffee black instead of with milk and sugar), the process ("change") builds on itself, becoming bigger (graver, more serious) and also (potentially) more dangerous, and even possibly disastrous (a "vicious circle" or "spiral of decline") as it builds, though it might also prove beneficial (a "virtuous circle").

In my brother's case, one of those chain reactions resulted in his divorcing Sheila.

•   •

I want to backtrack for a moment and talk more about Sheila, about my brother's wife, to whom I haven't done justice. Her part in this drama isn't large; it's barely a walk on, you could say. Still, every character in every story, fiction or nonfiction, however minor, deserves substance, should have a life not just on the page, but off it, that spills beyond the contours and boundaries of the "plot." So I told my Metropolitan Writing Institute students. The best way to evoke characters is through their motivations, their goals and what they're willing to do to achieve them. Characters who don't want anything or don't want much are the hardest to animate.

"Existential characters," I called them.

Take Sheila, my brother's wife. To someone who didn't know her well she may not have seemed like a person of great ambition or burning desires. She kept a cockatoo in her home office, wore loose-fitting Indian garments, and drank herbal infusions. She practiced yoga and meditation. She had a calm disposition. I couldn't imagine her losing her temper. And yet she was not without passion. Helping people, that was Sheila's passion.

Sheila helped me. I was going through a difficult period, one of the most difficult periods of my life. This was about twelve years ago. I was forty. I'd broken up with my girlfriend. We'd come to a bad end. I don't care to talk about it. It was that unpleasant. No, I won't name her. Another piece of advice I gave my students: if a character appears only briefly, for a line or two and never again except in passing, as a fleeting reference, an elevator operator, a waitress, the newspaper vendor—in the given case, an ex-girl-friend of mine—it's usually best not to name them, since once introduced by name the reader has a reasonable expectation of encountering that person, that character, again in some not insignificant way. Anyway, I'd just broken up with this girlfriend. In a state of despondency, I paid my brother and Sheila a visit at their Vermont home. While I was there, one evening Gregory had to do something at his college, attend some function. Maybe we weren't invited, or maybe we just hadn't wanted to go. Anyhow Sheila and I stayed in and dined without Gregory. Afterwards we went for a walk. Their house was on a lonesome unlit dirt road. It was a clear night with no moon. The stars were out. I don't think I'd ever seen so many stars. Shooting stars, too, dozens of them, one right after another. We spent a long while, Sheila and I, standing there in the middle of the road, watching shooting stars. As we stood there out of the darkness she spoke.

"You've changed, Stewart," she remarked. "You're not the same person you were when I first met you. I mean that in a good way. You used to be so much harder. You were too hard, I felt. I didn't care very much for you."

I stood there and said nothing.

"You seem a lot softer to me now. Mellowed. It's a good thing. Anyway, I like you much more now. I hope you don't mind, but I felt the need to tell you that. You don't mind, do you?"

"No," I said. "I don't mind."

We went back to watching the stars. I felt the thick lump in my throat and had to hold back the urge to burst out sobbing. Sheila must have sensed it, too, or maybe she heard me choke back a sob, but she took my hand and held it, like that. I realized then that my brother's wife was a remarkable person, someone who had probably saved a few lives, possibly more than a few, who had certainly done more good in the world than I would ever do. This, I told myself as she took me in her arms, my tears soaking the shoulder of my brother's baggy canvas L.L. Bean field jacket that she wore, is a good person, a truly good person. The world could use more people like her.

That was Sheila, who, as a logical extension of the changes *Coffee, Black* instigated and that had instigated it—my brother divorced. Greg let her keep everything: the house, the car, the cockatoo, even Kiki, their cocker spaniel.

• •

By then my brother's book was a national bestseller. It had gone through four printings, with more to come. He'd done the talk show circuit: *Oprah, The Today Show, Letterman, Charlie Rose, Dr. Phil.* ... Speaking invitations poured in from all over. It wasn't long before, in addition to his agent and publicist, he required a personal manager to handle his engagements and collect the fees for them, which rose commensurate with demand. Hoping not to lose him, the dean and department chair at his college did their best to accommodate his new speaking schedule. They reduced his teaching load from three to two courses per semester, then one, then to a single, one-day seminar taught during the Spring term, with a teaching assistant to proctor tests and grade papers for him. Even that became too onerous. Then the college offered him an endowed chair, if only he'd stay. By then my brother had had a half-dozen such offers from as many universities, all more prestigious than the one where he taught, each of which my brother declined.

By then, you see, my brother was a wealthy man—a wealthy man named Brock Jones, PhD. The "PhD" matters. As Gregory Detweiler, he never flaunted his academic credentials; he'd protest when students called him "Doctor Detweiler." "Please," he'd cringe and say to them. "Just Greg—or, if you must, Professor Detweiler." "Brock Jones, PhD," on the other hand, never left home without his Doctorate of Philosophy firmly in hand and fused to his new name. It was a key to his identity, also a key selling point. "Brock Jones, PhD" wasn't your average motivational guru touting the latest, state-of-the-art recapitulation of *think positive*. He was a Philosopher. A Doctor. A Doctor of Philosophy—which, doubtlessly, in the average person's not-very-sophisticated mind, translates to *philosophical doctor*: a doctor who, though versed in the medical arts, is just as well-versed in the study of knowledge, reality, and existence, while also displaying an imperturbably calm, phlegmatic approach to life's challenges. Though he didn't have to teach any more, Brock Jones, PhD was the perfect teacher. His subject: How to live a happier, more adventurous, more fulfilled and fulfilling life. A better life.

If there was one subject Brock Jones, PhD could teach by example, that was it. Materially speaking, live better he most assuredly did. With all the money from book royalties and speaking engagements, he bought himself a loft in a former suspender factory in Boston, and a bungalow on one of the nicer canals in Venice, California. There followed more bestsellers along similar lines: *Don't Just Stand There, Change!*; *Today is the First Day of Forever*; *An Amateur's Guide to Self-Reinvention*... profiles on *60 Minutes* and PBS fundraisers. Then the pied-à-terre in Paris, the condo overlooking the harbor in Portofino... cars, clothes, boats (sail and power), antiquities, fine art, vintage wines, rare books and manuscripts...

Am I making my brother out to have been an irredeemable, selfish materialist? He wasn't. He was generous. He contributed to charities, set up trusts and nonprofit organization, gave as much, more, than he got. He moved our mother into a new assisted living facility, a much nicer one, the best in the state. He bought Sheila *and* her mother new cars and paid for a transatlantic cruise that his ex- and her mother took together.

As for me, his twin brother, he would have been generous with me, too, had I let him.

I wouldn't let him; I refused his generosity. By the time he offered it, I was too upset by him, too livid—is that the right word?—too distraught, too disturbed, too incensed by what I interpreted as his complete disavowal of his identity, his past, himself: a self that was, had been, identical in almost every way to mine, that was *my* self. In disavowing that self, in eradicating it, as far as I was concerned, he'd eradicated *me*. In reinventing himself as "Brock Jones, PhD," he erased Gregory Detweiler; in erasing Gregory Detweiler, he erased me, his brother, his twin.

He denied my existence.

For were not our identities, had they not been, inextricably bound? Had we not been "the Detweiler Twins?" For as much as we'd chafed at that identity, as much as it displeased us, still, had it not been *ours*? Did it not define us—no less than the color of our eyes and hair and the shapes of our noses? Take one Detweiler twin away and—what remained? No Detweiler Twin. When he took Gregory Detweiler away from me, my brother took half of me with him. The better half.

That's right, Dear Reader: the better half. For though once upon a time I thought of myself as my brother's equal if not his better, starting around the time of what I will charitably refer to as Greg's "conversion" and rising to a crescendo several years later, I didn't feel that way. On the contrary, had someone asked me during that period "Who's the better person, you or your twin brother?" Without hesitation I'd have said, "My brother."

For I had come to doubt myself in every way.

That sounds portentous, I know. Not portentous as in foreboding, but portentous as in "said in a pompously solemn manner so as to impress." And why not, since I mean to impress you. This is a confession, after all, and confessions are meant—if not to impress, then to impress *upon* their listeners such extenuating circumstances as might paint the confessor in a more sympathetic light. That I had come to doubt myself in every way certainly counts as an extenuating circumstance.

And how, you ask, had I come to doubt myself in every way?

Listen: I'm going to tell you. It won't be a pleasant task and it may take some time. Still, I'll do it.

5. HOW I CAME TO DOUBT MYSELF IN EVERY WAY

"BACK-STORY (OR BACKSTORY): THE THINGS THAT HAVE HAPPENED TO a fictional character before you first see or read about them in a movie, television show, or novel."

In this case, that of one Stewart Detweiler: Renaissance Man, man of singular promise and potential, the tale—nay, the saga—of his precipitous rise and equally swift fall, a tragic tale of promises unfulfilled, of potential squandered, of one who, seeing his "bright future" swirl down the drain along with much of his hair, said to himself in disbelief, *This isn't happening. This can't be happening—to me!*

Oh, but it can happen. It *did* happen.

Some may argue that I got what I deserved, that the failures that met me with middle age were the price exacted by youthful hubris. In my younger days I was cocky, arrogant. I thought a good deal of myself. I had great faith in my future. I'd be an artist, an actor, a painter ... it didn't matter what sort. I'd make my mark. I'd be famous. That's what mattered.

When did I reach this conclusion?

When I was five years old. When Mrs. Norton, my kindergarten teacher, kissed me on the cheek. I'd presented her with a crayon drawing. And she kissed me.

That chaste kiss on the cheek — it was my first taste of artistic glory. No sooner did Mrs. Norton kiss me than I made up my mind: I'd be an artist.

Beginning then and for the rest of my life I dedicated myself to artistic pursuits. I wrote poems and stories, I sketched. I took guitar, singing, and art lessons. I signed up for the Thespian Society. I got leads in all the school plays. Rarely was I seen without a play script, a sketchbook, my notebook, my guitar … When other kids my age were playing sports or doing other things together, I'd be down in what before I claimed it as my studio had been the basement playroom, putting the final touches on my latest oil painting, typing my latest poem, standing before the full-length mirror I'd mounted on the furnace room door, gripping my yardstick prop sword, rehearsing King Arthur's Excalibur speech from *Camelot*. I sound like a fanatic; I was. But then I told myself: "To make it as an artist, Stewart, you have to be determined, disciplined, devoted. So what if nobody likes you, if you have no social life, no friends? When you're famous you'll have all the friends you want, and millions of fans to boot."

It's not true that I didn't have any friends. I did. They respected my artistic ambitions, they admired me for them. Maybe they considered me a fanatic; maybe they thought that I was showing-off. What of it? Artists show-off; that's what we do.

So: I devoted myself to my art, or to becoming an artist. The distinction matters. In the first case, one is devoted to a discipline, a vocation; in the second, to an identity. Now and then one of my MWI students would ask me privately if they had what it took to be "a writer." My response was always the same. "Forget whether or not you're a writer," I'd say. "The question is: are you *writing*. As long as you're writing," I'd say, "if it matters, you're a writer."

But it's not what I said to myself as a teenager, or in my twenties, or even into my thirties. Back then I wanted to *be* an artist, to be special; to stand out. I was driven by my ego. When we do things for imperfect reasons, that imperfection is almost always born-out by the results. I got lead roles in plays, but I was no actor; I painted, but I was no painter. I wrote poems, but I was no poet.

These hard truths wouldn't dawn on me until I left the small Connecticut town where Greg and I grew up, and in which very small pond I'd been an estimable fish, to pursue my fortunes in New York City. In that city not only did I learn that I was no big fish, I wasn't a fish at all. I was more like a plankton, or an echinoderm, an urchin, or a sea cucumber, or … or … a starfish! That's what I was. A starfish! Not a real star. Not even a real fish. A marine invertebrate clinging to the rocks at low tide.

Oh, I had minor successes here and there, bit roles in Off-off Broadway plays, paintings in hole-in-the-wall galleries, stories and poems published in obscure literary journals collated and stapled in someone's dining room, guitar-playing gigs in midnight bars and moribund cafés, performances attended strictly by other desperate artists awaiting their own pathetic turns at the microphone.

I was still young, still barely in my twenties. I hadn't given up hope. But I realized, too, that the Renaissance Man strategy wasn't paying off. I'd have to choose one discipline and give it my all. But —how to choose? Of all my nascent gifts, all those bright-feathered arrows in my artistic quiver, which to draw back and aim at the bullseye labeled "Success/Fame"?

• •

Professor Wallace made the choice for me. Wallace was a sad-looking man. He wore the same wrinkled, fusty, corduroy jacket always. His nose and cheeks were filigreed with purple capillaries. In the Brooklyn art school where I studied painting, film and theater, he taught remedial English, a mandatory course designed to fulfill the school's accreditation requirements. Though they drew and painted like angels, many students enrolled in the college were high school dropouts, immigrants, and others with but a bare grasp of the King's English. It didn't take much, therefore, to impress Professor Wallace, so unused was he to students who could arrange words into a grammatical sentence, let alone write a good story. Presented with a story of mine, one about my father, about that last summer visit I paid him in my sixteenth year, when I escaped in his rowboat to encounter an A-frame exactly like this one, Professor Wallace responded with unqualified enthusiasm.

"Now *this*," he said, snapping the fingers of one hand against the manuscript while holding it high with the other, "is a *categorically* publishable story." Though I had no idea what it meant, I loved that word: "categorically."

The Professor went on to sing my story's praises, its authentic images conveyed in limpid, lyrical prose. With those gin blossoms on his cheeks I couldn't say for sure, but I swear Professor Wallace blushed, so pronounced was his enthusiasm for my story. It wasn't until years after I quit art school, having flitted between artistic mediums for half a decade like a goldfinch flitting about the branches of an alder tree, after concluding that to have any shot at success I'd have to pick and choose one discipline and forgo the others, that Professor Wallace's encouraging words came back to me. The story that he praised? Though I'd published others since, I hadn't submitted it anywhere. It moldered in a desk drawer. I was afraid to submit it, afraid to discover that my professor's effusions hadn't been warranted, that in fact my story *wasn't* publishable, categorically or otherwise. Wallace's praise had meant so much to me, I wanted to protect it, to preserve it. So I kept the story under wraps in my desk drawer. But once I made up my mind to be a writer...I beg your pardon: once I made up my mind to dedicate myself *to writing*...I had no choice; I had to submit it.

I aimed high. *The New Yorker, the Paris Review, Harper's, The Atlantic.* It was taken by *The Chattahoochee Review.* Still: it got me an agent, a good one. She read the story, liked it, and wrote me asking if I had others and if by any chance there might be a novel in the works. The agent's name was Sally Treadwell. Note the power of that simple, declarative sentence. Something else I taught my MWI students: when things are stated simply, directly, with enough specificity, readers aren't likely to argue with them. Were I to tell you, for instance, that before becoming a literary agent Ms. Treadwell studied structural engineering at the Rose-Hulman Institute in Terre Haute, Indiana, and from there went on to a four year reserve commission in the Army Corps of Engineers during the course of which she researched the effects of fibers on the plastic shrinkage cracking of fresh concrete, you'd believe it, wouldn't you? Well, Sally Treadwell did none of those things, as far as I know. Why would a literary agent study engineering? But for a moment you were inclined to believe me, weren't you? Why? Because the degree of specificity along with the bold directness of the assertion left no room for doubt. Besides, who would make such a thing up?

A fiction writer, that's who.

But my agent's name really was—is—Sally Treadwell. If I'm ambivalent about which tense to employ, it's first of all because, assuming that Sally's still my agent, she won't be for very much longer. But that aside, it's unclear to me whether at present she is my agent. When an agent stops being your agent is often unclear. They may stop working for you, but rarely if ever do they come out and say "Oh, by the way, in case you haven't noticed, I've stopped working for you." Sally never quit. And I never fired her. But she has long since ceased to do diddlysquat for me.

That's where things stand with Sally and me now. But then, after discovering my work in *The Chattahoochee Review*, she became my stalwart. No, I didn't have a novel-in-progress, as I explained when I spoke with her by phone the day after getting her note. But I had more stories, some published, others not. "Send them all to me," Sally said. "Let's see what we can do."

Within four months I—or we, since Sally had a lot of input—put a collection together. We agreed on a title: *Penny Sufferings*. Sally sent it to six publishers. No bidding war ensued, however. For a first book of stories, the offer from Knopf was *very* generous; the others quickly dropped out. A year later, my first book was in print. Handsome, it was, with dark pennies floating over a blood-red field on the front cover, and the title and the author's name (*Penny Sufferings: a collection by Stewart Detweiler*) in a distressed brush font. Filling the back cover: a grainy black and white photo of me, the author, standing with arms folded against a craggy brick wall, wearing a pale polo shirt, one collar flipped carelessly up, looking mischievous, mischievous and rugged like the craggy wall (the suntan helped). Under the photo: my name, Stewart Detweiler, nothing more, as if nothing else needed to be said, as if to say, *Here, with no further ado, is your enfant terrible.*

The book garnered mostly favorable reviews. Starred notices from *Publisher's Weekly* and *Kirkus;* a positive, half-page review in the Sunday *Times* book section, followed in short order by equally glowing reviews in *The Washington Post* and the *L.A. Times.* An auspicious start to what would turn out to be a less-than-stellar career.

• •

I was still living in Brooklyn, no longer in a college dorm, but in a tenement in Brooklyn Heights, a fifth-floor walk-up with a "water closet" and a lion-claw bathtub squatting in the kitchen, a half-dozen blocks from Montague Street. With the advance from the book sale I took an apartment in Greenwich Village, on Cornelia Street. The rent was twice as high, but so what? Soon, I thought, the royalties will start pouring in, along with money for the sale of movie rights. There would be more books, more advances, more money. All I had to do was keep writing. At long last, I said to myself, I've done it; I've arrived. I've become the famous artist I always wanted to be!

So it was for three months. There were parties and readings and signings and more reviews and interviews and invitations to speak at libraries and universities and to book clubs and literary societies. Oh, it was lots of fun, tremendous fun, more fun than I'd ever had before in my life.

You must be wondering what Gregory, my twin, thought of all this. By then he was already ensconced in the small liberal arts college where he would remain for the next twenty-four years, following (too closely, some—including me—felt) in our philosophy professor father's footsteps, living a life of quiet, cozy, academic desperation.

How did Greg take my success? Well, or so it seemed, at first. He loved me, after all; he wanted me to be happy; he wanted me to be successful; we both wanted happiness and success—not just for ourselves, for each other. He attended my publisher's book launch party in Manhattan, at a place called Blue Smoke, a trendy barbecue joint down in the Flatiron district. I even signed a copy of my book for him. The book was dedicated to Greg, too, by the way. *To Gregory, my better half,* it said in understated italics in the middle of an otherwise blank page, as though whispered by me. It was the least I could do for my brother, who'd seen me through so many ups and downs, especially during those discouraging first years in New York. Now here I was, man of the hour, the toast of the town—well, the toast of that very small sector of the publishing community devoted to fledgling authors—signing books, drinking Prosecco, my editor and my publicist flanking me to one side, Sally Treadwell, my agent, to the other, and several dozen cheerful partygoers lined up to have me sign copies of my book for them. It was all very exciting, all very...what's the word? Heady. It was all very heady. I was gracious, and humble—considering. I wasn't the sort who would let fame go to his head, who'd forget the hardships, the humiliations, the insults, the setbacks, the hundreds of rejection letters, all those defeats and failures with which the road to my success had been paved. No: I wouldn't forget. I'd remember.

I was twenty-five years old.

Meanwhile I had another glass of Prosecco; I inscribed another copy of my book. I posed for more photographs of myself with my arm around the waist of one or more young attractive potential stalkers. As shutters snapped, I caught a glimpse my brother, of Gregory, dressed in a tweed sports coat and paisley tie, watching from the shadows, looking more preoccupied than celebratory. That, I suspect, is the moment when for the first time it may have occurred to him that I, his brother, had it in me to be ruthless and to possibly betray him. The penury and rapaciousness that he and I had rehearsed all those years ago playing the Pauper and the Millionaire had finally come home to roost. To both our surprises, it looked as though I'd be the Millionaire, the one with the fortune—an artistic fortune more than a financial one, but what difference did that make? I'd made it. I was a glowing, glimmering, glamorous success. A thrilling future lay before me. Meanwhile Gregory would plod on in his ho-hum academic despair.

Until then, I had considered Greg to be the successful one, the one with the charmed, secure existence: a PhD, a loving, strong, intelligent wife, a tenured professorship: he had everything to live for. Remember those seesaw-like phone calls back and forth to each other, with me bucking Gregory up one day, and him bucking me up the next? We were still riding that seesaw, Greg and I; we never stopped riding it. When Greg went up, I went down. When I went down, he went up.

The night of my book launch party, I was riding high on that seesaw, higher than Greg or I had ever ridden before. I think it made us both a little dizzy, knowing, as I'm sure both of us knew, that when it comes to seesaws in particular what goes up must come down. The concern on Greg's face as he looked up at me from his end of the seesaw? I see now that his concern was as much for me as for himself.

•   •

The night after the launch party, Greg and Sheila stayed with me in my Cornelia Street apartment. I gave them my bedroom while I slept on the couch. In the morning, while I brewed espresso to go with the bagels, lox, and cream cheese I'd bought, Greg sat on one of the cushioned bench seats by the bay window, gazing with abstracted interest at the naked ginkgo tree branches veining the pale street scene. He hadn't said a word all morning. Sheila sat at my kitchen table, leafing through the Sunday *Times* magazine, making idle chatter, filling the gaping hole left in the atmosphere by her husband's silence. At the launch party she had seemed genuinely happy for me. If there's an envy gene Sheila lacked it. There wasn't a trace of spite or vindictiveness in that woman. While Sheila and I chatted, Greg sat there, in the window seat, his stockinged feet resting on the bench cushion, his arms folded around the knees of his bent legs, gazing silently at nothing as we chatted on and a radiator valve hissed furiously. I wondered if he was nursing a hangover from the Prosecco. But I knew better. He was brooding—over our suddenly reversed fortunes, his and mine. I knew, since in his position I'd have done likewise. It was no fun being the Pauper, scratching at that mansion door in a snowstorm, begging to be let in by the Millionaire in his velvet smoking jacket (swirling his cognac, puffing his cigar). Greg may have taken some comfort in knowing it wouldn't be long before our roles would reverse again, as they always did, as they were bound to do. What goes up ... Or had Gregory already anticipated my downfall as well as his own? Could he see that far into the future? Was that the source of his abstraction? Is it possible that, on that gray morning through that bay window between the branches of that ginkgo tree, my brother foresaw this moment?

• •

My first book having done well, I set about following up on its success. No doubt you have heard of "the curse of the sophomore slump"—or "second book blues," as it is also sometimes called? Authors whose first efforts succeed beyond expectations are especially susceptible to it. In my case, the second book wasn't the problem. Or *writing it* wasn't the problem. It had to be a novel, of course. That's what was expected of me, not just by Sally, but by all those who had invested in my book of short stories, the point of which, if a collection of stories has any point, is to alert the publishing world to the existence of a new author, to serve as a sort of appetizer, an *amuse bouche,* if you will, something to whet the public's appetite prior to serving them the main course: a novel.

So I wrote a second book, a novel. Though titled *Reasonable People,* I still think of it as "The Hat Factory Novel." Its origins are traceable to two sources. The first source was a remark my brother made one day, an off-the-cuff suggestion that stuck with me. I forget in what context he made the remark, where we were or what we were doing. Anyway apropos of whatever, Greg said, "Why don't you write a story of pure atmosphere?" He said "a story"; he didn't say "a novel." But since a novel was what I had in mind, I took it that way. The second source was the display window of a hat store on Fifth Avenue in the low thirties (for all I know it's still there). Anyway, I happened to pass by there one day, on my way to or from where I forget. But I remember it was winter, and that it was not long after my brother made his off-the-cuff suggestion to me. I remember too that though it was winter it was unusually warm, bright and sunny, without a cloud in the sky. I'd taken my winter coat off and carried it in the crook of my arm. (Why these details should matter I don't know, but they do; at least I feel they matter.) I'd just taken my own hat off, too—an eight-panel cap of Irish tweed such as my father had worn, his "thinking cap," that he had given us for Christmas...He gave one to me and one to my brother. Identical caps...I'd just taken mine off when I happened to pass in front of the hat store and stopped to take in the display. I had no intention to buy a hat. But I enjoyed looking at them, something about hats comforted me. Maybe because the Connecticut town Greg and I grew up in had once been a hat manufacturing mecca, though by the time we lived there most of the factories were defunct and deserted while others had burned or would soon burn down, leaving only their brick smokestacks remaining to remind us of the town's once glorious industrial past. As I stood looking into the hat store window, admiring the array of fedoras and derbies and Panamas and trilbies and, yes, tweed caps like my father's—like the one jammed into the pocket of the coat I carried under my arm—I recall saying to myself, "Why don't you write a novel set in a hat factory town—a dying hat factory town in Connecticut like the one you and Greg grew up in?" Hats would feature prominently. Maybe the protagonist's father would work as a blocker in the last hat factory. Or maybe the young protagonist's (it would be a coming-of-age novel)...maybe the young protagonist's father would die or have died of mercury poisoning, as happened to many hat factory workers. The boy's mother would remarry—or would have remarried—the town's sole surviving retail hat merchant, a well-meaning fuddy-duddy for whom the boy would feel unalloyed contempt. Something like that. Suddenly as I stood before that hat store window display my brother's words returned to me, echoing my own challenge: *Why don't you write a [novel] of pure atmosphere?* That's it! My hat-centric novel would have a minimal plot. It would all be up to the setting, to ambiance, to atmosphere, to the charm of those things as conveyed by the work's limpid prose. In discussing it years hence (as they were bound to) people would say, "Oh, yes, that charming novel, the one set in the hat factory town."

Thus my second book—my first novel—was born. Why I ended up calling it *Reasonable People* is a long, unhappy story that I won't go into here. Anyway it was published. In publishing industry parlance, sales were "modest," which is to say not very good. On the basis of the success of my short story collection, Sally had gotten me a hefty advance, twice that of my first book. Consequently those "modest" sales amounted to a net loss for my publisher.

As for the reviews, though respectful, they were far from effusive. The worst was by an anonymous *Kirkus* reviewer who wrote (and I quote from memory), "If style over substance is your cup of tea, Stewart Detweiler's' *Reasonable People* may be the most stylish book of the year. Never before has so much perfect prose been lavished on so negligible a story."

With critics, publisher, and the reading public given reason to wonder if I might be a one-book wonder, the pressure was on. My next book had to be not merely better than the first and the latest, it had to be an unqualified triumph.

• •

Faced with the task of writing my third book, the sophomore slump took hold of me. Ideas weren't the problem. I had too many of those. Ideas are the novelist's *bête noire*. They're like cats. If you have more than two, you've got too many. This is why when non-writers buttonhole writers to tell them their "great idea" for a book, the one they always wanted but never had time to write, writers tend to be less than amused. It's like going up to someone who already owns an epidemic of cats and, with overflowing largesse, offering them—a cat.

It wasn't long before more than a few of my ideas turned into manuscripts, partial and whole drafts of novels that I shared with my agent, with Sally Treadwell. Dear Reader, there isn't time to share more than a few of them with you. Life is short, and I have only so many of these composition notebooks left to fill before mine comes to its brutish, inevitable end. And for sure you have better things to do than read about a failed novelist's failures, which is why you may want to skip the next page or two, where I'll touch upon them ever so briefly, just enough to give you a sampling, as it were. By all means, skip the rest of this page—and the one after it. After all, why should you care whether or not the next manuscript I shared with Sally Treadwell was called "The

Sidewalk Artist," or that it was about a New York City advertising executive who "chucks it all" to become a *Madonnaro*—those artists who draw on sidewalks with colored chalk? What can it possibly matter to you that in the novel's climactic scene, the hero rescues an array of "colorful" urchins from an inferno raging in the secret tunnels underneath Grand Central Terminal? The story was maudlin, trite, sentimental, saccharine, and grossly implausible. Making me wonder: why didn't Sally think it would sell?

"Write the next one," she told me.

I did. I wrote "Ariadne's Thread," a *roman a clef* about a relationship on the rocks set on a desolate Greek island, and "Perfect Strangers" (about another relationship on the rocks, a married couple this time, set in Venice), and "Walking Wounded," about an old man living alone with his cocker spaniel. To each of these efforts Sally's response was the same.

"Write the next one, Stewart."

But I didn't despair, nossir. I endured; I persisted. I drafted another novel, and another. My sixth effort, "Harris' Book," was my Land O' Lakes novel. You know Land O' Lakes? The butter company? The one with the box with the picture of an Indian maiden holding a carton of Land O' Lakes butter, etc.? "Harris' Book" was my novel about a blocked novelist's struggle to write a novel about a blocked novelist trying to write a novel (etc.). The book was written in "notebook form," with words, phrases, sentences, and entire passages struck through as Donald Harris edits his work-in-progress: the book we're reading. Harris' masterpiece accrues accidentally, in spite of its author. Though when I wrote it I was thirty-three, I made my protagonist older: fifty-three, my age now as I write these words. On the assumption that all middle-aged men owned enlarged prostate glands, I gave my protagonist one.

• •

It was my hero's enlarged prostate, among other things, that put Sally Treadwell off of this latest effort, as she told me when we met to discuss it one day over breakfast at Ladurée, an East Side patisserie on Madison Avenue, a dozen blocks north of the midtown office building where Sally's agency was located. A sunny late Spring day. We sat at a window table. I'd ordered a chocolate brioche with my latte. Sally looked fetching as always. She wore a yellow shift with a red polka-dotted scarf and a floppy straw hat. Taking the box holding my manuscript (there were still such things then as manuscript boxes) from her shoulder bag and putting it down on the small, round, marble-topped table, with a grim sigh she said:

"Write the next one, Stewart."

"Why? What didn't you like about it?"

"It's not a question of *like,* Stewart. I like your writing. I think you're a wonderful writer."

"So what's wrong with it?"

"Must we, Stewart?"

"We must."

"There's not enough plot."

"Oh, that again?"

"Yes, Stewart, that again."

"Could you be more specific?"

"All right." Sally sighed. "Not to put too fine a point on it," she said, tapping the cardboard box with her bright red fingernail, "what you've written here amounts to six-hundred and seventy-two pages of TMI."

"TMI?"

"Too Much Information. Sorry, Stewart, but I for one found myself less than enthralled by the excruciating details of your protagonist's midlife crisis. I'm not interested in his writer's block or the size of his prostate, or spending twelve pages alone in his room at his desk with him surfing disaster videos, or learning that he goes home nights with a stomach ache since his pants don't fit anymore because he refuses to admit that his waistline has betrayed him. I don't want ten pages about his receding hairline, or five pages of dandruff, or eleven pages of him visiting his urologist. It's all very authentic, all very real, all very honest. But it's *not* a novel. It's — it's more like an *assault,* an epic rant. Readers won't tolerate it. *No one* will tolerate it. They won't give a damn about your hero's prostate. *I* don't give a damn about your prostate. Not for six hundred and seventy-two pages I don't. And I like you, Stewart. I like you a lot. If anyone could possibly care about these things, it would be me. You asked me for my opinion. That's my opinion."

Me (softly, facing the crusty residue of latte in my cup): "It's not *my* prostate; it's Donald Harris' prostate."

"I don't care if it's Jesus Christ's prostate. Whoever's prostate it is, no one's interested."

"Everyone else is writing novels with plots. It's so unoriginal."

"Stewart, it's *boring.*"

"So are most men's lives. I can't help that. A novelist's job is to tell the truth. That's how I see it, anyway."

"Maybe you just need to be a little more imaginative."

"A dead body on page one, is that what you mean?"

"Not necessarily, though it wouldn't hurt."

"Whatever I write, Sally, whatever else it may be, it has to be authentic. That's my rule Number One. I'm not a … a fabulist."

"Call it whatever you like, Stewart, but I cannot sell this manuscript and I'm not going to try. I'm sorry. But at this stage of your career you must write a commercial book."

"With a dead body on the first page?"

"It doesn't need a dead body. It doesn't even have to have bestseller written all over it. But it has to have commercial potential."

•   •

I was thirty-four years old, hardly ancient, in the normal scheme of things, but by the standards of publishing long in the tooth. I'd given up my Cornelia Street apartment, the rent on which I could no longer afford, and moved—first to Washington Heights, then across Spuyten Duyvil creek, the waterway that divides Manhattan from the Bronx, to another walk-up, this one in Kingsbridge, an aggressively un-chic neighborhood of sooty tenements and brick row houses bisected by the ratty elevated. I'd long since spent every dime of the advance I'd been paid for *Reasonable People* and that said book would never earn back.

With no more royalty payments forthcoming, I was reduced to working menial jobs: dollar store clerk, dishwasher, barback. I also kept up a side-gig I started soon after my novel was published, writing occasional reviews for *Kirkus, anonymously.* I made more selling the publisher's galleys to The Strand than for the reviews, they paid so poorly, but they were fun to write.

Still, I hadn't lost hope. In fact I was brimming with optimism. Sure, I had my dark days, my periods of despondency, those times when as ever I'd phone Gregory, who as always would buck me up and see me through. But through it all I clung fast to my vision; I maintained focus, never losing sight of my goal. Namely: to write that truly great novel, the enduring masterpiece, one that would not only revive but cement my reputation.

Toward achieving that goal I'd arrived at several theories. The first theory was that to be truly great a novel had to be entirely authentic, meaning everything in it either had to be made up or nothing in it could be made up; everything had either to be drawn faithfully from reality, or a pure product of the imagination. As I saw it, the reason why most novels fail to be great works of art is because in service of that devil known as "verisimilitude" they falsify just about everything. They try to serve two gods at once: the God of Empiricism and the God of Romance. But the two gods can't be reconciled. The two gods hate each other. They're like a pair of fraternal twins who don't get along, who would rather tear each other to bits than be forced to play together. No: one must either embrace artifice wholeheartedly, never trying, let alone succeeding, to hold so-called "reality" up to a so-called "mirror," or create documents based purely on facts: on actual persons, places, events, emotions, feelings, with nothing made up or contrived, nothing added or artificial, nothing owing to the artistic imagination. If a dead body appeared in it, by God it had better be an actual dead body.

That was one theory of mine. Another theory was that to be great a novel should have no subject, or rather it should have nothing as its subject. I wasn't the first novelist with this ambition. "I'd like to write a book about nothing," Flaubert wrote in an 1852 letter to Colet, "a book with no exterior attachments, held together by the inner force of its style as the earth is suspended in space without support—a book with no subject, or one in which the subject is invisible." To write about nothing is much harder than it sounds. One way to do it, the only way, actually, is to write about everything, since—being equal opposites—everything and nothing are two sides of the same coin (Black/White, Dark/Light, Nega-tive/Positive, Love/Hate, Life/Death, Good/Evil, Truth/Falsehood, Failure/Success...). The interdependent interrelation of these duali-ties is fundamental to ancient Chinese cosmology and the so-called "natural order" of things (the Tao or "right way"): the path to One-ness as expressed by the Yin and Yang, represented thus:

My subsequent meeting with Sally took place over two years after the one previously recounted, in March of 1999, a month shy of my thirty-seventh birthday. We met at Laudrée again. It was mid-winter. Sally wore a purple fleece flapper cloche with a black flower. This time we met for lunch, on me. Sally had the frisée salad. I ordered a gruyere omelet. From my tattered briefcase I withdrew the fruit of those past two years: "Pure Flux," my novel about nothing, my dark matter masterpiece. That its plot (to the extent that it had a plot) borrowed heavily from that of "Harris' Book," didn't concern me. Like the black holes it emulated, a book about nothing was bound to suck everything proximate to it into its void.

"So," Sally said, eyeing the manuscript's title page skeptically. "This is your brand-new novel?" Emphasis on *brand*.

I nodded.

"Pure Flux?" she said dubiously.

"Pure Flux," I confirmed, smiling.

"Meaning—?"

"Flux is the action or process of continuous change—you know, as in fluctuation, variation, oscillation...as in 'All human societies, even those that appear to be fixed or stable, are in fact in a constant state of flux.' And pure means...pure."

Sally nodded. "What's it about?"

In purely abstract terms I explained as best I could.

"Plot summary?"

"Why not read it and see for yourself?"

"You said you had a new novel, Stewart. That was the purpose of this meeting, yes?"

"Correct."

"May I assume that the plot of this novel departs significantly from that of the last one?"

"Depends what you mean by 'significantly'."

"I mean does this one *have* a plot?"

"Oh. Yeah. Sure. It has *a* plot."

"Not the novelist writing the novel about a novelist writing the novel, etc.? Not *that* plot?"

I shrugged. "At least it's an *honest* plot, unlike most of them."

"In other words—nothing happens."

"I wouldn't say that. A lot happens. Internally."

"Internally, Stewart?"

"Existentially."

"*Existentially?*"

"Okay, nothing happens. So what? What happens in *Ulysses*? Two men cross Dublin on a summer day. *Under the Volcano*: a diplomat drinks himself to death. *Remembrance of Things Past*: a guy dips a cookie in his tea. The great masterpieces of literature. Guess what? Nothing happens in them! I could go on."

"Please don't," said Sally.

"Pascal's *Pensees,* Kenko's *Essays in Idleness,* Lautréamont's *Les Chants de Maldoror, The Decameron, The Stranger, Tropic of Cancer, The Golden Bowl, Eugene Onegin, The Magic Mountain, The Castafiore Emerald…* Musil's *Man Without Qualities,* Huysmans' *A rebours… Hamlet,* for Christ's sake. Not to mention everything Sam Beckett ever wrote. They're all about nothing!"

"They may all be masterpieces," Sally said, "but in this market I couldn't sell them either."

"Plot," I said, slapping my fork on my by then clammy omelet.

"I know this is painful for you, Stewart, and you may want a second opinion. But as your agent I have to tell you when I don't think something is right, and I don't think this book or one like it will do either of us any good." She stood up.

"Where are you going?"

"I have to get back to the office." Sally opened her purse.

"Lunch is on me, remember?"

"It's Laudrée, Stewart."

"Put your money away!"

She did. "Are you coming?"

I shook my head. "I'll stay here and finish my Crodino."

She reached down and touched my shoulder lightly. "Your time will come; I know it will, Stewart. You're a wonderful writer."

I nodded.

Sally gave my shoulder a squeeze and left the café.

• •

Nearly two more years passed before I sent Sally another manuscript. This time the rejection came over the phone.

"It may be time for you to get another agent," Sally said.

"You're firing me?"

"I'm not firing you, Stewart. Agents don't fire writers."

"You just said I should get another agent."

"I'm saying at this point in your career you may find it easier to work with someone else."

"You mean *you* may find it easier to work with someone else."

"Fine. *I* may find it easier."

"I'm difficult, in other words. Is that it?"

"Yes, Stewart, you're difficult."

"How am I difficult? What's been 'difficult' about me?"

"The truth? Watching you polish that turd of a novel for the last five years has been extremely difficult for me. Does that answer your question, Stewart?"

"Six years," I corrected her.

I was out of money, out of work (fired from my latest job, barista at the Starbucks at Astor Place, for correcting a customer who had asked me for an "*ex*presso"). My girlfriend of four years had broken up with me, plunging me into a deep funk. I could smell my despair. It smelled like a bald tire smeared with ripe Limburger cheese, set aflame, and rolled down a guano-covered hill.

The smell dripped from my lips, it leaked from my armpits, it wafted up from the damp depths of my rotting crotch. I lost my appetite. I couldn't sleep. My bowels froze up on me. My mouth went dry. I became impotent. I couldn't masturbate (well, I could, but to no end; not even to much of a beginning). I might have taken to drink, had I the stomach for it.

Instead I took to despising myself. From a deep well I pumped up bucket upon bucket of self-pity, shame, regret, remorse, reproach, and resentment. I drained that well dry. Yes, to anticipate your question, I phoned my brother; I called Gregory. But even Gregory's aggressive ministrations couldn't deliver me from this latest abysmal funk.

Here, Dear Reader, we enter the "bereft" stage of my narrative, the part where it looks as if our protagonist has finally hit rock-bottom, that things can't possibly get much worse for him.

Though of course they can. Of course they will.

Meanwhile there comes the reprieve—a flash of grace, a dollop of relatively good fortune, a scrap of hope, a dash of deliverance, the calm before the storm.

My deliverance took the form of a job offer from the Metropolitan Writing Institute.

So, eventually, did my doom.

6. BECOMING BROCK

*"Our identities are a collection of possibilities
that we have every reason to doubt."*

I SHOULD PICK UP THE PACE. IT'S ONLY A MATTER OF DAYS, MAYBE
even hours, before they come for me. I have to "beat them to the
punch." But it's out of my hands. Stories take their own time.

•   •

At this point in my back-story I am—or I was—forty years old.
Forty! Where, as they say, has the time gone? Strictly speaking,
nowhere. It sits frozen here on these pages where it will remain like
a fly trapped in amber until they crumble to dust. Until then the time
is, will always be, now. As the light of the distant stars reaches us
long after the stars themselves have burnt out, so my voice reaches
you through these words. Though my body has decomposed, these
words keep me alive. In reading them you graft your corporeal self
to my incorporeal spirit. Much obliged!

To return to the primary scene, the frame holding the flashback—the A-frame, that is. It's raining again. It seems as if it's
been raining forever, for as long as I've been sitting here, filling
these notebooks, since I arrived here to find my brother hanging

from a ceiling beam.

What happened next? you wonder (suspense).

Nothing. I sat there—here—as I'm sitting here now, with my back to this balcony railing, gazing out past the ceiling beam through the big triangular window.

How long did you sit there like that?

Long enough to lose track of all sense of time. It was as if I didn't exist. I passed out of my body—out of *both* of our bodies, my brother's and mine; one living, one dead; one sitting here, the other hanging from the beam from which our father once hung and from which—unless something interferes with my plan—I will soon hang. "A fugue state," the psychologists call it, known also as a "dissociative fugue" or "psychogenic fugue." A disorder characterized by reversible amnesia for personal identity, including memories, personality, and all the other identifying characteristics of one's individuality.

I've heard it said—possibly on an episode of *Star Trek*—that when matter and anti-matter collide, they cancel each other out; nothing of either survives. Something like that happened to me when I found my brother here. Matter and anti-matter, those equal opposite twins, met, collided.

The result: oblivion. Stewart Detweiler's oblivion.

● ●

The world returned slowly through each of my senses, starting with the sense of temperature. I felt cold; it was freezing. Within those fugue hours the thermometer dropped precipitously. It was the cold that made me open my eyes. Even with them open it took me a while to remember where I was, and longer to remember what was there behind me, beyond the rails supporting my back, and more time still to screw up the courage to turn my head and verify that this last horrible memory couldn't possibly be real, that the thing hanging from that ceiling beam—which I knew to exist—could only be the residue of a terrible, terrible nightmare.

But then why was I sitting (t)here, in my brother's lakeside house that used to belong to our father? What was I *doing* (t)here?

And why were my cheeks stiff with the half-frozen tears by

which I had presumably cried myself to sleep? *Had* I slept? (Ever notice how, when they don't know what else to do, authors ply readers with rhetorical questions?) It would have explained the dream fragments that, along with other perceptions, came swirling back to me, all having to do with my brother, with Gregory. The two of us riding in the back seat of our mother's car, her nauseating black boat of a '56 Mercury, bound for Danville, where she did her shopping in the stores along Main Street, at Genung's and McCrory's and Woolworth's. The smell of the car's houndstooth upholstery came back to me, along with its scratchy texture, and the horseplay Greg and I engaged in back there while our mother tried to concentrate on her driving, something she was never good at. One of the stores we went to, I forget its name or even what was sold there, kids' shoes, I believe, seemed to go on and on and on forever, stretching its way in a graceful endless curve toward some childhood Arcadia equipped with a carousel. Was that real or part of the same series of dreams all of which resolved themselves into the nightmare wherein my twin dangled from a ceiling beam behind me? Then we were sitting at the counter at Woolworth's — or was it Marcus Dairy? — eating hot dogs slathered with emerald-green relish. The next vignette had us running through the woods behind our house, laughing as we leapt in perfect synchronicity over fallen tree trunks and rocks. Building a fort in a field. Playing ping-pong in the gasoline-scented garage. Barbequing gypsy moth caterpillars on the hibachi grill. Scraping the dried soufflé of cut grass from underneath the lawnmower ... For a while I distracted myself with these and other dream fragments, forgetting again for as long as I could where I was and why I'd come here, and that I was freezing.

I couldn't go on delaying forever; I had to look.

So I looked.

But first I closed my eyes and counted

I counted to three.

When I got to three I kept counting to ten.

When I reached ten I counted to twenty.

Then thirty, then fifty ...

I counted to a hundred.

Then I opened my eyes. And turned.

That's when the sobs came.

Such sobs, Dear Reader, as I hope your body will never produce as long as you live. Like a series of bloodied rags my body expelled them. The sound of my wrenching sobs reverberated off the cathedral ceiling. It resounded off the fireplace's fieldstones and its heavy wooden mantelpiece. It roused me from one nightmare into a worse one from which there could be no waking.

I still had on my coat, my tweed cap, my leather gloves and a green plaid scarf (note the absence of the contentious "Oxford" comma, with which I normally comply, since "gloves and scarf" form a unit of their own). The condensation from my breath blurred the space between my brother's corpse and me. Beyond the triangular windows I saw nothing but whiteness filigreed with faint gray lines barely suggesting trees and a dock with two Adirondack chairs: a tentative pencil sketch, erased.

I rubbed my shivering self.

I remembered how on my visits there my father's home suffered frequent blackouts during storms. I remembered following him downstairs to the basement (unusual for Georgian homes to have basements, but this one did, does) to watch him flip the circuit breakers. I found a candle, lit it, and took it with me down the dark stairs. Since my last visit the basement had been refinished. I'm not sure who had it done, my brother or my father, but where before there'd been nothing but a bare concrete floor and walls (well-pump, heating unit, water heater, pipes, and drains), now there was a spare bedroom, a storage room for paint cans, tools and rakes, a laundry room with washer and dryer, and an artist's studio where the larger of two easels held a painting-in-progress, a naïve painting of the *Titanic* sinking. With the candle in one hand I pulled other paintings down from a shelf to see that they were all, every one of them, paintings of the sinking *Titanic*. Had my father done them? Or were the paintings my brother's? Had Gregory—Brock—had my brother gone into hiding for that reason, to reinvent himself yet again, this time as a painter of sinking ships? For a while when we were young Greg displayed a talent for drawing. No sooner did I declare myself "the artist" than he gave it up as a bad habit. More likely my father had done the paintings years ago, possibly in the last years or year of his life. But why the *Titanic*? What was the symbolism? And why paint the same subject over and over again?

I was reminded of that time I rowed away in my father's boat, of that abandoned identical A-frame full of paintings all of the same subject, or non-subject, paintings of absolutely nothing in assorted muted, pale colors. In point of fact with respect to draftsmanship the paintings were crude such that though bearing the name *Titanic* on their rearing counter sterns in some cases the sinking ships looked more like sinking rowboats—like my father's rowboat.

The last painting I pulled down from the shelf was a triptych on hinged Masonite panels. The first panel showed the *Titanic* approaching the iceberg. The second showed it rearing up for its final plunge—the iceberg looming in the background. The last panel showed the iceberg alone, isolated in its victory. I thought of the Holy Trinity, of the Father, the Son, and the Holy Ghost.

I replaced the last painting, then remembered my mission, and went in search of the circuit box, which I found in the laundry room next to the dryer. Sure enough, the breakers had all been thrown. I flipped them back. The heating unit roared to life. A chain dangling from an overhead light fixture tickled my forehead. I yanked it. *Mirabile dictum,* the light went on, dazzling me. I pulled the chain again, plunging the laundry room back into darkness.

With the candle guttering I made my way back upstairs, where already the sudden influx of warmer air had made a difference. The house smelled different. Odor molecules have more energy at higher temperatures. As the air gets warmer, the rate of emission increases. Those smells that I had noticed earlier—of must, mold, mildew, and the hideously indescribable odor in particular—were suddenly far, far more pronounced. Through my scarcely parted lips I sipped shallow breaths.

In the kitchen I switched on the electric stove and put the kettle on. Each of these actions I performed automatically, all the while pretending that my brother's corpse wasn't there, hanging there in the air behind and above me. I whistled as I opened cabinets and drawers to see what sort of food was in the house. I was suddenly starving. On an upper shelf I found a cylindrical box of Quaker oats. I put water in a pan and put the pan on a burner next to the kettle and added salt to it. I shivered. There was a small audio system on the living room shelf. I switched on the radio. It was set to the same station I'd been listening to in the car. According to the newscast, at least four people were dead and 295 missing after a passenger ferry capsized and sank off the coast of South Korea. Among the passengers were 300 high school students traveling with their teachers to the resort island of Jeju. The kettle whistled. The water in the pan boiled. I poured in a cup of oats. I found a tea bag and made a mug of tea.

It was all fairly ordinary, or would have been, save for the body hanging from a beam over my head, and the horrendous odor that, along with the frozen puddle of urine on the floor under its feet, I somehow managed to ignore the way the subjects in that test avoided the man in the gorilla suit. But mine wasn't a case of inattentional blindness coupled with inattentional anosmia. I was, as they say, "in denial." In the house where first my father and then my twin brother both hanged themselves, I pretended not only that those things hadn't happened, but that I wasn't there. I was somewhere else, in some other house, the house I discovered during the summer of my sixteenth year in my petulant bid to row myself beyond the reach of my father's pedantry in his beloved boat. Somehow I had come to that house again, for what purpose I had no idea, possibly to undertake a series of paintings of the sinking *Titanic*.

Meanwhile I sipped my tea.

As I sipped my tea the oatmeal boiled over. I stirred it, turned the heat down, replaced the lid on the pan. I've always liked the combination of oatmeal and tea. They were what my father ate for breakfast when I was a kid, before and after he left our mother, or (more likely) she left him. Those combined smells, tea and oatmeal, formed the olfactory soundtrack of those summers I spent with him through my sixteenth year. As an adult, in New York City, I became first a coffee then an espresso drinker. Before then I'd been a tea drinker like my philosophical father — and like Gregory, who, too, once preferred tea, but then, in his twenties, started drinking coffee with milk and sugar, and continued to do so until that now infamous moment in the first class section of a jetliner when he asked the flight attendant for his "coffee, black." Now here I was having tea for the first time in twenty-five years. There was a carton of milk in the refrigerator, but it had long gone sour. I found a jar of Coffee Mate (or the Kroger brand equivalent). As for my oatmeal, I sprinkled it with sugar and a pinch of salt and took it and my mug of hot tea with me and sat in the living room, on the wicker sofa, which faced the French doors overlooking the lake, though all they looked out on then was that erased pencil sketch. I ate calmly, with the radio on and classical music play-ing—a Bach cantata, if memory serves me. I sipped tea and gazed at the whiteness through the French doors, which reminded me less now of an erased drawing than of one of the blank prepared canvases I'd found in what I'll refer to henceforth as the "twin house." I thought of "The Painter of Grounds," the story that got Sally Treadwell to be my agent, about the artist so enamored of his lovingly prepared surfaces he refuses to paint anything on them. That's what my life felt like to me then, at that moment as I stared at the French doors while ignoring, or trying to ignore, the hideous smell. A freshly prepared canvas awaiting its subject.

Meanwhile I ate oatmeal; I sipped tea. As my brain warmed, I tried to think constructively; I understood that there were things to be done. But my mind was preoccupied: with memories, with images and events that rushed in to fill the voids between the whited-out French door windowpanes. There were Greg and I huddled behind that rock in the woods when we got lost and had the whole neigh-borhood out combing the forest in search of us. There we were farting in each other's pillows. There was my brother fixing the chain on my bicycle, and (next windowpane) bending over the dual carburetors of my first car, a dilapidated MGB, helping me adjust them (Greg was always handier at mechanics).

Whose turn to mow the grass?

One by one like a series of rectangular two-dimensional crys-tal balls each pane in the French doors served up another mem-ory, another image, something like what happened to me while driving my car here with the defroster failing and the windshield wipers slapping the frozen rain. The old house on a hill in Connecticut, the mulberry tree growing by the picket fence, sunflowers edging a sand pit, dappled sunlight, smells of cut grass and leaf smoke ... Who was that girl with strawberry-blond hair? Betsy Butterworth. Laughing. Waking up laughing at something Gregory said. What did you say, Greg? What was so funny it roused me—roused both of us—from our sleep?

Dear Reader, what makes up a life? A nasty, brutish birth. Screams, colic. The softness of a mother's breast. Tastes, smells, appetites. Discovering our bodies one organ at a time. Landscapes, colors, corners, crevices. Others enter the picture, strangers; friends. We learn to compete. School learning. Can you recite the alphabet? Can you multiply? Can you climb that rope? Masturbation: your newest friend who will be with you for most of the rest of your days. Girls. Sex. Hobbies and interests. What sports are you good at? What's your favorite TV show? High school. Travel abroad. Europe. Piazzas and fountains, trains, backpacks, hashish, hitchhiking, Toblerone bars, kissing that girl under a viaduct after getting kicked out of the youth hostel. A smoke-flavored kiss between cars on a train bound to or from Yugoslavia—or was it Budapest? A whitewashed room with a crucifix of twigs over the bed. A taxicab hurling across the Queensboro Bridge at dawn ...

When one set of panes filled in, I turned to the next.

I'd done just that, turned to watch the next set of French door windowpanes filling in, when something in my peripheral vision caught my eye ...

7. CHAPTER BREAK

...A WHITE CORD RUNNING FROM A WALL OUTLET NEAR A BOOK-case to a small flat rectangular object on the carpeted floor, partially concealed by a dead potted geranium. A cellphone. It had to be Gregory's...Brock's...my brother's. For sure it wasn't mine. I owned none, remember? Nor could it have belonged to my father, who had been dead for over sixteen years, and who like me never owned a cellphone. So it had to be Greg's. Brock's.

I'd risen from the wicker sofa, stepped over to and stood staring down at the thing as if at a copperhead or some other poisonous creature. It was an iPhone, that much I knew. I reached down and, hesitatingly, picked it up. I detached the charging cord and stood there, gripping the phone in both hands, holding it out in front of me like a priest holding the Sacred Host.

Do I dare?

I pressed the home button. The screen lit up. Over a plaid wallpaper pattern the time was displayed. 7.12 a.m. I pressed the home button again. The passcode screen appeared. As with pin numbers for bank debit cards, in my experience such things usually required a set of four numbers or letters, in which case, knowing or having known my brother almost as well as I knew myself, my guess was that, being lazy and disinclined to have to memorize things, like me he had used the last four digits—not of his own, but of his *brother's* Social Security number. My Social Security number. I input them. The phone unlocked.

No sooner did it do so than a flurry of missed call and voice message alerts appeared on the screen, from our mother, mostly, but from other people as well. Dawn Swopes. Adam Swann… and a procession of others whose names, though vaguely familiar, I didn't recognize.

I was reading one of those messages, still holding the phone in both hands, when it buzzed and quivered in my grip. I gave a cry and dropped the thing. It landed on the carpet, where it went on buzzing. As it did, I picked it up again and saw "Mom" on top of the black screen. Our mother was trying to phone my brother. God knew how long she'd been trying. Probably a dozen times a day every day for at least the last twenty days, relentlessly leaving messages, each more desperate than the last. She must have left dozens, a hundred messages. Now she was calling again.

The muffled buzzing persisted. Should I answer? I wasn't prepared to tell my mother the truth. I needed more time. The phone kept buzzing.

There's something called "Happenstance Theory," also known as "Krumboltz Theory," the brainchild of a man named John Krumboltz, which holds that indecision is desirable and sensible, since it allows us the opportunity to benefit from unplanned events.

As the phone kept buzzing, I looked up at my brother hanging there, thinking: Why did you do it, Greg? *How* could you do it? You had everything to live for. Money, fame, adoration. Bestselling books. All the things I'd dreamed of—you had them! A loving wife, a good job, a comfortable home, physical health, material success beyond most people's wildest dreams! You threw them all away. *Why?*

If one of us was destined to destroy himself, it should have been me. *I* should have been the one. But no, you had to beat me at that, too, the way you always beat me at everything. First born (by two minutes); first to lose a baby tooth; first to get strep throat; first to scrape his knee; first to ride a tricycle; first to read a book; first to kiss a girl (Betsy Butterworth: spin the bottle); first to go out on a date; first to drive a car. You did everything first. You were my older brother, after all.

And now you've done this, you bastard, you selfish prick. And what am *I* supposed to do? Tell me that! What am I supposed to tell *our* mother? That you, ever her favorite, the apple of her dia-betically blind eye, are dead, and that she's stuck with me — the loser? Jesus, Greg — or Brock Jones, Ph fucking D.

Why, goddammit? *Why?*

The phone kept buzzing.

But I knew the answer. We'd always suffered from depression, both of us. Just like our father. We got it from him. It was in our blood, in our genes. The D Gene. D for "Detweiler." D for "Depression." They say the children of a suicidal parent are twice as likely to commit suicide themselves, something like that. In our case one could argue that Gregory and I were a quarter or 25% more so inclined, having each inherited fifty percent of that predis-position, or half of "twice as likely."

The phone buzzed.

Few people understand the suicidal temperament. They can't get their minds around the fact that someone would want to destroy not only themselves, but all the people who love them. What isn't understood is that, by the time they commit sui-cide — in the moment before they blow their brains out or swal-low the poison or jump off the bridge or hang themselves from a ceiling beam — the suicide is already dead. Only the body remains to be destroyed.

There's this other theory, or syndrome, known as "vanishing twin syndrome." It happens more often than not, supposedly, when twins form inside the womb. One of the twins doesn't make it, is miscarried, dies while still in embryo, a zygote. Back when Greg and I were born, before there were sonograms, the mother in such a case might never even know about the "other" twin, since the tissue of the miscarried twin would often — usually, as a matter of fact — be reabsorbed either by the mother, the placenta, or by the surviving fetus.

Supposing, on the other hand, that each of the twins survives despite the fact that one was never meant to? Supposing reabsorption never took place? Supposing that the meant-to-be-dead twin arrived whole — if unintended — into this world? What then?

The cellphone keeps buzzing.

But I still haven't come to the craziest part of my theory.

Supposing that *all* identical twins that come into this world are an aberration, that in each case one of them was not meant to be, was meant to have died, but somehow, through a biological or metaphysical or cosmic glitch of some sort, never got the message?

Supposing, furthermore, that every person on earth was once an identical twin, but only briefly, in the womb, until their "tentative twin" did the right thing and vanished, got reabsorbed, leaving a single, unique, meant-to-be human being?

Do you see where I'm going with all this? What I'm saying, what I'm trying to say, is that one of us — Gregory or I — should never have been born.

One of us was an *aberration.*

Which one?

Answer: me, Stewart Detweiler: I was the aberration. I was the one meant to have died in my mother's womb, who ought to have been reabsorbed by my mother or by Gregory or by the placenta connecting us to our mother's uterine wall.

Now Gregory was dead. And it was up to me to absorb or be absorbed by him.

The phone kept buzzing. It buzzed four more times.

Then it stopped buzzing.

All the time while the phone buzzed I hadn't been breathing. Now I gasped for air. Oh God, I thought, gasping. *What will I do? What should I do?* I didn't know what to do.

The buzzing started again.

Oh God. Dear God...

I pressed the red button.

"*Hello? Brock? Brock, is that you? Are you there?! Brock — please — answer me! I know you're there! It's me, your mother, Brock! Are you there? Please, please...*"

The hardest thing about being absolutely free is you can do anything you want. Anything! Think of the weight of responsibility attending that level of freedom. Infinite choices up for grabs, as it were. And the choices all have to be made. With every page, every paragraph, every sentence, every word I write on this page, in this notebook, I create myself. The power of the declarative sentence! Say it's so and so it is.

Such freedom doesn't come free or even cheap. In my case to gain it cost me everything. I'd pay for it with my life.

My life!

"For God's sake, Brock! Brock, please—please…!"

In that moment, or rather in the one that follows, I realized the perfect subject for my pale, empty, mute, chaste, pristine canvas. Like my brother before me, I, too, would stumble upon my epiphany, the moment of my reinvention. As was the case with my twin aboard that flight from Burlington to whatever conference he'd been going to, when the flight attendant confronted him with her beverage request, the words I was about to utter would change me inevitably, inexorably, forever. But not for the better.

"Hello?" I said.

"Brock! Oh, Brock, dear Brock! Is it really, really you, Brock?"

Launching himself into a whole new identity had taken my brother precisely two words. It took me three.

"Yes," I said. "Yes, *it's really me.*"

8. GOD'S IMPALA

THE INVITATION TO INTERVIEW FOR THE INSTRUCTOR POSITION at the Metropolitan Writing Institute came two years after I submitted my application, which had moldered in a file drawer until a new dean came on board. Unlike his predecessor (who displayed a marked prejudice n favor of Iowa and Columbia grads), the new dean—whose name, I kid you not, was Dexter Bronze—took a more intuitive approach. In his email he wrote, "You have an interesting resume. Let's meet."

A few days later, wearing a dark blue sport coat handed down to me from Gregory (who had put on a few extra pounds and liked dressing his slob of a twin in his clothes), I arrived at the cramped midtown office of the Metropolitan Writing Institute, an enterprise familiar to all New Yorkers from the fluorescent orange catalogue kiosks bearing its name on every other street corner. There I met Mr. Bronze: a broad-shouldered, solid-looking man at least ten years my junior, with short-cropped gray hair and eyes that, matching his surname, looked like tarnished bronze. He spoke with a Texan drawl. In a cluttered conference room, he had me stand before the white board while he sat at the far end of the conference table.

"You've got thirty minutes," he said, checking his Rolex, folding his arms over his burly chest. "Teach me something."

I discussed scenes, how they are the basic building blocks of narrative, how, as Forster said, "we are all like Scheherazade's husband in that we all like to know *what happens next*," and what happens next is called a scene, how the word derives from the Greek word for the tent or shelter housing a dramatic performance. Putting my art school training to work, on the white board I drew one of those Victorian carpetbags, the kind Mary Poppins carries, a portmanteau, and explained how, like a portmanteau, scenes hold not only action and dialogue, the primary elements of drama, but summary, description, background, flashbacks, stream-of-consciousness, thoughts, memories, reflections, digressions. I went on to discuss framed narratives and flashbacks, taking Mr. Bronze on a guided tour through a superb example of the latter in Updike's *The Centaur*. I concluded my lecture with an appreciation of "circadian narratives": stories, novels, and memoirs set within a single day or scene (Woolf's *Mrs. Dalloway;* Joyce's *Ulysses,* Sebald's *The Rings of Saturn*), explaining how, in each of these works, mundane, grounding actions (a man walking along a stretch of shoreline; a woman preparing for a party) formed the still hubs at the center of their dramas.

"Whether we're narrating or reflecting," I said in conclusion, "writing exposition or action, summary or description, we should always—always—be writing scenes. Scenes are the coin of the realm of storytelling. They're what keeps King Schariar's sword off the backs of our necks."

I was hired.

• •

Starting then and for the next (nine? ten?) years I taught at the Metropolitan Writing Institute. I was a good teacher. "Evangelical" was the word Dean Bronze used to describe my pedagogic style.

There are rules to good storytelling, rules that can, and occasionally should, be broken. But before you can break the rules, you have to master them. Think of the great abstract impressionist painters (I'd say this—or something like it—to my students), of Pollock,

Rothko, Miro. They knew the laws of perspective, the effects of lighting, the fundamentals of color and composition. You see it in Pollock's drips, in Rothko's scumblings, in Miro's orbs and squiggles.

I taught my students that the fiction writer's essential task is to create experiences for the reader: not to tell us how a character feels, but to make us feel by putting us in the character's shoes. The difference between good and bad storytelling comes down to the difference between conclusions based on evidence and the evidence itself.

I taught them about point of view, how it comes down to the difference between the author and the narrator, how, when that distinction is lost, fiction dies. *No POV = No Story!*

I showed them how the best forms of suspense are attained with generosity rather than through coy withholding ("false suspense"), how great endings are both surprising ("Oh my God!") and inevitable ("But of course!"), how a great style is largely a matter of constraint, of the things an author resists doing, that the choices we make in the name of precision and clarity will ultimately serve both substance and style, while those made for style's sake serve only an insecure author's ego.

And I taught them about plot. In all works of fiction there are only two plots, really: Plot A and Plot B. Plot A gives us an unhappy character, a protagonist unsatisfied with her or his lot. With Plot A, I explained, the inciting incident is an opportunity seized by the protagonist in order to escape an unhappy status quo. Example: a failed author's successful identical twin brother commits suicide, providing him the chance to take his brother's place and gain the success that has eluded him. It doesn't end there, of course, since opportunity seized always brings complications.

Which brings us to Plot B, wherein an irritant or setback of some kind upsets a character's status-quo contentment, to wit: Having assumed the identity of his successful twin, our protagonist confronts the circumstance or circumstances that drove his successful twin to commit suicide in the first place.

In most stories, Plots A and B do a dance together, the opportunity/misfortune tango, with opportunity leading to misfortune, and misfortune leading to opportunity. And so on.

In fiction routine exists for one reason: to be disrupted by extraordinary events. Before disrupting it, however, it helps to enhance the status quo, to raise the stakes. If the status quo finds the protagonist content, give him *more* reasons to be happy, so when the status quo is subverted, he'll have a greater height to fall from. As your hero sits there on a high limb of his contentment tree, send a few butterflies of good fortune fluttering his way. As he snatches at them, bring him down with a salvo of stones.

Stone #1: My Enlarged Prostate Gland

It started just around the time I took the Metropolitan job. I couldn't sleep. I was getting up six times a night to pee. My prostate was to blame. (Yes, like the hero of "Harris' Book".)

Dr. Snyder, my urologist, assured me that, though I was young for the condition, it was neither serious nor uncommon. However, he went on to say, short of surgery ("Out of the question at your age"), there was no cure, and the drugs used to treat symptoms came with a laundry list of side effects, including hair growth, loss of libido, and something called "retrograde ejaculation"—an orgasm that backfires into the bladder, where it does no harm, but neither does it do any good.

"On the other hand," Dr. Snyder added sanguinely, "the pills may have no beneficial effect at all." In other words I might grow hair and be impotent and still have to get up ten times a night to pee. Rather than take any drugs, I chose to endure the occasional bout of insomnia.

Stone #2: God's Impala

You are already aware that I lived in a Bronx tenement with a bathtub in the center of its kitchen. I won't describe my neighborhood except for one detail that strikes me as pertinent if not symbolic: a car parked on the street in front of my building. Parked cars don't usually qualify as permanent features of a neighborhood. This one did. As testified to by a garland of fluorescent orange parking tickets tucked under its wiper blades, it had been there for some time: a boat-like Chevrolet Impala, its blue paint job faded to rust where visible under a mélange of bumper stickers, decals, flags, bunting, colored Christmas lights, plastic Jesuses, and other objects promulgating God and country. Spray-painted in blood red across the side of the car facing the street:

THERE IS ONE GOD AND MOSES IS HIS PROPHET

Why "God's Impala" qualifies as a stone will be made apparent in the course of time. For now suffice it to say that the vehicle was an ongoing source of perturbation.

Stone #3: My Brother's Odd Behavior

I'd been teaching at the Metropolitan Writing Institute for three years when the first clues emerged that my brother's "status quo" was undergoing a change. The first clue was a phone call from Sheila, Gregory's wife. The phone call itself was a departure from the norm. My brother's wife wasn't in the habit of phoning me; she'd never done so before. She asked me if I had spoken to Greg recently.

In fact, months had passed since our last real conversation. During it Greg had mentioned a project he'd been working on and that he seemed very excited about, his paper on the *Kybalion*. It was he who'd phoned me in an excited state, wanting to share his discovery of the phenomenon known as *Urphänomen*, one of the many German words for which there exist no equivalents in the English language: the notion that the smaller and more humble an object, the greater the likelihood of its containing the whole plan of the universe in concentrated form—a grain of rice, the atom. I listened patiently. It was, it turned out and as I've said, our last real conversation. After that two weeks passed with no call from him, then three, then a month, then two months…I tried phoning him a few times only to get his voicemail. More than once I left a message. When I finally got him on the phone his end of the conversations was as brief as it was perfunctory.

"*How are you?*"

"*Fine.*"

"*What's new?*"

"*Nothing much.*"

Put-off though I was by my own twin giving me the bum's rush, I chalked it up to Greg's being deep into his new project.

Nor was I unsympathetic. I was busy myself, revising my novel for something like the sixth time. I understood what it meant to be in the throes of creativity.

Then the call from Sheila.

"No," I told her. "We haven't spoken in a while. Why?"

"It's nothing, really. It's just that—well, Greg's been acting a bit strange lately, that's all."

I waited.

"It started with little things. Habits." She gave a little laugh. "He drinks his coffee black."

"What?"

"His coffee. He always used to take it with milk and sugar. He *hates*—or *hated*—black coffee. He used to give me a hard time for drinking mine that way. 'How can you stand it?' he'd say. 'It's so harsh, so *bitter,* so *nasty.*' Then, a little over a year ago, he comes home from this conference and the next morning at breakfast suddenly he's drinking his coffee black. Don't you think that's just a little odd?"

"I suppose," I said. "But it doesn't seem to be something that you need to worry that much about."

"Do you drink black coffee?"

"No," I said. "I take cream and sugar. I hate black coffee."

"And you don't think it's strange?"

"People's tastes change, Sheila."

"That's just the beginning. He started buying odd things, clothes and shoes. Things he would never have bought before."

"Like?"

"Black leather pants."

"You're joking."

"And a matching leather jacket. I teased him. I said, 'Do you plan to get a motorcycle to go with that outfit?' Well—guess what?"

"He bought a motorcycle?" I said.

"A Harley," Sheila said. "Used. He got it on Craigslist."

"Does my brother even know how to ride a motorcycle?"

"He's been taking lessons," Sheila said grimly. "And last week I came home from work and there's something in the driveway. A car, I assume, though I can't tell since it's hidden under a tarp. He greets me with this, this huge grin on his face. 'What's in our drive-way?' He dangles a set of car keys in front of me. 'Happy Birth-day,' he says. My birthday was three months ago. Then he takes me in his arms, waltzes me out to the driveway, and unveils the thing. A sports car, a Miata. Cherry Red. Not used. Brand new."

"Where's he getting the money for all this stuff?"

"That's a very good question. I asked him the same thing. 'Greg,' I said. 'Can we *afford* this?' Philosophy professors don't exactly make a killing. And I'm not exactly raking in the big bucks at the clinic. Plus we've got two mortgages to pay, thanks to your brother's decision to buy your father's house—which he still refuses to sell, even though your father's been dead for seven years and in those seven years we've spent a grand total of three weekends down there."

"What did he say?" I asked.

"About?"

"When you asked him—about the Miata, whether he could afford it?"

"He said, 'Don't worry about it.' When I pressed him, he refused to talk about it anymore. He said, 'You remind me of my mother, you worry so damn much.' Do you think maybe he might be gambling?"

"Greg—gambling?"

"Or...I don't know...cooking and selling methamphet-amines—like whatshisname, the bald guy in *Breaking Bad*?"

"Sheila, come on."

"Maybe it's something with his brain. I read somewhere that certain frontal lobe injuries can change someone's personality. Maybe he fell in the shower and banged his forehead on the fau-cet." She gave a little laugh but sounded desperate.

"Sheila, listen. He bought himself a motorcycle and you a car. If you ask me, it sounds like a classic midlife crisis. We're pushing fifty. Heck, maybe I should get a sports car." (I laughed, unaware that within a month by ironic coincidence I would inherit Julie's formerly spiffy Mazda. Sheila didn't return my laughter.)

"I'm serious, Stewart. Something's very wrong. For the past few months, every morning from five a.m. until noon he locks himself in his study. He won't let me or anything disturb him."

"He's working on a project."

"Why does he have to be so secretive about it? He always shared everything he wrote with me. He used to wear me out having me read every draft of everything. Now he won't share a word. He won't even say what he's working on."

"Something about the *Kybalion,* I think," I said.

"The what?"

"A book of ancient Egyptian philosophy. Anyway, Sheila, I really don't see why you're so upset. Heck, people change."

"Not like this," Sheila said. "Not that suddenly. I tell you, something is seriously wrong!"

Our conversation ended with me promising Sheila that I would phone my brother, that I'd speak with him.

Four days and a dozen phone messages later, Greg phoned.

"What's up, Stew?"

I didn't beat around the bush.

"Greg, what the hell is going on?"

"What do you mean?"

I reiterated my conversation with Sheila. Greg laughed.

"It's not a laughing matter. She's really worried."

"There's nothing to worry about. I told her so. Now I'm telling you. Everything's fine."

"What about all this money you've been spending?"

"There's not a problem."

"How isn't there a problem? What—did you win the lottery?"

"Look, everything's fine. Or it will be. Trust me."

"I'd trust you more if you were a little more forthcoming."

"There's nothing to worry about. Really. Sheila isn't comfortable with change. Most people aren't comfortable with change, even when it's for the better. You know what they say."

"No. What do they say?"

"If everyone had the chance to throw all their problems into a giant bowl and pick out new ones, we'd all grab the same problems back."

"Your point being?"

"My point is that everything's fine."

"Where's all this money you're spending coming from?"

"I came into a little money from a publishing project."

"Oh? What—a textbook?"

"Yes, that's right, a textbook. You could call it that."

"Greg, that's—that's great."

"Anyway, Sheila's got nothing at all to worry about and neither do you. All right? Listen, I've got to go now. I've got a meeting I need to attend. We'll talk again soon. Okay?"

•   •

For their nineteenth wedding anniversary my brother bought Sheila a diamond ring. The Greg I knew—had known—found diamonds ostentatious, vulgar even, like drinking champagne out of a slipper or eating breakfast in bed or doing anything whatsoever in a heart-shaped Jacuzzi. Notwithstanding which, on their wedding anniversary, in a resort hotel in Martinique, Greg and his wife undertook each of these activities, so Sheila told me with a mixture of delight and alarm shortly afterwards.

•   •

Less than two months after their wedding anniversary, my phone rang again. My mother this time.

"Have you heard?" she asked me.

"What?"

"Your brother—he's divorcing Sheila."

"What? Says who? Where did you hear this?"

"Sheila phoned. Just now. She's so upset! That's not all. He quit his job. I don't understand it. I'm so confused. Have you talked to your brother? Has he said anything to you?"

"No," I said. "Not a word."

"Oh God, Stewart—this is terrible. Terrible!" My mother sobbed.

"Mother, please, try to—"

"Why would your brother do such a thing? Quitting his job? Is he crazy? Might there be a reason? Do you think maybe he got fired? Did he do something crazy, like have an affair with a student, maybe? Or did Sheila ... do you think ..."

"Mother, please, it's best not to jump to — "

"Are you sure he didn't say anything to you?"

"Nothing, Mother, I swear. As far as I know their marriage was fine. The last I heard from Sheila, they'd just gotten back from Martinique. I mean, there've been some issues, but ... "

"What issues?"

"Well, you know, the usual stuff."

"Like *what*?"

"Oh, Mother, I don't know. I'm just guessing."

"When did you last speak with him?"

"I don't know. Two months ago?"

"Two *months*?"

"He's been busy, Mother. We've both been busy."

"I don't understand; I just don't understand ..."

"Mother, please, try to — "

"How can I calm dawn? This is terrible; terrible ..."

After getting off the phone with my mother, I phoned my brother at the college and got his voicemail as usual. Every day for the next few days I left messages, sometimes more than one. In my last message I made no attempt to conceal my anger. I was livid. How could Greg have done that to Sheila?

Greg never called back.

• •

A week later, I was on my way to teach my Thursday evening memoir class, riding the crowded downtown #6 local subway train (did I tell you this already?), clutching Janice Hauptmann's memoir-in-progress about her love affair with an octogenarian Brazilian former flamenco dancer, when I locked eyes with the long-haired, goateed, bespectacled, leather-jacketed author of *Coffee, Black* grinning at me from a poster advertising his bestselling book. As I think I've told you, I'd seen that poster and the photo in it many times, but without *really* seeing it, with that oblivion with respect to their surroundings that dyed-in-the-wool New Yorkers are so good at. A dead body in the street? A high-wire act between skyscrapers? You won't see us gawking. Why would I have given the time of day to a face in a subway ad? Yet there I was, locking eyes with this man I suddenly recognized as my own flesh and blood, my twin brother. It couldn't be! How was it possible? I remembered Sheila telling me of Greg's sudden dramatic changes in habits, among other things how he'd taken to drinking his coffee black. *And grown a beard.*

With the recognition dawning on me, the subway car's massed humanity and convulsing walls darkened and closed in on me. As the subway careened between Fourteenth Street and Astor Place, Janice Hauptmann's manuscript slipped from my grip and I fainted.

• •

How I got through that evening's class I'm not sure. Somehow I managed to perform. Still, my students knew something was wrong. I saw the looks of curiosity and concern in their eyes. Even Janice Hauptmann, whose manuscript I'd gone uncharacteristically easy on, seemed worried. After class as I was tucking papers into my briefcase, Janice of all people asked me if I was all right. I made excuses, thanked her, hurried off, hoping to get to the Barnes & Noble at Astor Place before it closed. Maybe I was wrong. Maybe the author of *Coffee, Black* wasn't my twin brother after all, but someone who happened to look exactly like him, my doppelgänger, not an impossibility when you take into account the fact that our faces were so unextraordinary.

Though I hurried, I arrived there ten minutes after the store closed. There, in one of the brightly lit display windows, was the same photo of my doppelgänger, blown up to Olympic proportions, mounted on a slab of foam core and propped up against a pyramid constructed out of a few dozen hardback copies of *Coffee, Black.* "No. 1 NYT Bestseller," the poster proclaimed in bright red typography across its top. At the bottom, underneath the author's grinning face:

Meet Bestselling Author
Brock Jones, PhD
Author Reading & Signing
Friday, Nov. 20, 7:00 p.m.

There was no need for me to take note of the time and date. It was twenty-one hours and forty-six minutes away, the very next day.

• •

That night, thanks to my prostate, I slept poorly. Before going to bed, I'd performed what had become an odd little ritual. I stripped off my BVD's, replacing them with a skimpy blue Speedo. From my top dresser drawer I took a balled heavy winter sock and stuffed it into the Speedo—not where you think, Dear Reader, as a visual enhancement, but farther back, closer to my anus. I discovered the remedy online. By applying mild pressure to that nether region of my body, the rolled-up sock squeezed my urethra, thereby suppressing my incontinental urges and thus sparing me from getting up ten times a night to pee. Sometimes the sock worked, sometimes it didn't.

It didn't work. Starting at around one a.m., and every half-hour thereafter, I rose to acquit myself of the latest phantom urge and token thimbleful of urine.

Dear Reader, should you ever need an argument against Intelligent Design, look no further than the male prostate gland. The word *prostate*, in case you're wondering, comes from the Greek word for "to put before." What my prostate had been put before I can't say; but that most growth-centric gland had wrapped itself around my urethra, where no intelligent designer would have put it, pinching it like a straw between fingers.

And though it's called Benign Prostatic Hyperplasia, trust me, there's nothing benign about being roused ten times a night and dragging your sleepy bones to the bathroom only to stand there, inert as Neptune's statue presiding over a fountain, yet unable to do what fountains do so well. You spread your legs like Ty Cobb with bases loaded, contemplate the fabulous waterworks at Tivoli Gardens, the Great Cascade at Petrehof, the spouting dolphins and spewing gargoyles of the Villa Lante. You harbor wistful memories of having once peed like a god. Never mind campfires: you could have extinguished the Great Fires of London and San Francisco combined. You recall how, as a boy of seven or eight, you'd sign your name in snowbanks, the strokes steaming with your body's golden effluence, a fleeting testimonial to the Palmer Method. You remember your suicidally dead philosophy professor father, the first person with whom you ever took a leak outdoors, standing side-by-side on the edge of his dock facing the twilit lake, pulling out father-and-son dicks, his tawny and uncircumcised, yours minus (thanks to Dr. Spock) its protective sheaf, pale as the bud of a white English rose. Together you aimed into the lake. Watching Dad's glittering soaring parabola, you'd think to yourself: *when I can pee that far, I'll be a man!*

Such fond memories do you no good as you stand there, blocked as a pipe full of concrete. Should mercy shine its dim light upon you, you might rid yourself of a soupçon of urine, enough to speckle the rim of the bowl or dribble down your leg. Ever the optimist, you keep standing there, your thoughts by now gone abstract. Urinous puns assail you: *To pee or not to pee. Let it pee. Piss on earth. Pee of good cheer.* Jokes, too. *Elderly patient: Doctor, I can't pee anymore. Doctor: How old are you? Patient: Seventy-six. Doctor: You've peed enough.* None of this helps. You feel furthermore that you are being watched, that this is a scene in a supposedly funny play scripted by Neil Simon at the top of his game in which you are the hapless lead. Based on past performances, even assuming that you manage to eek out that thimbleful of urine, should you return to bed you'll be back again in half an hour. Or you'll lie there trying but failing to ignore your bladder that keeps crying "Empty me! Empty me!"—like David Hedison in *The Fly*.

• •

Instead of going straight back to bed, I went into my "study" (the kitchen) and sat at my "desk" (salvaged door over tub). No sooner did I do so than the balled sock in my Speedo declared itself rudely. I ripped it out and slammed it to the floor, then yanked the Speedo off and flung it across the room, where it landed on my dead Mrs. Cox geranium.

Having nothing better to do, I Googled "Brock Jones, PhD." Aside from web pages dedicated to promoting his book, my investigation turned up nothing.

I shut off my computer, ate a bowl of Raisin Bran with water (I'd run out of milk). While doing so I made the mistake of looking out my kitchen window. There, wreathed by ginkgo tree branches, glowing—insofar as a rusty car can be said to glow—under the pink radiance of a mercury vapor lamp, sat the Godmobile, the Divine Impala. Patiently vigilant, it awaited the End of Days—or its owner, whichever arrived first. By its owner I don't mean the person to whom, assuming it was registered at all, the vehicle was registered—and who in all likelihood had skipped out on a DUI and was evading a bench warrant—but the Good Lord Himself.

Who, come to think of it, should have been arrested, too.

•   •

The next morning I went out and bought a copy of *Coffee, Black*. I had to go into Manhattan to get it, there being not a single bookstore in the entire borough of The Bronx. Two baseball stadiums, one soon to be torn down, the other brand new, each big enough to accommodate 50,000 illiterate Yankee fans, but not one damn bookstore.

I returned to the same Barnes & Noble, the one at Astor Place, to buy the book. Gramercy Park being closed to non-residents, I walked over to Stuyvesant Square. Having wiped the snow off a bench, I sat and started reading, or tried to, the printed pages having to vie with my sense of vertigo as I turned them, finding them to hold far more questions than answers. Could it really have been so simple a matter for my brother—for anyone, according to his book—to change…everything? As simple as ordering a cup of coffee without milk or sugar? Yet that, in a nutshell, was *Coffee, Black*'s premise.

Lest anyone doubted it, he had the example of his own precipitously changed life to submit as evidence. Now he'd go on to change more lives, millions more, according to the words spread across a horizontal band of gold ("OVER 1 MILLION COPIES IN PRINT") topping the cover of my already-in-its-third-printing trade paperback edition. The author's biography:

Brock Jones, PhD is whoever he wants to be.
This is his first book.

Dedication: *"To all my selves."*
Less than halfway through the book, having as yet come upon

no mention of the author's talented twin, I did what I had sworn to myself I wouldn't do: I skipped to the index. There, among S's, I searched for Stewart. Nada. Then, among the D's, I searched for my — our — last name: ... *depression ... determinism ... deus ex machina* ... But no Detweiler.

The park bench having become too cold, I repaired to Pete's Tavern, where I resumed my reading of *Coffee, Black*. I did so in the second booth from the front, the one where, according to local lore, the writer William Sydney Porter, aka O'Henry, known for the surprise twist endings of his stories, wrote "The Gift of the Magi," about an impoverished young married couple's quest to obtain Christmas gifts for each other. Della sells her beautiful hair to a hairdresser to buy a pocket watch chain for Jim, who has meanwhile sold his pocket watch to afford a set of combs for Della, voiding both of their gifts of all but their spiritual value. Hence the story's title.

I was two-thirds of the way through *Coffee, Black* when seven o'clock arrived. Fortified with two martinis, I made my way to the Barnes & Noble store. All this time I clung to the thread of hope that the author of *Coffee, Black* would turn out to be someone other than my twin. That thread was broken at the reading event to which I arrived late.

The event was packed. There had to have been at least a hundred warm bodies in folding chairs, and half as many more standing and squatting among the rows of bookshelves. He wore the Philip Johnson glasses, the leather sport coat, and a fedora — not the white Panama, a black one. Though his manner of dress was entirely different, though he had trimmed down, and though his mannerisms struck me as oddly unfamiliar, the moment he opened his mouth to address the crowd the last vestige of doubt dissolved. There was no question. Brock Jones, PhD was — had been — my brother.

I stood behind the crowd. From there the speaker's face was the size of a pea. Still I was left with no doubt.

The event lasted less than three quarters of an hour. He read a short excerpt from his book, then took questions from the audience. I listened distractedly, hearing every other word. I had a question of my own to ask. My question: "I heard somewhere that you have a twin brother. Is it true?" It took some time for me to screw up the courage to do so, but eventually I raised my hand.

My brother never saw it. Or maybe he did. Anyway, he never called on me.

The Q&A session over, I watched as fans, some holding as many as a half-dozen copies of my brother's book, stood in line to have their copies signed. It occurred to me that eighteen years had passed since Gregory had watched people standing in a similar line—albeit a much shorter one—to have me sign their copies of *Penny Sufferings*. I wondered if he had suffered half as much distress then as I did presently. But then I hadn't acted as though my brother didn't exist. Or had I?

The line of eager autograph seekers still stretched halfway across the floor when I turned and left the store.

• •

By the time I got home it was close to midnight. The streetlamp in front of my tenement building wasn't working. Though I could barely see it, I knew the Impala was there, parked in its usual spot. That car had a malicious presence. Like the discharge of ozone preceding a storm, it augured bad things. Before stepping into my tenement building and climbing the five flights to my apartment, I paid my respects to its curbed malevolence, its parked pathology, conjuring for its absent owner a series of increasingly dismal fates, from ensnarement with an NYPD tow truck to various forms of spontaneous combustion, vaporization, decapitation, Waterhouse-Friderichsen Syndrome, and other wasting diseases.

I had just done so and taken three steps toward my building's front door when I noticed the shadow sitting on the curb next to the car. At first I assumed it must be the car's owner, returned for it at last, a conclusion reinforced by the fact that the shadow looked no less derelict than the car itself. I was about to confront—him? her?—when the shadow spoke to me in a voice I recognized immediately. A woman's voice.

"Sheila?" I said.

Indeed, it was my brother's wife, his soon to be ex-wife, sitting on my stoop. Wailing, she threw her arms around me—or rather around my legs, for she was still seated on the curb.

"Sheila, my God!" I said, kneeling close to her, stroking her. "What—what are you doing here?"

"I had to see you," she said through her sobs.

"Let's go inside," I said.

Though Sheila was eight years my junior and physically fit from her relentless yoga regimen, on each of the five flights leading up to my railroad flat I had to stop and wait for her to catch her breath, so winded was she from sobbing. Once in my apartment, with her sitting on my uncomfortable faux-leather sofa, I offered her a drink. "Here," I said handing her the only cocktail I could manage. "It's rotten gin, but I've added a splash of olive juice to render it less toxic."

"Thanks," she said, drinking it down in two gulps as I looked on intently. "Mm—that hit the spot," she said breathlessly. Then, handing me the glass back. "Can you make me another?"

"Sure. Hungry?" I asked, doing so. "I've got a frozen fresh-caught salmon filet I can thaw and some green beans I can sautée *haricot verts* style."

"That sounds fine," she said with little enthusiasm.

"How did you get here, anyway?"

"I drove," she said. "The Miata. It's parked across the street. I hope that's okay. I don't understand New York City parking regulations."

"Who does? They're just a gloss on anarchy. You should be okay until morning."

"I guess you've heard? About me and Greg?"

I nodded. "Mom told me."

"When?"

"A few days ago. She phoned." I handed Sheila a second drink. "Maybe he'll change his mind," I said hopefully.

She shook her head. "He won't. I'm sure of it," she said, gulping her gin. "You don't know Greg anymore, Stew. He's changed completely. It started out like I said with little things, changes that I thought were cute at first, you know, wearing different clothes, eating different foods. One day just like that he's a vegetarian." She shrugged. "No big deal; I can live without hamburgers. He always hated cats. Suddenly he comes home with two kittens. He buys penny loafers—penny loafers!—and wears them with actual pennies. One day, we're about to sit down to dinner, he puts a CD of the *Blue Danube* on, picks me up out of my chair, and waltzes me from room to room around the whole house. Great, I thought. Why not? It was cute. He's like a new man—a happy man. What's not to like? But the changes—they keep on coming. The new cars, the impromptu weekend jaunts to Europe. Four-star hotels, five-star restaurants. Champagne and caviar. Suddenly I'm Zelda to his Scott Fitzgerald. I'm all smiles, but I'm not enjoying any of it because the man I'm with happens to be a total stranger. I mean who is this guy ordering room service at one in the morning, wanting us to have breakfast in bed? Back home he takes up gardening and golf. Golf! A membership in the local country club. Who knew there were country clubs in Vermont?"

As she spoke, while I snapped the ends off green beans, olive oil heated in the frying pan.

"When he's not playing golf or tending his gardenias, he's locked in his study, typing away on his secret project. I knew he was keeping secrets from me; I'm no dummy; I knew the signs. But what secrets? Was he having an affair? That would have explained a lot. The fancy trips, the flowers, the diamond earrings and other spontaneous expensive gifts: he's expiating his guilt. Meanwhile he's having a sordid affair. Only it's not an affair. Not with a woman, anyway. It's more like he's having a love affair with himself, or with his new *selves,* I should say, since there seems to be a new version of Gregory Detweiler every other day. Meanwhile I'm stuck with my same old tired self, watching helplessly as he becomes all these other people … Then, two weeks after our nineteenth anniversary, like *that*—" she snapped her finger, "—bam, he asks me for a divorce. Just like *that*! And the *way* he did it. He takes me to dinner. A Thai restaurant, this place in a strip mall. Not a bad place, but still. We're sitting there, eating Pad Thai and yellow curry, when out of the blue he says to me, "You know, Sheila, I've been doing some thinking. I think we've been married long enough." She shook her head. "The thing is, I can't fault him. I can't fault him because I can't judge him. I can't judge him because I don't know who I'd be judging. He's constantly remaking himself, like Proteus." She cried; I held her. "I just want to know why, Stewart. Why?"

"I wish I knew, Sheila," I said, stroking her. "I'm as much in the dark about all of this as you are. All I know is what I read in his book."

"Book?" said Sheila.

"It explains a lot, don't you think?"

"His PhD thesis? *Transindividuality in Spinoza?*"

I shook my head. "Come on, Sheila."

"I'm sorry, but what book?"

"The book."

She looked blankly at me.

"*Coffee, Black.*"

Her blank stare deepened.

"Sheila, for God's sake!"

"I'm sorry, but I have no idea what you're talking about." She looked alarmed, frightened.

"My God. He never *told* you?"

"Told me what? What book? What are *saying*?"

"Wait," I said. I went into my bedroom, got my still unfinished, heavily dog-eared copy of *Coffee, Black*, returned with it. I handed it to her. She stared uncomprehendingly at the cover.

She shook her head. "What's this got to do with anything?"

"Look at the back cover."

She did. There was my brother's—her soon to be ex-husband's—face plastered across the dust jacket.

"I still don't get it."

"You don't recognize him?"

She shook her head. "Brock Jones? I never heard of him."

"Forget the name, Sheila. Look closer."

She kept staring. Then:

"Oh, no. Oh my god. It's not... It *can't* be!"

I nodded. "It's Greg," I said.

"I don't believe it."

"I assumed you knew."

She shook her head.

It made no sense to me, either, at first. How could she not know? Then I remembered how long it had taken me to find out. Sheila and Greg never watched TV; since they'd been married they hadn't owned a television set. Neither of them paid much attention to pop culture. It was entirely possible that she'd never seen an advertisement for the book. For all I knew she'd never heard of *Coffee, Black.*

Still, I thought, even if Sheila had been completely unaware of the book or its author, surely some of their friends, colleagues, and acquaintances, hers and Greg's, had to have known about it. Surely one of them, at least, would have made the connection, would have recognized "Brock Jones, PhD" and outed him to Sheila. Unless...

Had they *all* failed the Gorilla Test? Was it *possible?*

Anyway Sheila had failed it.

"It may be cold comfort," I said to her, "but when I found out I was just as astonished as you are."

For the next half hour I told my sister-in-law what I knew about the book, what it was about. (And, if you're wondering, no: there'd been no mention in *Coffee, Black* of Sheila Detweiler's existence, either.)

"You think you know people," Sheila said as I poured her another drink and fried the green beans. "It's my business to know them, my profession. I help people know themselves better so they can do a better job of negotiating their own lives. That's what I assumed I'd been doing all those years. Now I see what a sham it all was, what a charlatan I've been. We can't know anyone. It's impossible. Just when you think you know someone, boom, they change —" She snapped her fingers again. "—like *that!*"

I said nothing. I sautéed the green beans. *Haricots verts.* Whatever.

"Here I am saying all these things to you as if I know you; as if you're who I think you are, when for all I know you're a completely different person, no less a stranger to me than your brother." She gave a little laugh. "Maybe you are your brother. The thought occurred to me, you know. You'd switched places, you and Gregory, the way you did that time in elementary school.

No wonder he hasn't been himself. He *isn't* himself; he's *you*. You pulled the ol' switcheroo on me, a practical joke. Is that what's happened? Are you really Stewart? Huh? Are you sure you're not Gregory?" She'd come up behind me as I faced the stove. She put her arms around my waist and rested her head on my shoulder. As she caressed me I concentrated on the *haricots verts*. What else could I do? Even if he was no longer himself, still, I wasn't about to sleep with my brother's wife. The salmon was in the broiler. She held fast to me as I bent to inspect it.

"Looks just about done," I said, the oven's breath hot against my cheeks. As I rose to get a fork to test it Sheila worked her way around to kissing me. The next moment served up a tableau of an aproned male fending off a woman's advances with two oven-mitted hands. "Sheila, no," I said with forced laughter, though I was terror-stricken. My brother's wife!

Just then an enormous thunderclap shook the apartment. With the oven still yawning we fell into each other's arms. Because it was on the top floor my kitchen had a skylight. Through it flashed the lightning that gave rise to the next explosion, and the one after that. With the fourth flash the lights went out.

I've always exercised a dutiful suspiciousness with respect to the weather as a metaphor in literature. Cleansing rain, illuminating lightning, chastising thunder, perplexing fogs, and moody mists … How meteorology, that dullest of all topics of conversation, became an acceptable subject for fiction, let alone one endowed with potent metaphorical implications, is a mystery to me. Who's to say if a thunderstorm is hell and damnation or just the sky doing its laundry? Sometimes — usually, in fact — a thunderstorm is just a thunderstorm.

That said, it was owing to a thunderstorm that I wound up sleeping with my brother's wife that night — slept with, I say, for we did not engage in sex of any sort. Instead we spent the night curled up in my twin bed like … I nearly said "like a pair of commas" … like the two halves of the Tao symbol, the yin-yang, head-to-toe, or as the French say, *tête-bêche*. How we ended up in that position I'm not sure, but I warrant it was in all innocence. To be sure I would not have forgotten had it been arrived at otherwise.

It was in that configuration that I found us on awakening a few hours later, my prostate-impinged bladder doing its thing, the thunderstorm having abated, Sheila's impressive snores rumbling through my apartment.

How I managed to sleep through the rest of that night I have no idea, but I awoke to sunshine and a disheveled but otherwise ordinary bed, neither Sheila nor anyone else but me in it. The power was back on. On my kitchen table under my Bialetti Moka espresso pot my brother's soon to be ex-wife had left a terse note: "Thank you." That was all.

That was the last time I saw or heard from Sheila.

• •

In the morning I phoned my mother.

"Your son is a bestselling author," I told her.

"Stewart — that's wonderful! Congratulations!"

"Not me, Mother," I said. "Gregory — or rather Brock Jones, PhD."

"Who?"

"You know nothing about this?"

"About what?"

"Gregory wrote a book. A bestseller. A huge bestseller. It's called *Coffee, Black*. It's a self-help book."

"Don't be silly."

"The reason you haven't heard of it, Mother, is because he wrote it under an assumed name." I spoke through gritted teeth.

"What are you talking about?"

"Brock Jones, PhD, that's what I'm talking about."

"All right, so Greg wrote a book. And it's a bestseller. Good for him. You make it sound like the worst thing in the world!"

"He changed his *name*, Mother!"

"Big deal. Authors do that all the time, don't they?"

"He's kept it a secret — from us, from Sheila, from everyone."

"I still don't see why you're so upset."

"Him keeping something like that from us? You don't find that upsetting? Of all the things that you get upset about, *that* doesn't upset you?"

"Calm down, Stewart, please!"

I asked: "Have you spoken with him recently?"

"Yes."

"When?"

"I don't know, Stewart. A week ago, maybe."

"And he said nothing to you—about any of this?"

"No."

"I'll be damned." I looked out my window. The crazy Impala was parked there as always. By now there must have been something like eighteen parking tickets on it, the thing was abloom with them, the fluorescent orange notices faded to a pale peach by a combination of sunshine and rain. Why hadn't the Chief of Transportation towed the damn thing away, already?

"Stewart? Are you there?"

"Yeah, I'm still here, Mother. Nominally."

"Maybe he wanted to surprise us."

"He surprised me, all right. He surprised Sheila, too, by suing her for a divorce. No wonder he quit his job. He must be rolling in money."

"Now you sound jealous."

"Oh, Mother, please!" Was I jealous? Yes, I suppose I must have been. Not only was my brother still the goddamn Millionaire to my Pauper; now he was the artist, too. Of all the ways in which a person can become obscenely rich, my brother had to go and do so by writing a fucking book.

"You're right, Mother," I said. "I'm jealous. I should be happy for him. I should be glad that my brother who no longer returns my phone calls and who I haven't spoken with in months and who denies my existence is suddenly rich and famous and lapping up his accolades under a pseudonym, with his wife, mother, and twin brother left completely in the dark. Wonderful."

"You'll see, Stewart. I'm sure he planned to tell us all about it."

"I don't want him to tell me about it. I don't want to *know* about it. I wish I didn't know. It's like some sort of bad joke."

"It must be a good book."

"Jesus, Mother!"

"You said it's a bestseller, didn't you?"

"Who cares if it's a good book or not? He lied to us, Mother! He lied to us all! He's been lying to us for a year—longer, probably."

"He's not lying, Stewart."

"What do you call it?"

"He just hasn't been very... forthcoming."

"A lie of omission is still a lie! Christ, Mother. How can you defend him like this? How can you take it so calmly, you who lose sleep over forgotten Christmas cards or a strange rash? For God's sake, look what he's done to Sheila!"

"Yes," my mother conceded. "Yes, that is a shame."

•   •

I still hadn't finished reading *Coffee, Black*. That evening, after teaching my intermediate fiction workshop, on the train back to The Bronx, abetted by two more very dry martinis drunk in swift succession at the Campbell Apartment in Grand Central Terminal, I read the last fifty pages.

Like the book's first hundred and thirty-five pages, its final fifty thrived on lurid analogies and overly broad abstractions, among them how most people—at least 95%, in Dr. Jones' estimation—are "prisoners serving out a life sentence." Their crime? Failure to see beyond their own "limited conceptions of themselves." From this metaphor the text stumbles into the next, how each of us is "an artist whose masterpiece is his or her own self," how those selves are "paintings-in-progress," how, just as the average, non-artist's ability to render accurately a face or a room or a chair or whatever else is directly in front of them is hindered by their notion—their preconceived idea—of what they are looking at, the average person's ability to clearly perceive and therefore realize his or her true self, to "paint their masterpiece," is encumbered by preconceived notions of who they are, notions suggested—nay, dictated—by who they've been, or worse: by who they believe themselves to have been. Or worse still: by who *others* perceive them to be. Around all these mixed metaphors *Coffee, Black*'s concluding sentence did a victory lap. "Such are the shackles," the sentence read, "each of us must break—not just once, but daily, sometimes more than once a day—if we're to achieve that Masterpiece known as our True Self." The End.

By the time I turned over the last page of *Coffee, Black*, all three martinis had been fully absorbed into my bloodstream. I was—to use Professor Wallace's word—categorically drunk.

It was in that state that I stood in the moonlit but still very dark (they still hadn't fixed the broken lamp) street in front of my building, scrutinizing the Holy Impala: the Pious Pimpmobile, Godly Gas-Guzzler, Sanctimonious Sedan, Righteous Rust Bucket, Reverent Wreck, the Jingoistic Jalopy. How I'd come to hate that car! I went up and stood close to it: close enough to view my reflection in the driver's side window. Pleased to have made my drunken acquaintance, I smiled. Someone had discarded an old floor lamp, the kind with a fancy wrought-iron arm, out on the curb with the rest of the week's trash. With both hands I picked it up, and—with little premeditation—bashed its heavy iron base through the window. It took two tries. Then I yanked the car door open, got in, disengaged the emergency brake. With the transmission in neutral, standing astride the vehicle, with one hand on the steering wheel and the other pushing and pulling it by its door frame, I maneuvered the car out of its parking space—no mean feat, considering that by then its tires were practically fused by inertia to the pavement.

With the car in the street I rolled it in the direction from which I had come, toward the hill for which Marble Hill, the adjacent neighborhood, is named. Assuming it rolled straight and true and no traffic interfered with its progress, it would roll all the way across West 230th Street and into the kiddie park there (where—the Parks Department being more vigilant with respect to such matters—it might possibly at long last gain the attention it deserved).

A running start; a final, categorical heave-ho...

Then I stood there, in the middle of the dark street, wiping my gloved hands, watching the Clerical Clunker gain momentum as it rolled down that hill of metamorphosed limestone. It might have rolled all the way into the kiddie park as planned, too, had the owner of a certain white Buick Enclave done a better job of parallel parking.

With the Buick's alarm cycling through its sequence of whoops, wails, yelps, and bleats, hands in my coat pockets, hugging the neighborhood's grim shadows, not once looking over my shoulder, I hurried back up the hill to my tenement.

9. CIGARILLO

I ENTERED MY APARTMENT TO FIND THAT SOMEONE HAD BROKEN into it. He sat there, at my kitchen tub-table, in the dark, or in what would have been total darkness except for the dim blue light through the skylight, the lattice of which stamped its lace-like pattern across the tabletop as well as the intruder's face. That the intruder was, or had once upon a time been, my twin brother is, for all intents and purposes, beside the point. To me then he was an intruder, a stranger, or might as well have been. I'd have been no more surprised and disconcerted had I found an African elephant or the Pope sitting at my kitchen table smoking a cigarette, dressed in a leather jacket. It might have been the same leather jacket he wore on the back cover of his book, or it might have been another leather jacket. Also as advertised he wore the salt-and-pepper goatee. A motorcycle helmet sat on the table before him, along with a pair of leather gloves. All this was revealed to me by the dim bluish moonlight drizzling down through the smutty skylight.

"Hello, Stewie," he said. The smoke from his cigarette or whatever he smoked wavered up through the skylight's lacy shadow. I switched on the overhead lamp. On my displeasure in seeing him Con Edison shed no light.

"Who let you in here?"

"I let myself in."

"You broke into my apartment?"

"You know you really should consider getting a police lock."

"What are you doing here—aside from breaking into my property and invading my privacy?"

"I came to talk."

"About what? What could you and I possibly have to talk about?"

"It's been a while, I know."

"You know it's *been a while*? What other astonishing displays of your uncanny grasp of the obvious have you come here to share with me this evening?"

"Aren't you even going to offer your big brother a drink?" It was an old joke between us, the "big brother" thing. Greg was born two minutes before me.

"I have a brother?" I said. "That's news to me. Put out the cigarette, please."

"It's a cigarillo." In the saucer he'd been using for an ashtray my erstwhile twin put his cigarillo, or whatever it was, out.

"Since when do you smoke, anyway?"

"Since I felt like it."

"Great. Now you've had your smoke and we've had our conversation. Now get out."

"Can I have that drink first, at least?"

"I have only shitty gin to offer you." I took the bottle of Fleishman's out from the freezer. "What you feel like. Is that your new code of ethics, your call to arms? Whatever I *feel* like: is that the flag you salute? Quitting your job? Divorcing your wife of nineteen years? Disowning your own family? Denying our existence?"

"How are you doing, Stewie?"

"Great, Greg. I mean Brock. Just great. Here's your goddamn gin. Drink up. Then go find somewhere nice and comfortable to go fuck yourself."

I slapped the glass down in front of him. Gin splashed onto the table and onto his leather jacket. He wiped it off with his fingers. "You're angry," he said.

"Really? What gives you that impression?"

"I understand. And I'm sorry, I really am. It's just that... well, sometimes we have to do what we have to do."

"Well, that casts a whole different light on matters. You were doing what you *had* to do, being true to yourself, obeying your instincts, fulfilling your destiny, following your bliss. And there I was thinking you were just being a goddamn fucking asshole. Fuck you, Gregory. Or Brock. Whoever you are. Fuck both of you."

"Are you done?"

I shook my head. "Not quite. I haven't told you to get out of my home yet."

"What are you waiting for?"

"Nothing. Get out of my home."

"I will. But first, can I tell you a story?"

"Make it short."

"Once there were two brothers, twins. They were both unhappy. As they grew older they became more and more miserable. Both suffered bouts of suicidal depression. But then one day one of the brothers saved himself. He escaped. He survived."

"And the other?"

"He committed suicide."

"That's the story?"

He nodded. "That's the story."

"It's a crappy story. The characters aren't developed. There's no setting or atmosphere. And the plot lacks tension."

"When you go to sleep at night, Stew, what condition would you say your bed is in?"

"What *condition*?"

"Is it made or not?"

"Not, usually." (I tried to mask my chagrin with impatience.)

"Because you didn't make it, right?"

"What's your point?"

"The bed you don't make, that's what you lie in. That's your life, Brother. I want to help you make your bed."

"I don't need you to make my bed for me. Or to tuck me in. Or to tell me shitty bedtime stories."

"You can change your life."

"Who says I want to change it?"

"There's a trick psychologists use," my uninvited guest said, scanning the surroundings, my home, appraisingly. "Maybe you've heard of it? You ask the patient, the subject, to imagine a house. You provide no other parameters. You say, 'Close your eyes and picture a house. Any house, anywhere.' You have them describe the first image that pops into their head. Some people describe a seaside mansion with terraced gardens and tennis courts. Others see a tumbledown shack in the desert with dangling gutters and tumbleweeds rolling by. The house they imagine—that's how they see themselves, what they think of themselves. It's your outlook on life, your spirit, your soul. This..." He gave another look around. "Is this what you think of yourself?"

"Screw you, you presumptuous prick."

"Do you know what your problem is, Stewie?"

"Apart from the ones you've already mentioned?"

"You want people to accept you just as you are. As you've always been and as you always will be. Accept me as I am or to hell with you. Tell me, how's that working for you, Stewart? Hmm? Why do you suppose you haven't been able to sell that novel of yours?"

I said nothing. I fumed. But I was thinking *he's got you there, pal.* I thought *no, goddammit, no.* I thought, *Dear Reader, Fuck You.*

"Face it, Stewie. You're not happy. You're not fulfilled."

"Finish your drink."

"You're as unfulfilled as I was, once, Little Brother."

"Finish it and go."

"I want to help you, Stew."

"I don't want your help. I don't even know who the fuck you are."

"Someone just like you. Someone who knows what it's like to be a Detweiler."

"Did you not hear me?"

"It's a curse, Little Brother."

"Don't call me that. I'm not your little brother. You're two fucking minutes older than me, asshole!"

"A death sentence—that's what it is. But there's a way out. I found it, and so can you."

"How? By turning my back on everyone?"

He shook his head. "By turning your back on that tumble-down shack in the desert. You don't have to live in that shack. You don't have to be deprived. You don't have to be depressed. You don't have to be a Detweiler. You don't have to die."

"Get out."

"Anything's possible, Stewart. Anything! Whatever you want out of this life, whatever you want to be, whatever you want to do, it's all within your grasp. The sky's the limit. *You can reinvent yourself.*"

"Yeah, yeah: I read your damn book."

"The point is, Stewart, everything's changeable, and the reason everything's changeable is because nothing's real. It's all a masquerade ball, that's all life is. It's just that we're all born with these masks we've worn for so long we assume we can't take them off, that we're stuck having to wear them forever. But we're not. We can take the mask off. Any time we want."

"And do what, then? Pick another mask?"

"Yes. Exactly. Pick another mask!"

"Motorcycle riding, cigarette smoking—"

"Cigarillo."

"—leather jacket wearing, goateed self-help guru? That your latest mask?"

"Possibly. For the time being."

"Or is it Famous Bestselling Author?"

"I wouldn't overrate fame, if I were you."

"Oh, you wouldn't, would you?"

"Being famous is just being misunderstood by that many more people. The point is, Stew, whoever I happen to be at this moment, I'm not stuck with him. I can change it. Any time. We're free, Stew. Or we can be, if only we'd realize it, if only we'd dare to let ourselves be free. If only we dare to allow ourselves to be something other than what's dictated to us by our habits and our histories, by what other people expect from us—or worse, by those stale, stingy, claustrophobic expectations that we hold for ourselves. Hell, Stewie—"

"Don't call me that either."

"—we could all be living in sprawling airy mansions. Instead most of us choose to live in the broken-down one-room shacks that we think of as ourselves."

"Jesus…"

"We could all be leading epic lives. Napoleon. Alexander the Great. Genghis Khan…"

"You're generalizing."

"—only most of us are stuck reading the same page over and over and over again."

"Why am I listening to this?"

"Stewie, if you could just—"

"Get out," I seethed.

"—I came here to—"

"Now!"

I opened a kitchen drawer, reached in, and felt around in it for the biggest, sharpest knife I could find, the one that I used for slicing and dicing onions. While gripping its handle inside the drawer I said to myself, *Are you crazy? What do you intend to do, slice him up, carve him to pieces, your own brother, your own flesh and blood?* Instead I let go of the knife, grabbed the motorcycle helmet from the kitchen table, and shook it at him, saying, "I swear, if you don't get out this minute, one of us is going to get hurt."

"You're not serious?"

"I am."

"Listen to yourself." He tsked me. "Threatening bodily harm to me, your own flesh and blood—your own brother."

"You are not my brother."

"No?"

I shook my head. "My brother was a gentle, self-effacing, soft-spoken scholar who loathed the limelight. He spent half his time with his head buried in books, and the other half mulling over the things he read in them. He was modest and sincere and self-critical to a fault. He detested pretense and ostentation and humbuggery of every sort and would have very much disliked you and your book."

"I'm sorry to hear that."

"Confronted with you in person, my brother would have gone out of his way to avoid you, if only to spare himself the inconvenience of hating your guts."

"That is unfortunate."

"You are not my brother. You're some cigatette—

"Cigarillo."

"—some cigarillo smoking creep who's broken into my home."
I shook his helmet at him. "Now leave—I mean it!"

"Or what, you're going to bash my skull in?"

There were two windows in the kitchen, the one that faced out
on the street, and another, much smaller one whose glass panes
were blackened with grime that opened to an airshaft that in its
slimness truly lived up to its name. With one hand I opened it; with
the other I held Brock's helmet suspended in the chilled gloom. "I
don't have to bash your head in. I'll let a New York City pothole
do it for me, when that hot rod of yours flies ass-over-teakettle over
it. Now I'm going to count to five. By the time I do if you're not on
your feet you can kiss your helmet and your skull goodbye."

"That's a two-hundred-dollar helmet, Stew, incidentally."

"And there's no access to this airshaft, Brock, incidentally.
One...two...three..."

"All right," he said, rising. "Have it your way. But I hope
you'll at least think about all I've been saying."

"I've heard you out. Now I *want* you out. Out of my kitchen.
Out of my life. Out of my consciousness. Do you understand?
I'll see you in hell before I engage you any further on the mortal
sphere." I dangled the helmet by its strap.

"Okay, okay. Just don't say I didn't try to—"

"*Now!*" I said and threw the helmet at him.

That was the last time I saw my brother, the last time we saw
each other.

Alive.

10. MOTHER / MOM

IN BOOK ONE OF HERODOTUS, THE LEGEND IS TOLD OF THE TWIN brothers Kleobis and Biton. According to the legend, the brothers were taking their mother, Cydippe, the Priestess of Hera, from Argos to Heraion to attend the feast of the goddess Hera. When the oxen that were to pull their cart failed to materialize, the brothers pulled the cart themselves—a distance of over five miles. So impressed was the Priestess by her sons' devotion, on arriving at the temple she prayed to Hera to bestow upon her children the greatest of all possible gifts that a god could give to a mortal. Hera attended her prayer. That night, following the feast, the brothers died peacefully in their sleep.

• •

"Brock, Brock — is it really, really you?"
   "Yes, mother Mom. Yes, it's really me."
   "Oh Brock, we were so—so worried about you!"
   "Yes, I know. I'm very sorry."
   "Do you have any idea how worried I was?"
   "I'm sorry."
   "Any idea?"

"Yes, Mom. I have some idea."

"How are you? Are you all right, Brock?"

"I'm fine. Really. I'm—I'm okay."

"Where are you?"

"Hmm? Oh, home."

"Home?"

"Dad's house, I mean. At the lake."

"Brock—*why*?"

"Why what, Mom?"

"Why did you do it—disappear like that?"

"Oh. Well—"

"You don't have to tell me if you don't want to. If it's none of my business."

"No. No, I don't mind. Telling you. It's just that … well, there's not all that much to tell."

"You sound different."

"Do I?"

"You do. You sound very different."

"I do?"

"You sound like your brother, almost."

"Huh," I said.

"Is he there? Your brother? He was coming down there to look for … to see you. He should be there by now. Is he?"

"Yes," I said. "Yes, he's here."

"Thank God. I was starting to worry about him, too. I couldn't take any more worrying."

"You worry too much, Mother."

"That's what Stewart says. Why shouldn't I worry, when my children disappear? You'd worry, too, if you had children. Why did you just call me that?"

"Call you what?"

"Mother. Just now, a moment ago. You never call me 'Mother.' You've always called me Mom. Stewart—he calls me Mother."

"I don't know, Mother; I mean Mom."

"Are you sure it's you, Brock?"

"Yes. Yes, I'm sure it's me. Mom."

I stood in front of one of the two sets of French doors. The rain had stopped. I looked out over the deck railing at the lake. As I did, a patch of blue opened up in what for days had been a gray or white sky, or maybe it had opened up earlier and I just hadn't noticed it before. The lake was calm. I saw the two Adirondack chairs sitting there on the dock, angled to face each other as if in conversation. Then I saw something else. A red boat. It drifted a few dozen feet from the dock. A fishing boat? I remember my father always complaining about boats fishing by his dock. Mornings after breakfast he'd stand right where I stood just then, in front of the French doors in his bathrobe with a mug of coffee in his hand and his face set with consternation, looking out at the dock, muttering to himself. Why the sight of people fishing by his dock perturbed him so I don't know. It's not as if they were doing him or his dock any harm.

My mother spoke.

"Are you sure you'll all right, Brock?"

"Yes, Mom. I'm sure. Really. Everything's fine."

"I was so worried. So worried. You have no idea how worried I've been. Everyone's been worried about you. Can you blame them, with you going off like that? Then that terrible dream... Oh, it was awful. Awful! I won't even tell you about it, that's how awful it was."

"What dream, Mom?"

"I can't tell you. I *won't* tell you. But it was awful, *awful*."

"It was just a dream, Mom."

"This was more than a dream. It was horrible. So horrible. And I kept having it over and over again. The same dream. Every night, almost. Anyway thank god you're still alive. I was so worried, so upset." My mother wept. I could hear her weeping.

"It's okay, Mom. Everything's okay."

"Where's your brother?" she said. "Where's Stewart? Is he there? Can you get him? I should speak to him."

"All right. Okay. Mom; I'll — I'll go get him."

I put the phone on the table, shuffled toward the downstairs bedroom, called out, "Stewart! Hey, Stewart, Mom's on the phone!" A beat or two later I shuffled back and picked the phone up.

"He's coming, Mom. So—how have things been with you?"

"You mean besides me worrying to death about you?"

"Yes."

"The food is terrible, as usual. They don't salt anything. The vegetables are a total disaster. They served Brussels sprouts the other day and I swear they tasted of absolutely nothing. The only thing good here is the strawberry ice cream. The strawberry ice cream is very good. If only they'd give us more than a thimbleful. That's when they don't run out."

"How's the weather been?"

"How should I know? They keep us caged up like animals."

"Hold on, Mom. Stewart's here. Hold on."

I passed the phone to myself.

"Hello, Mother."

"Stewart! Where have you been? Why didn't you call?"

"I don't have a phone, Mother. You know that."

"You could have used a payphone."

"There are no payphones anymore, Mother."

"You could have called collect."

"Do you have any idea how much a person-to-person collect call costs nowadays? Assuming they still do them."

"You still should have called. How long have you been there?"

"I got here yesterday." It seemed much longer.

"Why did it take you so long?"

"Mother, it's an eighteen-hour drive under ideal circumstances. And it rained the whole way. There was traffic."

"You should have called at least."

There was something odd about that red fishing boat, come to think of it. First of all, the fact that it was red—a bright, orangey red. Who goes fishing in a bright red boat? There were four men aboard. Two were sitting, the other two were standing, looking intently down into the water. That too struck me as odd.

"So—did you find your brother all right? I mean does he seem all right to you?"

"Yes, Mother. He seems fine."

"What is his problem? Why didn't he return my calls? Why didn't he return *anyone's* calls?"

"You know how he is, Mother."

"No, Stewart, I don't know how he is. No one knows how

your brother is. As soon as you think you know he changes."

"Well, that's how he is."

"Did he give you any idea why he disappeared like that?"

"Why don't you ask him?"

"I did."

"And?"

"He said it was none of my business."

"He didn't say that, Mother."

"Yes he did."

"He didn't, Mother. I heard."

"He might as well have."

"Maybe he just needed a break from it all. All these years in the spotlight. Fans, journalists, managers, publicists. Maybe he just needed a little time to himself. Anyway, Mother, there's nothing to worry about."

My mother harrumphed. "And how are you?" she asked.

"I'm—I'm okay."

"What does that mean?"

"I'm fine, Mother."

"Are you sure?'

"Yes, I'm sure."

"How long will you be staying there?"

"I don't know. A few days. A week. Maybe longer."

"I want you to make sure your brother's all right."

"I will. Don't worry."

"Don't let him swim."

"Mother—"

"Please! I don't want him in that lake. It's dangerous."

"I'll do my best."

"Promise me, Stewart."

"Okay, okay. I promise."

"Can I talk to him again, please?"

"Yeah, sure. He's uh—he's in the bathroom. Hold on a sec."

•   •

I put the phone down on a console table by the plant stand holding the dead philodendron. There were some papers on the table, a stack of opened and unopened letters. I rustled them around a bit, then went into the kitchen, walking on the balls of my feet on the wooden floor so my footfalls could be heard. Murmured exchange of two voices in kitchen. Moments later I returned, picked up the phone, and, in a slightly deeper voice this time (it always seemed to me that my brother's voice was deeper than mine, though this might not have been so; it may just have sounded deeper than my own voice sounded to me in my head), answered.

"Hey, Mom."

"Brock?"

"Yes."

"You sound different again."

"I do?"

"You don't sound like yourself."

"I'm a bit congested. I've got a bit of cold. It's getting better."

"Have you spoken to Dawn? Your assistant? Does she even know that you're down there?"

"Mom, listen to me, please."

"…"

"I checked myself into a hospital." Why I said this I don't know. Like that it just came out of my mouth.

"Hospital? What—?"

"It wasn't a hospital, really. It's a psychiatric facility."

"A *facility*? What—? Why—?"

"Anyway, that's where I've been for the past few weeks. Nervous exhaustion, that was the official diagnosis. In layman's terms it's what people call a nervous breakdown."

"A nervous breakdown? Thats *terrible*! Brock—why—?"

"It's not as bad as it sounds, Mom. Really. It happens. Overwork. Exhaustion. Still, it's not the sort of thing I want the whole world to know about. That's why I kept it a secret."

"I see."

"I'd prefer it if no one else knew."

"Not even Dawn?"

"Not anyone. If it should get out…well, it wouldn't do my career any good, do you know what I mean?"

"Yes, yes, of course. Nervous—what did you call it?"

"Exhaustion."

"What do you have to be so nervous about?"

"I doesn't matter. The important thing is I'm better now. I just needed to take some time away from everything."

"Why couldn't you just take a vacation like everyone else? Go to the Greek Islands—or Bermuda?"

"It's not so easy for me, Mom. I mean...Look, it's what I did, okay? It's what I felt I had to do at the time. Maybe it was a mistake. I don't know. All I know is...well, I feel better now."

"Well, that's good," she said unconvincingly.

"Really, Mom. I really do feel a lot better."

"I'm glad to hear it."

"I'm sorry you got so worried."

"So am I."

"How are you, Mother?"

"Why do you keep calling me Mother like that? Your brother always calls me Mother. You never call me Mother."

"I don't know. Stew calls you that; maybe it rubbed off on me."

"You still sound different."

"I told you I have—I had—a cold."

"Are you on some sort of medication?"

"Huh? Oh. No, Mom. I mean...for a while they had me on something, but I'm not taking anything now."

"What did they have you on."

"Just some drug, you know, to get me stabilized."

"What drug?"

"I don't know, Mom. I forget. Jesus, Mom, why the inquisition?"

"I'm curious."

"I don't know. Wellbutrin."

"Wellbutrin? That's serious."

"Maybe it wasn't Wellbutrin, maybe it was something else. I forget. Anyway it was just for a while. To get me, you know, stabilized."

"Where is your brother?"

"He's—in the kitchen, why?"

"Are you two getting along?"

"Yeah, we're getting along."

"That's good. How does he seem to you?"

"Stew? He seems … okay."

"What do you mean, 'okay'?"

"Well, honestly, he seems a bit … subdued."

"Subdued? How?"

"I don't know, Mom. Maybe I'm just imagining it. I haven't seen him in five years."

"Five years," she repeated with dismay.

"It was his choice, Mother, I mean Mom."

"You didn't exactly make it hard for him."

"It was his choice, Mom. The last time we spoke, five years ago, he told me in no uncertain terms he never wanted to see me again. What was I supposed to do?"

"You could have forgiven him."

"Who said I never forgave him?"

"You could have seen that his anger was out of love."

"Oh, sure." As I spoke these words, a part of me couldn't believe they were escaping my lips. And yet they made perfect sense to me; I couldn't disagree. Had my actual brother spoken those same words, not only would I have found no measure of truth in them, I'd have responded with wounded righteous indignation. "Anyway, you asked me how Stew seemed," I said.

"Subdued," my mother repeated.

"He hasn't been happy, Mom. Things have been hard for him. Not getting his book published. Doris breaking up with him."

"I wish she'd held on just a little longer. It might have made all the difference in the world."

"You don't know that."

"It wouldn't have hurt."

"It was probably inevitable, Mom. Their troubles may have been deeper than either of us knew." (They were.)

"She was a stabilizing force for him. He needed that. Your brother was always more volatile than you, more sensitive. The artist. He's always needed someone stronger than him to guide him. Growing up, you used to be that person for him. Now he has no one. He tries to keep it from me, but he's unhappy. I know it. I always thought that of the two of you you were the strongest.

That's why when you disappeared I couldn't believe...it didn't make any sense."

She was crying.

"Mom," I said.

"Try to cheer him up. Try to be a brother to him again. He drove all that way to see you."

I nodded—to myself, obviously. "I'll do what I can," I said.

I heard my mother sigh. "You're so moody, both of you. I was never that way. Not a bit. Your father was never that way either, until...well...How did we raise such moody children?"

"We probably shouldn't talk about this now, Mom."

"I don't understand it."

"Listen, Stew's coming back." More exaggerated foot treads, paper rustling. "Hold on, Mom. I'll pass you back to him. Stew? Stew, talk to Mom," I said, handing the phone to myself.

"Yes, Mother."

"Are you all right?"

"Yes. I'm alright," I said, sounding duly subdued.

"Are you sure?"

"I'm fine, Mom. I mean Mother."

(Jesus. Who was I supposed to be? I'd forgotten.)

"It's time you two started getting along again."

I said nothing.

"At least now you two are talking. Your brother loves you. That's the important thing. You both love each other. He's your twin. Whatever differences you may have, they're nothing compared to what you both have in common. Nothing can change that. Right?"

"Yes. You're right."

"Can I speak to your brother again?"

"Huh? Oh...yeah...uhm...sure, okay. Lemme see if I can got him for you." Shouting. "Greg? Brook?"

More rustling sounds, etc.

"Yeah, Mom."

"Please don't stay down there too long. I mean, fine, take some time to yourself if you have to. But enough is enough."

"A couple more weeks, Mother. That's all."

"Now you sound like Stewart again."

I said nothing.

"People are depending on you. Your fans. Dawn. Your brother. They love you. I love you. Everyone loves you. Your brother especially. He needs you. You both need each other. Now more than ever. But right now he needs you more than you need him."

Of course she was right. Mothers always are.

II. BUTTERFLIES & ROCKS

BACK (AGAIN) TO OUR BACK-STORY:

The referral came indirectly through my journalist friend Julie, the one who gave me the Mazda that brought me here. Through her I had been introduced to bestselling author Laura Welles, who contacted me one day to ask me if I would be willing to take her place on a panel ("Second Acts in American Literary Lives: Are There Any?") at a writer's conference in Saratoga Springs, she herself having been food-poisoned by a spoiled batch of lobster bisque. Possibly because I had vented abundantly to her about it, Laura was aware of the sad saga of my perpetually evolving opus, and of the fact that Sally Treadwell, my agent, refused to represent it. To my surprise she asked to read the manuscript. To my greater surprise, a week later I found the following email from her in my inbox:

> Hi Stew,
>   I found your novel interesting. Why don't you send it to my agent, Elizabeth Watson? I've told her about it.
>   Cheers,
>   Laura

I'm going to say that this was back around June of 2012, though I can't be sure. In case you haven't already guessed, I'm not at all good with dates, mainly because I don't care. What difference does it make, I'd like to know, if something happened in June or July, on a Saturday or a Sunday, in this or that year? Still, there are those readers (you may be one of them) who, equipped with built-in calendar algorithms and having nothing better to do, will catch an author's every chronological slip-up and write finger-wagging letters to their publishers.

At that time, Elizabeth "Bitsy" Watson was the most powerful literary agent in New York City. Less than a year before, she'd placed a first novel by a nineteen-year-old Vassar undergrad for six figures—not any six figures, but six figures starting with the number 5. News of the transaction spread quickly, filling gossip columns with the sort of spiteful buzz that sells books while increasing by an order of magnitude an agent's clout. Overnight, in literary households anyway, "Bitsy" became a household name. To have her as your agent—just to get her to read something of yours—was no mean feat, she having in the wake of all that publicity declared a moratorium on unsolicited manuscripts, especially those of authors whose previous efforts had sold "modestly." Notwithstanding which, Bitsy had agreed to read my manuscript. At least she would read the first few pages. The rest would be up to the work itself.

Since the last time Sally Treadwell rejected my ever-evolving opus, ten years and as many drafts had come and gone. But technically at least I still *had* an agent, so I told myself, albeit one who refused to represent the greatest of all my creations; who refused to even look at it, in fact.

Still, I had faith in my novel. I believed in it. All it lacked was the right agent to champion it, someone of impeccable taste with lots of clout. Someone like "Bitsy" Watson.

• •

Sometimes butterflies and rocks come in the same package. Example: Ashley Bridges. One of my Metropolitan Writing Institute students. Pretty. Twenty-six years my junior (do the math). Here I confront the fiction writer's frequent dilemma: to show or to tell? To dramatize or not to dramatize? Narrative or exposition? Summary or scene?

Scene: The femme fatale arriving late to her first class. "Strawberry blond" hair. Healthy-looking but pale skin, pale as a blank sheet confronted by a blocked writer except where touched by rouge—or is she blushing? Wearing a crisp frilly white blouse over tight tight designer jeans.

"I am so *so* sorry I'm late, Professor—" Breathless, extracting a tattered folded page torn from a Metropolitan Writing Institute catalogue, searching for her instructor's—my—name in it. "Professor ...?"

"Detweiler," her instructor—I—say[s]. "Mr. Detweiler." (For he is not, has never been, a professor.) "Or just Stewart, if you like."

"You see, Mr. Stewart, I'm an intern reporter with Fox News, and we had a breaking story this afternoon." Her breathlessness gives way to what strikes him as a spurious deep-southern-fried accent. "Maybe you heard about it? Late this afternoon this guy jumped off the Manhattan side stanchion of the Brooklyn Bridge. And he lived! I saw the whole thing. They took him to Bellevue. They say he was probably high on something. Oh, it was so *exciting*! Anyway, after filing my report, I went back to my apartment to take a little ol' nap and ... well, I must have slept right through my alarm! That's why I'm late."

Were he any less intent on her "jewel-like" eyes, less—in a word —"*taken*" by her, our protagonist might have seen her for what she was: a burlesque of feminine seductive charm, with her fluttering lashes and pupils that sparkled at will. A neophyte reporter? Hailing from the Deep South? Who was she kidding?

A more vigilant author would have deleted her then and there.

Instead, with ears ringing, holding the class roster over his midriff to hide the involuntary erection (who asked *your* opinion?) asserting itself against his Dockers, our author-protagonist studies his subject, describing her to himself in the present tense. *Her breasts are ample if not especially large; the frilly blouse cut precariously low over them, sending a rush of warm blood to my face.* She smiled. Attractive, to be sure, but in a transparent, superficial way, what E.M. Forster called a *flat character*, dispatchable by a sentence or phrase: "All surface, no substance."

Yet there was something else, too, something he couldn't place at first, someone of whom, with her fiery reddish blonde hair, her triangular chin, her freckled skin and bow-shaped smile, she reminded him. Then it came to him. Betsy Butterworth: the girl for whose affections the Detweiler twins once wrestled savagely to no end other than a pine needle up the nose. She who once upon a time had for him been the paradigm of unattainable glory, and—retrospectively—a harbinger of ignominious defeats to come. Now here she stood, reincarnated, bearing a different name, come to be taught by him in his classroom. Her double. Her twin. A second chance?

Summary: He fell for her.

Not that I assumed we'd be lovers; I was neither that naive nor that vain. She merely gave her middle-aged teacher hope that even at his age he stood a chance of engaging her non-platonic interests, that she found him attractive—and not just mentally: that, however over fifty, Stewart Detweiler might still be, as it were, "in the running." Or anyway not totally over-the-hill.

• •

That impression accrued over a series of shared taxi rides, she to her apartment on Central Park West, me to Grand Central Terminal, from where I caught my train north to The Bronx. The fare having risen to over five dollars, splitting it made sense—for me, anyway, my compensation for dispensing my pearls of wisdom to Metropolitan's matriculants having peaked at thirty-five dollars per classroom hour, not counting prep time.

The first time Ms. Bridges and I shared a cab was in early September, after that first class together. Splitting the cab was her idea. It wasn't like me to chum up with my students, especially early in the term when establishing an air of aloof authority was crucial. Whether they say so or not, deep down students want to look up to their teachers; they don't want us to be their equals. It's what they are paying for. In letting students feel that you are in no way superior to them you take the bread, as it were, from their mouths.

But half of five bucks was half of five bucks, so I agreed.

The first taxi I flagged pulled over. I held the door open for her; she bowed first before sliding across the roomy seat (the cab was an old-style Checker, one of the last of its breed). She held her pale slender hands out for my briefcase. "I'll take that for you, sir, if you like."

As we rolled up Lexington Avenue I smelled her perfume, a scent of verbena and hothouse gardenias that I'd been aware of only subliminally in the classroom, but that in the closed darkness of the taxicab swelled to full amplitude. I've never been a fan of perfume or makeup of any kind, those expedients behind which some women enhanced their animi. I rolled my window down. As I did, Ashley asked, "How long have you been teaching?" Seeing the parade of stalled red taillights winking ahead of us, wondering was it too late to take Park Avenue, I made a quick calculation and answered, "This term will be [ten?] years." Then, more to myself, shaking my head, "Amazing how quickly the time has gone."

"You must be enjoying yourself."

"Oh? How did you reach that conclusion?"

"Times flies when you're having fun."

"Tut-tut. Cliché."

"Some clichés are true."

"Most of them are. That's not what's wrong with them. Anyway, as they say, *tempus fugit*." I studied the rhythmic patterns of winking brake lights.

"You sound somewhat morose," she observed.

"Somewhat morose? I'd have said wistful."

"Wistful with a twist of cynicism."

"Sounds like a cocktail. Bring me a wistful, straight up with a twist of cynicism."

"Shaken, not stirred."

"Very good. It comes with age, to answer your question."

"What?"

"Whatever modifier you want to paste on me."

"You're as old as you feel. I know: cliché." I felt her smile in the dark next to me.

"In that case I feel fifty-three years old."

"How old *are* you?"

"Fifty-three."

The driver said something. I turned to see him, under his turban, speaking into a cellphone. Though by then they had eroded civility for over a decade, I still couldn't abide having to listen to one side of another person's conversation, let alone in the back of a taxi and on my dime. But my fellow passenger had already accused me of cynicism. I had no wish to provide her with yet more targets for her pop psychology squirt gun. Traffic was at a standstill.

"Aren't you going to ask me how old I am, Professor?"

With a sigh: "How old are you?"

"Guess!"

"I'd rather not, thank you."

"Why not?"

"I'll flatter or offend you, and I don't care to do either."

We had yet to reach 23rd Street. I tapped on the Plexiglas divider. "I've got a 10:20 train to catch. Why don't you try Park?" I suggested. Into his chin microphone the taxi driver murmured something. I tapped the Plexiglas harder. "Did you hear me? Who are you talking to, anyway?"

"They talk to each other," Ashley answered for him. "It gets them through the long lonesome days and dark, lonely nights."

"Well it's not getting me to Grand Central, that's for sure."

"You'll make your train, don't worry. If not, I'll just have to buy you a drink at the Oyster Bar. And maybe some oysters, too. Do you know what the French poet said about eating oysters?"

"No," I said.

"*Eet eez like keezing ze see on ze leeps!*" She tittered.

I almost said something apropos being her teacher, being too old, being any number of things that would have rendered said drink with or without oysters inappropriate. Then I thought better of it. Why go there? Meanwhile I silently vowed not to let this wily attractive clever young woman insinuate herself into my private life.

At five minutes to my train the cab pulled up in front of Grand Central. With the taxi door opened and me standing on the curb and the cab driver still on his phone, I handed Ashley a five-dollar bill.

"Don't be silly," she said, waving the money away. "You can pay next time."

There will be no next time, I thought, but had no time to argue.

I jammed the five back into my trouser pocket, said goodnight, and was about to slam the taxi door when Ashley shouted, "Hold on!" and presented me with my very own worn leather briefcase.

"Much obliged," I said, taking it.

"See you next week," said Ashley.

"Next week is Rosh Hashanah. No class."

"Oh, right. Forgot." That smile again, those batted eyelashes. No denying it: she had a lovely face.

I had started across the street when I heard:

"Mr. Detweiler—Stewart?"

I turned to see her waving a manila envelope out the taxicab window.

"I know it's not my turn yet, but I would be so *so* very appreciative if you'd give a quick look to these few pages of mine that I've written, and let me know if I'm on the right track?"

"I really shouldn't," I said, taking the envelope.

"I *so* appreciate it," said Ashley Bridges.

I nodded, then ran to catch my train.

• •

Before submitting it to "Bitsy," I had planned to spend a weekend or two putting the final polish on my novel. I spent two months. When waking was necessary—when not in the grip of insomnia—I woke up every morning at 4:30 to work on it. This was my big chance. I didn't want to blow it.

For this version, I decided that maybe Sally Treadwell had been right after all; maybe I should give my novel more of a plot. Not just any plot, a sensational one full of surprises and twists. I'd incorporate my idea for my twin novel. Remember? It's basic premise: twin brothers trade lives with each other. Sound familiar? Yes, just as Greg and I traded places back in sixth grade. This time, though, the prank would take a macabre turn, with the blocked novelist twin ("Writing a novel about a blocked novelist..." etc.) assuming the identity of his brother, whom he murders. Yes, murders: why not? Oh, it would be dark, very dark, possibly the darkest novel ever written, its darkness mitigated in part by a rollicking, unhinged, rant-prone, maximally unreliable narrator, its imagery, meanings, and motifs bursting with metaphor, its narrative suffused with essayistic digressions on topics ranging from Determinism, Cartesian Dualism, Manichaeism, and Physical Cosmology, to the Paradox of the Cretan Liar and the Coincidence of Opposites (*coincidentia oppositorum*), all combined with assorted postmodern metafictional bells and whistles.

How, you wonder, did I manage to orchestrate all of the above into a sensational page-turning novel? Trust me, Dear Reader: I did it. And with only minimal recourse to metaphysics.

You must wonder, too—or is marvel the better word?—at the coincidence by which my sensational plot replicates the plot of this, my confession? I admit, it *is* an enormous coincidence, one that stretches credulity to—if not beyond—the breaking point. Yet I take no blame for that; it simply happens to have been the case. Bear in mind, too, that the book that I wrote (or re-wrote) was a novel, whereas what you are reading is nonfiction. One has nothing to do with the other.

But even were this a novel, and I, its author, a student in one of my own Metropolitan Writing Institute workshops, I would enforce the rule that erects a firewall between author and narrator, between creator and creation. Though we authors may be guilty of fabricating characters and thrusting them into a challenging situation or situations, we can't be held accountable for what those characters do or for what happens to them subsequently. That includes coincidences owing to nature or destiny, therefore beyond the author's purview.

What's that? You don't *believe* it? It's *too much* of a coincidence?

You're forgetting something, aren't you, Dear Reader? Namely whose words these are that you're reading: those of a dead person. Complain all you want. Your complaints fall on dead ears. Bulletin: I CAN DO WHAT I WANT. I can cut my thumb and drizzle blood all over this page. I can drool on it or set in on fire. I can insert a recipe for borscht or chicken soup. I can quote from *The Merck Manual of Diagnosis and Therapy* (*"Much of the mystery surrounding drug action can be cleared up by recognizing that drugs affect only the rate at which biologic functions proceed..."*) or *The Origin of Consciousness in the Breakdown of the Bicameral Mind* (*"Justice is a phenomenon only of consciousness, because time spread out in a spatial succession is its very essence. And this is possible only in a spatial metaphor of time...")*, or from *The Kybalion ("In addition to the changing of the poles of one's own mental states by the operation of the art of Polarization, the phenomena of Mental Influence, in its manifold phases, shows us that the principle may be extended so as to embrace the phenomena of the influence of one mind over that of another...").*

I can recite De Morgan's Laws:

> The negation of a conjunction is the disjunction of the negations.
> The negation of a disjunction is the conjunction of the negations.
> *"not (A and B)"* = *"(not A) or (not B)"*
> *"not (A or B)"* = *"(not A) and (not B)"*

I can burst into song, if I bloody well feel like it. A Union Song, maybe, *Joe Hill* or *Cotton Mill Colic,* or something sappy from *The Umbrellas of Cherbourg.*

And while it's true that with respect to the commerce between reader and writer that you, the reader, hold all the cards, that you have not only the right but the power to cast these words of mine aside at any moment, to put this confession down and never pick it up again, or tear its pages out one by one and use them for kindling, I'm betting you won't. I'm betting you'll read at least as far as this sentence and beyond. It wouldn't surprise me if you've done so already.

Anyway, believe it or not, I'm telling the truth. The dead have no reason to lie.

So—I revised my novel again. I considered calling this version "Quantum Entanglement," but after considering fell back on my working title: "Duplicity."

● ●

I seem to have gotten ahead of myself again. We're still on the 10:20 local to The Bronx.

Having found an isolated seat, as the train tunneled its way out of Spanish Harlem, with the manila envelope Ashley had given me lying on the baize seat beside me, I snapped open my briefcase, extracted the day-glow orange folder marked "Metropolitan," and perused my students' workshop submissions. A few lines was all it took usually to arrive at a summary judgment. For instance, a story by Michael Quigley, the guy in the J. Crew plaid flannel shirt and wire-rimmed glasses, a former I.T. geek who, like so many Metropolitan students, lost his job during the crash. His serial killer novel opened with an italicized diary entry by one Albertos Morpheus, aka "The Burger King Butcher," *that twisted cannibal who grinds his victim's flesh into hamburger meat and cooks them on his parents' barbecue grill...* or words to that effect. Clearly Michael wanted to be the next Stephen King or Thomas Harris, a process that by his estimation would take about six months and earn him a high six figures—and that was just the advance on royalties. I'd have had little sympathy for Michael and his kind had they not been so meek and self-effacing, saving all their bloodlust for the pages of their prospective blockbusters. That said, if I never had to read another story about serial killers again, it wouldn't have been too soon.

Next: a short story by Margot Abrons, who sat off to the side of the class presumably so her nail biting would escape notice. It began, "On a stark cold winter night, my boyfriend's best friend, Bernie, drives me to the clinic." Another abortion story. I could anticipate one per term. Not that there's anything wrong with abortion as a subject for fiction per se. Whatever side of the issue one stands on, it's a sad part of reality. The problem with the abortion stories my students wrote was that they never failed to pick the lowest hanging—no, not the lowest-hanging, but already on the ground and rotting—sentimental fruit. Instead of challenging the reader's feelings as good fiction does, they merely exploited them. Odds favored Margot's story ending as eight out of ten such stories did, on an ironically symbolic note, with heroine exiting through alleyway behind clinic to avoid mob of protesters out front, to be met with the rosy-fingered dawn forming itself into the shape of a human fetus.

Next:

How striking her beauty was to me! Ever since I first
spied Lilith's cloaked and bound figure as she was forced

by the royal guards to kneel before her Majesty, Queen
Kali Morab III, I foresaw a temptation that even I, fiercely
devoted Second to Princess Ourania, could hardly resist...

The perpetrator of this abominable tripe was Alice Nordland.
She sat in the last row and rarely spoke, her face buried in a notebook wherein at first I assumed she dutifully transcribed my every
pearl-like utterance. In fact—and as I saw while distributing my
handout—she was doodling Rapunzel-haired "damsels in distress"
and "knights in shining armor," complete with visors and, I kid you
not, jousting sticks. As much as I disapproved of reality, I found it
easier to stomach than fantasy. The best thing to be said of students
like Alice is that one rigorous critique was all it took, usually, to get
them to drop the class and retreat back into their dungeons.

All this time Ashley's envelope sat on the seat next to me. I
hadn't forgotten it. Reluctantly, I picked it up. The lickable flap
wasn't sealed. I pried open the brass clasp, and—slowly, with a
blend of curiosity and dread—drew out the manuscript. With it
resting in my lap I counted the girders of the Park Avenue Bridge
as they swept by. What made me hesitate? The prospect of having
my worst fears confirmed, or seeing them nullified? Odds favored
her being less talented than she believed, in which case it would
be up to me to break the news however tactfully. But supposing
she turned out to be brilliant? Or worse: a far better writer than
I? There was always that fear-encased possibility, or that fear-encased hope, since I wanted my students to be good; I wanted them
to succeed, truly I did. Notwithstanding which I didn't want them
to outshine me, at least not straight out of the gate.

If my years of teaching at MWI had taught me anything, it was
that the odds of that happening were slim to nonexistent. Most (I
nearly wrote "the vast majority"—how wily the cliché!) of my students were at best modestly gifted. Had they been truly talented,
they would have gone to Columbia, to Brooklyn, to Hunter...to
any one of the accredited graduate programs sprouting "like mush-
rooms" across the country, many of which offered tuition assistant-
ships. The dabblers, the dawdlers, the dilettantes, the dregs—they
took classes at MWI. Now and then a truly gifted student slipped

through the cracks to land in a class of mine. To date none had posed a threat to my authorial supremacy.

I picked up Ashley's manuscript. I read the title page:

Leaving Whynot
a novel???

I sighed. If you had no story to tell, a novel was as good a place as any to hide it. Spill enough ink on enough paper and you're bound to produce—if not a masterpiece, a *manuscript*. Turning the page (as the train clattered along the Harlem River) I read:

> "Oh my dear, dear, *dahlin'* sister, oh Lordy, I feel so *sorry* for you, I surely do. Those New York City folk, those bobcats—why they'll chew you up and blow you out in tiny little bubbles, I sweah to God, they will, little sistah!"
> My mulatto half-sister Rosalie lay sprawled in her flowing, white chiffon nightgown across the disheveled surface of her tall, pink canopy bed, looking every inch of her like something a swarthy angel had dragged in from way up high in the cottony Mississippi clouds…

It's brash, I thought. I'll give her that. "Swarthy angel" wasn't half bad. Striking the word "surface," I replaced it first with "sheets" then with "covers." I read on, cutting a modifier here, rearranging a sentence there. Good God, I told myself. *I'm editing her!* I had long since forsworn line-editing students' efforts. It was too much work, for one thing, and they rarely appreciated it. My doing so to Ashley Bridge's pages could only have meant one thing: I was enchanted. By her charms, by her work. By both.

I turned and peered across the aisle through the scratched window at the lights of Harlem spilling their reflections into the black river. Meanwhile in my own window the floodlights of Yankee Stadium dazzled, a night game running extra innings. With my forehead resting against the cool glass I closed my eyes. As bridges, buildings, and viaducts floated by, I imagined the train being lifted off the tracks, seized by the grip of an enormous gorilla, soaring through the darkness. While aware of its power to crush the train, I was simultaneously touched by the solicitous restraint of the monster's grip. From that brief dream I awoke with a start, convinced that I'd missed my station, to see that the train had just pulled out of University Heights.

• •

Though I lived in Kingsbridge, closer to the Marble Hill station, I preferred to get off at the next stop, one with an odd, Dutch-sounding name: Spuyten Duyvil. From there I walked home. At that hour the station, situated along a stretch of desolate marshland, was deserted. At the platform's far end, near the overpass, among a phalanx of newspaper vending boxes, stood a fluorescent orange Metropolitan Writing Institute catalogue "kiosk" — a term that evoked in me Technicolor footage of Gene Kelly hoofing it through the twisted cobblestone streets of Montmartre, though it was only a plastic box and empty at that. It had been empty for months, either because demand by Bronx residents for creative writing courses greatly exceeded supply, or because my employer hadn't gotten around to refilling it. Those intent on a catalogue were met with

Sorry, we're out of catalogues.
For further information please call

followed by a toll-free number. However technically correct, that "further" bugged me. We're supposed to be a writing school, damn it. Why seek "further" information? Further than what? Than information close at hand? *Way out there* information? *Far out* information? "I'd like the *furthest* information available." Having contemplated doing so for weeks, with a black Sharpie from my briefcase, glancing furtively over each shoulder like a schoolyard pervert, I changed "further" to "more."

No sooner did I make my editorial contribution than an electronic voice cried: *"Alarm … Alarm!"* —followed by a series of apocalyptic whoops and bleats. One of the ticket vending machines on the overpass had malfunctioned. It had been doing so for days. I breathed "a sigh of relief." Imagine: arrested for assaulting bad usage! I wouldn't have put it past them.

Then I climbed the stairs from the train platform to the street.

It was a mostly uphill two-mile walk to my building...(yeah, I know, you're impatient, wanting me to get on with the story: not that of an insomniac writing instructor arriving home to his status-quo situation, or that of the same author falling for one of his female students, or even that of a struggling author perturbed by his twin's not only having written a bestseller, but having kept it a secret from him, not *those* stories, but the one you started some hundred and fifty pages ago, of a man who encounters his double hanging from the ceiling beam of a lakeside A-frame, *that* story. You'd like me to dispense with digressions, ditch the past perfect, pick up the pace, get to *what happens next.* I know; I wasn't a Senior Instructor at the Metropolitan Writing Institute for nothing. But this is no mere flashback, it's my back-story, which is to say: *my life.*

(And why should you want me to get on with it, knowing, as you do, what awaits me at this confession's end? Yet there you stand with your scimitar aimed at my neck. Dear King Schariar, please be patient with your Scheherazade. I promise I'll get back to the main plot! I just need to establish a few more things first, to give you a clear understanding of the circumstances that inspired me to assume my dead brother's identity. Just a few more pages, please. Then—if you must, if you're still so inclined, have at me with your fucking sword.)

Now then...where were we?

It was a three-mile walk to my building. Blah blah, atmosphere, moonlight, neighborhood, stream-of-consciousness musings. Home.

Before bed I check the mail (note tense shift). My American Express statement, along with other bills, including one for $378.13 for an oil pan reseal and brake job for the Mazda. Junk flyers. A rejection slip from the *Tallahassee Review.*

The United States Postal Service having delivered its usual injuries and insults, I switch on my computer and click the email icon, inviting a barrage of spam, including several enticements for male member enhancement, one come-on for which ("Gain a HUGE PENIS in your sleep!") evokes the image of Gregor Samsa waking to find himself transformed not into a giant beetle, but into a giant phallus. How the story might proceed from there I'm deliberating when a fresh email pops onto my screen.

From: *abridges@hotmail.org*
Subject: *taxi shanghai*

hi stew,

Stew?!

i hope you don't mind my emailing you at this late hour, but i
had to tell you how much i enjoyed my first class with you and
how grateful i was that you volunteered to read what I gave you
tonight though you didn't volunteer really i pretty much shang-
haied you anyway you'll think its totally amateurish i'm sure but
still i can't wait to hear what you think

pleasant dreams

ashley

Should I answer? Heck no! It's past midnight!

I close my computer, eat a bowl of Raisin Bran with water (my
quart of milk having turned), shower, take half an Ambien, go to
sleep—or to bed, sleep and bed having become disassociated with
each other of late. Forty minutes after nodding off, I'm up.

Curious, isn't it, how my enlarged prostate mirrors that of the
protagonist of "Harris' Book"—which, in case you've forgotten,
was absorbed by "Pure Flux" and all subsequent iterations of my
novel. Curious, too, is it also not, how these novels of mine, or this
one perpetually ameliorated novel, anticipated with Cassandran
clairvoyance its author's fate. Be all that as it may, my impinged upon
urethra with its Chicken Little urgencies *("Alarm!...Alarm!...")*
has once again awoken me.

Sleep being off the table, I contemplate various pursuits prac-
ticable at two o'clock in the morning, to wit:

a) floss teeth
b) trim:
    1. eyebrows
    2. toenails
    3. nostril hairs
c) scrape dried crud off electric toothbrush charger base
d) water plants
e) organize linen closet

f) gargle

g) read (not a novel; heavens no; too enervating. Something companionable and edifying, a random dip into Erasmus' *Copia*, Burton's *Melancholy*, or the *Zibaldone*.)

Should those activities prove insufficiently engaging, I can always get drunk and/or commit suicide.

Instead, I re-read Ashley's email. However obsequious, it beats being told that I owe eight hundred dollars to a credit card company or that my latest short story sucks or that my penis is a candidate for enhancement. I type:

Dear Ashley,

(Yes, I'm one of those email troglodytes who insists on salutations, valedictions, punctuation, and, yes, capitalization.)

> Thanks for your note. I too enjoyed meeting you and our shared taxicab ride. I haven't yet read the material you gave me, but I look forward to doing so and am sure there's nothing to be embarrassed about. In fact — and unless you have any objection — I'd like to Chamber it when we meet in two weeks' time for our next class.
>
> Meanwhile — have faith!
>
> See you in two weeks.
>
> Yours,
>
> Stewart

Before hitting "send," I append my surname. Then I change "Yours" to "Best."

Then I delete the exclamation point.

Then I reinstate it.

Then I delete it again.

Then I cut "and our shared taxicab ride."

I'm about to hit "send" again when on second (or third—or fourth—thought), I delete my surname. *Then* I hit "send."

My gut muscles contract, relax.

I fart.

Then I return to bed and sleep "like a baby."

12. BURYING BROCK

THE GENIUS OF KAFKA'S "THE METAMORPHOSIS" RESTS MAINLY in its fantastic opening. *"When Gregor Samsa woke one morning from uneasy dreams, he found himself transformed right there in his bed into some sort of monstrous insect."* With one declarative sentence, Kafka establishes his alternative universe. No explanations, no arguments. Take it or leave it.

No sooner did I answer my mother's query (*"Is it really you, Brock?"*) in the affirmative, than I became my brother. One moment I was Stewart Detweiler, failed novelist and disgraced Senior Metropolitan Writing Institute Instructor; the next I was Brock Jones, PhD, bestselling author and motivational guru.

The metamorphosis—that wasn't the hard part. All I had to do was believe it. *"There's no such thing, really, as reality. What we think of as 'reality' is nothing more than an unbroken series of convictions. The empiricists got it backwards. Perceptions don't shape beliefs, beliefs shape perceptions."* —*Coffee, Black.*

And I did believe it; I had no trouble believing it. The differences between my brother and me had always been negligible, matters of degree and chance, a twist of fortune here, a roll of the dice there, this road taken, that one left behind. Compared to the things we had in common, the choices that led each of us on to our distinct paths were as superficial as the clothes we wore, the brands of toothpaste we used, the way we combed our hair. Deep down in our DNA, we were—had always been—identical.

It wasn't even a question of belief. One needn't believe in a demonstrable fact.

•   •

Since Greg Detweiler and Brock Jones, PhD were, had been, one and the same, and since Gregory Detweiler and I had likewise been identical, by logical extension Brock Jones, PhD and Stewart Detweiler were identical.

As for Stewart Detweiler, the reality…potentiality?…the unique set of possibilities and conditions that until that moment had gone by his name no longer existed. They'd been replaced, usurped by a new set of probabilities and possibilities. Had I bothered, I might have remembered them, but only the way one remembers parts of a dream.

But to answer your anticipated question: no, I never looked back. Why look back into a black, empty abyss when one can look forward into a bright future?

Besides, there was no time for looking back. I had too much to do.

•   •

For starters, there was the question of what to do about Stewart Detweiler. Now that I had become Brock, what was to become of him?

The obvious answer was that Stewart Detweiler could no longer exist. He had to die, to be dead. In fact he already was. His putrefying corpse hung by a length of rope from the ceiling beam above my head. That's right. Now that I was Brock Jones, PhD, logically he who had been Brock Jones, PhD, the one hanging from that beam, was now my erstwhile self, Stewart Detweiler.

But wait! you say. Before you go on to describe said undertaking (a word that, in the given context, is doubly apt), did you not stop to consider the ethics of what you were doing? Assuming your twin's identity? Taking his life? Couldn't you see how *wrong* it was? *Taking?* Dear Reader, I wasn't *taking* anything! No, no—I was giving, as I saw it, as I still see it. My twin, who from where I stood had had a fabulously good life, was dead; while I, whose life was a botch, lived. Greg/Brock had had everything to live for, while I, his wretched twin, had few if any good reasons left to carry on my demeaning existence. Yet my brother had died while I went on breathing. It was all wrong! It made no sense!

But it was a wrong that I would set right.

How? you ask.

By giving this perfectly healthy but wasted body of mine to him, to my dead brother. Not just a kidney or an eye or a lung or even a heart or a brain, but all eleven organ systems: circulatory, respiratory, digestive, reproductive, nervous, skeletal, muscular, endocrine, excretory, immune, and integumentary…the whole kit-n-caboodle.

That's how I saw it, how I still see it. Besides, Dear Reader: what else could I do? Having already led my mother to believe my brother, her precious son, the apple of her worrisome eye, was alive and well, having relieved her of that one monumental worry, could I possibly get back to her and say, "Hey, guess what, Mom? When you talked to Brock? That wasn't Brock. That was me. Brock is dead. He hanged himself. I was just—you know—*pulling your leg.*" How cruel a person do you suppose I am?

No, I couldn't do that. The moment I led our mother to believe that my brother was alive and well, I was committed to making it so.

But wait, you say. What about *you*? Sooner or later, your mother would have to find out that *you* were dead. In which case wouldn't she be just as upset?

You're right; that's true. Of course she'd be upset. I'd taken that into account. But instead of losing a successful son, she'd lose a miserable failure. Which would be the lesser loss?

Besides, she loved my brother more. She worshipped Brock. She even kept a shrine to him in her assisted living facility apartment, on her vanity in front of the mirror, with signed copies of his books and autographed publicity photos and clippings from

People and other magazines. The same vanity held no shrine to Stewart Detweiler.

How, you wonder, was it possible for a mother not only to favor one twin over another, but to favor the twin who'd changed his name, who had denied his—her—identity?

Here I can only theorize. My theory is this: that for our mother, her son's, my brother's, change of identity was a relief. She'd been grateful for it. It gave her hope that at least one of us had slipped out from under Malcolm Detweiler's suicidal shadow, that he had freed himself from the Detweiler curse. To our worry-prone mother this must have constituted a tremendous weight off her shoulder. Hence her worshipful embrace of Brock Jones, PhD, the hero who'd rescued one of her sons. In her dimming vision his was the brightest of stars.

That was my theory, anyway.

But do you really expect people to believe you weren't motivated by greed? By the pied-à-terre in Paris, the beach bungalow in Venice? Not to mention all the opportunities attendant to gaining your brother's fame? Do you honestly expect people to believe your motives were purely altruistic, that you weren't thinking also if not mainly of yourself?

Whoever said that to be noble motives need to be pure? What's pure in life? Sure, I was thinking of myself. One way or another every choice we make in life is designed to give us some form of pleasure, whether that of satisfying a hunger or expiating some form of guilt or just the pleasure of doing a good deed. Those were secondary motives. My primary motives were selfless; they were noble. Nothing you say or think will convince me otherwise.

Now may I get on with it?

• •

The question remained: what was my former self doing hanging from a ceiling beam in the home that had once been our father's and to where my present self had absconded, seeking refuge from his notoriously successful life? How to explain that to myself, let alone to anyone else?

The first explanation that came to me was the most virtuous

in its simplicity. Summoned by our panicked mother to my father's lakeside house to learn why no one had seen or heard from me in two months, having found me in hiding but otherwise in good condition, after spending a seemingly pleasant day with me, one night, in the middle of the night, while I lay sound asleep in my downstairs bedroom, my identical twin, whom I had left asleep in the loft, awoke, got hold of a length of blue nylon rigging rope, and—most inconsiderately, I might add—hanged himself from the ceiling beam as our father had done years before. You see, I would tell whoever asked me, my poor brother suffered from depression. He had been deeply depressed for some time. How did I know? He'd told me, that's how. In our last conversation, before I'd gone to bed that night, we'd spoken about it. He made it clear that he'd been terribly depressed. I could go into all the gory details, if I had to, if compelled to. I could tell whoever it was about my brother's—about Stewart's—slow but steady descent from bright early promise into disillusionment, despair, depravity, and decrepitude, about his failed literary career and his disastrous dalliance with a young woman less than half his age, as a result of which he had lost not only what little remained of his dignity but his job, a job that, though he may have complained about it from time to time, had been his one remaining anchor in life. I could say all those things by way of explanation. Or I could just say, "He'd been depressed," and leave it at that, since, as with good fiction, it's often best to give readers an impression supported by one or two authenticating details and leave the rest to the imagination.

What was wrong with this idea? Nothing, except that I'd have to report the suicide to the authorities. The police would have to investigate. True, Stewart Detweiler had no life insurance, so there'd be no insurance company involvement. Still, there would be an investigation, and possibly an autopsy. What were the odds that no one would suspect a possible switcheroo on the part of the deceased's reprobate twin? Dental and other medical records would be consulted and compared. Did we have identical cavities? I had three root canals, two crowns, and, on the bottom left side of my mouth, a missing molar that only showed when I smiled widely, which I did rarely. What chance was there that my twin had the same missing molar? And even if he did, still, there would be other discrepancies.

No: it wouldn't work. I had to get rid of the body, to dispose of it. But where? How? By what means? I had to decide. Having decided, I'd have to act swiftly. I'd also have to be careful. I'd have to make it look as though Stewart—my former self—had committed suicide, but in such a way as left no body to be found.

Here again, almost immediately a simple solution presented itself: drowning. Stewart would have to have drowned. Yes: my depressed brother had consigned himself to a hideous watery death. One night—the same night as in the previous scenario—while I slept, he got up, got dressed, went down to the dock, jumped into the freezing water and drowned himself. No, that wouldn't do. Eventually his body would turn up. He'd have to weigh himself down with something. He'd have to fill his pockets with stones, like Virginia Woolf before she waded into the Ouse. But first he'd have to somehow get himself out into deep water. He couldn't swim out, not with pockets full of stones. He'd have to do so by some other means. Of course! Our father's boat! That's how he'd do—how he had done, how he *did*—it. It's important to put the story in the past tense, to think of it not as an idea, but as a *fait accompli,* something that has already happened. This is what I'd tell my students at the Metropolitan Writing Institute whenever they would come to me and say, "I have this idea for a story" or "What if my character were to do X?" Forget about ideas, I'd say. Readers don't want ideas; they want a story! Never mind what your characters *would* do; what *do* they do; what *did* they do? Conceive of your stories *as if they've already happened.*

Ergo:

He'd filled the boat with stones, then, having rowed himself far out into deep water, with his coat on and its pockets filled with stones, he climbed (jumped?) overboard. Being a strong swimmer like his brother, even weighed down with stones he might have put up a bit of a struggle. He might have grabbed onto the side of the boat and tried to save himself. Or he might have given the boat a shove, preempting any such effort. In any event, with the water as cold as it was, even if somehow he'd managed to empty the stones from his pockets and keep himself afloat, still, he would be too far out in the lake to make it back to shore before succumbing to the below-fifty-degree water. No, there'd be, or would have been, no way for him to change his mind and then to rescue himself. And the boat? That was the beauty part. For the boat would eventually find its way to someone's dock. True, that someone might not report it; that someone might just want to keep such a beautiful boat while breathing not a word to anyone. On the other hand, they wouldn't be able to use the boat, now, would they, especially once word got out about its having gone missing in the middle of the night along with one Stewart Detweiler. Once the missing boat was found, one could only conclude that the missing person had been its solitary passenger and sole crew. From there could one come to any conclusion other than suicide? Especially given the stones left in the bottom of the boat's hull, along with an empty vodka (no, better make that gin: I, or rather my brother, preferred gin) fifth, and a likewise empty vial of Diazepam or some other prescription drug from his—my former—travel kit?

It was, I told myself, a good if not a flawless plan.

True, someone *might* suspect something. If so, there'd be no witnesses to confirm their suspicions. But then why would anyone suspect anything? By what twisted logic would anyone be drawn to the conclusion that the wealthy, famous, successful, respected and adored Brock Jones, PhD, had, for some bizarre reason, killed himself?—rather than his failed, miserable, embittered, impoverished, obscure, friendless, clinically depressed brother?

But—

Wait! Oh no no no no no no no. It won't work. The boat. It can't be found. If it's found, then it was missing. If it was missing, then I—Brock Jones, PhD—must have known that it was missing along with my depressed, possibly suicidal brother. In which case, I would have had to report both the boat and my brother as missing. I'd have to tell everyone: my mother, the police. And I'd have to do so right away, as soon as *I* knew: meaning the moment I noticed that the boat and my brother were both gone. Right?

But supposing... supposing I didn't notice the boat was gone? Supposing all I knew was that my brother Stewart had gone missing. How did I know? When did I know? After a week or two. You see, he'd—he'd driven off one day. That's right. He drove off in his car, in his once sporty, now decrepit Mazda RX-7. Naturally I assumed he was headed home. Naturally. So when I heard nothing more of him, that was no surprise to me. After all, prior to this last spontaneous and unplanned visit we hadn't spoken to each other in—how long? Years. Five years. So why would I call—or expect a call from—him? I just assumed he was fine. Naturally.

The missing boat? I assumed that it was behind the house, under the deck. That's where I last left it, having been too lazy to bring it indoors and deal with the hoisting mechanism. So I'd put it under the tarp. After Stew and I took it out. Oh, yes: and I'd also let him take the boat out once or twice by himself. He'd asked me if he could.

"What are you asking me for?" I'd said.

"It's your boat."

"It's Dad's boat," I said.

"It came with the house. The house is yours."

"Nonsense. It's as much your boat as it is mine. Anyway by all means take it out. I never use it. I'd rather swim. Enjoy yourself."

So he'd used it a few times. That's right. Anyway, I forgot that it had been left under the deck. So I didn't notice it was missing. I never looked back there. Why would I? The only other things I keep back there are a wheelbarrow and the deck furniture, likewise under tarps. But it being winter I had no use for either. So how was I to know the boat was gone? That my brother had taken it on the roof of his car? Yes, that's right: he'd tied it down with some blue rigging rope and driven off with it. (Can you do that with a convertible sports car, tie a boat on top of it? Who knows? Sure. Why not?) Maybe I knew he'd driven off with it. Maybe he'd asked me if he could drive off with our dead father's boat on top of his car. Why? How should I know? What would he want with a boat in New York City—in The Bronx, no less? Maybe he'd take it out on the Hudson River. I don't know. Why are you asking all these questions? I never asked so many questions. All I knew was he'd driven off with the boat on top of his car, on top of the Mazda. What he planned to do with the thing was his business.

Little did I suspect that it was all part of a suicidal plan.

And just what was that plan, you ask? Your Honor, or who-ever the hell you are, the plan was this: that he'd drive the car with the boat on its roof to a secluded boat ramp, where he would launch it along with himself, a fifth of gin, a vial of (name prescription sleep-inducing drug), and a bunch of rocks. He'd row himself out into the depths of the lake, and then he would...

But why go to all that trouble? Why not take the boat into the water here, at the house? Better still, why not just jump off the dock? Why bother with the car and the boat and all that?

Your Honor, I honestly don't know. On the other hand, where is it written that in order to commit suicide you have to be in your right mind, or even rational, let alone efficient or practical? Maybe he wanted to confuse me; maybe he didn't want me to know that he had done what he did, at least not right away. Or maybe he planned it that way; maybe he didn't plan it at all. Maybe he acted on a series of impulses, blindly, out of distress and despair. I don't know; I really can't explain it. All I know is my brother is gone, Your Honor, and so was my—our—boat, until someone discovered it weeks later washed up on his or her lawn.

(See why I've struggled with plot? I no sooner engage one than it becomes convoluted and implausible. Better to have no plot at all, I felt and still believe. In this case, though, a complicated plot would have to do. Anyway, it would buy me some badly-needed time.)

Wait a minute! Of course. What was I *thinking*? There was no need to kill off Stewart Detweiler. Why bother killing him off, when he was barely alive to begin with, when all it would take to make him "live" was a phone conversation with my mother three or four times a month, and only as long as she lived—which, let's face it, wouldn't be all that long, not with her advanced diabetes and her kidneys already well on the way to failing. No other family, no job, no friends, no literary agent, no fame, no fortune, no beach bungalow in Venice or *pied-à-terre* in New York or Paris or Portofino, no one calling or checking up on him with any frequency (the last person to do so had been Julie, the Pulitzer Prize winner who gave him her car, her used Mazda, the one who'd moved to Paris)...There was the landlord where he lived, but a check once a month would take care of him. What about his land-line? What if people phoned it? I'd disconnect it! Who uses land-lines anymore? I'd have the phone company provide a message with my—with Stewart's—new cell phone number. No. Wait. Why would I do that? I'd simply tell my mother myself to use the new number. What about everyone else? To hell with everyone else! What about the mail? I'd send a forwarding notice to the post office. No I wouldn't! I'd do no such thing! No one would know. Who else might notice that I—I beg your pardon—that Stewart Detweiler, was gone, missing? No one!

There now, you see? There are *advantages to alienating people!* Nice job, Stewart! Thanks to your miserably circumscribed existence, thanks to your misanthropy, your pettiness, your spite, your bitterness, your lack of warmth and grace and humor, your generally negative attitude toward life, you've made *my* life—the new one—that much easier! I don't have to kill you off after all! For all intents and purposes, for *my* intents and purposes, you're dead enough!

So much for Stewart Detweiler.

•   •

There were further complications, of course. A simple rule of life: everything is more complicated than you think it will be. That's especially true, I discovered, of disposing of bodies, especially when the disposal has to be undertaken clandestinely. There's nothing simple about it.

First there was the matter of getting the body down from that ceiling beam. I couldn't just go up there, cut the blue rope, and let it fall. For one thing, it was a fifteen-foot drop, which, with his body already in a state of decomposition, would have made quite a mess, not to mention the mental mess that method, with its attendant thud, crunches, splashes, splatters, and splats, would make in my already distraught, disheveled mind. Also the bar unit, with its panoply of bottles of various colors, sizes, and shapes, and assorted cocktail glasses, was in the path of the fall, adding to the potential gruesomeness. I had to arrive at a means by which to lower the body gradually.

No sooner did I pose this challenge to myself than my mind's eye projected the engraved image of a shrouded corpse being lowered by rope from the Asch Building after the Triangle Shirtwaist Factory fire. Where I had come across that image I'm not sure, but there it was. Yes: that was the obvious if not the only solution: lower the corpse by rope with the beam as fulcrum. I'd need a good strong rope, as strong as the blue nylon rigging rope with which my brother had hanged himself, but longer, at least forty feet long: long enough to reach from the floor up to and around the ceiling beam and down to the floor again. Then I could control the speed of the body's descent from the ground, like a boy flying a kite.

Here, too, a solution presented itself almost instantly, one that would kill two birds with one stone—a practical bird and a literary bird, as it were.

The solution hung over my head next to my twin brother's corpse: my father's boat, or rather the pulley system by which it clung to the rafters. It looked like this:

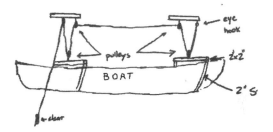

The system sported the same blue nylon rigging rope a length of which my brother used to hang himself (in fact he had sliced a length suitable to his needs from the end of that very rope, the slack portion of which our father would normally coil and stuff next to the cleat; I saw the jagged end where he'd probably cut it with a steak knife) By my estimation, the rope had to be at least forty feet long. Since a matter of yards separated the pulley mechanism from my brother's corpse, it struck me that if somehow I could slide the noose by which it hung down the beam toward the mechanism, having lowered and detached the boat from it, I could use the same mechanism to lower the body. How to slide it over?

Considering that he'd been in excellent physical shape (having taken up swimming and bodybuilding), with his muscular build, though he looked a lot slimmer, my brother probably weighed only about twenty-five pounds less than I, meaning around one hundred and eighty pounds, enough to put a lot of friction between the noose and that beam. Supposing I greased the beam? Then, with the grappling hook my father used to change lights and put on his ceiling fans, I could pull the body along it toward where the boat hoisting system hung. Yes: that could work. In the sink cabinet of the loft bathroom I found a jar of petroleum jelly — a big jar, half-used, to what end I didn't care to know.

To grease the beam I'd have to climb out on it, there was no other way. I have always been afraid of heights, always. It's why even with Coach Hunt and an army of sixth graders egging me on I could never climb to the top of the rope in Phys Ed or get enthusiastic about tree forts. Now, though, I was sufficiently motivated.

With the jar of petroleum jelly I returned to the balcony railing and stood contemplating my next move. From there I could reach the beam, but only eight or so feet of it; from that point the stairs went down, while the beam stayed where it was. To get to it I'd have to put a ladder on the stairs — a tricky business. Even then to reach the beam I'd have to lean too far over.

I was about to abandon the whole plan when I realized if I stood on the stair railing I could easily reach the rest of the beam. The only problem was that the railing was slanted. I decided to risk it. To be on the safe side, using another length of rope from my father's boat — not the blue rope by which it hung from the ceiling, but a yellow rope that I found in the hull after lowering the boat to the floor — I made myself a harness. It's not hard to do. With one end of the harness around my waist and the other secured to the beam, I climbed on the slanted railing and, trembling the whole time, coated the top and sides of the beam with Vaseline, imagining while doing so what someone would think were they to enter that house and discover — not one, but *two* Detweiler twins hanging side-by-side from the same oak beam? With my heart pounding I climbed down off the railing. Using the grappling hook, having snared the noose, standing as far as

I could to give myself leverage, I dragged the corpse down the length of the beam to where it lined up with the pulley system for my father's boat.

The boat hoist mechanism worked perfectly. Of course it was badly off-balance, with one of its pulleys—the one that normally supported the bow of my father's boat—bearing the full weight of my brother's body. Still, it did the job. My brother's body came to rest gently on the leather sofa, with the boat lying next to it on the floor. Perfect. All I had to do was put the oars in the boat, pull the boat down the leaf-covered lawn to the strip of sandy shore near the dock, and get my brother into the boat.

Thanks to a method known as the "fireman's carry," the last part turned out to be easier than you might think. Lest the name doesn't make it obvious, the "fireman's carry" is the method by which firemen rescue—or used to rescue—unconscious people from burning buildings. With the subject lying face down, shift your weight to your right leg and stick it between the subject's legs. With your left hand grab the subject's right hand and pull it over your shoulder. With your head under the victim's right armpit, wrap your arm around the back of his or her right knee. Then squat and lift, distributing the subject's weight evenly across both your shoulders and proceed with the evacuation. Using this technique, you can easily pick up and move an unconscious person of equal or lesser body weight than your own. In fact the technique is no longer favored by firemen, since it requires rescuers to be in an upright position, increasing the risk of smoke inhalation. Still, it served my purpose perfectly.

Anyway, getting the body into the boat wasn't the problem. Getting it out of the boat was a different story. In deep water there would be no way to lift and shove it over the side—not without swamping or capsizing the boat and sending us both into the freezing water. For a while this had me stumped, but to this problem too eventually a solution presented itself.

As I've mentioned, in his incarnation as Brock Jones, PhD, not only did my brother lose weight and become physically fit, he became something of an athlete. Among other martial arts and sports he took up swimming. He was quite the inveterate swimmer, apparently. He swam in all kinds of water and all kinds of weather, explaining the wetsuit I found in one of the A-frame's closets. Could I fit into it? I could, more or less. The legs fit, so did the arms. But I couldn't raise the zipper, which was in the back, all the way up; in fact I broke the strap attached to it for that purpose trying. Still, with seven-eighths of my body protected (including my head by a separate thermal hood and my feet by booties I found in the same closet), it seemed to me that I should be able to survive at least thirty minutes in fifty degree water: a fact that I confirmed via the Internet. In all likelihood I could survive longer than that.

Now things were really taking shape. An hour before sunset, with the wetsuit still on (damned if I was going to take it off and put it on again), I drove my car—my former self's former car—to a location less than a mile as the crow flies from the house, but about four miles by road, close to a boat ramp that, according to a map of the lake on the wall in the downstairs bathroom, would serve my purpose. A towel, a robe, a change of clothing, a thermos bottle of hot tea, some stale cookies from a box I found on top of the refrigerator: all these things went into the Mazda with me. I parked the car a few dozen yards from the boat ramp, which was right where it was supposed to be. I hid the keys under the floor mat. In my wetsuit through a pink-gold twilight I walked the four miles back to the house, arriving there just as the sun was about to set, a glorious sunset, the best I'd ever seen there. I took it as a good omen, a sign that—in case I still had any doubts—I was doing the right thing, the noble thing, making a glorious (if con-voluted) sacrifice to a cause far more worthy and significant than the only cause Stewart Detweiler had ever served: himself. Soon all that selfishness, all that bitterness and fear and anger and regret and sadness and self-pity, would be behind me; soon Stewart Det-weiler would be behind me. To be more precise, he would be at the bottom of Lake S——.

• •

The trouble with most thrillers is they make so little sense. Their sensational plots depend heavily if not exclusively on characters whose actions are determined by pathology rather than greater or more reasonable motivations.

Even if we accept the motivations, even if we don't mind reading several hundred pages of pathology, still, their plots don't usually hold up under scrutiny. However talented he may be, can anyone really believe that Patricia Highsmith's Mr. Ripley gets away with it? After clubbing Dickie to death with an oar and accidentally falling overboard, he chases the whirling runaway motorboat "heedless of the propeller's blades." If there's one law that applies equally to real and fictional people it's the one stating that those intent on their physical well-being don't argue with propeller blades. Apart from which the whole plot of that enormously popular novel depends on the ineptitude of a vast network of law enforcement officials.

Such is the stuff of bestsellers and why I can't write them. I'm too hung up on logic, on the false god of verisimilitude—as if a novel of any sort were a reasonable place to look for, let alone find, credibility. *The Audubon Society Field Guide to North American Trees,* maybe, or a cookbook. But a *novel?*

The truth is this: the stupider a novel, the better it will sell. Any hack willing to foist a gratuitously arrived at corpse on a gullible public can write her way to bestsellerdom. Suspend logic and disbelief, throw caution, good taste, and one or two laws of physics to the wind, and you're off and running.

I hold myself to higher standards. Even presented with a fortuitous corpse on Page One, as fate had seen fit to equip me, I resisted all temptation to, as it were, dispose of the matter gratuitously, in ways more intent on shock than on conveying the literal, concrete, authentic truth.

So—I'd taken the body down: the body, that's how I thought of it. Not as my brother's body, or Gregory Detweiler's body, or Brock Jones, PhD's body, or my body (it was as much mine by then as anyone's), but simply and non-specifically as "the body," a thing belonging to no one. I wrapped "the body" in a large blue tarp I found covering a wheelbarrow under the deck. By one arm jutting out of the tarp, using the fireman's method, I lifted it up and over my shoulder and carried it to the boat that by then was already down by the little beach, along with the oars, some stones I'd collected, a roomy jacket with big pockets, a cinderblock, and a large knife—the biggest and sharpest I could find. Also the same yellow rope that I'd used to get the body down. All these things I stowed in the boat's hull. With the body stowed with them and my, or rather my brother's (though it was mine now, wasn't it? Wasn't everything that had been my brother's mine, now that *I* was my brother?) wetsuit on, I cast the boat off. As it glided into the lake, I climbed in myself.

I'd forgotten how tippy the boat was. As it pitched and jostled I almost lost my balance and fell overboard. Somehow I regained equilibrium. Soon I was in my seat, rowing out into the dark lake. By then it was after midnight. There was a half moon out that night—a gibbous moon, to be technical about it, though I used to get on my Metropolitan students' backs when they'd use that word, one of a long list of words I had come to distrust, along with "spot" (as a verb), "spy" (ditto), "place" ("put"), "frame" ("body"), "glance" ("look"), "seemingly" and "gingerly"—words that reek of author-at-work, a literary stench: one-word clichés that suggest to me an author not fully awake at the wheel.

A scattering of lights burned in homes dotting the shore, along with brighter dock lights. Otherwise no evidence was to be seen of quotidian human existences or activities excluding the disposal of human corpses by water after midnight.

Except for the gentle splashes my oars made in the water and a dog barking in the very far distance there wasn't a sound to be heard, not even the peepers and crickets one usually hears up north. Nothing. As I kept rowing, I heard the rasp of an engine overhead, and looked up to see the flashing lights of a small aircraft. I had rowed several hundred strokes and was about three-quarters of a mile from where I'd started when I heard a spluttering sound and turned to see a fishing boat coming up from behind. Its occupant had to have seen me. He steered a wide birth and came within no less than several hundred feet as he passed; he couldn't have seen much of anything.

That was the only other boat I saw that night. I rowed for another half hour or so, until I reached my destination, one I identified by a configuration of dock lights, including a green one at the dock's deep end—yes, that's right, Daisy's green dock light straight out of *Gatsby*. How it got from a fictional West Egg, Long Island, to a lake in Georgia, I have no idea.

In deepest water, with at least a thousand feet separating the boat and me from the shore in all directions, I stopped rowing and laid the oars against the gunwales.

Now for the hard part—the second hardest part. I had to pull the big coat around the body. It was one of those baggy canvas L.L. Bean field coats, with generous snap-down pockets. I'm not sure if it had been my father's or my brother's. In any case, it was perfect for the job, or would have been save for one thing: I should have put it on earlier, with the boat still on dry land. I now saw that doing so out in the middle of the lake would be next to impossible. At the very least I'd have to move carefully. If the boat tipped over before I did what needed doing, all would be lost.

Anyway I proceeded. Carefully, as if diffusing a bomb, with the boat threatening to capsize with every movement, I managed to work the coat under the body, which lay with its back against the keel, then manipulated both arms into their sleeves. At last, with the coat on, one rock at a time, I filled the pockets with stones, careful to balance the stones perfectly to keep the boat stable under me. With the pockets full to bursting with stones I snapped them shut. I secured one end of the rope around the cinder block, the other end around the body's midriff.

Now the first-hardest hard part, anyway the part that terrified me most, and that explains the need for that big sharp knife. With respect to disposing of human bodies by water I'd done my due diligence. At Yahoo Answers I asked, "Why does a dead body float on water?" and got this:

> When people die, bacteria normally present in the walls of the stomach and intestines escape from the weakened tissue into the abdominal cavity, where, as the tissues rot, they produce methane, hydrogen sulfide, carbon dioxide, and other gasses, causing the torso to bloat, lowering the density of the body until it is less than one gram per cubic centimeter ($1g/cm^3$), the specific gravity of water, putting into effect Archimedes' Principle, which

states that the upward buoyant force that is exerted on a body immersed in fluid, whether fully or partially submerged, is equal to the weight of the fluid that the body displaces and acts in the upward direction at the center of mass of the displaced fluid. For this reason without exception a corpse lying on the bottom of a lake or river eventually will surface owing to gases formed in its tissues as a result of decay and the action of internal bacteria resulting in a dramatic reduction of specific gravity, explaining why witnesses have reported corpses breaking the surface of ponds and lakes with dramatic force, like corks popping.

While an article in a science webzine titled "Drowning Investigations" offered this discouraging tidbit:

The amount of time required for a body to surface depends on several factors, including water temperature and depth, fat distribution, and foods and beverages consumed prior to drowning. Bacterial action takes place more slowly in deep cold water. In that case the corpse may not appear for weeks. With time, however, as the body becomes distended with gas, its buoyancy will continue to increase. This is why, despite being anchored by objects as heavy as outboard motors, homicide victims dumped into lakes will eventually surface.

I'd have given up then and considered some alternative plan had *Answerbag* not provided this simple if ghastly solution:

To allow the gasses to escape and bubble up to the surface rather than becoming trapped within the body, the easiest thing to do is to cut the stomach open, since that's where most of the gasses will accumulate. However gasses may get trapped in other places, too, so it's best to puncture the body all over.

Dear Reader, I know what you must be thinking. How *could* I? Disembowel *my brother's corpse*? But it wasn't "my brother's corpse" anymore. It was "the corpse," a thing: a decomposing putrid thing belonging to no one: not to my brother, and not to me. It fell to me to dispose of the thing, a grisly but necessary part of the surgical procedure whereby I replaced what had been my brother's decaying body with my healthy living one. Had I donated my kidney to save his life, would you or anyone else give a damn what became of my brother's old, useless kidney, if it ended up in the trash or got flushed down the toilet? Would you get sentimental about it?

No. Of course not.

Well all right then.

Knife in hand, with one bootied foot to either side of the corpse, straddling it, I went to work. Though I tried to ignore my emotions (I almost wrote "my gut feelings"), there's no word in English for what I felt as — with the corpse's bloated belly glaring up at me — I introduced the knife's serrated blade to just below the sternum and started slicing, headed through the naval down to the pubic bone. All the neurons in my brain seemed to fire at once. The chalky flesh wrestled with the blade. Through my knuckles I felt the tissues tearing. A dark translucent fluid rolled out over the sides of the wound to pool in the bottom of the boat. At the same time as the blade sliced into skin as rubbery, gray, and cold as the wetsuit I wore, I experienced something else, another feeling I'd never felt before, a sense of heroic concentration, as if I were a surgeon performing a risky operation under extremely adverse conditions that would save the patient's life — which, as I hope I've explained by now, was the case. At the same time I had the distinct sense that I was being watched, as if that little boat bobbing out in the middle of the lake were an operating theater, with a ring of first year medical students gazing down at me, the master surgeon, from the viewing gallery above. *Ready...set...incision.* As my scalpel — kitchen knife — pierced the skin, a shudder went through me — not an unpleasant shudder, but a shudder of satisfaction such as in the past I'd experienced having applied a precise brushstroke to a canvas or nailing a perfect sentence to the page. In that moment, with that slice of that knife in that belly, I achieved a perfect balance of detachment, concentration, and creative bliss. *This incision must be perfectly straight. Work through the subcutaneous fat. Easy, now. Careful....* After the initial gag response, I felt not a trace of nausea or faintheartedness. And though a hideously putrescent odor arose from the incision, it didn't bother me, either: it merged with my bliss, becoming part of it. I was the artist at work, bent to his labors, immune and immutable.

Have I mentioned that there was a gibbous moon that night? It was that gibbous moon's milky glow that bounded off the corpse's distended belly, that moon's lactescent glow that glistened in the goo oozing from its abdomen, that gibbous moon that doubled as my surgical lamp. Three slices it took me to cut through the layers of tissue, each its own shade of moonlit gray. The same focused intent that guided the blade kept me perfectly balanced aboard that ultra-tippy boat. I might have been standing on *terra firma,* I felt so centered, so grounded.

Meanwhile an idea floating just under the level of my consciousness held me no less firmly in its grip: namely, that I was performing not just the task of a surgeon, but of a novelist, exposing to daylight — or a gibbous moon — the "innards" of my character[s], though as any novelist worth his or her salt will tell you the innards they tear out and expose to the readers' scrutiny are none other than their own. It's the novelist's human soul that she cuts open and bares to the world, herself in the guise of her characters that she eviscerates. If when starting a novel the novelist has secrets, unless the dismal novel is a failure by its end all will have been revealed: there should be nothing left to tell, nothing to expose. Every novel is a confession and a vivisection, every novelist a surgeon — not of the flesh, but of the spirit — whose operations are performed strictly on paper.

What is being confessed? The sum total of everything the novelist thinks, feels, knows, understands, intuits, remembers, and believes.

As I sawed through my equal opposite, another thought occurred to me. Instead of merely slitting the corpse open from sternum to pubic bone, I'd go on, forming two perfect halves: twin halves, equal opposite halves. Nor would I stop there; I'd keep slicing clear through the keel of my father's boat, splitting it in two. But I wouldn't stop there, either. As the two sundered halves of that always bipolar boat, the port side (Gregory) and the starboard side (Stewart) drifted away from each other, with my legs spreading farther and farther apart like a cheerleader doing a split, somehow I would keep slicing, splitting everything — the lake, the county, the state, the country, earth, heaven, the solar system, the Milky Way … splitting all of creation into two perfectly equal halves. Bifurcating the universe.

There, I said to myself. Finished. The operation is complete.

No sooner did I say it than I was torn abruptly from the trance that had kept me and the boat trim. I tottered to and fro, wobbling like a drunk in a tempest—like a drunk *in a boat* in a tempest. I grabbed one gunwale, rolling the boat to starboard, then its equal opposite, rolling it to port. With each roll the low-riding boat swallowed a few gallons of lake water. My legs gave out from under me. I pitched forward, landing on top of the corpse I had just gutted, our bellies and lips meeting. Slowly, with both hands gripping the gunwhales, I drew myself back into the seat, where I remained for a few moments, catching my breath, covered in mephitic goo.

After a while, with my heart beating reasonably again, on quivering thighs I rose and zipped up the field coat with its pockets stuffed with stones. Then I checked to see to it that the rope was still secure around the cinder block.

Now the easy part—as easy as falling out of bed, or a boat. I took a deep breath and, purposely this time, rolled the boat, capsizing it, dumping the body and myself into the lake.

Wetsuit or no wetsuit, that lake was bloody cold. It was like falling into a ditch full of icy razor blades. That was the least of my problems. The cinder block rope must have caught itself on an oarlock or something. The cinder block proceeded to drag—not just the body, but the rowboat down with it to the bottom. The boat's two floatation chambers, one in the bow, one in the stern, weren't sufficient to countermand the combined weight of the block and the body attached to it. As the bow—or was it the stern?—nosed under, the stern (or was it the bow?) reared *Titanic*-like out of the water.

Luckily before capsizing I'd had the presence of mind to grab the knife. As I struggled to cut the rope, another section of it snagged my right ankle. Boat, body, block, and Brock: all went down to meet their watery dooms. While thrashing away in the cave-dark water I recalled my mother's dream, the one she had of my brother drowning, the dream that prompted the phone call that would ultimately deliver me to this moment. With my red blood cells screaming for oxygen I succeeded in grabbing hold of and slicing through the rope, sending one disemboweled corpse and one cinderblock to Neptune's locker or its freshwater equivalent, releasing the boat, which bobbed upside-down to the surface. I bobbed and spluttered alongside it.

I still gripped the kitchen knife. I hurled it away.

Next challenge: canoe self-rescue. I had read up on the procedure online and practiced in the shallow water by the dock. True, my boat wasn't a canoe, but its size, shape, and weight were similar. Depending on how strong you are, there are two methods.

#1: Get under the center of the boat, lift it up, and flip it over.

#2: Roll the boat over full of water, find the bailer, and bail until the canoe is stabilized, them jump back in the boat.

#2 is what I did, or tried to do, only I'd neglected to bring a bailing bucket. I did the best I could with my hands. The best way to get back in a canoe when alone is to pull yourself to the stern, grasp the boat by both gunwales to keep it balanced, partly submerge yourself for greater momentum, then—in one smooth motion—heave yourself out of the water and plant your chest firmly onto the stern gunwale.

It took me six or seven tries. With my chest on the gunwale, using it as a pivot, I twisted and turned until my legs fell into the boat. From there I rolled myself over, got into the seat, and went on bailing until my fingers froze.

I'd forgotten the oars, which by then had floated off in separate directions. With my two freezing hands I paddled to and retrieved the nearest. Using one oar, my ass half-submerged in freezing water, I paddled the half-swamped boat home.

It took something like an hour. By the time I beached the boat I was shivering so fiercely I could barely control my muscles.

Back in the house, with my teeth chattering and every muscle in my body quaking, I put the kettle on, and—somehow, despite trembling fiercely—got a fire going. I sat on the wicker sofa with a mug of hot tea and the fire belching and a stack of blankets and throws smothering me.

Shivering, with the fire blazing, I fell asleep.

13. "I AM NOT A BAD MAN"

TWO WEEKS PASSED (WE'RE BACK IN OUR BACK-STORY) BEFORE I saw Ashley again.

Meanwhile I put the final touches on the latest version of my novel. For this version, in addition to changes previously mentioned, I reinforced the narrator's unreliability. All unreliable narratives are first-person, and all first-person narrators are, to some extent at least, unreliable—though that doesn't make them unreliable narrators. This is as true for nonfiction as for fiction.

Take this back-story apropos my fall from grace. While it's true that the narrator's (my) situation may not have been ideal, that we may not envy him his unpublished novel or his enlarged prostate, his circumstances were far from dire. He had a job. He wasn't starving or dying of cancer or living in a war zone or being slowly poisoned by totalitarian state-sponsored thugs. Apart from that one pesky reproductive organ, his health was good. True, his brother had forsaken him. Still, things could have been worse.

One thing I advised my Metropolitan students against: sentimentality. As defined by me: *emotions in excess of experience.* Readers shouldn't be expected to have feelings for what they themselves haven't experienced. Efforts to make them do so are likely to be met with resentment. If I say, "*Stewart Detweiler came to doubt himself in every way,*" I'd better be ready to prove it.

Better still, I should put you into the circumstances that add up to that sentiment.

• •

The day of my next visit with Ashley started off auspiciously. A chilly late September Wednesday, the temperature down below freezing. Wearing my mock turtleneck and cuffed khaki Dockers, I walked to the train station, taking note on my way of hoarfrost clinging to car windshields. I walked briskly, a spring in my step, my battered briefcase swinging, my breaths condensing, the frosty air yanking tears from my eyes, whistling Bach's Suite No. 2 for flute (the first rondeau movement). I hoped to catch the 8:15. The sky overhead was a providential (who says modifiers can't earn their keep?) blue patched with... make that scumbled... scumbled with scrappy clouds.

I had a big day ahead of me. Among other things, to make up for the class that had been pre-empted by Rosh Hashanah, we had four students' works-in-progress to chamber that evening. The "chamber" in question was the figurative one wherein Metropolitan students were isolated during critique sessions of their work. This prevented them from defending their efforts and thereby inciting their peers to ever more savage assessments. When I first taught at MWI I balked at the convention. With time, though, I came to appreciate it, having learned that when it comes to criticism, given the thinnest, shortest, shoddiest length of rope (blue? nylon? rigging?) writers will find a way to hang themselves. So I accepted the protocol. I even took to using the verb form of "chamber," as in "Next week we'll be chambering so-and-so's story."

That Wednesday we would be "chambering" Ashley's work-in-progress, which I'd added to that evening's schedule and for which I had spent the better part of an afternoon composing my response, striking a perfect balance, I thought, between advice and encouragement, directness and tact, holding her to high standards while allowing for her youth and lack of experience.

In addition to my student papers, my briefcase held the manuscript of "Duplicity," a photocopy of which I intended to hand-deliver to the then-most powerful agent in New York City, Elizabeth "Bitsy" Watson. But not before my appointment with Dr. Snyder, my urologist.

(Back to unreliable narrators for just a moment. I confess to finding the whole idea of an "objective narrator" frankly absurd. It's why in general I disapprove of third-person narrators, and by extension of most novels, since most novels are written in the third person. The conceit of a detached outside observer, an entity without family or friends, with no hobbies or interests, no foibles or failings, having no hopes or dreams, no past or future, not even a name, existing for no reason other than to relate to us Emma Bovary's fate or chart the history of the French invasion of Russia and its impact on five aristocratic families, is—to put not too fine a point on it—stupid. Such narrators, we're told, are god-like in their omniscience. I say they're godlike in that they don't really exist.)

Now back to our back-story-in-progress, but first this reminder from *Essays in Idleness* author Yoshida Kenkō: "You should never put the new antlers of a deer to your nose and smell them. They have little insects that crawl into the nose and devour the brain."

• •

Seated on the icy platform bench, I read over my comments on Ashley's pages. Had I been too critical? She was a tyro, after all. I should have made more of her strengths. Students tended to assume that whatever wasn't singled out for praise had been found egregious. On second thought, I'd been too kind. She'd see through it. She'd find me patronizing, or worse, pompous: an arrogant, egotistical phony. She'd scoff at my critical appraisal, smirk at it, shrug it off with a toss of her shimmering golden blond hair burnished here and there with touches of copper and brass. She'd share my appraisal with her lover, with her phalanx of lovers. They'd have a good laugh over it, seeing it for what it was, a pathetic bid on the part of a graying, middle-aged, once briefly celebrated but since gone to seed author-cum-writing-instructor to seduce his pretty young student with a bundle of highly-scented unctuousness. *Now just a minute,* I said to myself. *Who's seducing whom? She's not even your type!*

You like dark sophisticated Europeans. She's a blond haired, blue-eyed Mississippian. To borrow another writer's description, Ashley Bridges is "the classic Surfictionist creation—a blur of insouciance, a touch of disingenuousness, a waft of grit." The eyelid-batting femme fetal, a flagrant stereotype. Had you come across her in a student's story, you'd ask that she be developed or recast.

On third thought, my critique of Ashley's novel-in-embryo was thoughtful, honest, gracious—not to mention quite well-written, if I say so, on a par with my best prose.

A ping sounded from the loudspeaker. A tinny voice announced the train's delay. A chilly gust charged up the platform. I flipped up the lapels of my sport coat. I'd underdressed. With the papers back in my briefcase, I walked up the stairs and into the enclosed over-pass, wherein the kind folk at Metro North had installed a heater beneath which a cluster of rush-hour commuters stood huddled, armed with coffee containers, cellphones, and/or early editions of various newspapers. From amid the huddle came a familiar cry:

"Alarm! ... Alarm!"

They still hadn't fixed that damn ticket vending machine. Twice in the past two weeks I had phoned the so-called station-master, whose smiling photograph along with a telephone number for complaints or suggestions was displayed in a glassed-in bulletin board and whose name was either Hector Gonzàlez or Hector Rodrìguez, I forget which. Each time I called I was treated to the same recording assuring me that my call was "very important" and that someone—presumably the smiling Mr. Gonzàlez or Mr. Rodrìguez himself—would return my call "as quickly as possible." Which of course he never did.

"Alarm! ... Alarm!"

Maybe there *was* something to be alarmed about, some empirical or theoretical threat of which the vending machine alone was aware. Or was it giving voice to my existential dread?

Fishing a quarter from the pocket of my Dockers, I made my way to the payphone. Once again I dialed the stationmaster's number—incorrectly, it turned out, waking up some hag in her Medusa's Raft of a bed. I hung up and made my way back through the mob to face the bulletin board again. Mouthing the phone number, I returned to the payphone and redialed, only to get the same recording assuring me that my call was important and asking me to leave a phone number. Instead—in a clear voice but with the receiver tucked close to my lips so as to avoid making a spectacle of myself—I said, "Yes, this is Stewart Detweiler calling you at—" I checked my wristwatch; the 8:15 was six minutes late, "—at eight-twenty-one a.m. from the Spuyten Duyvil Metro North station to report a malfunctioning ticket vending machine. This is my third call to you, Mr. Rodrìguez." Or was it Gonzàlez? Hell, the guy probably didn't exist. "Frankly," I continued, "I'm not sure why I'm bothering to make this call, since by now it's fairly obvious to me that this whole 'stationmaster' crock is nothing but a public relations ploy, one that as far as this customer is concerned has badly misfired. I mean if you're going to put up a person's photograph and give him a name and a phone number and call him the *stationmaster*, you might as well go the whole hog and have him return people's calls." I tried to think of something more to say—something blistering, something "wound[ing] to the core," something that would compel the entire Board of Directors of the Metropolitan Transportation Authority to hurl itself *en masse* off of one of its taller bridges—but I faltered. "Uhm...that's it, I guess...uhm...thank you." I hung up.

Then I realized: I hadn't left my phone number. From the depths of my Dockers I fished out another quarter. I had started dialing again when the crowd scrambled and jostled around me. Through the overpass window I saw the train arrive.

• •

Some pages ago you heard me say that I'm against novels with plots. It's not that simple. I don't oppose plots in general. What I'm opposed to are the the-Queen-died-and-then-the-King-died-of-grief sort of plots one gets with ninety nine percent of novels, where causal relationships are as artificial as they are obvious. Which isn't to say that I don't think things should happen in a story. On the contrary—and as I'd insist with my Metropolitan students—a story or a novel should present us with, if not a plot, a series of incidents or events, preferably of escalating dramatic import.

Such is the basis of the epic—the oldest of all plot forms, poised between the legend and the so-called chronicle. Epic plots are almost always chronological, presenting the hero's actions in sequence, resulting in something akin to an anthology of heroic deeds. Heroic epic provided the footing for the "picaresque" tale, wherein we're presented with the doings of a less-than-noble character or rogue in a contemporary world as seen through the rogue's eyes.

Though not the oldest, of all forms of plot the picaresque is the most primitive. In theory if not in practice its episodic nature allows it to proceed from event to event without resolution, freed from the exigencies of cause and effect, unfettered by the obligation to organize itself toward a mythic or meaningful climax. Its vitality—nay, its existence—depends on its pointlessness.

What follows, Dear Reader, is a picaresque of my unheroic existence boiled down to a single day in September of 2012.

• •

Having detrained at Grand Central, I rode the subway down to the Village. There, at Copies Plus ("Where We Treat Every Customer Like an Original; 4¢ per page, No Minimum"), assured by the young Asian man behind the counter that my copies would be ready in an hour, I surrendered the manuscript of my novel. From there I walked one block south to the Café Virgil.

Of all the cafés in the city, the Virgil was my favorite. It featured cryptic lighting, flea market paintings, sagging upholstered furniture, and patrons hunched over small, marble-topped tables. The sun shined; the day had warmed. There were three tables outdoors, on the sidewalk. Two were occupied. On the third my heart was set. At one of the others a distinctly European-looking woman sat hunched over a notebook, writing. Something about a woman writing in a notebook I found irresistible. Sunglasses, black sweater, gold earrings catching the sun...

The management had changed. In place of opera music a hybrid of disco and salsa blared from strategically located speakers. In place of the raspy old Mafioso who normally presided over it a young woman stood behind the hammered copper counter. Her flushed cheeks looked freshly scrubbed; her eyes bore the shocked look I had come to equate with transplanted Midwesterners, fresh off the Greyhound from Broken Bow, Nebraska. To this farm-fresh barista I was reduced to explaining my order: a latte with two-percent milk, no foam, and a half shot of decaf espresso (my urologist having urged me to cut down on caffeine). I tried to be clear and precise, the same qualities I urged upon my Metropolitan students.

The new barista gaped at me. I repeated my order, more slowly this time. *Caffellate. Small. Two-percent milk. Half a shot. Decaf. No foam* (N.B.: had I, rather than my brother, undergone his airborne epiphany, you would have been spared the following scene). The barista gaped on.

"Is there a problem?" I asked.

"We don't sell half shots."

"Why is that?"

"We just don't," the barista elaborated with a shrug.

"Tell you what," I proposed. "Make it a whole shot. Pour half into a regular sized cup of hot, foamless, two percent milk, pour the rest down the drain, and charge me for a full shot. How does that grab you?" I asked, meaning nothing untoward.

The barista's perplexed, somnolently-parted lips gave birth to a dubious bubble.

"Look." I forced a smile. "I must be making this sound more complicated than it is. I just want some hot milk with a little espresso in it, half a shot. Decaf. That's all." Smile.

"Two-percent milk," the barista queried.

"That's right! Two-percent milk." I approved a little too enthusiastically. "Exactly!"

They didn't have two-percent milk, I learned.

"Have you got whole milk?"

The barista affirmed that they did.

"Have you got *skim* milk?"

Again, affirmative.

"Would it be possible, somehow, by any means, for you to mix the two together—by *any* means?"

Under her bangs the barista looked at me questioningly. The fellow behind me in line grumbled.

"I mean," I clarified, "give me half a regular cup of skim milk, hot, plus half a cup of regular milk—likewise hot, then pour in half a shot of—"

"Christ," said the fellow behind me.

I spun around to face him who was not only impatient but tall. "I waited my turn, you can wait yours." To the barista: "—then pour in half a shot of decaffeinated espresso. Sound good?"

The barista asked what size. "Regular," said I, to be told that the present establishment offered no such size. "Only tall and *grande*," said the barista, pronouncing it "gron-DAY."

"For Pete's sake," said the fellow behind me.

"Supposing you give me whatever size fits in your average, regular cup?"

The barista inquired as to what I meant by "average" and "regular." A woman in line somewhere behind the slender fellow said, "Come on!"

"A plain, regular, old-fashioned, garden-variety coffee cup, like *that.*" I pointed to a cup on top of the espresso machine.

"That's for regular coffee," the barista informed me.

"Great."

"We don't serve lattes in that kind of cup."

The slender fellow: "This is ridiculous."

"The smallest size latte we have is a tall, which is this." The barista produced a tall glass vessel with a handle, the kind in which inferior Italian restaurants serve cappuccino with whipped cream and cinnamon. Appalled, I said, "What about one of those cups over there?" I pointed to a wall of shelves holding an array of hand-painted ceramic mugs.

"Those aren't for customers," said the barista.

The slender guy stormed off. The woman behind him followed suit.

"For whom are they?"

"They're for sale."

"How much?" I said, extracting my wallet, calculating that victory would be worth almost any price. The barista said they were all priced differently. I said, "Okay," and pointed to a yellow one with brown polka dots. "I'll take that one."

"What *is* your problem?" said someone else in line behind me.

"My problem," I faced the young woman and explained with admirable forbearance, "is I'm trying to get a cup of coffee here." The woman said something that I ignored.

"So," said the barista holding my polka-dotted mug. "You want *half* whole milk, half skim, and *one* shot of espresso—"

"Half a shot," I corrected. "The other half you may save for posterity."

With what I interpreted as a dirty look the barista resumed: "...half a shot of espresso—"

"Decaf," I clarified.

"...and no foam. Right?"

"Fabulous," I said.

• •

Though the outside table was still vacant, the distinctly European-looking woman was gone. I got my notebook out, a composition notebook similar to that in which I write these words. Sipping my hard-won *caffelatte* (the twit had put cinnamon on it, but never mind), I entered my latest idea for a title, *Young Suicides Live Happily Ever After*, one of countless stars in an expanding universe of titles in search of works-in-progress. *Geography is My Major, Waltzing Among the Ruins, Skylarking Away from Home, A Dream of the Death of God, Everything Bad is Happening at Once*...I had hundreds of such titles, bastard verbal orphans in search of their fathers. Occasionally a vagrant title would launch me into a story, or, like a frame from the rack, perfectly fit an already finished canvas. Mostly, though, the titles piled up in my notebooks: caps without pens, flowers with no stems.

At that outdoor café table, I planted another:

"The Worst Man in the World"

Then sat there awaiting inspiration, biting my lip, my pen hovering over my notebook like a police helicopter on *America's Most Beloved Car Chase Videos*.

(Please trust that this is leading somewhere, Dear Reader. Every novel worthy of its name redefines the concept of "plot."

This one just happens to be shaped like an ouroboros: the snake swallowing its own tail. It starts where it ends, and ends where it starts: like infinity:

)

I had been sitting there, at my café table, sipping my *caffelatte*, waiting for the copy shop to produce three copies of my manuscript, one of which I'd hand-deliver to "Bitsy" Watson, enjoying my view of MacDougal Street, when in rapid succession two delivery trucks blocked it: a Boar's Head Provisions truck, its feral hog baring gilded tusks, and one from the Golden Flow Dairy, an unfortunate name, it seemed to me, for a purveyor of comestibles secreted by the glands of domestic animals. The truck engines grumbled; their diurnal emissions polluted my coffee. The distinctively European-looking woman's table was presently occupied by someone reading the sports pages of the *New York Post*.

I fleshed out one of my titles.

Title: "Throwing a Baseball." Man confesses adulterous affair to wife, put to the task by the discovery that he can no longer throw a baseball, i.e. he's no longer a boy. He's crossing the baseball field adjacent to the apartment building/house where he's been having the affair, when he comes on some boys playing baseball. A foul ball is struck and flies his way. How he picks it up and reels back to throw. As he reels back, suddenly he realizes, his brain working in slow motion, that he is about to make an ass of himself: that the muscles that once existed to throw baseballs are gone and nothing has taken their place. His pathetic pitch lands several feet short and a dozen feet left of his target, a twelve-or-so year-old boy on the pitcher's mound, who eyes him with a mixture of contempt, disgust, amusement, horror, and pity: this with him having just cheated on his dear wife, with his throwing hand still smelling of his mistress' sex: cursed. The confession, when it comes, sucks every regret the man has ever had in his life into it, though all he gives voice to is the mishap with the baseball, a symbol for all he has lost and forsaken and abused and thrown away in his life. How he is wretched. How his poor wife (thinking it cute that her husband feels so torn up about a silly thing like throwing a baseball) rubs his forearm, comforting him. "Aw, Harvey, what do you care about throwing baseballs at your age?" The more sympathy his wife gives him, the more Harvey suffers, until he can't bear her goodness anymore and wants to break down and confess all, but he won't; it would only make things worse in the short run, though in time his confession and its consequences might teach him a badly-needed lesson and at long last grow him up, but without this good woman in his life: divorced but emancipated, evolved. A moving, ironic story. Or maybe the wife dies. His guilt turns her oddly-shaped benign mole malignant.

Alternative title: "Foul Ball."

I'm about to flesh out another title when a young man sits down at the other table, the one not occupied by the avid *Post* reader. No sooner has he done do so than he gets out his cellphone. I wait, knowing I cannot write—or think, for that matter—with a cellphone in use in my vicinity. The offender has crisp, self-satisfied, effeminate features. He wears a leather jacket and T.S. Eliot-style horn-rims and speaks loudly, more loudly than necessary. I muster my impatience, my *caffelatte* growing cold. A dozen minutes later he finishes his conversation only to take another call. Again I wait, my sighs morphing into grunts, my blank gaze transmogrifyied into a bloodletting stare.

When Call #2 gives way to Call #3 I gather up my belongings and leave the Café Virgil, thinking: *When we're young we're vulnerable in countless ways. As we age the ways grow fewer until we face one big vulnerability.*

"Everything else," I recite aloud in my father's voice, approaching McDougal Street, "is icing on that cake."

The weather had taken a turn for the worse. Dark clouds menaced the sky across the river. I returned to Copies Plus to see if my copies were done.

• •

When I saw what the young copy shop employee had done to my manuscript I "couldn't believe my eyes." Instead of producing three collated copies of the full manuscript, he had made three copies of each individual page and bound them together with a paper clip.

I said, "Are you out of your mind?"

The young man stared at me. (What is it with people these days? They ruin your life and they stare at you.)

"They're not collated," I explained.

"Collated?"

"Collated! Collated!" I made a gesture more indicative of pulling taffy than of collating a manuscript. Then, under my breath, or so I thought, "Idiot." The manager must have heard. Also Asian but older, his crew cut gray, his trapezoidal face wrinkle-free, he wedged himself between his employee and me. With hands flat on the countertop he said:

"What's the problem?"

"I asked for my copies collated."

The copy shop manager turned to his employee and said something I couldn't hear. The manager asked to see my receipt. I presented him with it.

"It doesn't say collated," he pointed out.

"I don't care what it says."

"If you had said collated, the boy would have written it down. You asked for three copies. You didn't say collated."

"Well I sure as hell didn't ask for three distinct copies of each individual page!"

"It's not written down, see?"

I looked around for the young man, but he had disappeared into the back room apparently to commit ritual suicide. "It's a four-hundred and seventy-four page manuscript. Obviously I wanted it collated!"

"You say obviously, but if it's not written down..."

"You mean to tell me," I said, wiping my bone-dry forehead, "that when a customer comes here with a four hundred page manuscript and says, 'I'd like three copies,' your first instinct is to take each page and make three copies *individually*? Is *that* what you're telling me you do as a matter of course?"

A gift for you

Dear Jessica, Season's greetings! Thanks again for all your help. I will follow-up with a signed book plate! Warmly, Peter From peter selgin

 **amazon** Gift Receipt

Send a Thank You Note

You can learn more about your gift or start a return here too.

Scan using the Amazon app or visit
https://a.co/cMdE2HD

Duplicity
Order ID: 111-5954646-4520202   Ordered on December 11, 2020

"Had you asked him to collate the copies," the manager said, "he would have done so. You may have said 'each'."

"I said no such thing. I certainly didn't tell him *not* to collate the copies, or to un-collate the original, which was collated. What does the word 'copy' mean to you people, anyway?"

"Give me the manuscript," said the manager, holding out his hand. "I'll do it over for you."

"There no longer *is* a manuscript," I was obliged to explain. "What was a manuscript is now four-hundred and seventy-four discrete pieces of paper." With that and on the verge of tears I took my package of not-collated copies and made ready to go. The copy shop manager must have inferred my despair, for when I looked up his face registered a dint of pity.

"I'm sorry," he said. "The boy is new. It's only his second week. He's very conscientious, but sometimes he takes things too literally."

"Well," I said, "I'm sorry, too."

I turned and started out of the shop, then stopped.

"Tell the boy…" I said. "Tell him… it was a misunderstanding, that mistakes happen. I should have made myself clearer. I'm sorry," I said, and left, thinking: *I am not a bad man.*

• •

I rode the Broadway local to Dr. Snyder's West Side office. Snyder's waiting room was painted (appropriately) yellow and already at that early hour crowded with mostly elderly people bearing the disgruntled expressions of the incontinent. I was given the usual form to fill out, asking me about my "voiding history," a phrase that when I first encountered it five years ago struck me as having more to do with the current presidential administration than with my nocturnia. On a scale of one to ten I was to rate stress, urge, overflow, waking, dribbling, volume, and frequency. With the same sense of doomed resignation as when I had taken my last Standard Aptitude Test, I filled in the answers.

At last I was seen by Dr. Snyder, an aggressively bland-looking man in a white smock whose taste in neckwear was highly questionable. I'd put out my hand for him to shake, but he was already leading me to his examination room. (I confess here a prejudice against doctors who don't shake your hand. I don't care if they've been shoving their digits up patients' bums all day. The right of refusal should be mine.)

We chatted; he took notes. Having distilled my symptoms down to a few phrases on a sheet of yellow lined paper, he led me into another, more formidable room, where he had me drop my trousers and, with my back to him, my head thrust forward, and my elbows resting on the padded gurney, bend over. *Now* came the handshake, urologist style.

"Well," Dr. Snyder said, feeling around in there. "Your prostate is a bit bulky." Bulky: just what did that mean? "Bulky" as in ungainly, like the character Hoss in *Bonanza*? Or "bulky" as in broad and muscular, like Charles Bronson in *Death Wish*?

"I'd like to do a cystoscopy."

I knew what that meant. Mind you, I've nothing against having something shoved up my penis *per se*, but when the something is about the size of the Mt. Palomar telescope I find cause for alarm. Before I had time to demur, the doctor's frowning associate had wheeled in a metal cart bearing what looked to my eyes like a plumber's snake. As if the thing were a ballpark frank wanting mustard, she slathered it with K-Y jelly.

Naked but for a paper examination gown, I sat on the equivalent of a rubber diving board, one with a U-shaped opening carved out of it, the better to let my parts dangle unencumbered. Until that moment I had maintained something on the order of dignity. Now all bets were off. Taking my limp member into her gloved hand, with as little interest as she'd have shown a common garden slug, the doctor's assistant said, "This will make you numb." No sooner did she offer this inadequate prediction that, with a hypodermic needle, she squirted something into my dick. I felt a brief shiver of icy coldness, then nothing beyond the lingering impression that I had just been violated, along with sympathetic confusion for my poor put-upon penis, which must have thought it odd indeed to have something ejaculate into *it*.

Enter Dr. Snyder again, snapping on a fresh pair of latex gloves. "Bend your knees and try to relax" (apparently I look anxious). "I'm going to explain everything I'm doing." True to his word, the doctor outlines every inch of his offensive. "Now I'm introducing the probe into your penis," he informs me, yet all I feel is a vague imposition, a rigid coolness rising deep within me. I'm told to cough. "Again," the doctor orders. With each cough the snake advances another brutal inch. "We're approaching the prostate now," Dr. Snyder announces with the cool Midwestern drawl of a veteran airline pilot pointing out the Rocky Mountains below. And how about that royal *we*? Does it refer to him and me, or to him and his Apollo 11-sized apparatus? "You may feel a little something right about now." Quite so, only the little something is a hurt the size of Alabama. Bent on impressing the doctor's assistant with my manliness, I suppress a scream. *Should I cry out, who will hear me among the angelic orders?* My cheeks meanwhile are awash in involuntary tears.

"Looks like you've got yourself a ball-median valve," Dr. Snyder observes, going on to explain that a knob-shaped outcropping of excess prostatic tissue has plugged the opening of my urethra like a ball in a hole, hence the name. "We could do a minimally invasive procedure to get rid of the growth," he goes on to say. "But at this stage I still think drugs are your best option."

Having seen enough, Dr. Snyder makes ready to remove his instrument, or rather he makes me ready for its removal. "There will be approximately three seconds of discomfort." Translation: I am about to feel as if the fires of hell are passing through my penis, as if my tool has been dipped into a pit of molten lava, as though all nine circles of the Inferno have relocated themselves inside it. "If you can't endure the pain, let me know." Sure thing, doc. I'll send you a postcard.

The urethral baptism by fire over, the doctor gives me some pills. "These will turn your pee bright orange." Yes, I wonder, but what will they do for my smile? "You may feel a slight burning sensation when you urinate." More diminutives. A *little* discomfort; a *slight* burning sensation. I picture my cock as *Brennkommando* flamethrower spouting bright orange terror.

• •

A stiff breeze pried up the leaves of the ginkgo trees lining West 68th Street. The sky had gone dark as the bottom of an iron skillet … no, an elephant's belly … no, an iron skillet. At 68th and Central Park an odor of impending rain suffused the air. I considered buying a five-dollar umbrella to add to my burgeoning collection of always-at-home-when-you-need-them cheap umbrellas. No peddlers in sight. But why be a pessimist? Let the Garden State keep its clouds!

I looked at my watch. A quarter to four. To collate all three copies would take at least an hour. … I had still to buy a manu-script box and make my way to Elizabeth Watson's office at 56th and Park. To cross the park alone would take thirty minutes. Bit-sy's office closed at five. I'd have to collate one copy and leave the rest for later. Thanks to Julie (Mazda/Pulizer Prize) I had a card for the New York Society Library at 79th. I went there.

While collating I recalled the airy hotel room on Lago Mag-giore where Doris (girlfriend) and I had stayed, cold marble floors, cypress trees. I spent my mornings at a café, writing, the words run-ning so deep I neglected the searing sun arcing over my head. Then home to the feast Doris had set out in the hotel garden: olives, pro-sciutto, cheese, bread, modest-sized glasses of *frizzante vino rosso*. After lunch sitting in the shade reading to each other, Doris from her Italian crime novel, me what I'd written that morning. Doris smiling, laughing—indulging me, possibly, but I didn't think so. I wondered, while collating, if there'd been any correlation between Doris' diminished interest in my writing and my loss of interest in her? From that airy hotel on Lago Maggiore my memory pivoted to one of me returning home from an affair, the first of two … or three … three and a half … how, walking toward the subway at Fourteenth and Broadway, I felt the Lower East Side's squat build-ings glowering down at me, their cornices furrowed like brows, how that same evening in the apartment that Doris and I rented, I took inventory of everything: houseplants, books, the shared spices in our shared cabinets, how tempted I'd been then to confess all—not just to Doris, but to God, to get down on my knees on the icy kitchen linoleum and by the streetlamp's glow seeping through the kitchen window cry out, "*I am not a bad man!*" A fresh title occurred to me: "Evidence of My Bad Character."

I kept collating. Making out in that Viennese park after dusk with the girl I met at the youth hostel. Swedish? Norwegian? Our bellies aslosh with Grüner Veltliner, surrounded by signs saying *"Verbotten!"* ... how American I'd felt, how much a child of a country founded on rebellion, on a middle finger raised to an intolerant Anglican king ... "Oh Beautiful for Spacious Skies!" How I'd sung it for her, for Astrid or Ingrid or Gretta, on the *verbotten* lawn whilst fondling her *verbotten* breasts beneath the *verbotten* stars. Was it Lawrence who claimed that Americans are oppressed by their tolerance? As I keep collating yet another title springs forth along with another idea for a story: "True Omniscience," about a couple seeking lodgings along an interstate after midnight with infant son in tow. The story begins with a disclaimer by the author—pardon me, the narrator—explaining that he has no business telling the story he tells: no wisdom, no perspective, no insights to offer, no particular gifts of empathy or sympathy, no philosophy or world view, no objectivity, no great passion for his subject (then again he's not convinced that he *has* a subject). However, as we go on turning pages, slyly, masterfully, mysteriously, this "worthless" narrator evaporates, abandoning us to the viewpoints of the story's main characters: mother, father, dreaming child ... but also to other characters: the state cop who pulls them over for a burned-out taillight, the clerks at various motels. We even get the viewpoints of things: the highway, the car, a suitcase, a stretch of motel carpeting, an elevator ... The story could as well be called "Empathy," since it would demonstrate that not only is everything around us, animate or otherwise, invested with a point-of-view, by extension the entire universe is invested with feelings, attitudes, opinions, and—by further extension—with pity, therefore with pain. Having arrived at this singular concept for a short story, I settled on two superficially similar yet crucially different candidates for an opening sentence:

"In a sense, I am telling this story."
"In essence I am telling this story."

I finished collating...
[break here?]

14. OLD PHONE AND TWINKLE

EVERY GREAT NOVEL OPERATES ON TWO LEVELS, ONE LITERAL, ONE figurative, with the literal interpretation merely a means toward the metaphoric end. One should never take great novels literally. *Lolita* isn't about pedophilia, it's about a contest between poetry and prose, with language — specifically American English — holding the stakes. It's the English language that Humbert (poetry) ravages, that he probes and fondles in a series of motel rooms. An interstate tug-of-war ensues, with Quilty (plot) in pursuit of Humbert, intent on claiming the nymphet for his own prosaic ends. In the end, Plot is riddled with bullets (of lead, but really of words). Plot murdered, contest won, poetry triumphant. Only dimwits think *Lolita* is about pedophilia.

Taking any great novel literally is a mistake. The greater the novel, the greater the mistake.

• •

The odd red rubber boat was back, trolling the waters of Lake S —— a hundred or so yards beyond the dock. Since the weather cleared it had been out there every day, resuming its dogged zigzag pattern, inching toward the middle of the lake — not fishing, by the looks of it, but searching for something, accompanied by the winding rasp of a gasoline-powered generator.

What could they be searching for? I asked myself, seeing it out there for the third day in a row. Not a dead body. Certainly not Brock Jones, PhD's dead body. Why would they be searching for it? Even assuming that he had been reported missing to the authorities, still, they had no cause to presume the bestselling author dead, and less cause to conclude that his corpse had wound up at the bottom of this lake. At the very least before dredging the whole lake (or whatever they're doing out there) they would have searched for him here, whereupon they'd have discovered … me — Brock Jones, PhD — alive and well, suntanned and fit and brimming with optimism, a man with everything to live for.

Maybe (I said to myself) they're looking for someone *else's* body?

Oh, come now, really! What are the odds of *that*? In the same lake where, it so happens, you disposed of your brother's corpse a few days ago? Even Charles Dickens couldn't get away with such a coincidence! Who would believe it?

Would *you* believe it?

Of course not. No one would believe it.

No, I told myself. They must be searching for something else. A sunken boat, maybe? Or alligators. Since coming here as a child I've heard rumors of alligators roaming the lake, former pets whose owners abandoned them when they outgrew their cuteness, or wild creatures that, for some reason or other (climate change?) had wandered north of their normal habitations below the Fall Line, and whose sightings by fishermen enlivened the pages of local newspapers.

Yeah, that's it, I told myself.

Alligators. That's what they're searching for.

They are not searching for alligators.

• •

I had only just begun my transformation into Brock Jones, PhD, a process that, with the disposal of one extremely inconvenient corpse, had merely been initiated. Removal, that had been Stage One of the process.

Leaving four other stages: Recuperation, Research, Renewal, and Reconnaissance. *Coffee, Black* and books like it notwithstanding, and though it may seem that way retrospectively, from outside, changing your life involves a lot more than snapping your fingers. It takes a lot of work, much of it tedious. Which is why I haven't looked forward to telling this part of my story.

Frankly, it's not that interesting.

Take the research component. What did it involve? Mostly hours on my brother's laptop (which I eventually discovered under wads of socks and underwear in a pair of studded black leather motorcycle saddlebags in a corner of the bedroom), familiarizing myself with his bank, credit card, brokerage, and other statements, acquainting myself with his business interactions and social pursuits, his calendars and contacts—all the activities that defined his quotidian existence, insofar as a chameleon can be said to have had a quotidian existence. I read or scanned thousands of emails, most of little import. Like cramming for an exam.

As for passwords, as different as Brock had been from Gregory (let alone from Stewart) Detweiler, I counted on the well-documented fact that, when it comes to identical twins, certain things never change. This has been demonstrated many times through scientific studies of twins separated at or soon after birth, who, despite having spent years and even decades apart, still share many of the same habits and traits. Both siblings use Vitalis and part their hair one inch from the center on the left, hate button-down collars, roll their socks down to two inches above their ankles, flip backwards through magazines, chew off their fingernails rather than trim them with clippers or manicure scissors, sleep with a night light on under three plaid blankets to the sound of crashing waves generated by a white noise device ... intimate traits so deeply engrained in them they may as well be coded—along with the color of their eyes and shapes of their nostrils—into their DNA.

Sure enough, though he had changed so many other habits, Brock Jones, PhD still used the same password system as Gregory Detweiler (who used the same password system as Stewart Detweiler): his twin brother's middle name along with the last four digits of the same brother's Social Security number. Our middle names were "Peter" and "Paul." The trouble was that both Greg and I used them so seldom that even now, writing this at this moment, I have to consult my old driver's license to tell you which middle name is—was—mine.

I tried both.

One worked.

Like both of our prior selves—and as carelessly—Greg used the same password for his tablet and his phone. Along with pin codes and other security information, he kept an encrypted key to his passwords in a document stored in a Google Drive folder, with dashes, asterisks, and other symbols replacing numbers and letters. It didn't take Alan Turing to decipher them.

Since he'd used the same password or a close variant for all of his online transactions, it took only half a day for me to access most of his personal accounts.

• •

It was a good thing, too, since I, or rather since Stewart Detweiler, was running low on cash, with less than twenty dollars in his wallet and next to nothing in his bank account. As for my former self's Amex Card (not a Gold card like Brock's; a humble green one), he was in considerable debt to said credit card company, enough to have entered a so-called "debt consolidation program" that allowed him to pay off his debt at pennies to the dollar, provided he did so at an exorbitant rate of interest for the rest of his mortal existence.

None of this would have been any of Brock Jones, PhD's concern, had Brock Jones, PhD not been equally cash poor. His wallet, which I discovered in the same studded leather saddlebag, contained a grand total of six dollars. The same saddlebag also held ninety-seven cents in loose change: three quarters, one dime, two nickels and two pennies. All tolled, my past and present self had $24.97 in cash.

Aside from oatmeal and a few ancient jars of Prego tomato sauce, there was nothing to eat in the house.

So—first things first: I needed cash. And food.

And so, on the splendidly clear morning after my gruesome

watery burial adventure, with Brock Jones, PhD's *and* Stewart Detweiler's wallets and debit/credit cards in my pockets, I drove the spluttering Mazda into town. The ride took twenty minutes (it would have taken less time had I not gotten stuck behind a logging truck). The center of the town I won't bother describing here, since I ignored it, knowing pretty much what to expect there: lowdown burger, pizza, and/or taco joints, barbershop, a tattoo parlor, ratty so-called antique stores, the truck-damaged marquee of a movie theater that had long since ceased showing movies: all the trappings of Main Street, USA, post Great Recession. One of those towns where the fronts of buildings look like the back, and the backs look like ... you don't want to know what the backs look like. (The description fits many who live in such places, too.)

As I said, it was a splendid morning. The southern sky served up notably muscular cloud formations in that region prone to estimable clouds. Where not stuffed with clouds the sky was a providential (have I used that adjective already?) blue. I drove with the driver's side window all the way down, one hand steering, the other playing with the breeze. Maybe it was the fact that by then my gray stubble had evolved into a beard, but catching my face in the rearview mirror, I no longer recognized my former self. I no longer looked like Stewart Detweiler.

First stop: a bank teller machine. Of the pin numbers that occurred to me, the third turned out to be the charm. I withdrew three hundred dollars. Make it three hundred and sixty.

With eighteen crisp sawbucks tucked into Brock Jones, PhD's wallet, feeling rich beyond my dreams, I drove to Kroger along the tawdry strip at the north edge of town, filled my shopping cart to brimming, and stood in line to pay.

It was while standing there that I learned that our mother wasn't the only one obsessing over Brock Jones, PhD's disappearance. On the magazine rack to my left, tucked in among the covers of other supermarket tabloids, in a replay of the Invisible Gorilla Test that I'd failed all those years ago aboard a crowded New York City subway car, I recognized a face, my own—or what might as well have been my own face, complete with gray beard, scowling in the direction of the photographer as its owner exited what looked like a municipal building. In italicized gothic type, the caption above the grainy photo read, "GONE GURU!" I forget which tabloid it was, the *Globe* or the *Star* or the *National Enquirer.* It wasn't the lead headline, which, if I recall correctly, had to do with the latest outlandish solution to the JonBenét Ramsey murder, but a side headline. I did a quick scan of the other rag sheets, expecting to see a similar photo with an analogous alliterative headline ("AWOL AUTHOR!" "WHAT'S BECOME OF BROCK?"), but there was just the one. Still, it was enough to paint my forehead with clammy sweat and make me wonder: Why this sudden interest in Brock Jones, PhD's absence? Before I'd headed off on my journey south, there hadn't been a single buried news item about it. Now of a sudden my erstwhile twin's disappearance was worthy of at least one front-page story. Someone, apparently, had alerted the authorities, had pressed the panic—or was it the publicity stunt—button? If so, did that stunt include its object's self-inflicted end?

I would not have put it past Brock Jones, PhD.

I edged my cart out of checkout line and rolled it to the pharmacy section. There, from a rotating rack, I chose a pair of cheap sunglasses, the kind with mirrored lenses to better obscure my eyes. With them on I took my place in another checkout line.

• •

It was while waiting in that second line that my eyes met another headline, this one on the front page of the local newspaper:

Police Comb Lake S——
For Missing Alabama Man

Having taken the paper off the rack, I found the article:

> M———, GA. Since Friday morning, state and local police have been searching the woods and surrounding areas of Lake S—— for an Alabama man who was reported missing two weeks ago, and whose car, a late-model Ford Mustang convertible, was found partly submerged near a boat launch in Turtle Cove, a shallow inlet at

the southeastern end of the lake a mile from the dam. The car's owner, Lester Figes, a 42-year old self-employed exterminator of Wetumpka, Alabama, was reported missing on April 1 by his sixteen-year-old half niece, Melody Baker.

A woman waiting behind me in line cleared her throat.

"Sorry," I said, and tossed the paper into my cart.

• •

The cashier was a pretty young teenager with orange hair and matching bright fingernail polish. Among items that I'd transferred from my cart to the conveyor belt: a bottle of top-shelf Chianti to christen my new existence. The cashier said:

"I'll need to see some ID, sir."

I smiled at her. "You're kidding."

She returned my smile. "We have to card everyone, sir. It's store policy."

I nodded. "I was about to start humming 'You Make Me Feel So Young'."

"Sorry?"

"An old song."

"Oh," said the cashier.

I handed her my—Stewart Detweiler's—New York driver's license. Like most drivers' license photos, this one captured nothing so well as the fluorescent-lit glumness occasioned by a two-hour wait at the DMV. The cashier looked at the photo, then at me, then at the photo again. I waited for her to remark on the dissimilarity between the photo and the person standing before her.

She asked: "Do you have a Kroger card?"

"A what?"

"You know—for Kroger points?"

"No. Oh, wait. Yes, I think I do!" I fished around in the wallet and found a Kroger card.

The cashier went on ringing up items, including a 1.25 lb. grass-fed Angus beef tenderloin (Unit Price $8.95 per lb.; total with Kroger discount card: $12.55) ... Just when it seemed to me I was in the clear, the cashier remarked:

"Has anyone told you you look familiar? You're not famous or anything?"

"Not to my knowledge."

"Maybe it's those sunglasses. You buying those?"

"Hmm?"

"There's a price tag on them." She pointed.

"Oh!" I reached up to remove it.

"It'll be easier if you take them off."

"I've got it," I said, fumbling.

"Here, let me help." She reached and pulled the tag off for me.

"Thanks."

"Maybe you just have a familiar face."

She *was* cute. (I know, I'm supposed to say *how* she was cute, in what particular, concrete ways, but I don't feel like it. I will mention the faint freckles dusting her nose.)

"*Very* familiar," she said, "like I saw you recently on TV or on the cover of a magazine. Do you mind me asking where you're from?"

"What makes you think I'm not from around here?"

"You don't sound like you're from around here." She rang up the Brussels sprouts. Onions. Grapefruits. A bag of frozen fresh-caught salmon. "Lemme guess. I bet you're from New York!"

"No. Not New York."

"Near New York?" Blueberries.

"Not far from there."

"Someplace I've heard of?" Low-fat yogurt.

"Do you know Wappingers Falls?" The name just came to me.

"Nope," said the cashier.

"That's where I'm from."

"What are you doing down here, if it's any of my business?"

"Just... you know... visiting," I said.

"You have friends or family here?" Three cucumbers.

"Hmm? Yes. Friends. Well, a friend. A good friend."

"That's nice."

Wheat germ, crumbled gorgonzola, olive oil, capers... I bagged the groceries myself.

"You enjoying yourself?"

"I am. Very much."

"It's a nice town. Small, but nice. How big is—Where'd you say you were from?"

"Wappingers Falls."

"How big is Wappinger Falls?"

"Wappingers. Pretty small."

"Smaller than here?"

"I'd say so. Yes. A bit." I had no idea how big or small Wappingers Falls is.

"You been out to the lake yet?"

"No. Not yet."

"It's pretty." Tomatoes. A bag of spinach.

"Is it?"

"It's the cleanest lake in the state. I read it in a magazine. Ask your friend to take you."

"I'll do that."

"There's this restaurant called The Bowline. Right on the water? You can watch the sun set while you're eating dinner. They have really good burgers. And French-fried pickles!"

"French-fried pickles?"

"Yes, sir. They've got other stuff, too. It's a nice place. Maybe you and your friend can go there some time. Your friend a lady?" Oatmeal. Peppermint and rose hip tea.

"Yes, a lady."

"She'd like it, I bet."

"Thanks for the tip."

"You're welcome."

The cash register vomited a three-foot long receipt.

"That's two-hundred and thirty-six dollars and fifty-two cents. You saved twenty-seven dollars and ninety-four cents and earned 236 Kroger fuel points." She handed the receipt to me.

Together she and I finished bagging my groceries. As we did the cashier said: "I still say you look like somebody."

"Well," I said. "Don't we all?"

•   •

At the Kroger station, using my (Brock's) Kroger card for the discount, I gassed up the Mazda.

Next stop: Lowe's, where, along with a roll of blue painter's tape and a trim brush, I bought a quart of high quality exterior latex paint of a certain bright color.

Last stop before returning home: the Verizon store, where, with Brock's American Express card, I obtained another cellphone. Thanks to the phone companies in their infinite greedy wisdom, you can't own two cellphones with the same number, which suited my purposes. I didn't *want* the same number. The new phone would be Stewart Detweiler's.

What else did I need?

Nothing.

I drove back to the house, where, after a quick swim and a few hours' more research, I put on an apron and went about preparing my first official meal as "Brock Jones, PhD": steak, roasted baby red potatoes, *haricots verts*, spinach and gorgonzola salad. I preheated the oven to 425 degrees, rubbed the one-and-one-half inch steak on both sides with garlic-infused olive oil, salted and peppered it, then seared it in a cast-iron skillet to a deep brown on both sides, three minutes per side. Slide skillet into oven and bake for 20 minutes, turning once. Let cool for 10 minutes before slicing thin on bias. Enjoy with room temperature top-shelf Chianti facing sunset-smeared lake through French doors with fire burning gently in hearth. While taking in the view, chewing, drinking, listening to the chorus of hisses, snaps, and belchings of the fire, say to yourself: *Welcome back, Brock Jones, PhD.*

• •

Starting the next morning with breakfast (1 cup plain low-fat yogurt with a mixture of fresh raspberries and blueberries, 254 calories) followed by windmills (30), jumping jacks (75), push-ups (25), sit-ups (25), a three-mile jog and a twenty-minute swim, I launched my diet and exercise regime. Lose twenty pounds in two weeks: that was my goal. Limit carbs, sugar, all fats. Lots of vegetables and fruits eaten raw. Spinach and apples. A little meat and olive oil now and then. At sunset I took the boat out for long rows. I swam — with a wetsuit at first, then without, back and forth to the neighbor's dock. The cold water didn't bother me; I grew to like both it and the forty-five minutes of shivering that invariably followed such dips and that subjected every cell of my body to its own aerobic workout. Afterwards a cup of hot herbal tea by the fire. Then more floor exercises. Crunches, stretches, isometrics…

Less than two weeks into my regimen for the first time I dared to look at myself in the full-length mirror, the one behind the door to the downstairs bedroom. By then the bare patches in my gray beard had filled in nicely. Was I imagining things, or did my shoulders look broader? My stomach was flatter. To myself anyway I looked better than I had in a long time. Pounds shed: sixteen. After less than two weeks! Not hard to believe, given my single-minded determination and total lack of distractions.

A few days later I tried on a pair of Brock's jeans.

Snug, but they fit.

• •

Mother called. A few times. More than a few. Sometimes she'd call us both, Brock and Stewart, on the same day. I kept both cellphones fully charged and made sure to remember which one I was answering, and as whom. Different ringtones helped. Stewart's phone had a classic ringtone ("Old Phone"); Brock's played a synthetic rendering of "By the Seaside," until I grew sick of that aural equivalent of saltwater taffy and changed it to "Twinkle." In time I came to think of my past self as "Old Phone" and my present self as "Twinkle."

It was Twinkle who answered his mother's call the sunny Sunday afternoon when I first noticed the red boat trolling the lake.

"Hey, Mom."

"Brock, is that you?"

"Yes, Mom. It's me. Who else would be answering my phone?"

"I swear you don't sound like yourself."

"How are you, Mom?"

"I'm fine. What do you want me to say? The food here is boring. I wish they'd let us do our own cooking."

"Mom, you're blind."

"I am not blind! I'm *legally* blind. That just means I can't drive. I see enough to be able to cook. It's not like I'd burn the place down. They won't even let us keep a hot plate in our rooms. It's like a gulag here. A concentration camp. Terrible."

"How are things otherwise?"

"What can I say? I'm old. My kidneys are shot. And I'm still worried about you."

"There's nothing to worry about. Really."

"I swear you sound like your brother."

"It's the connection. The signal's poor here. And I'm a bit congested. Allergies, probably."

"I never had allergies. Neither did your father. Are you taking anything? They have good things for allergies now. Over the counter. There's one that starts with a Z. It was on the TV."

"I'll look for it, Mom."

"Do you have blown air?"

"What?"

"Central air conditioning. Is that what you've got down there? I hope not. You may have mold in your ducts. I hope it's not mold. They say once mold gets in your ducts its impossible to get rid of. You probably have to replace all the ducts. What are you doing, anyway?"

"Doing? You mean now? This moment?"

"Yes."

"I'm sitting on the dock. Reading." This was true. I was sitting on the dock, reading. Sartre's *Nausea,* a foxed, dog-eared and heavily marked-up paperback found on one of my father's shelves. I'd had a light lunch, a *salade Lyonnaise* I'd fixed for myself after taking the boat for a six mile morning row, and that I'd paired with an ice-cold, pinch-dry Lanquedoc rosé for which I had driven all the way to Athens and back, and that I continued to sip with my mother on the phone. The odd red boat was out there, zigzagging.

"How much longer are you planning to keep this up?"

"Keep what up, Mom?"

"This...whatever it is you're doing? Hiding from everyone. How much longer do you plan to stay down there in that moldy old house, letting everyone in the world worry to death about you? It's in the news. Did you know that?"

"It is?"

"Someone showed me. One of the other prisoners here. She has a subscription to the *National Inquisition*—"

"*Enquirer.*"

"What?"

"The *National Enquirer*, Mom."

"Whatever. One of those awful newspapers. There you were plastered all over the front page. I couldn't believe it. Such a terrible photograph. Is your beard really that long?"

"Anyway, Mom, there's no need for anyone to worry."

"You could at least tell them where you are."

"I will. Eventually."

"Eventually *when*?"

"I just need a little more time."

"Time for *what*? What are you accomplishing? Are you writing another book?"

"Yeah, Mom. I'm writing another book."

"What's this one about? Or can't you tell me? Not that I'd tell anyone. Like you can't trust me, your own mother."

"You know how it is, Mom."

"You can talk about it or you can write it."

"That's right. You've got it."

"Shouldn't you at least let Dawn know that you're all right?"

"She knows, Mom. I told her."

This was so: I had emailed Dawn Swopes, my (Brock's) personal assistant (or manager or whatever he'd called her) and let her know—in the vaguest terms possible—that I was all right, that she needn't worry about me. In my terse email I explained that I was taking some personal time off, that I would be indisposed "for an indefinite period," that she should cancel all my appointments for the next month, and furthermore that I was not to be disturbed by anyone—herself included, that any emails or other correspondences received by me would not be answered, nor did I intend to take phone calls or check email. As for my whereabouts, I preferred not to disclose them to anyone, herself included. I said all this knowing, assuming, that it would all be of a piece with Brock's protean nature, that Dawn would see it as just another phase in his ever-evolving odyssey of eccentric self-reinvention. Meanwhile it would buy me the time I needed to slip gently into the vague waters of my new life, rather than plunge headlong like Burt Lancaster in *From Here to Eternity.*

"Thank goodness for that," my mother said.

I sipped my rosé; I watched the red boat.

"Weren't you supposed to do some big thing for television soon? Some big fundraising special or something?"

There had been several emails and phone messages to that effect, increasingly frantic in tone, mostly from Dawn, but also from one Adam Swann. "That's all on hold for now," I said, earning one of those pregnant silences at which my mother was so adept.

"What about Sheila?"

"What about her?"

"Shouldn't she know where you are?"

"Mom, we've been divorced for over four years."

"She still cares about you. Can I at least tell her you're all right, if she calls?"

"Sure, fine. Just don't let her know where I am. Don't let anyone know. I mean it, Mom."

"All right, Mr. Mysterious."

"Seriously, Mom."

"I said all right."

The red boat passed in front of the dock again.

"What about Stewart? Have you called him? You should call him. He loves you. He drove all that way to see you, to make sure you were all right. That's how much he loves you. He thinks you don't care for him anymore, but I know that's not true. If you'd just call him once in a while it would mean so much to him. It would mean a lot to me, too. I worry about that brother of yours. No career, no girlfriend. He doesn't seem to have any close friends. He says he's doing fine, but I don't believe it. He should have left the city long ago. It's obvious that he's depressed. I'd be depressed, too, if I were your brother. He hasn't had much luck, that's for sure."

"No," I said. "He hasn't."

"You should call him once in a while."

"I will."

"They're serving lunch now. Something boring. I can smell it. It *smells* boring. I have to go. Take care of yourself."

"Right, Mom. You, too."

"Call your brother."

"I will."

"It'll boost his spirits. You're such a positive person. I wish your brother had some of your positive spirit. He's so negative."

I nodded to myself.

"Good bye, Brock."

"Bye, Mom."

• •

Seconds later the other phone—"Old Phone"—rang.

"Stewart!"

"Hello, Mother."

"Where are you?"

"Home. Why?"

"I just tried your landline. It's disconnected!"

"I know, Mother. I had it disconnected."

"I thought you hate cellphones? You swore you'd never get one."

"Things change. Got to keep up with the times."

"You should have kept your landline. I'd have paid for it."

"What do I need a landline for?"

"What if there's a blackout?"

"There hasn't been a major blackout in the city in twenty years."

"But what if there is? If there's a blackout your cellphone won't work. You'll be stranded. Alone in the dark in your apartment with riots going on in the street. What if there's a terrorist attack? Or heaven forbid a nuclear war?"

"Please, Mother. If the world should end, my having a landline won't save it or me."

"Don't be a smartass."

"Can we change the subject?"

"What have you been doing with yourself?"

"The usual." I shrugged—pointlessly, since my mother couldn't see it. "Working on my book."

"The same one?"

"Yes, Mother. The same one."

The silence that followed came with a shift in sound. The generator's winding roar had suddenly ceased. I looked up to see the red boat bobbing. I heard the voices of men aboard it, saw one of them gesturing, shouting, but couldn't make out what they were saying.

"I spoke with your brother."

"Did you?"

"A few minutes ago. He's still at your father's house. He's writing a book, too. He won't say what it's about. Mr. Mysterious. You know your brother. Do you need any money?"

"Thanks, Mother, I'm fine."

"I don't see how with no job."

"I'm managing."

"You're not selling drugs, are you?"

"No, Mother."

"Or your blood?"

"Mother, Jesus—!"

Aboard the red boat one of the men pulled a slender object from the water. A broken-off piece of dock planking? A lost water ski?

"Your brother says hello, by the way. He cares for you. No matter what you think."

The generator re-started; the red boat moved on.

"Are you sure you don't need money, Stewart? I have a CD that's due to mature soon. When it does I can send you some."

"That's okay, really."

"They're serving dinner. I have to go. I'll call again soon."

"Use this number."

"What other number is there? Your landline's disconnected."

"That's right."

"They're serving so-called chicken Marsala again. I can tell by the smell. I may be legally blind, but my nose still works."

"Have a nice dinner, Mother."

"It's the second time in nine days. I know; I keep track."

"Take care, Mother."

"*You* take care."

"I will."

15. MALCOLM'S MISSING MASTERPIECE
[ALT. TITLE: "DREDGING"]

IN ADDITION TO READING ALL MY BROTHER'S EMAILS AND TEXT messages, studying his calendar, reading (and re-reading) his published books as well as his outlines, notes for and drafts of various works-in-progress I found in various Google Drive folders, as part of my reconnaissance I read many of my father's books and papers too. In many ways he and my brother were more alike, more "twinned," than Greg and I had been. Up to the time of his transformation, down to his choice of profession, the books he read, the clothes and shoes he wore, Greg had walked in our father's footsteps, or in his shadow. If I was to become Brock Jones, PhD, I would have to absorb Brock's basis, Gregory Detweiler. And the basis for Gregory Detweiler was, had been, our father, Malcolm Detweiler.

Before dishing out the next course of my confession, I feel the need to inject a preface, or, if you like, a warning. You may recall my brother once offering me a rare bit of literary advice. "Why don't you write a novel of pure atmosphere?" The inspiration behind this suggestion of his was a late nineteenth century novel by a Frenchman to whom my father (from whom Gregory took most if not all his reading cues) first introduced my brother. The author was Joris-Karl Huysmans, and the novel was À Rebours—or, in

English depending on the translation, *Against Nature* or *Against the Grain*. Considered the ultimate example of so-called "decadent" literature, it tells the story of a reclusive eccentric named des Esseintes, who, loathing contemporary society, abandons Paris and retreats to his country estate, where, one by one, he indulges his senses as well as his intellect in an ideal aesthetic realm of his own invention. Among des Esseintes' various indulgences: an array of tiny liquor casks controlled by a series of valves and spigots, with each liquor corresponding to an orchestral instrument, from which he sips "harmonic" combinations and that he calls his *"orgue a bouche"* ("mouth organ"); a giant tortoise whose carapace he encrusts with so many flashing jewels the miserably laden beast can no longer move; a garden of monstrous and poisonous flowers; a "black mass" feast consisting exclusively of foods that are black ("turtle soup, Russian black bread, ripe olives from Turkey, caviar, mule steaks, Frankfurt smoked sausages, wild game served in sauces colored to resemble liquorice water and boot-blacking, truffles in jelly, chocolate-tinted creams, puddings, nectarines, fruit preserves, mulberries and cherries") served on black-bordered plates by "naked negresses" and accompanied by wines "of... Tenedos, the Val de Penas, and Oporto, drunk from dark-tinted glasses. Following the course of coffee and walnuts came other unusual beverages, kwas, porter, and stout." Chief among des Esseintes' many indulgences—the subject of an entire chapter—are the books in his orange and blue library, one that excludes all the monuments of Golden Age Latin in favor of works embodying cultural disintegration, including De Sade, Petronius, and other pornographic classics.

I say Huysmans' novel "tells the story of" though there's very little story to tell. The beauty of *Against the Grain*—one of many beautiful things about it—is that it's a novel not so much of "pure atmosphere" as of pure *description*: a novel that, more successfully than any other I can think of, does away with plot and characters and all that silly stuff. A novel about nothing.

Consider the section that follows my tribute to Huysmans.

•   •

Every room in this house is full of books. Where not packed onto shelves the books are staggered in piles on the floor, on tables, on the kitchen counter: everywhere. The place reeks of books: a fusty, musty, mushroom– or sperm-like, faintly sexual smell, the smell of decaying paper and moldering thoughts. Though some of his books are arranged alphabetically or by subject, when it came to his library my father had no special ardor for order, or he did once, but lost it over time. Freed of any organizing principle, the books wandered promiscuously from room to room, with history books frolicking with volumes on the natural sciences, novels conjugating with text and reference books, *belle-lettres* fraternizing with biographies, Plutarch rubbing shoulders with paleontology and Pound, not to speak of the orgies of literary miscegenation unfolding on the floor and in closets.

In one place alone my father's books are organized: a bookcase in the little office he made for himself in what had been the basement. Unlike the others, this bookcase is draped over by a royal blue chintz cloth held in place by pushpins. I parted it to reveal books neatly arranged by subject, some—many of them—with dozens of sticky-notes and paper clips marking their pages. Among headings written on strips of masking tape affixed to the shelves: *Twins/Twin Studies, Dualism, Taoism, Nature vs. Nurture, Mythology, Nietzsche, Nothing, Plato/Unity of Opposites...* On smaller vertical strips these are sub-categorized (under "Dualities": Radical Dualism, Mitigated Dualism, Cartesian Dualism, Naturalistic Dualism, Moral Dualism, Dualistic Cosmology, Manichaeism, Parallelism, Double-Aspect Theory, Doctrine of Double Effect... "Mythology": Apollo & Artemis, Castor & Pollux, Romulus & Remus, Amphion & Zethus, Gulgamesh & Enkidu, Kleobis & Biton...).

Among the books shelved above "Dualities" is a slim bound volume titled *The Kybalion: Hermetic Philosophy*, yes, *that* book, the one on which Greg was en route to deliver a conference paper when he had his epiphany.

The fourth shelf from the top is devoted to fiction, to novels mostly, all to do with twins or doppelgängers: Stevenson's *The Strange Case of Dr. Jeckyll and Mr. Hyde*, Dostoyevsky's *The Double*, Plautus' *The Two Menaechmuses*, Nabokov's *Despair...*

At the far left end of the bottom shelf are six marbled composition notebooks very much like this one I'm holding, filled with notes in my father's jagged handwriting. The notebooks are dated, numbered, and titled as follows:

Twins I (June 12, 1993)
Twins II (Sept. 19, 1995)
Twins III (Dec. 12, 1995)
Twins IV (May 13, 1996)
Doubles (Oct. 23, 1996)
Double or Nothing (July 1997)

From the first five notebooks, a sampling of quotes:

Ouroboros drawing from the early alchemical text The Chrysopoeia of Cleopatra (Greek: Η χρυσοποιία της Κλεοπάτρας) dating to 2nd C. Alexandria encloses words hen to pan (Greek: εν το παν), "one is the all." Black and white halves represent Gnostic duality of existence. Western equivalent of the Taoist Yin-Yang symbol.

Yin and yang symbol represents philosophy of balance wherein opposites co-exist in harmony and transmute into each other. Dot of yin in yang qua dot of yang in yin symbolize interconnectedness of opposite aspects of Tao, the First Principle. Contrast makes reality discernable. Without contrast we experience nothingness.

Castor and Pollux share a bond so strong when Castor dies, Pollux gives up half of his immortality to be with his twin. Ergo the Discoursi or Gemeni is seen only half the year as twins divide time between underworld and Olympus. Whether immortal not consistent among accounts, nor whether twins hatched from one or two eggs.

In the Yoruba religion, deity representing twins called Orisha Ibeji or Orisa Ibeji. "Ibeji" literally "twins." Carved figures, up to ten inches high and carved with the family mask, house soul of a dead twin called ibeji. Yoruba people believe that this care and tending ensures survival of remaining twin.

Zurvanism derives from Zoroastrian notions of Free Will. Like Mazdaism (extant branch of Zoroastrianism), sees contest between good and evil as mortal choice rather than willed by nature. Apply to modern concept of "evil twin," not wholly or intrinsically evil but mirror image or opposite of "good twin."

Not entirely to my surprise there was even this entry:

Duplicity *(n.) early 15c., from Old French duplicite (13c.), from Late Latin duplicitatem (nominative duplicitas) "doubleness," in Medieval Latin "ambiguity," noun of quality from duplex (genitive duplicis) "twofold." The notion of being "double" in one's conduct (compare Greek diploos "treacherous, double-minded," literally "twofold, double").*

> *1: contradictory doubleness of thought, speech, or action especially the belying of one's true intentions by deceptive words or action*
>
> *2: the quality or state of being double or twofold*
>
> *3 (legal): the technically incorrect use of two or more distinct items (as claims, charges, or defenses) in a single legal action*
>
> *When you are being duplicitous there are two yous: the one you're showing and the one you're hiding. And—key to the idea of duplicity—you're hiding that you in order to make people believe something that's not true.* [father's underscores]

Though his handwriting can be hard to read, by and large my father's notes in the first three notebooks are decipherable. By the middle of the sixth notebook—which is two-thirds full—the notes are incomprehensible, at least by me:

> *... existence stubbornly refuting Parmenides', still taken seriously by Socrates and Plato. Aristotle gives serious consideration but concludes "opinions follow logically in dialectical discussion, yet seem next door to madness when one considers the facts." Atomist Leucippus' attempts to reconcile with everyday observation of motion / change. Thing that exists = absolute plenum but no motion in plenum because full. Same scenario macroscopic objects not-being by means of coming together /*

moving apart / constituent atoms. Russell also finds both sides mistaken believes no motion in plenum. Bailey notes Leucippus first thing (the void) might be real without body points out the irony of idea coming from materialistic atomist. Leucippus first to identify "nothing" as having reality attached. Void (as "nothing") differentiated from space as in removed from consideration. Characterization reached pinnacle Newton / existence absolute space. Modern quantum agrees space ≠ void, concept of quantum foam exists in absence all else, though general rel. no longer supports absolute space. Refer to Descartes and Parmenides' argument denying space existence; matter and its extension leave "no room for "nothing." Idea of space actually empty still unaccepted; invoke Hegel / plenum reasoning...

Some pages later:

Thesis: The Absolute is Pure Being
Antithesis: The Absolute is Nothing
Synthesis: The Absolute is Becoming

Below this my atheist philosopher father wrote:

Law of identity *(A = A; a thing is identical to itself)*

Law of excluded middle *(either A or not-A; a thing is either something or not that thing, no third option)*

Law of noncontradiction *(not both A and not-A; a thing cannot be both true and not true in the same instant)*

However:

Law of identity is inaccurate because a thing is always more than itself

Law of excluded middle is inaccurate because a thing can be both itself and many others

Law of non-contradiction is inaccurate because everything in existence is both itself and not itself

This is followed by:

2/0 = point at complex infinity on complex projective line on Riemann sphere. 0/0 not = 1 since multiplication only trivial for FINITE values. 1/0 = per above, division by 0 = multiplying by ∞. Note: some expressions that appear to approach 0/0 may have other values that are finite. See L'Hopital's rule:

If $g'(x) \neq 0$ for all $x \neq a$

and if $\dfrac{f(x)}{g(x)}$ has the indeterminate form $\dfrac{0}{0}$ or $\dfrac{\infty}{\infty}$

then $\displaystyle\lim_{x \to a} \dfrac{f(x)}{g(x)} = \lim_{x \to a} \dfrac{f'(x)}{g'(x)}$.

provided that $\displaystyle\lim_{x \to a} \dfrac{f'(x)}{g'(x)}$ exists or $\displaystyle\lim_{x \to a} \dfrac{f'(x)}{g'(x)} = \pm \alpha$

And then:

When one body exerts a force on a second body, the second body simultaneously exerts a force equal in magnitude and opposite in direction on the first body.

$$F_A = - F_B$$

Finally, in red ink on a page all by itself:

$$0 \times 2 = 0$$
$$0 \div 2 = ?$$
$$0 \div 0 = ?$$

There the last notebook ends. Possibly these are the very last words—or numbers—my father ever wrote.

What grand dissertation had my father intended to pull together from all these notes? Though I searched every file drawer and folder for a manuscript-in-progress or anything else that might have shed light on what he'd been up to, I found nothing.

Still, one thing was obvious: my father was obsessed with twins. Having twin sons just as obviously provided the basis of this obsession.

Whatever stood behind his obsession, clearly Malcolm Detweiler had been pursuing some grand unifying theory of equal opposites, of the twofold, double-sided nature of existence. A theory of everything and everything's identical twin: nothing.

• •

Throughout the rest of my ... what should I call it? My sojourn? My squat? My retreat? My obscuration? ... Throughout my time at my father's A-frame, I made a point of reading or at least skimming through every book behind that blue chintz cloth, taking a volume to bed with me each night and staying up late reading, sometimes most of the night. Despite doing so, for some reason, even on as little as two or three hours of sleep, I never felt exhausted; I didn't even feel tired. If I did, I'd take a catnap, something I'd never done in my *other* life, not without waking up drenched in a cold sweat, feeling more nauseated and disoriented than refreshed.

Here, on the other hand, in my "new life," on my father's hammock strung between a pair of sweetgum trees at the edge of the lake, to the sounds of boats buzzing by and water splashing against the lake wall, I'd drift off into short, sweet, relaxing slumbers, and awaken feeling as fresh as the breezes that swept over me in my rocking woven cotton cradle.

• •

In addition to books, an entire shelf of my father's "Twin" bookcase is devoted to videocassettes of old movies (my father, who died in 1997, never lived to see the age of Netflix and live streaming). After dinner, before bed, I'd watch one of those movies, all of which had something to do with twins, doppelgängers, or switching identities.

A partial catalogue:

The Black Room. After a ten-year hiatus, Anton returns to the castle occupied by his twin brother Gregor, a tyrannical baron. When Gregor's subjects storm the castle, he turns his title over to his beloved twin, whom he then murders and whose identity he assumes, thereby reclaiming his baronetcy. But what of the prophecy that foretold Anton's murder of his brother?

The Prisoner of Zenda. On the eve of his coronation, the King is drugged by his twin brother, Prince Michael. To prevent Michael from assuming the throne, the king's attendants get his identical twin cousin Rudolf to impersonate him. While the king is imprisoned in a castle in Zenda, Rudolph falls in love with the king's betrothed.

Among the Living. John Raden, son of the town patriarch and owner of the now-idle mill that was the town's raison d'être, believes his twin brother Paul died in an accident twenty-five years ago. In fact he was brain damaged as a result of the beatings of his overbearing father, and has been alive all the while, ensconced in a room in the decaying Radon mansion, tended to by a doctor and a servant. The plot kicks in when, after a quarter century of isolation, insane Paul escapes the mansion and heads into town.

A Stolen Life. When manipulative, man-hungry Pat Bosworth (Bette Davis) drowns in a sailing accident, her shy, demure twin sister Kate (ditto) assumes her identity as well as her husband, Bill, whom her sister had stolen from her in the first place. But Bill, who'd had it with Pat, wants a divorce. To tell or not to tell?

The Dark Mirror. Identical twins—one loving, the other severely disturbed—are murder suspects. Only one committed the murder, and each can provide an alibi for the other.

Paranoiac. Simon—a spendthrift alcoholic—plots to drive his sister insane so as to inherit the estate of their rich parents. His plan is foiled, however, when a mysterious stranger appears, claiming to be Simon's brother Tony, who supposedly committed suicide by jumping off a seaside cliff and whose body was never found. Though "Tony" claims to have faked his death, Simon knows the truth: after forging a suicide note, Simon murdered his brother and buried the body behind a wall in the chapel of the estate.

Dead Ringer. Desperate and broke Edith (Bette Davis again) murders her wealthy twin sister Margaret and assumes her identity.

Suture. Destitute Vince plots to murder his twin brother Clay with a car bomb and pass off the corpse as his own so he won't have to share money from father's will and can start a new life.

The premise of nearly all twin/double stories boils down to this: since the laws of nature dictate that one thing can't exist in two places at once, a person and his or her double can't both remain alive: for the laws of the universe to be respected, one of them must perish.

Said premise, needless to say, fails to take into account Quantum Entanglement.

• •

When not reading books or watching movies from my father's bookshelves, or gathering clues about my brother's life, or swimming, or doing floor and isometric exercises, or rowing my father's boat or napping in his hammock, I taught myself how to ride my brothers' motorcycle, a late model BMW R1200C Phoenix Cruiser with a yellow gasoline tank. I'd never ridden a motorcycle before. The closest I'd ever come had been on the Greek island of Naxos thirty years earlier, when I nearly killed myself and my girlfriend on a rented Vespa. I started out cautiously, learning what I could online before climbing on the machine, which to my surprise started on the first try. I wore my brother's helmet, gloves, and full regalia of protective gear, and practiced along the stretch of one-lane road leading to the house, and later riding circles in the cul-de-sac, until I felt confident enough to ride all the way to town and back.

Meanwhile the Mazda went under its own tarp next to the sagging aluminum carport, under which, you may recall, my dead father's Alfa Romeo cowered under its own tarp, beyond repair. Its tires were flat, its convertible top reduced to leather rags, its bucket seats torn and occupied by spiders, mice, and carpenter ants, its pistons welded by rust to their cylinders. Through gaps in the corroded floor chickweed and crabgrass sprouted.

• •

I did other things. I tended the yard. With the riding mower stored under a tarp beneath the deck (whose pistons, unlike the Alpha's, hadn't rusted) I mowed the lawn. I seeded bare patches in the grass. I got the sprinkler system pump up and running again. I replaced the splintered boards on the dock, filled in the sinkholes that had formed along the seawall where the muskrats got to it, and repaired breaches in the wall itself. I planted new shrubs and pruned old ones. I'd always had a black thumb. Back in New York the few potted geraniums I'd kept in my apartment withered under my neglectful stewardship. Now, despite the unsuitability of the season, the same geraniums or ones just like them out on the deck here burst into boisterous blooms. The hands that ministered to them were identical, but the results were entirely different. Ditto the five azaleas, the four gardenias, the three hydrangeas, and the one camellia bush I planted. I noted other significant changes as well. Several hundred or so pages back in this document, paraphrasing the section of my brother's first book wherein he describes the changes that he underwent during the days, weeks, and months immediately following his airborne epiphany, I wrote and you read: "He felt... like a different man; indeed, he *was* a different man. There could simply be no question about it. He felt different in his gestures; he felt different in his bones and in his blood. His skin felt different on his face. When he smiled, he felt the difference in the tension of his muscles and nerves, and he smiled much more than he ever had before. He felt it in the movements of his bowels and in the spasms, flow, and contractions of his bladder. His erections felt different; it might have been the power of suggestion, or a placebo effect of all the other changes, but it seemed to him that they were a good deal stronger and lasted longer, and that, furthermore, his sexual organ, by what could only be called immaculate enhancement, had grown markedly larger in all three of its primary states: erect, tumescent, and flaccid... His breath was sweeter; his teeth struck him as whiter; his hair was thicker; and his hairline, which had been receding or threatening to recede, seemed no longer to be doing so. He had much more energy and enthusiasm...." If I've duplicated this passage, it's not out of laziness, but because during my first weeks here my brother's experience was indeed duplicated.

Along with these physical and emotional changes there came a change in outlook and philosophy. No longer did I doubt, much less hold in contempt, the premise of my brother's book.

How could I doubt it, when I was its living embodiment? What more proof did I need that one really *can* change, for the better, with a snap of one's fingers, just like *that*!

As simple as ordering coffee, black.

•   •

However, along with black coffee, trouble, as they say, was brewing.

First, there was that red boat, which, gone for a week owing to inclement weather, had returned, now plying the waters nearer to the lake's center—yes, Dear Reader, a short distance from where

I had disposed of my brother's corpse. Still, that they could have been looking for my brother made no sense, none at all. As for Lester Figes, whoever he was — he had nothing to do with me. For that matter, what could he have had to do with my brother?

Since no one but my mother had its number, I left Old Phone's ringer in the "on" mode. Meanwhile I silenced Twinkle. Apparently my brother had shared his cellphone number with only a very few people, including Dawn Swopes, whose messages, before I instructed her via email to cease and desist, lit up the screen no fewer than two-dozen times a day. There were other phone and text messages, too. Most of them I gave a cursory glance to and forgot about.

One message, however, was harder to ignore.

what did u do to my uncle?

I was sitting in one of the two chairs on the dock, in the shade of a new sun umbrella I'd bought, a blue-and-white striped umbrella with a hand crank and a fifty-pound iron stand. A few minutes later:

i know u did something

Another minute:

they found his car

Twenty seconds later:

the police

The next few messages arrived in rapid succession:

i know it was u

u wont get away with it

i wont let u

answer me

goddam u

The number associated with the messages had a 334 area code. I looked it up. Alabama. Specifically, the southeastern side of the state, including the Montgomery, Auburn-Opelika, and Dothan metropolitan areas, as well as Phenix City.

A thought occurred to me.

I found the newspaper I'd bought at Kroger and re-read the front-page story.

334 was also the area code for Wetumpka.

A coincidence, to be sure.

I searched for other messages and calls from that same number, but found none. Had my brother deleted them? What was going on? What could he possible have had to do with someone from Wetumpka, Alabama, or his/her uncle? It made no sense.

For the rest of that day and that night and most of the following day I kept one eye on that phone screen. Each time it lit up I winced.

No other messages from that number followed.

Probably some crazed fan, a stalker, no doubt. Brock Jones, PhD must have more than his share of them.

I put it out of my mind.

16. FOR I HAD COME TO DOUBT MYSELF...

BACK TO NEW YORK CITY AND MY (ADMITTEDLY OVERLONG) back-story.

As I exited the Society Library at 79th and Madison raindrops speckled the sidewalk. I carried my battered briefcase and two plastic bags, one in each hand. The plastic bag in my left hand held "Bitsy" Watson's copy of "Duplicity," the one in my right held the other two un-collated copies. I still had to get a manuscript box. If you haven't done so all this time by now you must be wondering why I couldn't have just emailed Bitsy a digital version of my novel, why I insisted on this antiquated and cumbersome approach. Call me a Luddite, but I could not bear the thought of Bitsy reading my virtual words. I wanted her turning pages — not digital pages, real ones. For the same reason I can't bear the thought of so-called "electronic" books. I have never bought one and can now safely say I never will. Like an electric fire, it may do the same job, but it's also equally unprepossessing. Anyway I wanted the chance to meet my novel's savior.

It took me four stationers to find one decrepit enough to still carry manuscript boxes. By then I was twenty-seven long blocks from my destination. The sky was as dark as a coalminer's lungs. Should it start pouring, I thought, my freshly-copied manuscripts and I will both be soaked.

It started pouring.

There was a Starbucks on the corner. Normally I'd have gone out of my way to avoid that establishment, finding its coffee only slightly less deplorable than its pastries, and those in keeping with its pseudo-bohemian but ultimately bland corporate ambiance. I ducked inside and took a corner table. With the wet world going by outside, I collated the other manuscripts. As I did, another title occured to me, along with the outline of a story: "Desecration," about a woman (middle-aged? older? Joan or Joanne. Realtor? Grade-school teacher? Lawyer?) whose dead best friend in her will has asked her to look over the grave of her niece who died in a car accident, to make sure that it's not desecrated by contemptuous youth. The graveyard has an iron gate around it. Driving by it one afternoon, this woman, call her Jo, sees another, younger woman sitting on the niece's gravestone eating potato chips. She thinks she knows who the woman is: the estranged hippie daughter of her dead friend. When she drives by again the girl is gone, however the potato chip bag has been left on the grave mound. To the litterbug daughter of her dead friend Jo mails a mildly chastising letter but gets no reply. A week later the same thing happens, more or less. Unwilling to confront the young woman (who, she suspects, is insane), Jo composes a second letter, sends it by regular post to her dead friend's daughter, and tapes a copy of it to the graveyard gate. To it she receives a reply by post from the hippie daughter saying, essentially, "I don't know what you're talking about. For the past three weeks I've been at an artist's residence in Downeast Maine." A week later Jo visits the graveyard again. Raining. Autumn. She sees the young woman sitting there eating potato chips as before. This time she parks her car, gets out and confronts her, to discover that the young woman is of no relation whatever to her dead friend, in fact she's a total stranger, wild-eyed and obviously unstable. "Who *are* you? Did you know X? What are you doing here?" Metaphysical implications. Accusations. Kafkaesque twist. Delmore Schwartz' "In Dreams Begin Responsibilities." Alternative title: "Wreck of the Hesperus."

"A good simile refreshes the intellect." —Wittgenstein

• •

Four-forty. The rain still fell, but not as hard. Having gathered my
collated life, I stepped out into the watery world. Halfway to the
building that was my objective, at Park and 56th, the sky, as they
say, "opened up." *Burst open? With a vengeance?* Clichés, I thought,
leaping over a sewage drain overflowing with *caffelatte*. The del-
uge soaked my jacket sleeves. It glued the backs of my Dockers to
my calves, pasted my mock turtleneck to my shoulders. At least, I
thought, dodging a discarded broken five-dollar umbrella, it's not
raining cats and dogs. Then again, every cliché once had its *day in
the sun.* Raining cats and dogs! Whoever came up with that could've
given Wild Bill Shakespeare himself a run for his money (another
puddle; another deft dodge). Shakespeare, now there's someone
who could write up a storm. *Blow winds, and crack your cheeks!
Rage! Blow!* Note emphasis on punchy Saxonate monosyllabic
verbs (a taxi blares its horn; a man rushes past me with a newspaper over his head). *You cataracts and hurricanes spout / Till you
have drench'd our steeples, drown'd the cocks!* A little alliteration
never hurts (someone's umbrella spoke nearly pokes out my left
eye).... *You sulfurous and thought-executing fires.* Note the adjec-
tival phrases: *thought-executing; oak-cleaving* (another cab heaves
a puddle into my briefcase), verbs pressed into service as modifiers.
(A bicycle messenger gooses me.) *Singe my white beard!* My next
puddle-jump I miscalculate, baptizing my Doc Martins... *Crack
nature's molds...* (rain batters car tops, leaks from my nose)... *all
germens spill at once that make ingrateful man!...* "Ingrateful"—the
one pure abstraction in Lear's storm. Even the Bard nods, occasionally. *Rumble thy bellyful! Spit fire! Spout rain!...*
      At 64th Street I stop to catch my breath. I haven't run like
this in a while. My heart pounds in my chest like a wire beater
thumping a rug. My face drips; the weight of water has unrolled
my Docker cuffs. The world gone gray with rain. *Change, light!*
When it does, I vault into a puddle. My Doc Martins morph into
amphibious landing craft, the opposite curb into a Czech-hedge-
hog fortified Normandy beach. Under a fusillade of rain, amid
a profusion of sodden fellow soldiers, I storm the sidewalk. An

ambulance careens by, screaming.

From there it's half a block to the vestibule of 2650 Park Avenue. Before surrendering to the security guard, I try to reconstitute myself into something presentable. Having phoned up to the agency, the guard hands me an adhesive tag with my name and a number written on it. While awaiting the elevator I inspect the contents of my bags. The padded envelope holding Bitsy's copy of my novel is soaked, the recipient's and return addresses both badly blurred. The manuscript in it has fared only slightly better, its upper edge crinkled as the hem of a crinoline petticoat, the page headers smudged beyond recognition.

Like everything else, my reasons for wanting to hand-deliver the manuscript are twofold: first, a reluctance to entrust the matter to the United States Postal Service; second, the off chance that I might encounter said powerful literary agent, shake her hand, smile, crack a joke, dispense a little of my charm, something for her to remember me by apart from one more in a boundless sea of novel manuscripts. Making nice with her administrative assistant wouldn't hurt, either.

Under the circumstances, though, I had to reconsider. Did I really wish to present myself to Elizabeth Watson looking like a drowned duck? Did I really want to hand her the blurred, crinkled, smudged outcome of my infinite labors? Having already kept her waiting months, would another day hurt?

I tore off my security clearance badge, picked up my plastic bags, stepped back out into the pouring rain.

• •

Before the boy's lavatory mirror at the Friends Quaker School, I tried to regain some semblance of my venerable middle-aged self, or at least to not look completely disreputable. In doing so it occurred to me not for the first time that the last traces of my youth were slipping away. It wasn't just my hair going, or the incipient turkey wattle below my once taut jaw that quivered like

— a rigger working the underbelly of a bridge
— a leaf clinging to a branch in a storm
— a pubescent baby boomer perusing a Playboy
— a quart of raw chicken livers

—a grieved child's lower lip
—the back of a tickled toad
—a hanging drop of viscous fluid ready to fall
—a bowl of *blancmange* ...

... it was something else, unappetizing yet unnamable, though if I had been forced to name it I would have chosen "sour," as in "sour-puss," a word that my second-grade teacher, Miss Szost, applied to me in concern or disgust. I could no longer remember the last time I had smiled at myself in a mirror as I once did routinely, as a means—not of tempting, but of disarming Narcissus, yet not without fondness for the face (however undistinguished) that returned my grin. Lately, though, when I looked in mirrors, I didn't care much for what I saw, not the making of a venerable gentleman, but an old fart in embryo. Was it Fitzgerald who said that the face you own at forty is the one you've earned? Or is it "deserved"? Combing back my wet thinning hair, I thought: it's my luck to have earned the face but neither the income nor the esteem. My lips looked thin. I did some mouth-stretching exercises. Time for a beard? Nah.

Another reason for my spending so long in front of that mirror: I was waiting for the other person in the lavatory to leave so I could pee. Though his back was to me at one of the urinals, he was undoubtedly one of my students, the building being otherwise unoccupied at that hour. Despite a bursting bladder, I knew too well that until I had the lavatory all to myself I would be unable to make my own offering to the porcelain god. My prostate was the main culprit, but there was also a psychological element at work, what Dr. Snyder called "a shy bladder," the same phenomenon that prevented me, as a boy, from pissing in proximity to strangers. With the onset of my disease the phenomenon had reasserted itself with a vengeance. Called upon to produce a urine sample at Snyder's office, with the rubber-gloved nurse waiting dutifully outside the bathroom, I could no more deliver myself of the requisite thimbleful of urine than I could have piloted an F-16 or gone fifteen rounds with Muhammad Ali. Once freed of the psychological inhibitor, however, I'd manage. Having gained the initiative, the trick was to get it over with as quickly as possible before the next inhibition arrived.

With the student gone, I seized (so to speak) my opportunity. I'd forgotten the pills Dr. Snyder had given me, one of which I had already taken, and his warning that they would turn my pee bright orange and cause a "slight burning sensation" when I urinated. Predictably, the "slight burning sensation" felt more like I was trying to piss a wire tube-brush.

I had loosed a mere squirt of Metropolitan Writing Institute orange urine when the lavatory door swung open and another of my students entered. The Ken Doll. This was my uncharitable nickname for Arnold Beckman. *Tall, dark, and handsome,* immaculately outfitted in designer sports jackets and suits, looking as if he'd come to class straight from a GQ shoot. Though by then I had given up the habit of assessing, or trying to assess, my students' levels of talent or ambition based on their appearances, with Arnold, the Ken Doll, I found it hard to resist. Saul Bellow once quipped, "The unexamined life may not be worth living, but the examined life makes you want to kill yourself." As I saw it, my role as Senior Instructor at the Metropolitan Writing Institute was not merely to teach creative writing, but to initiate my students into the examined life, to get them to be not only more keen and accurate observers of the life within and around them, but to analyze their observations, question them, turn them over and over, then repeat that process—not once or twice, but as often as necessary to render those observations as precisely as possible in words on a page.

And while it was a fact that in direct consequence of attaining said level of acute existential examination my students might, occasionally, like Mr. Bellow and me their instructor, wish themselves dead, what of it? If you planned to be a writer, especially one of substance, the examined life wasn't something you could hope to get around. It was the cross you had to bear, the price you had to pay. Arnold Beckman would never pay that price. He was too well put-together. Not merely too handsome (in and of itself that was no disqualifier; I'd been pretty decent-looking myself at his age). His cosmological outlook was too well-ordered. He needed a planet or two out of alignment, an errant moon or a recalcitrant asteroid. He was too well-adjusted to be a great or even a middling writer—or, for that matter, to wish to be one. Why spend the better part of your mortal existence alone in a room stringing sentences together while trying not to jerk off and/or fall asleep when you could be out in the world laughing, dancing, feasting, flirting, and fucking—and getting paid for it to boot? Why waste your impeccably groomed, camera-ready presence in front of a dumb computer screen writing stories for others—who, all things being equal, were more suitably disposed to exist alone in *their* rooms—when you could have the likes of Ashley Bridges eating, so to speak, out of your perfectly manicured hand?

To sum up, whatever it took to wish oneself dead, the Ken Doll just didn't have it in him.

Arnold (jovially, bellied up to the adjacent urinal, brazenly unzipping): "Hey, there, Mr. Detweiler."

Me (grimly trying to piss, my dick a needle; my pee a camel): "Hello, Arnold."

Arnold (unleashing The Flood): "How's it going?"

Me (nodding, grimacing, struggling): "Fine, just fine."

My rival in micturition stood a good three inches taller than me. His other dimensions I chose to ignore. As Arnold released a stream to rival Angel Falls, I stood beside him, my cheeks burning, blocked as the tomb of the Holy Sepulcher, put in mind of the following doggerel:

> There once was a man from Stanbul
> Who soliloquized thus to his tool:
> First you robbed me of wealth / then you took all my health
> And now you won't pee, you old fool!

Should I quit while ahead, I asked myself? Flush nothing and get it over with, or pretend to? As Arnold's outpouring resounded off the lavatory's tiled walls, I felt myself growing smaller and smaller, until it seemed to me that I could more easily flush myself than any amount of my urine down the drain. I thought of this line of Kafka's: "When you stand before a man you stand before the gates of hell." In the given instance the man was Arnold Beckman and the gates of hell a urinal.

"Catch you inside," said Arnold, flushing.

•   •

Five minutes past the hour, I strode into class. I liked nothing better than to arrive strategically late to a classroom full of deferential students, sitting there waiting like baby birds with mouths gaping for the juicy worms of wisdom I dispensed so copiously.

Seeing everyone there but Ashley, I felt my heart gutter. It happened sometimes on the day of their first chamber: second thoughts, cold feet. As her classmates sat there silently, I wondered: Where is she? Has she stood me up?

Minutes later, as I finished taking roll, she appeared in a gleaming lipstick-red trench coat that looked as unperturbed by the rain as the rest of her.

"Sorry," she said breathlessly. "It's just about impossible to get a taxi in the rain in this city, isn't it?"

As if she were an embarrassment, the other students resisted looking at her. Or was this moment somehow perceived as a private one between teacher and pupil in which they did not wish to intrude? Ashley took off her raincoat. Under it she wore a blouse as low-cut as the one she'd worn on the first day of class, with a lacy neckline—if something that swooped down past one's sternum could be called a neckline. In the semi-circle of one-armed desks she took the seat two desks to the left of Arnold Beckman's, throwing first him then me a toothy grin, her triangular chin jutting. For my part I did my best to look graciously disgusted, when really I was relieved almost to grateful tears. All day I'd yearned to see her.

"Well," I said, looking up from the manuscripts arranged on my desk. "We've got four pieces to chamber. Shall we get started?"

We did the other three pieces first, saving the best (not Ashley's work, my critique of it) for last. First chamber sessions were tenuous affairs, with students exercising supreme diplomacy, doling out compliments like soup kitchen volunteers dishing out turkey with all the trimmings to the homeless on Thanksgiving Day. By the third class the gloves would come off and they'd be at each other's throats, going at each other's earnest efforts like drivers at a demolition derby. In that regard anyway they would have become seasoned authors.

But it was early in the term, and that evening's class was still on its good behavior. I'd have to cajole and coax them to get them to say anything critical, while dissuading them from launching their critiques with, "I liked this story," or words to that effect. "Our purpose here," I'd say, "is to get at what's working or not in a piece of writing. Reserve your value judgments for after class." It was a speech I gave early in the term, one that framed me as a tough but fair taskmaster, someone disinclined to let his classes devolve into mutual back-patting societies or critical food fights.

I started with Alice Nordland's story, the one about the Second to Princess Ourania, daughter to Her Majesty Queen Kali Morah III and his love affair with the cloaked, bound, ravishing Lilith. Might as well put it out of its misery. Like a dentist lining up his sterile implements on a tray, I spread the pages of the manuscript out on my desk, their margins slathered with my thoughtful ink. As there were no volunteers to start off the session, I called on the student in the farthest desk, Michael Quigley, who'd written the story about the serial hamburger killer. "Michael, give us your thoughts, if you please," I said.

"Well," he began. "First of all, I really liked the sto—"

"Stop!" I said, raising my hand. I gave The Speech, then gestured for Michael to continue.

"Well, the characters were interesting, and I admired how you—"

"I'm sorry to have to interrupt you again," I said. "But please say 'the author'."

"Oh, yeah, right. Sorry. Um…I really admired how the author captured the whole feeling of that time and place in history."

What time and place in history? I thought, smiling. *Queen Kali Morah III?* What land was she queen of if not the Kingdom of Cloying Cliches?

"Go on."

"Well," said Michael, adjusting his Buddy Holly horn-rims, looking increasingly myopic under them as he blathered on. "I liked how Alice—oops, sorry—how the author developed the plot, the way she built up all that tension leading up to when they're…you know…gonna burn Lilith at the stake."

What tension? I thought. It was a foregone conclusion that the "knight in shining armor" would rescue the slave object of his "burning desire." Even if by some miracle one didn't assume as much, the specifics of the executive burning were rendered so cartoonishly as to turn anything approaching suspense into a series of belly laughs or a case of mild indigestion.

"Please go on."

"Well," said Michael. "I know we're not supposed to say what we liked, but I have to say I liked the setting a whole lot."

What setting? I thought. An auction lot of battered plaster and lath props carted from deep within the Quonset huts at MGM, where they waited to be boxed up for storage or burned.

"Do continue," I said.

"And the costumes. I really like how she described all the costumes."

Costumes indeed! Straight off the superannuated rack at Western Costume, tagged with the long-forgotten names of every central casting knave ever to scuff the B-lot pavement at Paramount.

"Anything more?" I said.

"Well," said Michael. "I did find the writing a little bit flowery in some places."

Now we're getting somewhere, I thought, though "a little bit flowery" was putting it mildly, considering that Alice's prose was like a stroll through the orchid hothouse at the Enid Hauptman Conservatory, but instead of orchids what flourished there were metaphors and similes.

"Is that all?"

"That's it, pretty much," said Michael. "Overall I really liked— oops, there I go again!—I mean, I think it's a pretty good story."

The other student's appraisals of Alice Nordland's story fell along similar lines, variations on a theme of "it was pretty good"—meaning no one liked it, but nor did they feel threatened by it. To my disappointment, Ashley sugarcoated her response along with the rest of them. Or did she really mean it when she said, "Gee, I am just so *impressed* by the author's imagination. I mean, I can't *imagine* making up a whole *world* the way she's done it here, with... oh, I don't know, so much *passion* and *conviction*."

I thought: is she *kidding*? Was Ashley exercising charity, or was she softening up the jury in anticipation of her own critique session? Or both?

Eager to arrive at her piece, I whipped the class through the other two submissions. Though tempted to make mincemeat of Michael's hamburger-centric serial killer, I held back. It was, after all, our first chamber session: no need to go ballistic. Over Margot Abrons' abortion story I tiptoed, aware that she seemed on the verge of tears even before the first words of criticism had been spoken. To each of these stories the class was likewise charitable. It never failed. The least promising works earned the most praise, while those with true potential drew the harshest criticism, occasioning vitriol or apathy or a blend of both. So I wasn't surprised to hear Ashley's submission damned with faint praise.

"I think the writing's all right," said Darcy Hedgeworth, the financial auditor who, despite advanced middle age, wore her gray hair in double pigtails. "I'm just not sure I buy the whole transplanted Southern belle thing. It reminded me too much of Tennessee Williams and Holly Golightly, and all that."

"Are you saying that the central character seems derivative? Or worse—stereotypical?"

"I guess that's what I'm saying, yes."

"Hmm," I said.

The others chimed in. From the moment when she walked late into that first class, I sensed antipathy on the part of some of the other students toward Ashley. Hadn't I felt some of the same antipathy myself? Yet any ill will I harbored then had long since worn off, had altered into something else entirely, whereas the other students' animosities seemed to have hardened. Like vultures they descended, knowing nothing tastier than the raw flesh of a draft manuscript. However much this disgusted me, I found it pleasing, for it set the stage for my favorite part of the chambering process, the part where, as my own type of bird, I displayed my plumage, the moment of truth when I'd pronounce my verdict. In fictional terms this is called the "reversal," the part of the story where "against all odds" (and to mix metaphors) the heroine is rescued from the burning stake by her knight in shining armor: *moi*.

I cleared my throat.

"I must say," I began, "I have a different take on this story than the rest of you seem to." Oh, how Stewart Detweiler loved pulling the rug out from under his students! "Frankly," I went on, "I'm baffled by some of your responses. Not that I disagree entirely, as far as—" a considered pause "—as far as the issues raised. What baffles me is the tone of the criticism, the tepid if not altogether absent enthusiasm for a piece of writing that, though clearly a first draft of a work-in-progress by a novice author—is, I happen to think, nevertheless, in its way, rather ... stunning."

Vacant faces, as was to be expected. After all, what could they say? It was my classroom. Over the world of baristas and copy shops, of cellphone abusers and rainstorms, of evangelistic Impalas and hysterical ticket vending machines, of editors and literary agents, I could claim no dominion. Here, however, within the scum-colored walls of my basement classroom in the Friends Quaker School, I was Master of the Universe.

Though I had planned to read from my written critique, inspiration seized and carried me off beyond the limits of my carefully crafted prose, to the timberline—nay, the snowy summit—to the snowy summit of critical perspicuity.

"Clearly the author," I said (tossing Ashley a conspiratorial grin), "has a strong native talent. There's much vim and vigor in her prose, not to mention skill, though at times these are at odds with the material, and her cleverness interferes—again, not always, but at times—with her saying precisely what she means." I produced two examples, then went on. "You may recall, some of you, my mentioning in our first class the two loves that no fiction writer can do without. The first is the love of language. That's obvious enough. The second is a love of truth. That's less obvious, since here we're talking fiction. By 'truth' I don't mean the *factual* truth; I mean the essential, the emotional, and, yes, occasionally, the literal truth. In my opinion this author brings ample portions of both kinds of love to her creation.

"However," I proceeded, "instead of uniting them, she pits those loves against each other with words often chosen as much or more for her fondness for quirky diction than for their precise meanings. There's a lot of showing off in these pages, a lot of energy given over to charming the reader, to flirting with him. And as I'm sure all of you know, flirting can be enjoyable for both the flirter and the flirtee. Still, at some point flirtation must come to an end and real lovemaking, again if you will, if you'll grant me the analogy, must begin. Otherwise, for the reader anyway, the result—to put it as generously as possible—is frustration. On the other hand," I was quick to add, "to commit these particular sins requires considerable talent. But let's deal with the specifics..."

●   ●

Having delivered myself of my global assessment of Ashley's submission, I turned to the nuts-and-bolts portion of my critique. I was in fine fettle that evening, balancing wit with seriousness, levity with rigor, kindness with strictness, praise with censure. Unlike most of my colleagues, who frowned upon giving prescriptive advice, I considered it my obligation. If a solution to a problem occurred to me, why not share it? To have done less would have been stingy. Only once in recent memory had a student dared to question the efficacy of my doling out prescriptive advice. "After all, it's her story, isn't it?" The student in question, Melissa Cosgrove, was by day a dental hygienist. Long nose, seborrheic skin, a permanent frown etched onto her face. No one liked her. Once during a break, through the street-level casement window I watched her smoking alone on the dark sidewalk, and felt brief sympathetic pity for her, until, as they exited the basement door, she flicked her still glowing cigarette butt at the backs of a contingent of Alcoholics Anonymous members. To her remark I responded with a speech I'd worked up for the occasion. Imagine, I said, a mechanic telling the owner of a car that keeps stalling, "It's your carburetor." Or a heart surgeon saying to his patient, "Heck, it's *your* left ventricle." No, I said. If one has solutions to offer, to do less than offer them would be selfish.

And I had plenty of solutions to offer. Hard-pressed as I was to meet the demands of my own creations, when it came to student efforts I never hesitated to storm the battlements—slings, arrows, and vats of boiling oil be damned. I'd spend hours—days, even—engineering spines for their non-existent plots, conjuring solid themes from the thin air of their vapid premises, breathing life into characters as flat as flounders. To the smoldering ruins of their efforts my students had only to apply my remedies for phoenix-like masterpieces to take flight. Thereof gave I of myself.

"As always," I added in closing, "I reserve the right to be wrong. If anyone disagrees, by all means please say so."

Blank stares, dazed silence. What could they say? My critique had left no room for dissent.

"Other comments or questions?"

With a prophylactic smile I varnished the classroom.

"In that case, I'll see you all next week."

• •

"Professor Detweiler!"

Downpour had diminished to drizzle. I had just left the building and was walking slowly, hoping she'd catch up to me. She did. There she was, like magic, at my side.

"Would it kill you to call me Stewart?" I asked.

"I like your last name, Detweiler. It sounds so much sexier than Stewart, don't you think? It's like a detective's name. Didn't George Peppard play a detective named Detweiler?"

"George Peppard? Isn't he before your time?"

"I like old movies. Anyway I can't imagine calling you Stewart. Or worse: Stew. Yuck!"

"Thank you."

"Anyhow to me you're Professor Detweiler."

"Can we at least dispense with the 'Professor'?"

"Okay, just Detweiler then. Hey, there, Detweiler! How's it going, Detweiler? That's what I'll call you. Do you mind?"

Suppressing my delight, I asked whether there was something in particular she wanted to ask me.

"Not exactly. Not a question, anyway. A statement."

"State away, in that case."

"All right. I think you're holding back on me."

In the dimness between streetlamps I stopped to look at her. She looked lovely, of course. That we were alone and the street was wet and dark heightened this impression.

"I know that you mean to be kind, that you want to encourage us beginners and all that, but frankly, Prof — ... Detweiler ... well, to be honest, I haven't got the time."

I studied her, wondering just how disingenuous she was being. "I thought your piece got a thorough, rigorous critique. And as for being kind, your fellow students — "

"Please, I don't give a fuck what they think." The word *fuck* leapt so unexpectedly from her perfectly shaped lips it stopped me, as they say, dead in my tracks. "Sorry," she said. "I didn't mean it that way. But then you have to admit, most of the people in our class ... well, let's just say they're not serious. Honestly, I don't know how you can *stand* to read some of that stuff! Alice Nordland — my *god*! You should get — what do they call it? Hazardous duty pay! Anyway it's your opinion that matters to me, not theirs. They're amateurs: what do *they* know?" A dainty shrug. "Though I'm a beginner, at least I'm serious about my writing, dead serious. That's why I want you to be ruthless with me, to pull out all the stops, let me have it with both barrels. Don't gild the lily!"

Like a boxer by a flurry of landed jabs, Ashley's barrage of clichés left me stunned. Could anyone capable of such a salvo possibly become a serious writer? Yet she wrote well, and her earnestness seemed genuine if over the top. Furthermore there was something conjointly exquisite about walking side by side with her down a dark wet street, the heels of her red leather cowboy boots (into which she'd tucked her jeans) clicking along, the traces of her perfume scenting the damp night air.

"What makes you think I'm holding back?"

We had started walking again. "I'm a woman," she replied with a shrug. "I know when a man's holding back. Look." She squared up to me. "I know what you're thinking: that if I were really a serious writer I wouldn't be here talking to you; I'd be at some way better school."

She obviously regretted this remark. I watched her turn away to reconsider. "And that's not any reflection on you," she added sheepishly. "You're a wonderful teacher, I know you are."

"You've had me for all of two class sessions."

"I know, but I also read all your evaluations."

"Did you? How is that possible?"

"The dean—he let me. Well, he didn't *exactly* let me, but...well, let's just say I ingratiated myself to him."

I thought *I'll bet you did,* picturing Ashley in her tight jeans and low-cut blouse perched like a hood ornament on Dexter Bronze's solid lap while scrutinizing my employee file. We passed my subway station.

"Plus I read your books," she added coyly. "*Penny Farthings.*"

"*Penny Sufferings,*" I corrected her. "A penny farthing is a bicycle."

"And *Reasonable People.*"

"I'm surprised you were able to find a copy. There must be all of four left in the world, of which I own three, the rest having been pulped. So? What did you think?"

"It's a wonderful novel."

I eyed her dubiously.

"You're an impeccable stylist."

I laughed. "So you've dug up my reviews, too!" I recited: "'If style over substance is your cup of tea, Stewart Detweiler's *Penny Sufferings* may be the most impeccably stylish book of the decade. Never before has so much perfect prose been lavished on so negligible a story.'"

"Do you commit all reviews of your books to memory?"

"When it's that memorable, yes. You have to admit, the reviewer has a way with words."

"He's a jerk. Or she. Who wrote it, do you know?"

"Some anonymous prick."

"I want names. I'm making a list of assholes."

"Actually he's someone very close to my heart."

"I hope he's not still close to your heart after that."

"He is indeed. As close as ever."

Ashley stopped walking and faced me, dumbfounded.

"You reviewed your *own book*?"

"I did."

"And you gave yourself a *rotten review*?"

"Rotten?" I drew back indignantly. "It wasn't rotten. It was quite respectful, I thought, on the whole. 'The most impeccably stylish book of the decade.' Hell, that's not exactly what I'd call a drubbing."

"Why would you do that to yourself?"

It was my turn then to shrug. "I gave myself a fair review, which is about all one can ask for. Hell, I even read the book, which is more than can be said for most reviewers." Wherefore the urge to admit these things had sprung I hadn't the foggiest, but it felt good. Cleansing. *Like an autumn drizzle.* I looked at my watch.

"I'm missing my train," I said.

We had reached Park Avenue. The drizzle had softened to something benign that muted lights and traffic noises. Silently without collusion we turned and headed uptown.

"I still say you're a wonderful writer."

"Thanks."

"And a terrific teacher. Your students love you. You know that, don't you, Detweiler?"

"Some of them," I said.

"*Most* of them. Anyway, I'm glad I picked you."

I smiled, thinking if that was true, why hadn't she remembered my name on that first day of class? I dismissed the thought.

"And I want you to know," she said, coming closer and taking the arm that held my briefcase, "that I'm determined to write this little ol' novel of mine or whatever it is. I'm giving myself three months."

"Three months? That's a bit tight, isn't it, considering you've never written a novel before?"

"If I can't do it in three months, it's back to TV news for me."

"What do you mean 'back to'? You haven't quit, have you?"

"Call it an unpaid leave of absence."

I shook my head.

"What are you shaking your head at me for?"

"Nothing wrong with writers giving themselves deadlines," I said. "I'm all for it. I think you *should* give yourself one."

"Should I?"

"Yes. In fact let me give you one. As long as it takes. That's your deadline. You don't want to be treated like a beginner? Don't act like one. The difference between a real writer and a beginner is real writers give it everything they've got—and not just for three months, or even six months or sixty years, but until they're dead and buried. For God's sake, Ashley—." My speech and I both came to a stop on the corner of Nineteenth and Park. "You're—how old, twenty-eight?"

"Twenty-eight?" said Ashley, aghast. "Twenty-six!"

"A child, practically. Hell, you're just beginning. Look at me." Yes, I thought, *look at me*. "I'm past fifty; I've published two books and spent the last twenty years working on the third. Where do you think I'd be if at you're age I'd given myself three months?" *Some place better than this, that's for sure.* "You talk as if writing is something you plan out like any other career, like passing the bar or getting a medical license. Writing's not a career, it's a way of life. You don't choose it; it chooses you. You have no choice, not if you're a real writer. If you're a real a writer you'll starve before you quit. You'll see all your friends get high paying jobs, watch them raise lovely children in beautiful homes while driving magnificent cars. Meanwhile you'll scribble away in your lonesome garret as your health declines and the rejections pile up like snow on Mt. Fuji. Still you won't quit, no matter how badly you want to, not till you're dead. And even then you'll keep on writing, if at all possible."

We looked at each other. As we did I wondered what this young woman in her prime made of her teacher's middle-aged rant. Did she find me brave, determined, self-pitying, pious, pathetic, grandiose, grandiloquent...destroyed, but not defeated? A staring match ensued. Generally I discouraged my students from leaning on eye color when describing characters. Who cares if the heroine's eyes are green or blue—or polka-dotted, for that matter? But it mattered just then, to me. Ashley's eyes were a dusty cuprous oxide with bright bits of copper shining through. It made a difference too how they gazed unblinkingly into mine, their lengthy lashes curling inward. These were qualities I would not have wanted to miss on the page or elsewhere.

"My stars—that was some speech!"

"You liked it?"

"Does that mean you won't tear me apart?"

"Heck no. If it's tearing apart that you're after, tearing apart's what you'll get. Where do you want me to start?"

"The beginning will do fine."

"Let's keep walking," I said.

We continued uptown, the lights of shops and cars blurring peripherally as traffic zipped through rain puddles. "What say we start with your title."

"What's wrong with my title?" Ashley asked, gripping my arm.

"Nothing's wrong. It's a perfectly good title. But it's got nothing to do with your novel, based on what I've read so far."

"You only read seventeen pages."

"Your novel's not about leaving anywhere. It's about arriving here, in New York City."

"That's the whole point," said Ashley, clinging tighter. "It's called irony, I believe."

"There's a difference between being ironic and being misleading."

"Go on," said Ashley.

"Do you care to get some coffee or something?"

"Don't you have a train to catch?"

"I'll catch a later one."

"Okay, but my treat."

•   •

We crossed Madison and ducked into a diner, one of those Hellenic marvels flooded with wasted light. Ashley treated herself to a malted, while I ordered a slice of apple pie with my decaf, à la mode. I carried the same torch for coffee shops as for cafés, almost. Having taken a few sips on her straw, from her bag Ashley produced a notebook and a pen.

"Please go on," she said, flipping the notebook open like a reporter.

"Are you interviewing me for Fox News?"

"About my book, silly!"

"Oh, right. Well, about your prologue—or prologues, I should say, since you've got at least two."

"What about it, them?"

"They should go. Both of them. I said so in my critique."

"So what should I do? Where should I begin?"

"At the beginning, with the inciting incident."

"What?" Crinkling her unblemished brow.

"With the moment that launches Isabella's world out of its status quo. Better still, begin *in medias res,* in the middle of things, with her already arrived in New York, in the midst of her struggle to survive." I took a bite of my apple pie and spoke with my mouth full. "A rainy day. She sits on the front stoop of her new apartment in the Village—the East Village; she can't afford the West—holding an umbrella over herself, waiting for the moving van to arrive from way down south in Dixie with her furniture. The van is two days late, explaining the bags under her eyes, since she's been sleeping in a sleeping bag on the cold parquet floor. At long last, the van shows up. None of the furniture fits—the priceless heirlooms, the dining room table, the armoire, the china hutch, the crested oak headboard—everything's gotta go. Everything—" I took a swallow of coffee, "—everything but the fox hunt painting, the one in the hideously gaudy gold leaf frame, bequeathed to her from Grandmother Beauregard, a painting Isabella can stand no more than she could stand the embalmed, sherry-guzzling snob who gave it to her, a painting that in its subject as well as its style represents to her everything she despises about her Southern aristocratic roots, and why she's torn herself from same. Yet she must keep it; it's a legacy, and valuable, and Mama Beauregard would never forgive her for stowing it in the closet. She hangs it over her bed—her mattress, that is—on the wall she painted a lush mocha brown, hoping to warm the place up a bit, but it turns out that in her dark apartment it's more like living inside a vat of fudge. Meanwhile her ancestral furnishings lie in the street being rained upon. Only her antique spinet desk survives the move. She sits at it now, at the end of your first chapter, with tears in her eyes as rain shivers down the dark window, and opens her diary—excuse me, her journal, since she's a journalist—and scribbles her first entry, which takes the form of a letter to her dear departed granddaddy, Cyrus Stonewall-Beauregard or whatever, Mississippi Newspaper Tycoon, the man who inspired her to be a journalist in the first place." I looked up from my empty pie plate, whose residue of melted ice cream I had been trying to eat with my fork, to see Ashley bent over her notebook, scribbling frantically. Done scribbling, she faced me, lips parted, triangular jaw hanging.

"Chapter One," I said.

"Wow! That was amazing!" said Ashley.

"I got a bit carried away."

"Are you kidding? It's *wonderful!*"

"You like it?"

"Like it? It's great. It's—magnificent! It's just what this darn book of mine needs. I'll have to tweak it a bit, of course, here and there. But otherwise—it's perfect!"

"You really think so, huh?"

"I really do!" Ashley's eyes sparkled (I know, I know; but that's just what they did).

"Of course," I said, "you'll go about it your own way, in your own style. Heck, it's *your* novel." I said this despite the fact that Ashley had as yet neither a novel nor a style in which to execute it. She was too young yet to have a style. Like most writers—like me—she would struggle through years of permutations before arriving at hers.

"You don't mind if I use it, do you?" she asked.

"What—what I just described? Of course not, by all means use it. Mind you, I was shooting from the hip."

"Well you're a great shot, Detweiler."

"Well..."

"I'm going to use every detail."

"Listen," I said. "Do you want my real advice?"

"*Mais certainement, monsieur!*"

"Write a pitch paragraph."

"A what?"

"A paragraph that spells out, in no uncertain terms and in as few words as possible, the plot of your story, *what happens to who, where, when.*" I offered some concrete suggestions. "Give your southern belle ingénue a love interest," I said. "Better yet, give her two diametrically opposed love interests: *Gone with the Wind* set among skyscrapers and newsrooms. Make one of her two paramours a young idealist, the other an old cynic. Make one poor, the other obscenely rich and powerful. Make one a young, idealistic, leftwing liberal investigative reporter, the other a sep- tuagenarian conservative media mogul. Young Jimmy Stewart vs. grizzled Claude Rains. Do that and you'll have a pretty good idea of what your book is about. Take a stab at it," I said, "then show me what you come up with."

"A paragraph?"

"One paragraph."

She put her notebook and pen back in her bag and had pulled one sleeve of her raincoat on when she stopped, weighing some- thing. Rising, leaning over the table, she planted a quick kiss on my cheek. As she did, I was given a bird's-eye view through the parted curtain of her lipstick-hued raincoat into the warm tawny depths of her considerable cleavage. Then—while I felt myself flushing—she sat back down, took a compact from her purse, and fixed her lipstick.

"Sorry," she said, patting her hair. "But I couldn't resist."

"In the future," I said clearing my throat, "I think it might be best if you try."

"What time have you got?" she asked mechanically.

"Quarter to eleven. I can just make my next train."

"And I have a date to meet," said Ashley.

"A date? At this hour?"

"Land sakes, it's not even eleven o'clock! My social life doesn't even roll up its sleeves till after midnight, usually."

"I'm glad to know we weren't socializing."

"For you I'm willing to make an exception."

She stood up. She seemed just then to tower over me.

"Let me get this," I said, picking up the check, though she'd scarcely acknowledged its presence. Flinging a few dollars on the table, I myself rose.

We stepped outdoors. The drizzle had ceased. The lights of the city burned neatly. Though I hadn't hailed it, a taxicab pulled over.

"I am so so very grateful for your advice."

"*De nada*," I said getting in.

"Sorry about the kiss. That was out of line, wasn't it?"

"I've been kissed before and survived."

"I believe it." She winked.

"Grand Central," I told the driver.

17. DINKUS

WITH GOOD FICTION, ANYWAY, THERE'S ALWAYS A SOLID PRESENT, a *here* and *now* from which events are described and in which everything is anchored and grounded.

But even that "here and now" can be deceptive. If "here" is the loft of a lakeside A-frame, and "now" is a rainy afternoon in May of 2014, is it the case that I am, in fact, "here" "now"—at this moment? Excepting some unpredictable occurrence, as to where I *really* am all I can tell you with any certainty is that I am no longer anywhere in particular. And as for the time, I can say only that for *you* the time is *now*. For me, having entered eternity, the time may best be described as a baffling blend of those equal opposites: forever and never.

Putting that aside, let's agree that my here and now consists of the moment on this balcony on this rainy day when, having spent the past eight or so hours writing my confessions, I am, for the first time, taking a break. Speaking of breaks, white spaces (or "space breaks," as they're sometimes called) are among a writer's best friends. They tell readers that a transition of some sort—spatial, temporal, topical, emotional, or formal—is about to occur, and best of all they do it without words. All one has to do is hit the return key an extra time and *voila*: instant transition. Add three asterisks to the white space and you create a "hard break," implying a more extreme transition. Traditionally, the three asterisks were arranged in a triangle to form an "asterism." Literally, "a group of stars."

In some cases, typographers replace the three asterisks with a "dinkus," a small drawing or artwork or other typographic symbol. Quite often the dinkus has its own symbolic import. For this confession, for instance, for reasons that ought to be plain enough, in keeping with my theme I've opted for twin bullets. That they are bullets isn't significant. That they are twins is.

So — space breaks communicate through implication. And as I often told my Metropolitan students: why state a thing when you can imply it? If you can suggest an emotional response by way of a facial expression, gesture, or action, for goodness' sake do so. *Never state what you can imply.* That's a golden rule of fiction writing, one you can "take to the bank" with you.

As for the break in question, the one I'm taking *here, now,* apart from two interruptions, one to go to the john and one to eat an insufficiently ripe Georgia peach, it is the first real break I've taken in eight (or so) hours. In that time I've filled four composition books and drained a half dozen fine-point Flairs (of which my professor father kept an ample supply for marking student papers) dry. With each page filled my handwriting has grown increasingly sloppy and cramped; my ass aches. I had to stop. I couldn't write another word.

Now the rain has stopped, too. The sky is clear. The same sun is setting — spectacularly. When my father bought this house that would make him so happy and that he'd eventually hang himself in, he must have been aware that it faced west, that its two large triangular windows would serve up spectacular sunsets such as this one, with its garish oranges, purples, magentas, and pinks, stretching behind trees on the far bank of the lake. No wonder in retirement, despite his drastically reduced income (the college provided no pension), he couldn't bear to leave. My brother's offer to pay his mortgage — to become his landlord, essentially — must have meant a lot to him. On the other hand it may have added to his sense of shame: a son shouldn't have to provide for his father. My guess is that in the end our father felt trapped here: that this house meant too much to him. It became a coffin wherein he felt buried—or he buried himself—alive. It was his soul, this house. I see that now. In my short time here it's become my soul. I suspect something of the sort could be said of my brother. Something about this place touched all three of us Detweiler's deeply.

It could even be said that this place overwhelmed us, that it did us in. "Beauty that kills." Where have I heard that phrase? Oh yes, I remember now. "The Story of an Hour," by Kate Chopin. Joy, not beauty. "The joy that kills." … *she had died of heart disease—of the joy that kills.*

Our father's love for this house, it removed him from the world, from his children and their mother. He couldn't have them and us. He'd had to choose.

He chose this house.

And it killed him.

Then it killed my brother.

Now it's going to kill me.

Like everything else at this hour, the oak beam over my head is burnished by the sunset's ruddy glow. I've filled four and a half composition books. I expect to fill several more. …

When I wrote that I was taking a break, I lied. While it's true that I took one, by the time I said I was doing so, said break had already occurred. I'd gone downstairs, brewed some coffee, and drank it with a rice cracker spread with avocado. When I wrote "I'm taking [a break]," obviously I was still writing, as I'm writing now. Anyway so much for my break.

• •

I'd been here three weeks when I saw the ghost, or ghosts. Or dreamed I saw them (or him).

Ghosts usually come at night. Not this one. He arrived one morning. I was painting my front door, re-painting it. The red that my father painted it decades earlier had faded badly, leaving the ghost of a red door. I chose a color verging on vermilion, a pigment originally made by grinding the mineral cinnabar (mercuric sulfide) into powder, and whose name derives from Old French: *vermeillon,* from *vermiculus,* the diminutive of the Latin *vermis,* meaning "worm." You could say I was painting my front door "worm-colored" when I heard the sound of a vehicle approaching. Since few cars enter or leave my cul-de-sac, the sound would have commanded my attention even if it hadn't been that of a European engine, and not just any European engine, but a vintage engine, and not just any vintage engine, but that of a sports car, and not just any vintage European sports car, but what despite the passage of forty years I recognized instantly as the silken splutter of a 1962 Alfa Romeo Giulietta Spider Veloce. Not my father's Alfa, that functionless heap rusting under a tattered tarp, but—as I saw stepping around the corner of the house with a two-inch trim brush in one hand and a freshly opened quart of "Scarlet Daze" in the other—a mint-condition version of the selfsame vehicle. The car's convertible top was down, the person behind the wheel plainly visible as he pulled into my driveway.

Its driver was my twin brother.

I just wrote (and you just read) "Its driver was my twin brother," but by that what do I mean? Do I mean "my twin brother" as in Gregory Detweiler, or "my twin brother" as in Brock Jones, PhD? Neither possibility was possible, or they were equally impossible. Greg Detweiler had become Brock Jones, PhD, who was dead: I knew, having buried him in the lake. That left Stewart Detweiler as the only impossible possibility.

Be all that as it may, my twin sat in the idling Alfa, smiling, smoking a cigarette: a younger, slicker, sleeker, more polished version of myself, about twenty years younger, thirty-five or so: the age at which all but the most hopelessly ugly men look handsome. He wore sunglasses, not cheapo knockoffs like the ones I'd bought to disguise myself at Kroger's, but stylish designer shades such as Marcello Mastroianni wears in 8½. His face was deeply tanned. He was the spit and shine of the person I'd wanted to be at sixteen, the summer I fantasized about driving off with my father's car and ended up rowing off in his boat instead.

The Alfa was the same red as my father's had been in its heyday, i.e., vermilion, the exact same shade as the paint in the can I held and that I had set to work refreshing the front door with, the color of molten lava, of … of … of Cunard Line passenger ship funnels, of the Tori Gates of Fushimi, of a hot midday sun seen from under a closed eyelid. Of blood (pigment) and buttermilk (binder). Scarlet Daze. Worm-red.

The Alpha's tube radio blared one of the following two songs:
1. *"Mais Que Nada"*
2. "The Girl from Ipanema"

By then it was obvious that I was experiencing either a ghost or a dream, or a ghost *in* a dream. About ghosts in fiction I feel more or less as I do about dreams. Unless you count that time in tenth grade when my brother and I visited Mr. Pennington, our chemistry teacher, in the big old Victorian where he lived between the firehouse and the train station, I never believed in ghosts. Mr. Pennington, who wore yellow cardigans and looked like TV's Mr. Rogers, claimed his house was haunted. As evidence he showed us the frayed badger hair shaving brush his "ghost" had dropped into his toilet every night for a week without fail while he slept. It mattered not whether the toilet lid had been up or down, or whether Mr. Pennington left the brush in the medicine chest or on the sink counter: come morning he would find it bobbing in the commode. Seated at his kitchen table, Gregory and I took turns holding the evidentiary shaving brush, marveling at its battered hairs and chipped brown Bakelite base, feeling as though we were holding the ghost: as if that shaving brush were the thing haunted or doing the haunting. That Gregory and I were both stoned on a joint Mr. Pennington shared with us didn't hurt.

The Alfa Romeo ghost tipped his Ray Bans.

Not that ghosts haven't played their part in literature. Without its phantom king there'd be no *Hamlet,* nor could Macbeth exist without Banquo's Ghost. Poe's telltale heart wouldn't beat on under the floorboards were it not animated by the ghost of a guilty conscience. And what of those wretches who populate all nine circles of the *Inferno?*

In some cases, ghosts and dreams come hand-in-hand. Dickens' *A Christmas Carol* is the prime example. As for dreams, if not for the false hope raised by a dream contrived by Zeus, Agamemnon might not have mustered his troops to siege Troy, therefore no Trojan War, therefore no *Iliad.* Before he murders the pawnbroker, in a dream symbolizing the soul's dual nature, torn between bloodlust and compassion, Raskolnikov revisits the time when as a boy he watched a group of peasants beat an old mare to death with pipes and crowbars. What is Alice's looking glass but a doorway to her dreams?

The trouble with fictional dreams is that in turning their nebulous objects into pellucid prose they tend to be too artificial. Whatever stuff dreams are made of, words aren't it. And since a work of fiction is its own dream, reading a fictional dream is like kissing through—not one, but *two* screen doors. So I'd tell my Metropolitan Writing Institute students.

• •

As the Alfa Ghost lit another cigarette (here the dream gets confusing as dreams will) a second vehicle wound its way down the unpaved road toward my cul-de-sac. Without looking up, by its splutters, belches, and backfirings, I'd have known it for a Mazda RX-7 with a blown muffler. It had the same cracked windshield, the same cockeyed pop-up headlights (one retracted, the other not), the same faded paintjob. It pulled alongside the Alfa, which had pulled alongside *my* Mazda, which I had parked alongside my dead father's rusty Alfa under its magnolia-leaf strewn tarp, so that in all a quartet of convertible roadsters, each a different shade of red, populated the driveway.

As it sat there with its beleaguered muffler system ticking, through the Mazda's cracked windshield I observed that the second ghost driver also looked like me, like Stewart Detweiler, but an older, grayer, heavier, decidedly un-snazzy Stewart Detweiler. Under a frayed alpaca sportscoat he wore a mock turtleneck.

From their respective roadsters both drivers emerged to confront each other. Words were exchanged. The next thing I knew both versions of myself were going at it in the grass and gravel while I stood there, watching, as Betsy Butterworth had watched Greg and me wrestle in that pine copse. I wanted to intervene, to break up the fight, make these twin ghosts see that they loved each other, they needed each other, they *were* each other. But I couldn't; I was frozen, paralyzed. I tried to cry out, "Guys, please,

please—*stop!*"—but the words caught in my throat. Meanwhile they kept fighting, rolling across the lawn, the dust clouds growing thicker, the sun shining higher and brighter, the air growing warmer, until the unsettling tableau before me resolved itself into a series of paintings, a Pollock, with its whirling dervishes of spattered paint, then a Miro, with its orbs and squiggles, then a Rothko, with its scumbled fields of incandescent color, until at last things coalesced into a dazzling vermilion blur. I blinked to find myself looking up through the branches of a sweetgum tree at the blinding bright noonday sun, drifting on a boat of some sort, bobbing and swaying on ocean waves.

It wasn't an ocean. It was a lake. There was the dock with its rusty ladder. There were the two badly weathered Adirondack chairs. The swaying boat was the hammock in which I'd dozed off after painting the front door red.

18. ROCKAWAY

IF ONLY NOVELS AND BOOKS IN GENERAL WERE LESS PREDICTABLE. Once I've grasped an author's intentions, once I've got the gist of the premise, the plot, the characters, the theme, the style—once I pretty much know what I'm reading—I lose all interest. I'm reminded of the opening of Dazai's *No Longer Human,* in which the narrator explains how, as a young boy, he'd been entranced by a railway overpass near to his home, how he'd stand at the center of the overpass for hours watching the trains pass to and fro beneath him, believing that the overpass had been built for that purpose, to feed his aesthetic poetic enjoyment. No sooner did he discover that in fact the structure served the prosaic utilitarian function of letting commuters cross the tracks that he lost all interest in it.

That's pretty much how I feel about most novels that I read.

What I'd really like to see for a change is a book that truly surprises me on every page. Not the skin-deep surprises called "plot twists," but surprises that cut down to the bone, deeper, to the roots, as it were, of a book's essence, its nature, making it entirely unpredictable and impossible to classify. With such a book no matter how many times you open it, or what page you open it to, it feels like you never read it before.

Such is the book I dreamed of writing. Indeed, I had written it. Not only had I written it, I'd written it several times. And now, with it thoroughly, *categorically* written, I had secured Elizabeth "Bitsy" Watson's promise to read it. At this juncture in my overextended back-story, that book — my book — is figuratively if not literally in Bitsy's hands.

The Damocles Sword of Bitsy's verdict hanging over my head made concentrating on other things impossible. Since I'd handed it to her — or rather to her assistant — myself, there could be no question as to Bitsy's having received the package. Assuming she had the package, had she opened it? If she had opened it, had she started reading? If she had started reading, how many pages had she read? I pictured her sitting in a comfortable upholstered arm-chair in her office — or no, on one of those couches associated with psychotherapists, the Edwardian kind with one end raised and a scrolled headrest: a fainting couch, yes: a fainting couch. Or in the living room of her East Hampton home, or the den — or the library — or a den that functioned as a library, with book-lined walls, or on a chaise longue on her porch, or her deck, or a wicker chair, yes, a wicker chair on her deck overlooking the Sound, or the bay, or whatever it was that her two million dollar Hampton home overlooked, in her bathrobe with a mug of tea or cof-fee at hand and the sun freshly risen, then reading on through the day, on the beach with the surf crashing and gulls wheeling and squawking, and on the train back into the city — or did she take the Jitney? — scowling at the conductor when he interrupts her to ask for her ticket in the middle of one of my best scenes, the one where Harris has trapped himself in the bathroom of a muffler repair shop. Or maybe she doesn't scowl; maybe she shakes her head and laughs as she absently hands the conductor her ticket or monthly pass. (*Would* she laugh at that scene, or would she find it in frightfully poor taste, with its loving depiction of public washroom decrepitude? No: she'd laugh; of course she'd laugh. Bitsy Watson is no prig!) ... Then back to her midtown office, to her fainting couch, where she keeps reading, refusing all calls, cancel-ling all appointments, unable to put the thing down ... and so on, for days, until   having not once interrupted her reading except to eat or drink or to attend to one or another mandatory bodily need—with tears in her eyes she turns the last page, jumps for joy, gets on the phone, ignites a bidding war, procures for her newest client an advance that breaks all records and enters the annals of publishing history. I smiled over my own morning coffee, letting myself wallow in this fantasy for another moment before shaking it out of my skull, thinking, Come now, Stewart, ol' boy; mustn't get our hopes too high. Oh but they were already as high as could be. You see I had faith—infinite faith—*(think positive!)* in Bitsy Watson. She'd recognize my achievement; she'd be my savior.

Something else was on my mind that morning, something at once bothersome and oddly assuring. Here you see me hesitate (okay, you don't *see* it, but take my word for it), since the thing that bothered me—that coated my morning with its icky residue—was: yes, another dream, for which I apologize. Then again I did warn you, didn't I, that this tale or confession or whatever it is contains two of everything? Be that as it may, before going to bed the night before I'd taken half an Ambien as I sometimes did when I felt a bout of insomnia coming. I did so reluctantly, knowing it probably wouldn't do any good, and if it did, I'd probably have strange dreams.

As things turned out I slept; and, yes, I had a strange dream.

In the dream I was in a library or office of some kind, don't ask where, when on a shelf I noticed a slim paperback bearing the title *Harris' Book*. Curious, I took it down. Sure enough it was *my* book, or a book I had apparently written, but unlike any book I'd ever known myself to write or imagined myself writing, first because it was such a slim volume, as thin as a volume of poetry, the spine no more than a quarter of an inch thick. The cover showed a torn segment of an American roadmap (for some reason I felt it was in the South or the Midwest, a city and environs, someplace like Athens, Ohio, or Macon, Georgia); at its peripheries the map faded to brown, so it looked as if it were emerging from a puddle of brown water, a mud puddle. It was an old-looking paperback, the paper already foxed at the edges. As I thumbed through it, I noticed that some pages were of slightly different sizes and had been pasted loose into the book, while other pages were missing. In some cases whole sections of the book were gone. Judging by the book's size, I calculated that at least two-thirds of its original contents had been eradicated. Taking the volume (by then I'd concluded that it was a galley and not a finished book) with me, I went in search of my publisher to find out just what in blazes was going on. The publishing entity turned out to be none I'd ever heard of, not even a known small or university press, but a New York publishing house called "Coliseum Press" or "Corinthian Press"—something like that. Since in the dream I was already in the city, I rode the subway to the address on the copyright page, some desolate, gloomy part of Queens, a district of warehouses and transit sheds in or near Flushing Meadows Park, where remnants of the '65 Worlds Fair were still to be found, also the site of the ash pits in *The Great Gatsby,* the ones lorded over by the billboard eyes of Dr. T. J. Eckleberg. On a desolate street a few blocks from the subway I found the building housing my publisher's office. Swollen with indignation, clutching the offensive galley, I made my way to the editor's desk, to find him stooped over a drafting table, smoking a cigar, wearing a clerk's visor and frilly sleeve garters, a character straight out of *The Front Page*, Eddie Robinson as Barton Keyes in *Double Indemnity*. Seeing me, he smiled around his stogie and extended a hand as stubby as his cigar for me to shake. Instead I shook the emaciated galley in his ruddy face and demanded of him theatrically:

"What is the *meaning* of this?"

"Why, that's your book," says the editor.

"What do you mean my *book*? You mean the galleys of it?"

Editor (waving cigar): "No, that's the finished book. We were just getting around to having a copy mailed to you."

Me: "Why wasn't I informed? What about copy edits?"

Editor: "Oh, we've taken care of all that."

Me: "This is a quarter of what I wrote! Where's the rest of it?"

Editor: "Sure we cut it. It was too long."

"Look at this thing! It's like a starved dog! It's hardly a book at all! It's more like … like a … pamphlet. And look at this cover!"

Editor: "What, you don't you like it?"

Me: "It looks like a scrap of roadmap in a mud puddle."

Editor: "Well—."

Me: "You've ruined my book! I'll sue you!"

Editor: "Whaddya mean, 'ruined'? It's published. Aren't you glad it's published?"

Me: "I want my name taken off this monstrosity! I want every last one of these so-called books pulped and my original manuscript returned to me! I refuse to have any part of this—this *insult!* ... you—you—"

Editor: "Calm down, or I'll ask you to leave or have you thrown out. Better still ..." From a shoulder holster that had escaped my notice he withdraws a snub-nose and waves it under my jaw. "... I'll blow your brains out and teach you a lesson in manners."

• •

Despite this and despite my fretting over Bitsy's response to my novel, I tried to get some work done. It was a Sunday. I had two classes to prepare for that week. For ten[chk?] years I'd been teaching at Metropolitan. Ten[?] years I had spent mucking the Augean Stables of my students' works-in-progress, shoveling manure-fouled sawdust and straw, replacing it with golden hay and fresh clover. For ten[?] years like Rimbaud I had dragged myself through stinking alleyways of putrid prose, breath held, eyes closed, waiting for the day to dawn when at last I'd make my own offering to the muses.

At my table bright with morning sunshine, with the fluorescent orange Metropolitan Writing Institute folder open before me, wearing my half-moon reading glasses, a demitasse of *espresso macchiatto* at arm's reach, I read Alice Nordland's latest offering. My assault on her previous effort had failed to induce the Dungeons and Dragons Queen to drop the class. In my response to it—the one about the love affair between the Second to Princess Ourania and her slave Lilith (or was it Princess Lilith and her slave Ourania?), I'd suggested she try writing "something a little closer to [her] own experience." Apparently Alice, a dog walker by trade, had taken my suggestion to heart. Abandoning her medieval milieu, she applied her spurious imagination to a contemporary setting and theme, a story about a professional dog walker. Well, I thought, reading on, it's an improvement. But as I kept turning pages my sense of relief dissolved into something more like horror. As the story progressed, the female dog walker identified more and more with her charges, taking on their behaviors, sniffing at flower beds, chasing vehicles, growling, sniffing, barking at, and biting people. At one point, she squats to pee on a fire hydrant. The climactic scene has the protagonist not only sniffing but eating another dog's shit, standing on a Park Slope sidewalk on a sunny afternoon smearing feces over her face as pedestrians avoid her.

I closed the folder and sat there, at my sunshine-flooded table, my face buried in my hands. What could I possibly say about this? Unlike the ugly Duchess in *Alice in Wonderland*, I struggled to find a moral or anything redeeming in Ms. Nordland's tale. Then again, it couldn't be said that she hadn't accomplished something. She'd invented a new genre: the Coprophagious Dog Walker Story. That's it, I thought: I'll praise her originality; I'll applaud the boldness of her premise.

Then I thought: are you *kidding*? This doomsday formula must never leave the biological weapons facility. It should be buried deep within a mountain in the Nevada desert, alongside drums of assorted nuclear waste and the carcasses of mad cows. With my Sharpie on the story's last page I wrote: *You've taken some big risks here, which is admirable.* My Sharpie and I hesitated. *Then again,* I almost but didn't add, *this story should be leashed, guttered, and cleaned up after.*

I turned to the next submission.

But that was it for me; I couldn't go on.

• •

It was a sunny day. Why not take it off? Take a walk in the park. Visit a museum or two. I was checking the Met's Sunday schedule when a ping announced an incoming email.

From: *abridges@hotmail.org*
Subject: *guess what?*
Message:

Elizabeth Watson wants to read my novel!

My reply:

What???

What had happened was this: Based on her instructor's tongue-in-cheek suggestions, per his recommendation, Ashley had written a pitch paragraph, but then, with neither his prior knowledge nor his consent, she'd fashioned it into a query letter—a letter from an author to a prospective editor or agent inviting them to read their manuscript. Said letter Ashley printed and signed fifty copies of and sent off to as many agents, including Elizabeth "Bitsy" Watson, who had responded in the affirmative.

Nor was Bitsy alone. Of fifty agents queried, twenty-six had requested the manuscript of "Leaving Whynot," Ashley's novel. Some did more than request: they cajoled, implored, pleaded. A few even offered sight unseen to represent it.

I ask you, if at all possible, Dear Reader, to imagine the mixture of feelings that were mine at this moment. You would have to imagine an amalgam of outrage, horror, self-pity, spite, envy, confusion, admiration, insult, and amusement all at once, just for openers. Following a banshee wail and assorted furniture kicking, I took comfort in the fact that Bitsy would never read Ashley Bridge's novel, for the simple reason that Ashley Bridge's novel did not exist.

No sooner did it materialize than my comfort turned to shame. There I was, Stewart Detweiler, Senior Instructor at the Metropolitan Writing Institute, counting on the failure of one of his own students, wishing for it, hoping for it. I felt awful then, so awful I went to my refrigerator, opened the freezer, found the bottle of gin I kept cold in there, poured a jigger's worth into a glass, and—with the clock on the kitchen wall reminding me that it was not even noon—drank it down in one gulp. Unabetted by vermouth or even olive juice, the lousy gin went down like battery acid, which did not stop me from pouring and gulping another jigger's worth.

Thus fortified, back at my computer I responded to Ashley's email:

You haven't <u>got</u> a novel!

To which she replied:

I know. What should I do?

—a smiley emoticon rode shotgun next to "I know."
I asked her where she was and what she was up to.

Headed to the Rockaways. Wanna come?

• •

Each of us imagines a time and place in the not-too-distant future when we will be happy, healthy, successful, loved, and respected. In this magical place the weather is always good. We are in love. We are not sick or old or out of shape or exhausted or sad or angry or petty or spiteful or petulant or dyspeptic or cynical. Our clothes fit perfectly. Our shoes are polished and in good condition. We're not losing our hair. We are wrinkle and blemish free and altogether photogenic. The things that annoy, perturb, terrify, haunt, humiliate, dispirit, and demoralize us don't exist there. Something about the place suggests an island. There may be palm trees or olive groves; that the ocean is nearby is unquestionable, but it matters not. What matters is that in this place you feel like the person you were always meant to be, the person you are, really, except that you haven't had the chance to be that person in a while. Instead you've been this other person who is cynical, dyspeptic, petulant, going bald and getting fat ... whose ears ring and whose prostate is enlarged ... all the things that, in this other place, this magical place, you aren't and never were. What's curious about this place we're talking about is that you, who believe in so few things, who are in no sense religious and find the idea of heaven laughably absurd, not only accept its existence as something devoutly to be wished for, but consider it to be real, proximate, and inevitable.

Nor are you alone. Everyone believes in this same, or a similar, place. Not only do they believe in it, they spend much of their emotional lives there.

That sunny Sunday afternoon, for me, Rockaway Beach was that place.

• •

I met Ashley there. She stood alone on the deserted boardwalk, framed by sky and water: a sailing yacht in mid-ocean, lightly sparred. Over her usual painted-on jeans tucked into vinyl boots she wore a scarlet cape with a dark fur collar.

"Hello there," she said, offering me first one cheek then the other to kiss. She wasted no time taking my arm. "Shall we?" she said.

The day was as windy as it was bright. We walked into the sun and wind. The surf was powerful. I couldn't remember when I had last been to the shore. I'd forgotten just how good it feels to exist in close proximity to that salty nauseating expansiveness. There were few people out on the boardwalk and fewer still on the beach itself. Recalling Frost's "Once by the Pacific," I recited the poem from memory, a recitation I would refrain here were I not prohibited from doing so by the greedy executors of the Frost estate, who, should this confession ever find its way into print, would charge its publisher an arm and a leg for my having quoted it, given which said presumed publisher, being a fucking cheapskate like them all, would cease and desist. Ergo I cannot quote the poem's first line, describing how the "shattered water" generated a "misty din," or the second, in which the "great waves" overlook other similar waves "coming in," or the third, in which the same waves consider "doing something" to the shoreline, or the fourth line, which goes on to say that the "something" under consideration by the waves (water) was unlike anything that it/they had ever done to "land before."

"That's beautiful," said Ashley. "Did you write it?"

"Robert Frost."

"I know him. I mean, I've read some of his poems."

I considered letting her in on the demons lurking behind every line, Frost's depressed mother, his alcoholic father, a sister dead at 53 in the state mental hospital to which he had committed her, the poet's own dark impulses and depressions, then thought: why spoil a perfectly good beach poem? "It may be the first and only apocalyptic sonnet ever written," I said. "Frost chose the form for its rhyming couplets, since they sound like waves crashing."

"How do you know so much?"

"Hey, it's what they pay me the big bucks for."

"Have they paid you for this?" Stopping abruptly, she pulled me close and kissed me ... well, let's just say she kissed me *hard*.

"You shouldn't do that," I said.

"Why not?"

"Because."

"Because what?"

"Need I remind you that you're my student?"

"Need I remind you of *this*?"

Again she kissed me, even harder this time. I couldn't remember when I'd last been kissed like that, possibly the last time I'd been to the beach: a long time. On my suddenly chapped lips I recognized the taste of lipstick, something else that hadn't occurred to me in a while. While being kissed by her for a moment I imagined that the lips pressed to mine weren't Ashley Bridges' but Betsy Butterworth's, that I was back in fourth or fifth grade playing spin-the-bottle at a party, but instead of my brother scoring Betsy's kiss it was my spin of the empty Coca-Cola bottle that had won me the Grand Prize of her lips.

"You keep this up," I said when she stopped, "I may have to apply for that hazardous duty pay you mentioned."

"Plus overtime!"

Once more she kissed me, or we kissed each other, it being reciprocal by now. Alongside Ashley's kisses her yet-to-be-written but already sought-after novel lumbered elephant-like in my consciousness, but as that space was large enough to accommodate Ashley's kisses and the Atlantic Ocean, for the time being at least the beast was easily ignored. Ashley's tongue, I noted, tasted of vanilla. Between breaths I said:

"You know, I'm old enough to be your father."

"Talk about clichés!" said Ashley with a blend of breathlessness, disgust, and delight. "The perpetual professor. The perennial pedagogue. Know what I say to that?"

"No. What do you say?"

"*Goodbye, Mr. Chips.*"

This time when she kissed me, she simultaneously grabbed the hand in which I held a bag of saltwater taffy I'd bought on my way to the boardwalk, bringing it forcibly to the hollow (gulf? bay?

tidal basin?) of her bosom. The taffy fell into a sand dune.

"I'm out of practice," I announced, coming up for air.

"Out of practice or out of shape?"

"Both. I should get back into doing push-ups. Would you believe I used to be able to do seventy-five? No fooling. Now I probably can't even do fifty. Matter of fact…"

What impulse overtook me I can't say for sure, but there and then I dropped and did a set on the boardwalk, managing only thirty-five before my arms quivered and gave out on me.

"You all right?" she said as I rose, wiping my hands. "Goodness—your face is beet red!"

" 'Beet red.' Now where have I heard that before?"

"Red as a brick? A lobster? A Valentine?"

"How about just plain red and to hell with it?"

We continued along the boardwalk.

"May I ask you something, Ashley?"

"Shoot."

"Have you always gotten everything you want?"

"Gadzooks! Of course not! What makes you say that?"

"What haven't you gotten?"

"Everything!"

I looked at her searchingly.

"That's what I want. Everything. And I haven't gotten it—yet! My turn to ask you something now."

I braced myself.

"What made you want to be a writer?"

With a wistful sigh I explained: How from early on I'd wanted to be an artist. How my kindergarten teacher kissed me. How I'd sought to distinguish myself from my twin brother.

"You're a *twin*?"

I nodded. "Gregory, that's my brother's name. Or was."

"What does he do?"

"He's a motivational guru," I said, failing to hide my distaste for the term.

"A what?"

"He teaches people how to reinvent themselves."

"That sounds really interesting. Are you and he close?"

"We were. No longer. We don't speak anymore."

"Oh, no! Why not?"

"It's complicated to explain. Let's just say he changed."

"It's sad when brothers don't get along."

"Yes, it is. Very sad."

"What's it like being a twin?"

It was a question I'd been asked often. I gave the same answer as always: "What's it like to not be one?"

"Did you ever change places?"

In drastically abridged form I relayed the tale of the substitute teacher in the portable classroom.

"Is your brother—Gregory, right? Is Gregory happy?"

"I suppose," I said. "You'd have to ask him."

"Are you?"

"Am I allowed to plead the fifth?"

"No."

"In that case, I guess so."

"You *guess* so? That's a very qualified yes."

"What can I say? I lead a very qualified existence."

"Why is your happiness so qualified, Detweiler?"

"Where would you like me to start?"

"Anywhere will do fine."

"Heck, Ashley, I don't know. I suppose I'm a bit—cliché alert—artistically frustrated. I thought I'd be further along in some way. A shelf of books. Two novels at least. A small but loyal readership. My name in 'Who's Who of Contemporary American Authors.' Something like that." I shrugged. (What would authors do without shrugs?) "But then I look at the bright side. I'm healthy, more or less. My ears ring, my knees creak. I've got a prostate the size of a sovereign landlocked microstate. But I've got a strong ticker and for a northeasterner my lungs are pretty clear since I never smoked. And look here," I said, stopping to pinch an inch, or three. "Hardly any belly fat! Pretty good for a guy who's more than halfway to the grave, eh?"

"Oh stop it!"

"I'm ambulatory, let's agree on that much. And now might I ask you something?"

"Go on."

"Why are you and I always talking about me?"

"It must be our favorite subject."

"It's not *my* favorite subject."

"'*Mankind is not a subject of fiction; he is the only subject.*' You said that the first day of class. Remember?"

"Forster. And he said 'man', not mankind. For sure he didn't say Stewart Detweiler."

"Stewart Detweiler's a man."

"Stewart Detweiler's a bore. Let's change the subject. Let's talk about you. Tell me something I don't know about you. Anything."

"When I was little, I used to be an aural Tom."

"A what?"

"A Peeping Tom, only instead of my eyes I used my ears."

"An eavesdropper, you mean?"

"No, I mean an aural Tom. That's what I called it. It started the first summer my parents sent me off to a sleepaway camp in the piney hills of Central Mississippi. 'Twin Lakes', that was the name of the camp, since there were two lakes, one right next to the other. We had swimming and boating and crafts and drama productions. One of the counselors was Miss Hathaway. She had the most beautiful hair and eyes you ever saw. And she dressed so beautifully, too, in long, sheer, white summer dresses. The rest of us all wore jeans. She played piano. One night, in the middle of the night, she was practicing alone in the music studio. I woke up and heard it. It must have been three or four o'clock in the morning. I couldn't sleep. In my pajamas I went out for a walk. The studio was a dozen yards from my cabin. It had these big plate-glass windows looking over one of the two lakes. Between it and the lake was this big rock. The Dog Rock, we called it, since it sort of looked like a dog. I spent the next hour hidden behind that rock, listening to Miss Hathaway practice, playing Poulenc's Fifth Nocturne, the same eight bars over and over. I was mesmerized. Not by the music, or not just by the music. It was the fact that I was listening to her playing without her knowing it, without her having any notion that I was there listening, that she had an audience, that she was performing *for me*. You know the thing about if a tree falls in the woods and there's nobody there to hear it, does it make a sound? Poulenc's music was the tree. Miss Hathaway's playing was the axe that made it fall. And thanks to me hiding behind that rock, it made a sound. Anyway that's how I became an aural Tom. From then on for the next year and a half I never missed an opportunity to eavesdrop whenever I could."

"What made you stop?"

"One day my mother caught me eavesdropping on her from underneath the dining room table while she was gossiping on the phone with one of my aunts. She had my daddy give me a whipping. That did the trick. From then on I did my eavesdropping on paper."

"On paper?"

"In my imagination. Eavesdropping on my own made-up stories and characters."

"Speaking of which," I said, "what about that novel of yours, the one you haven't written yet, the one twenty-eight agents including Elizabeth Watson want to read."

Ashley stopped walking and faced me, bouncing on her feet. "Isn't it terrific?"

"Sure, it's great. But now what? You can't stall forever. If you want to keep those agents hooked, you'll have to come up with something—fifty pages, a couple chapters. Otherwise they may just call your bluff."

"My bluff!"

"Isn't that what they call it when you bet on an empty hand?"

"My hand is *not* empty!"

"With all due respect, you don't have a novel. You've got a few random scenes that don't add up to twenty-five pages. To keep an agent interested you'll have to send them a kickass first chapter at the very least. And as soon as possible."

"Are you offering to help?" Said with an enticing smile.

• •

To understand my response to that question some psychology is in order, for as best as I'm able to interpret things at that precise moment Ashley's novel—the one she hadn't written—and mine (the one already in Elizabeth Watson's hands), became quantumly entangled. Yes, I wanted to help Ashley, but largely because in helping her I hoped to help myself or at least to take my mind off my own helplessness, there being no greater helplessness than that of a dejected author whose manuscript is under consideration by an agent. Having delivered their child to the freshman dorm on the first day of college, parents must feel something of the sort. On one hand they hope their progeny will succeed and be happy; on the other they pray they won't be lured into a Satanic cult or a terrorist organization or gang raped by the varsity football team.

But something less conscious lay behind my desire to help Ashley: my inability to bear the thought of her achieving in a matter of weeks what in thirty-plus years I myself had failed to and might never achieve. The triumph of shallow cunning commercialism over authentic artistic struggle, of surface over substance, of youthful dazzle over depth. That I couldn't bear.

Helping with a selfish motive: this was the grave sin for which I would pay dearly. But then—that day—the weather was fair. The sun shone. The wind blew. The surf roared.

"Yes," I said, returning Ashley's smile. "I'm offering to help. I just hate to see you blow this chance." My words were prophetic in several ways.

•   •

With arms encircling each other's waists we walked east along the boardwalk as far as Jacob Riis Park. By the time we got there Ashley and I had agreed to spend the following weekend, and, if necessary, the one after that together working on her novel.

"This is so generous of you," she said. "I'm not sure how I'll be able to thank you."

"You'll think of something," I shouldn't have said.

Out of nowhere clouds had rolled in. Soon they filled the sky, black and ominous. When the rain came we joined the water bottles, used condoms, and other trash under the boardwalk.

"Now what in heaven's name do you suppose we should do while waiting for this little ol' monsoon to pass?"

"Don't look at me," I said.

"That's just what I'm doing."

She did more than look: she gazed, her eyes sparkling again. (Ashley is the one person I've ever met able to make them do so at will.)

"I must warn you," she said, planting a series of kisses along my jawline. "I don't believe in sex on the first date. Not until after a dozen kisses." Another kiss. "That makes eleven."

The rain fell harder now, dribbling down between the board-walk's planks, forming a nearly solid transparent curtain where it rolled over the sides. She kissed me once more—this time on the lips. "...and...twelve!" she said, and reached for my buckle.

Dear Reader, apart from a few choice passages of my father's copy of *My Secret Life* that I read clandestinely for educative purposes at age twelve, I've never gotten much out of sex scenes in books. That applies to reading *and* writing them, something I've never been good at, owing mainly to a lack of interest—not in sex, mind you, but in the mechanics of who does or did what to whom. Beyond that the characters engage in activities in excess of kissing that fuse them fervently through all of their senses, what more needs saying? Were I to tell you, for instance, that on that ultimately stormy afternoon beneath that lubricated boardwalk at Rockaway Beach, with the knees of her designer jeans buried in the sand and my brown corduroys hugging my ankles, Ashley Bridges fellated me to a shivering, stuttering, knee-jerking climax, that, having swallowed my considerable discharge of semen, using the back of her small pale hand for a napkin, she wiped her lips, and, having done so, offered me the most candid and reassuring of smiles—what, if anything, would such details add, really, to the bald fact of her having sucked me off?

"Did you enjoy that, Professor?"

"Beats putting socks on wet feet," I said.

• •

When the rain subsided, we made our way to the nearest shelter, a falafel joint where, over what turned into dinner, we discussed Ashley's—I almost said "Ashley's novel"—Ashley's novel-in-embryo.

"Listen," I said. "I don't think you should send your book to Bitsy Watson."

"You said she's the best agent in New York."

"I said she's the biggest agent, I didn't say she's the best — not for you, anyway. She's old. She's got a million authors, most of them already more famous than you or I will ever be. She's not what you'd call hungry. Even assuming Ms. Watson (I couldn't bring myself to say 'Bitsy') does take you on, you'd be a speck of dust in her galaxy, a grain of sand on the beach of her bestselling authors client list." I shook my head. "You need someone young, someone hungry, someone who'll really pay attention not just to this one project of yours, but to your entire career."

"Who might that be?"

"Sally Treadwell. My agent. I'll speak with her. I'll do better than that. I'll pitch your project so hard she won't know what hit her."

"You'd do that — introduce me to your agent?"

"I'll be doing you both a favor, sending her someone as young and talented as you. It won't make me look bad, either."

"I don't know what to say."

"Say nothing. Leave things to me. Meanwhile let's focus on how to get this book of yours into halfway decent shape."

We solidified our plans to get together and work on it.

Afterwards, holding hands all the way, we rode the subway back to Manhattan. At Grand Central, per what had become our routine, we parted ways and I caught my train up to the Bronx, but not before stopping at a Duane Reade (Duane Reade ... Dear Reader ...) in the terminal to pick up the prescription Dr. Snyder's office had phoned in for me.

19. VISITATIONS & CONSTRAINTS

LIKE DES ESSEINTES IN HIS FONTENAY FORTRESS, I, TOO, HAVE MADE eccentric improvements during my time here to what, for all intents and purposes, has become *my* lake house. I will describe some of those improvements presently. First, some prefatory remarks.

Occasionally as a Senior Instructor at the Metropolitan Writing Institute I would give my students exercises. My favorite was the "Boring Exercise." It consisted of writing two one-minute pieces, each about a page long. The object of the first piece was to gain and hold our attention by any means possible. The object of the second piece was to "bore us stiff." When they had written both pieces, without saying which piece they were reading, in the same tone, with another student keeping time, I'd have them read both. Afterwards, we'd take a hand vote to see which of the two pieces we preferred. More often than not, the piece that was meant to be boring won.

When students tried to be interesting, they invariably succumbed to clichés of substance and style. They described car crashes, fist-fights, murder, or pornographic sex scenes in panting prose studded with perfunctory modifiers ("suddenly", "cautiously", "silently") and worn-out catch phrases ("the next thing she knew", "to her complete surprise", etc.).

When they tried to be boring, on the other hand, their better writing angels guided them. One student wrote an enchanting description of white paint drying on a wall; another portrayed a doddering old man's quest to arrive at the perfect soft-boiled egg, with amusing results.

While anyone can be unintentionally boring, to be boring on purpose takes great skill. In fact it's impossible, since any such effort is doomed to give rise to ingenuity and originality.

Something of the sort can be said of any constraint we impose on ourselves as writers. The more challenging the constraint, the less predictable and dull the result.

Sometimes I'd even bring a literal bowl of constraints to class, an Indian offering bowl of hammered copper inlaid with a brass and turquoise mosaic of Lord Ganesha, the elephant-headed deity of abundance, son of Shiva and Parvati. According to Hindu myth, one day, wishing to bathe in private, Parvati had her son guard the front door of their house. In due course Lord Shiva arrived home only to be told by his son that he couldn't enter. In his fury, Shiva severed Ganesha's head, whereupon Parvati vowed to destroy all of creation—a threat Lord Brahma averted by replacing Ganesha's head with that of an elephant. This bowl I would fill with constraints, each printed on a fortune-cookie-like strip of paper, and pass around the conference room table. Each student would pick one constraint from the bowl (those wanting an extra challenge could pick two).

• •

Back to my need to describe to you some of the improvements I've made to this house in my time here. With respect to thrills, the subject holds little intrinsic promise. Apply a draconian constraint or two, however, and suddenly matters take on a brighter, more favorable aspect.

Constraint #1: Begin each sentence with the next letter of the alphabet. An aesthete my father was not. Books decorated his home. Call it "library chic." Dust jacket spines determined the colors of whole walls. Entire floors were carpeted with plush paperbacks. Forming a frieze over the fireplace: Will and Ariel Durant's

The Story of Civilization—all eleven volumes. Garnishing the gateleg table: Gibbon's *Decline and Fall of the Roman Empire.* *Constraint #2: Write only sentences of 100 words or more.* Given how, with its battleship gray siding, its steep pitched, prow-like roof, its forecastle-like deck, its triangular bridge windows facing the lake's wide waters, my father's A-frame resembled a WWI gunboat, in redecorating it I emphasized its nautical aspects, taking as my inspiration D'Annunzio's *Vittoriale degli italiani,* his hillside estate in Gardone, for which, with Mussolini's blessing, the decadent author and fervent nationalist had the entire bow section of the cruiser *Puglia* (aboard which he'd served during the Battle of Fiume) dismantled and reconstructed, its prow pointed over Lake Garda toward the Adriatic, poised to "re-conquer the Dalmatian shores."

Constraint #3: Write only sentences or phrases of 6 words or less. Walls: sea mist blue. Kitchen cabinets of knotty pine. Rattan shades. Navy pillows with white piping. Captain's chairs. Decorative oars over French doors. Green/red port/starboard deck lights. Conch shell and seahorse bathroom wallpaper.

Constraint #4: Sentences backward only write. Of natural sisal fibers derived from the long green leaves of the *agave sisalana* cactus plant would the loft stair carpeting be made.

Constraint #5: Describe things strictly in terms of smell. Opened, each drawer, closet, and cabinet emitted a maritime perfume, a nautical ectoplasm, a symphony or sonata of seagoing scents featuring (but not limited to) the following essences:

1. funnel smoke
2. camphor
3. salt marsh
4. pipe tobacco
5. marine grease
6. bilge water

The N+7 constraint (courtesy of Jean Lescur): Excluding proper nouns, replace every noun in a given text with the seventh following noun in a dictionary of your choice. Or choose a different following noun. Original: "This house is like an ocean liner. At night, her mast and deck lights ablaze, she cuts through a frothy sea of moonlit hydrangeas and iceberg rhododendrons. Her decks ascend toward the starry sky: A-deck, B-deck, saloon, shelter, promenade, and lifeboat. Listen: *The Blue Danube* pours from her portholes."

N+7: "This household is like an oddball link. At nightlight, her mastiff and decoy light-years ablaze, she cuts through a frothy seal of moonlit hydrangeas and identikit rices. Her decoys ascend toward the starry slacker: A-decoy, B-decoy, salver, shield, pronoun, and lift. Listen: *The Bluff Danube* pours from her posers."

N+1: "This houseboat is like an octagon linesman. At nightcap, her mastectomy and deckhand lighters ablaze, she cuts through a frothy seabird of moonlit hydrangeas and icicle rhombuss. Her deckhands ascend toward the starry skydiver: A-deckhand, B-deckhand, salt, shepherd, promise, and lifeguard. Listen: *The Bluebell Danube* pours from her porticos."

N+3: "This housebreaker is like an octogenarian lingo. At nightdress, her mastermind and decline lightings ablaze, she cuts through a frothy seafood of moonlit hydrangeas and iconoclast rhythms. Her declines ascend toward the starry skylight: A-decline, B-decline, salute, sherbet, promoter, and lifer. Listen: *The Bluebird Danube* pours from her portmanteaus."

N+4: "This housecoat is like an octopus linguist. At nightgown, her masterpiece and decongestant lightnings ablaze, she cuts through a frothy seafront of moonlit hydrangeas and idea ribs. Her decongestants ascend toward the starry skyline: A-decongestant, B-decongestant, salvage, sheriff, promotion, and lifespan. Listen: *The Bluebottle Danube* pours from her portraits."

Haiku constraint: Turn your sentences into poems of seventeen syllables, in three lines of five, seven, and five:

House Cuts through Ocean
Blazing that Ship Decked Out
To the Night in Lights

• •

The house being small and my budget being limitless, I could indulge my every whim. The window of the front door—the exterior of which I had already painted red, and that, to insure privacy, my father had covered with a striped bedsheet—I replaced with a made-to-order window of stained-glass based on a design made after one of those paintings of the sinking *Titanic* I'd discovered in my father's basement studio. It seems fitting to me now, given the lives that had met or would meet their doom there, that this vessel-like house should greet visitors with that symbol.

The entire house, I decided, inside and out, should be painted a panoply of seaworthy shades, from Gale Force Gray to Bay of Fundy Blue; from Coastal Fog Sapphire to Breezy Point Beige; from Driftwood Umber to Nitrogen Narcosis Azure…Perusing the names on the paint chip racks at Lowe's, I wondered if perhaps I'd missed my calling as a designator of Paint Colors. I pictured a bespectacled man in a lab coat tucked away in the bowels of the Sherwin William's factory doing nothing else all day but coming up with names for paints. A pigment poet. A tint tagger!

"All art is quite useless." —Wilde.

"Everyone knows the usefulness of what is useful; but few know the usefulness of what is useless." —Zhuang Zi.

• •

What, you have every right to ask, does all this have to do with my getting a phone call from Adam Swann? Nothing, except that the call happened to come while I was in the throes of painting the deck boards White Star Line Buff. I really shouldn't have answered. The call, that is. The phone was on the deck rail next to the screwdriver with which I had pried open the paint can. Though I recognized the area code as that of my recently disconnected landline, the number that followed was unfamiliar to me. It was one of many unfamiliar phone numbers that surfaced daily on my cellphone screen, most of which I noted but otherwise ignored. Those that recurred persistently I blocked. Though many callers left voice-mails, usually I kept the volume down or off so I wouldn't have to hear them. If I listened to the messages at all, I did so usually long after they'd been left.

This time, though, I'd left the volume on, and, for some reason—maybe because my fingers were covered with paint and I didn't want to get any on the phone—I listened:

Hello there, Brock! Adam Swann here. How are you? Listen, I've been trying to get in touch with you. Looks like I'm not alone. I spoke with Dawn, who said that you're still taking some time for yourself. That's great; we all need to take some time for ourselves. It's something I've been meaning to do myself for a while now, only I never seem to get around to it. Anyway I hope you don't mind my calling you at your personal number. It's not something I'd normally do. I absolutely respect your privacy. But as you know the taping for the upcoming PBS pledge break lecture program is scheduled for less than two weeks from now up in Kingston, where we've booked studio time. Anyway, Brock, based on what Dawn said I gather this leave-of-absence or whatever you're calling it is indefinite? That you're not sure, or she isn't sure, when you plan to be back in action? Meaning you're not sure (or she's not sure) if you'll be available for the taping? Because if that's the case, I mean it's fine in the sense that at least technically we have a 72-hour cancellation window. With the studio, I mean. So we can definitely postpone taping—if absolutely necessary, if we have to. Naturally if you're uncomfortable with going ahead at this time for whatever reason we don't have to. I sure don't want us to go ahead if you're not feeling totally there with it. You should feel comfortable. That's crucial. I mean what point would there be otherwise, right? What I mean, what I'm saying is, anything I can do to accommodate you, I'm absolutely...If we have to put it off for, say, you know, a week or two, or even a month, that's not a problem, not a huge problem. We could even postpone until the next pledge drive, if it comes to that. The thing is, what I need from you, Brock, the reason I'm calling, the main reason aside from just to, you know, touch base and see how you're doing, is to find out exactly what it is that you'd like to do, that you need, if there's anything, anything at all, that I myself or anyone else can do to accommodate your needs at this time and make this project come together as smoothly as possible so it's a great experience for everyone. Of course, you know, needless to say there are legal and reputational ramifications should we be forced for whatever reason to postpone beyond a certain date, or, God forbid, to can-

cel—which, frankly, wouldn't be in anyone's best interest, in fact
it would be a pretty bad thing at least as far as any future contracts
with PBS would be concerned, yours and mine. I mean it would
leave a pretty sour taste in quite a few mouths. Which is why I'm
hoping to hear back from you as soon as possible so we can make
some decisions here. As I said, we can go ahead with the May tap-
ing; or we can possibly postpone in time for the next pledge drive,
which is something they may go for. Either way, if you possibly
can, do please give me a call ASAP. And I hope you're doing—

Sticky hands or no, I picked the phone up.

"This is Brock Jones, PhD."

"Brock! Man—wow! This is great. I mean, it's great to hear
your voice. I mean... How *are* you?"

"Fine."

"Great. I mean—gee, that's great!"

"When is this show supposed to be?"

"Show? Oh, the taping, you mean?"

"This taping. When is it?"

"The studio's booked for the weekend starting on Thursday the
Fifteenth, a little over two weeks from now. But we can always—"

"Where?"

"Excuse me?"

"Where's the studio?"

"United Media. In Kingston, New York. But if we need to—"

"What time?"

"Sorry?"

"What time do you need me there?"

"Well, normally we start rehearsing the day be—"

"No rehearsal."

"What?"

"When will you be ready to start taping?"

"You mean before the live audience?"

"Yes, before the live audience."

"The sixteenth."

"Friday?"

"Yes, Friday. But—"

"What time?"

"Nine."

"A.M. or p.m.?"

"A.M."

"Fine. I'll be there nine a.m."

"No rehearsal?"

"No rehearsal. Or you can call the whole thing off. Whatever you prefer."

A pause during which I scanned the lake for the red boat. At first I didn't see it, but it was there, all right, way out at the lake's center, a pinprick of red on that pale blue expanse; a drop of blood on the horizon.

"Okay," said Adam Swann. "Fine. If that's what works best for you."

"It works best for me," I said, and hung up—or did whatever it is that one does these days to terminate a phone call.

Thus I set the publication date for "Brock Jones, PhD," only instead of print my masterpiece would debut on semi-live television. Only then would I be born—or re-born. Like a butterfly from its chrysalis, on Friday, May 16, at 9 o'clock a.m., or whenever the taped program aired, Brock Jones, PhD would emerge, or re-emerge, and take flight. There would follow in short order my latest book—the one I had gone into hiding to compose. A breakthrough work, entirely without precedent, one of imposing literary merit, unlike any ever written before. The book about twins; about a twin who assumes the identity of his dead equal opposite. "Duplicity." I saw the cover: a mottled blue sea, the title treading water at its center in austere sans-serif ALL-CAPS, framed by one or two austere rectangles, its only other embellishment a schematic of an impossible object known as the "Penrose Square":

I might even call the book "Penrose Square"—not a bad-sounding title at that. The cover would have much in common with the covers of the old Albatross Edition and Olympia Press paperbacks respectively of the '30s and '50s, the latter infamous for its motley mix of serious literature and smut (both, in the case of *Lolita*); one of those covers whose sublime starkness sets it far apart from all others but that publishers seldom risk.

And here was the beauty part: since no one in the world knew that Brock Jones, PhD had a twin, or *had* had one, the book would be read as a novel, one rich in metaphoric implications. Like *Moby Dick*'s white whale, the twin metaphor would operate on multiple levels: self-invention, the divided self, how our contradictory natures and impulses destroy and create us: Poetic vs. Prosaic; Empirical vs. Romantic; Memory vs. Imagination; Soul vs. Body; Pauper vs. Millionaire... how, though many try, 95% of us fail to break through the prison walls of our divided natures: how we fail to absorb, and thereby triumph over, our equal opposites. And so on.

• •

It never occurred to me that my brother might have taken his own life for a good reason. On the contrary and despite my mother's dire predictions, when I saw him hanging there I was entirely perplexed; astonished. I couldn't imagine why he had done it. *He had everything to live for.* He was so successful, so recognized, so admired. He'd realized every one of his—my—dreams.

So I assumed.

As the initial horror subsided, however, it struck me that my brother's suicide wasn't so astonishing after all. In fact, the more I thought about it, the more inevitable it seemed.

Like me—like all the men in the Detweiler clan—Gregory suffered from depression. I knew his deepest, his darkest despairs. I knew them because I suffered dark, deep despairs of my own, identical deep dark despairs. Still, of the two of us Greg had been more like my father. They were close to each other in ways that I was never close to my dad. As I think I've said, it felt to me at times as if my brother and my father were more twinned than Greg and I, they were so close. It was no surprise to anyone—more of a foregone conclusion—when, like his father, Gregory became a professor of philosophy. In other ways too they were closer. They got along better. As we both grew older my brother enjoyed summering with my father at this lake house much more than I did. While I grew to resent those summers away from my friends and the familiarities of home, Greg thrived on the same deprivations. I imagined them taking the same morning and sunset walks my father and I had taken, but with Gregory lapping up the same philosophical monologues that had me gnashing my teeth. He'd come home bearing the latest thick tome from our father's library—*Critique of Pure Reason, Fear and Trembling, Being and Nothingness*—books I'd dip into when he wasn't looking and that within a page or two induced in me a blend of nausea and narcolepsy.

Given how closely my brother followed in our father's footsteps, is it any wonder that his life came to the same end? As I've said before, it's a statistical fact that the children of suicides are twice as likely to commit suicide. For Greg the odds were probably higher, first because he looked up to and emulated our father, and secondly because—as if the incubus of our father's suicide had not in itself posed a sufficient burden—he suffered the trauma occasioned by the manner in which he learned of it.

It was Gregory who, fifteen years ago to this day, found our father hanging from a ceiling beam, the one three feet above and two feet behind where I'm sitting now. It was a rainy winter's day much like this one. As would be the case with my brother fifteen years later, no one had heard from our father in a while. It was assumed that he'd sailed into what he called his "Intertropical Convergence Zone," the Doldrums, as he tended to each year during the winter solstice. But when December turned into January and January to February with still no word from him, my brother made up his mind to find out what had happened.

Greg asked me to go with him. I declined. I was too busy. I was at a "crucial point" in my novel, in the midst of one of my countless revisions. I didn't want to break the flow.

Meanwhile in his self-imposed lakeside solitary confinement, all of our father's doubts, his depressions, his despair, his view of himself as a failure at all things, as a philosopher, a father, an author, even as a professor, progressed from an occasional acute ailment to a chronic condition, one that eventually consumed his every thought and feeling, paralyzing him, infecting every cell in his body. The everyday chores of his existence—making the bed, brushing his teeth, watering the geraniums on his deck, feeding himself—confronted him with a monumental sense of futility and hopelessness. The perfect life that he'd taken such pains to construct for himself had left him dead and empty at his core. Had his stomach been sturdier he might have taken to drink. Instead he took to his own sentiments, which was worse. Day by day, month-by-month, his sense of hopelessness grew stronger, assuming monstrous proportions. As it grew so did his paralysis and his rage. Since the parasite fed on his substance, the only way for him to destroy it was to obliterate himself.

One winter's day, with a length of blue nylon rigging rope and a convenient ceiling beam, that's what our father did. Two weeks later, my brother arrived by car to confront the result. He found our father stripped to his soiled undershorts, hanging there, in the shadowy putrescence of his Cathedral-ceilinged A-frame. As when I found my brother, the main circuit breaker was thrown. Like me he must have stood there for some time in that gruesomely gloomy space disbelieving his own eyes as tears rolled out from them, cooling as they slid down his cheeks.

Gregory never told me any of these things. From a gas station phone he called me to tell me that our father was dead, that he had hanged himself. And though I pressed him for details, he refused to say anything more. It was up to me to phone our mother. Her reaction to the news was telling. With a sigh she said, simply:

"Well, that's that."

Gregory's love affair with self-reinvention was a natural outgrowth of his desire to escape his father's fate, to cheat the destiny programmed into him by his genes as well as by the fact that he had modeled much of his own life after our father's. In a double sense, by way of both nature and nurture, he'd lived in that man's shadow. So he changed. For all intents and purposes, by all appearances, he became another, completely different man. So we all thought.

But a man can't escape his basic nature any more than a tiger can outrun its stripes. For all his self-reinvention, he wound up hanging from the same ceiling beam.

That's how I explained my brother's suicide to myself, until I learned there was a better reason, or anyway a more immediate one. Her name: Melody Jenkins Baker. She was sixteen years old. She lived with her uncle in Wetumpka, Alabama.

His name was Lester Figes.

20. CHARLIE & CHARLEY

I LEARNED ON A FOGGY MORNING, ONE OF THOSE MORNINGS WHEN a thick fog turned everything gray, that non-hue arrived at by combining white and black, those antithetical impossible colors: so what I saw through the French doors where the lake and the sky should have been was a union of equal opposite impossibilities. If there was a red boat out there I couldn't see it.

The afternoon before from the mysterious 334 area code I had received the following text message:

i no where u live

Followed seconds later by:

so do they

I heard the sound of a car engine followed by the crunch of tires rolling on gravel. Two car doors slammed. I heard two pairs of crepe-soled shoes making their way down the boards to my side of the deck. A female voice called:

"Yoo-hoo! Dr. Jones? Is anyone there?"

In life as in art, clichés exist at every level. There are linguistic clichés, character clichés, clichés of substance, structure, and style. There are sentimental clichés, intellectual clichés, clichés of the mind, of the heart, and of the soul. What sets great writers apart comes down to the degree of sensitivity to which their cliché meters ("shock-proof shit detectors" Hemingway called them) have been calibrated.

Yet even the most finely calibrated cliché meter can't rescue you from cliché any more than a Geiger counter can prevent radiation. It merely warns you of the danger. But unlike radiation, clichés can't be avoided. They're everywhere. Since they can't be eliminated, the trick is to subvert or enhance them, as one enhances jar spaghetti sauce by adding sautéed onions and red wine.

Sometimes, though, authors go too far. They overcorrect, carrying their characters so far from cliché they strain credulity.

• •

So it was on that foggy May day when, at seven a.m., crying, "Yoo-hoo! Anyone in there?" two Atlanta Field Office Special FBI Agents came calling, a man and a woman, he a black man, she white, both sharing the same first name, and both wearing suits of dark seersucker with bowties and carrying plated silver hip flasks in their breast pockets—filled, presumably, not with bourbon but with sweet tea.

Okay, the seersucker suits and bowties are embellishments (as to the hip flasks, I can't warrant that they carried them; but then nor can I warrant that they did not). Nor was I summoned with the words *Yoo-hoo*! But they were two FBI agents, and their given names were Charlie—though hers was "Charley," C-H-A-R-L-E-Y, while his was "Charlie," C-H-A-R-L-I-E. I had long enjoined my Metropolitan students against assigning incredible, too similar, or otherwise confusing names to their fictional characters. But this is non-fiction so it can't be helped.

To make matters even worse, the agents' surnames were, I kid you not, "Smith" (hers) and "Jones" (his)—and so one of them shared my newly-inherited ultra-generic last name.

Apart from female Charley's high cheekbones and male Charlie's chunky build and flaccid face, I have little more to say about these two, descriptively, beyond that they were without question FBI agents who filled the threshold of my freshly red-painted front door.

One of them, the man, asked:

"Are you Mr. Gregory Detweiler?"

I had to think about that.

"Or Brock Jones?"

I thought harder. "That all depends," I answered.

"Is this 67 Turtle Cove Drive?" asked the woman.

"It is indeed."

"And this is your home?"

"That, too, is subject to debate."

"Do you live here?" he asked impatiently.

"Yes—and no."

"What's that supposed to mean?" asked his partner.

"Yes, I am living here. Provisionally."

"Provisionally?"

"For the time being."

The woman turned to her partner, who fished a photo from his portfolio case and handed it to her. She held the photo up next to my head.

"Yep. It's him, all right. Take a look."

Her partner took a look.

"Uh-huh," he agreed. "It's him."

"I guess it must be me," I said with what I hoped was a mordant grin.

"You're Mr. Brock Jones—the author?"

"Brock Jones, PhD," I was tempted to say, but resisted. "Yes. That's me."

In unison they flashed their credential wallets, complete with polished gold badges.

"Charlie Jones, FBI," said the man.

"Charley Smith, FBI," said the woman. "May we come in, sir?"

I'd been in the middle of my morning exercise regimen, on my way to fifty sit-ups, when I heard the knock. I wore a pair of blue sweatpants and nothing else. I stepped aside; they entered.

"Nice place," said Ms. Charley Smith, looking around.

"Do you mind if I put on a shirt?" I asked.

"Be our guest," said Mr. Charlie Jones.

In the bedroom I threw on a t-shirt and returned to find Charlie Jones eyeing the screen of my tablet, which I'd left open on the dining room table, while his partner looked up at the boat that I'd brought back inside and re-hoisted to the ceiling. I closed the tablet.

"Nice canoe," said Charley Smith.

"It's not a canoe. It's an Adirondack guide boat."

"Is it just for decoration or do you actually use it?"

"I use it occasionally. Very, very occasionally. Almost never, as a matter of fact. Do you mind telling me your purpose here?"

"What would be your guess?" said Ms. Charley.

"A missing persons investigation?"

"Good guess," said Mr. Charlie.

"Congratulations," I said. "You found me."

"Actually, Mr. Jones," said Charley, "you are not the person that we have been looking for."

"Oh?"

"Might I have a seat?" said Charlie.

"Huh? Oh. Sure. Uh…Can I get you both something? Coffee?" I felt a touch of nausea.

"We're fine, thank you."

They occupied the two wicker chairs; I sat on the wicker sofa.

"So—who *are* you looking for?"

From a pocket of his suit Charlie withdrew a photo of a not very good-looking man in his thirties or early forties, a quite ugly man, as a matter of fact, with a long, flaccid face, blotchy pale skin, sleepy eyes, a droopy nose, and a spiky crew-cut.

"You wouldn't happen to know this person, by any chance, would you?" he asked.

I shook my head. "I've never seen him." I hadn't. Seen him.

"Does the name Lester Figes mean anything to you?" Charley asked, pronouncing it "Fie-jess," with a soft "g."

I shook my head. "Never heard of him. Why? Is it supposed to mean something to me?" My heart was racing—or doing whatever hearts do when you know you're lying.

"He heard of you, apparently," said Charley.

"Yes, well. So have many people." I smiled.

"My wife's a big fan of yours," said Charlie.

"Is that so?"

"So is she." Charlie nodded with his chin to Charley.

"I'm halfway through your latest," Charley affirmed. "*The First Day of the Rest of Your Life*. I've got it in the car."

"Good for you," I said.

"Read the other one, too, the first one. You know, the coffee one?"

"*Coffee, Black*."

"Yeah. It was great."

"Thank you."

"I read that one myself," said Charlie Jones. "Interesting theory you put forth."

"You don't sound all that convinced."

He frowned. "In my experience, people can change all they like, sooner or later they go back to being who they were. Like water in a well."

I turned to Charley Smith. "Do you concur?"

Charley Smith shrugged. "It's like they say, you can't outrun your own shadow."

"A tiger can't outrun its stripes," Charlie Jones capitulated.

"But I still loved your book," Charley Smith put in quickly.

"So—you believe human beings are powerless in the face of destiny. A pair of fatalists."

The two agents exchanged looks.

"Makes you wonder," I said, smiling but with an edge to my voice, "why we even bother trying to make anything of ourselves. I mean, what's the point?"

"We have no choice," said Charlie. "Like you say, we're fated to do so."

"To outrun our own shadows, even though it's impossible," added Charley.

"That's right," said Charlie. "Even though it's impossible."

"Hmm," I said.

"Then again, what do we know?" Charley said. "I mean, heck, Mr. Jones—"

"Dr. Jones."

"—you wrote the book on it."

"Actually, I've written four books," I corrected her.

"Four books! And here we are talking like it's any of our

business!" said Charlie.

"What *is* your business?" I asked, my patience running thin. "Just what is it that I'm supposed to have to do with this Lester whatshisface, whoever he is?"

"Figes," said Charley. "Lester Figes."

"We have reason to believe that he may have come here to see you," said Charlie.

"Here? To my home, you mean?"

"To this house."

"To see you," said Charley.

"See me what for?" I said.

"To transact some business."

"Some business. What sort of business?"

"If you don't mind, Mr. Jones," said Charlie, "it would save a lot of time if you let us be the ones asking questions."

"You say you never saw him?"

"Never."

"Never spoke to him on the phone?"

"No."

"Never texted or emailed him?"

"Nor telegraphed. Nor smoke-signalled. Nor communicated telepathically. As far as I know."

"How far is that?" Charlie wished to know.

"What about Melody Jenkins Baker? That name ring any bells?" asked Charley.

"Never heard of her either," I lied.

Charlie: "You've had no contact of any sort with or by someone by that name?"

"Not to my knowledge." I felt sweat gathering around the elastic of my undershorts.

Charley: "Mr. Jones, I urge you to please consider the possible repercussions of your not telling us the truth."

"I *am* telling you the truth, what little I know of it."

"Let us tell you what we know, Mr. Jones." said Charley. "We know that starting back in early January of 2014 you and Ms. Baker had a series of communications via the Internet, via Skype but also via email. As for the nature of these communications—"

"There's no need to go into all that at this moment," said Charlie. "Is there, Charley?"

"Suffice it to say that you were in touch with each other over a period of approximately two months starting that January until about the end of March. According to records obtained by our office. Do you deny it?"

"There's no point denying it, Mr. Jones," said Charlie.

"I'm not denying anything. I don't happen to remember any of it, but I don't deny it. What does all this have to do with Lester whoever?"

"Melody Baker is Mr. Figes' niece," said Charley.

"Lester Figes is Melody Baker's uncle," Charlie clarified.

"Fine. So he's her uncle," I said. "So?"

"She's the person that reported him missing. She's also the person who suggested to us that he may have come here to see you."

"Really? Did she say why?"

Charlie: "Like I said, some business transaction."

"What sort of business?"

Charley: "That's something we were hoping you'd tell us."

"I would if I knew."

"So you deny that you ever saw Lester Figes?"

"Never saw him. Never knew him. Don't know him. Don't care to know him."

"He never came here?"

"Never. At least not while I've been here."

"As far as you know, you never spoke with him?"

I stood up. "I'm sorry, Mr. Smith, Ms. Jones—"

"I'm Jones," Charlie corrected, pointing. "She's Smith."

"This conversation is over. If you want to speak to me any further, it will have to be through my attorney." Did I *have* an attorney? As Stewart Detweiler I never had one. But to be sure Brock Jones, PhD. had a small army of them.

Agent Smith smiled. "I was wondering when we'd come to that."

"You've come to it."

Charlie and Charley stood. Charley looked up at the boat.

"Sure is a pretty canoe," she said.

"Guide boat," I corrected.

"How much weight do you suppose a boat like that can carry? Off the top of your head?"

"I haven't the foggiest."

"At least two people, wouldn't you say?"

"No. I'd say no such thing. In fact I believe I've said enough. So long, Miss Jones. Mr. Smith."

They started toward the door. As she reached it Charley turned. "Stewart Detweiler, that your brother's name?"

I stared at her.

"Your *twin* brother? Right?"

"What about my brother?"

"Who is he when he's at home?"

"He's a writer."

"Oh? What has *he* written?"

"Nothing that you will have heard of."

"Are you and your brother close?"

"Not especially, no."

"When did you last see each other?"

"It's been a while."

"A while?"

"A … few years."

"Does your twin brother — ?"

"Good day, Ms. Jones."

"Smith. He's Jones."

"Good day to both of you."

"We'll be in touch," said Charley Smith.

"Through my attorney if at all," I said.

"Enjoy the rest of your day," said Charlie Jones.

Both agents extended their hands. I held the door open.

• •

The fog had started to lift. I stood outside watching them walk to the green vintage Willy's Overland station wagon they had arrived in, complete with faux wooden side-panneling. Something occurred to me then. As he opened the wagon's door, I called out to them:

"Yes, Dr. Jones?"

"I would very much appreciate it if you'd please do your best to respect my privacy. Keep my whereabouts out of the papers, if you can. If at all possible."

"We'll do our best," said Charlie Jones.

"Long as this investigation's ongoing," said the other Charley, "your secret is safe with us."

"From the tabloids, anyway," said Charlie Jones, smirking.

"I appreciate it."

"We'll keep it under our hats," said Charley, tipping hers.

They climbed into the Overland.

I watched them drive off through the lifting fog.

21. ETC.

AMONG MY FONDEST AUTHORIAL ASPIRATIONS HAS BEEN THAT OF
pulling off the greatest literary red herring in all of literature. In this
endeavor my role model would have to be Chapter X of Gogol's
Dead Souls, wherein a postmaster tells the story of one Captain
Kopeikin, a soldier returned from the campaign of 1812 minus
one arm and with a wooden leg and who may or may not be a
figment of another fictional character's imagination. The story, told
in elaborate detail, purports to account for the mysterious identity
of Chichikov, the book's main character, a corrupt former govern-
ment functionary who, in a get-rich-quick scheme, wanders the
countryside purchasing "dead souls" (serfs no longer living but for
whom, owing to a flawed census system, their landlords still had to
pay taxes). The postmaster's monologue goes on for some ten pages
before one of his listeners interjects, "You have said that Kopeikin
had lost an arm and a leg; whereas Chichikov..." At which point
the postmaster smites his forehead and excuses his glaring error,
saying: "...in England the science of mechanics had reached such
a pitch that wooden legs were manufactured which would enable
the wearer, on touching a spring, to vanish instantaneously from
sight." Imagine a whole novel culminating in such an obvious error
on the narrator's part, one that, as you turn the last page, obliterates

everything that preceded it. Who could forgive—or forget—it?

My second fondest authorial aspiration, of a piece with the first, is to produce a narrative that disintegrates—imperceptibly at first, then like a meteor burning through the atmosphere—into random notes and jottings, a debris-trail of contingent passages, sentences, phrases, images, data, ideas, inspirations and insights. A novel reduced to rubble.

A self-destructing novel.

Why is this idea so attractive to me?

• •

The Saturday following our afternoon in the Rockaways, I met Ashley at the Café Sabarsky, a Viennese café annexed to the Neue Gallery on the corner of Fifth Avenue and 86th Street. I was in an unusually good mood, having slept well three nights in a row, thanks to the capsules Dr. Snyder prescribed for me, a drug that addressed the worst symptoms of my BPH by relaxing the muscles of the bladder neck as well as the tissues of the prostate itself, making it easier for me to urinate. True, it had its unpleasant side effects, including hypotension (low blood pressure) that made me black out when I stood up too quickly—as happened to me that time on the shuttle platform at Times Square when, in a hurry to catch my train, I blacked out to find myself engulfed by solicitous fellow passengers, the looks of concern on their faces deeply touching—and the aforementioned possible "retrograde ejaculation," though I'd yet to experience the latter, having had neither the curiosity nor the inclination to test-drive that aspect of my manhood. As for the drug's other potential side effects, a list as long as my forearm, I put them out of my mind. The point is I'd been sleeping well; I felt good. "Like a new man," as it were.

With a notebook open in front of me, over Viennese coffee and apple strudel Ashley and I arrived at a rough outline for her opening chapters. From there we cabbed it across the park to her Central Park West one-bedroom co-op, where we were greeted by Ashley's uniformed doorman. We spent the rest of the day there, working in her well-appointed dining room, with its Chippendale table and matching highboy, with me pacing behind Ashley as she clicked away at her MacBook using all ten of her slender, French-manicured fingers.

We made a good team. The sentences I fed to her Ashley improved and vice-versa. It was like playing tennis with a good partner. You hit the ball hard, I hit it back harder.

By noon we'd arrived at what we both felt was a solid first chapter. It found the heroine and her octogenarian ultra-conservative media mogul paramour, Bernard T. Rex, in a Plaza suite bed together. Ashley and I took equal pride in the novel's first sentence, wherein the wheezing mogul comes up for air following a prolonged session of cunnilingus. It was Ashley who provided the touching detail of having the mogul's puffing, blood-engorged, liver-spotted cheeks "glisten" with her heroine's bodily fluids, lifting a pedestrian scene from its humble origins into sublimity. With giddy satisfaction she read the passage out loud to me. As opening gambits go it was quite effective. It got things off, so to speak, to a good start.

By three o'clock we had a half-dozen good pages.

"This deserves a cocktail," Ashley announced, extracting a bottle of chilled *Veuve Clicquot* from her freezer.

One window of her apartment (the rent on which had to be over six grand) overlooked a church. You could see the stained-glass windows. As I stood admiring its convivial colors Ashley came up from behind me and handed me my drink.

"Here's to a successful collaboration," she said, kissing my cheek, her other arm around my waist. "Care to see the rest of my digs?"—meaning her boudoir, the one room I hadn't seen.

If I expected a massive poster bed with a frilly canopy like the one she had described in those early pages of hers, I was disappointed. The bed was plain as was the room itself, its walls painted a pale pistachio green. One thing stood out: a painting over the bed, a landscape in thick impasto strokes, with a pair of vague draped figures and a smeared yellow sun smack dab in the center of a sickly sky. At first I assumed it was a reproduction, but a closer examination proved otherwise.

"This is an original Rouault," I said.

"A what?" asked Ashley.

I faced her. "You own a Rouault."

Ashley's eyes deepened with emptiness.

"Georges Rouault. The Fauvist master?"

She kept staring.

Among the other paintings in Ashley's bedroom were two more whose artists were known to me. A Vlaminck and a Dufy—Jean, not Raoul.

"Have you any idea what these paintings are worth?" I couldn't help asking.

Ashley shrugged. "They're not mine. They're my mother's. She bought them a long time ago at different auctions. She didn't have room for them in her house, she said, so she asked if I could store them for her."

Store them indeed, I thought.

"Gadzooks, quit looking at me like I just kicked you in the teeth! They're just little old paintings, for goodness' sake!"

"They belong in a museum," I said.

"What has a museum got over my bedroom?"

She had me there.

"Know what your problem is, Detweiler?"

"Do please tell me: what's my problem?"

"Your problem is you take everything too seriously. Well I've got a secret for you. Life isn't serious. Not *that* serious. I say that as someone who used to report the news."

As someone who owns a Rouault, I thought.

"Are we going to stand here yakking about art?" she said. "Cuz I don't know about you, but I for one can think of *way* better uses for our time and this bedroom."

So saying, she relieved me of my flute, tore me from the Dufy I'd been admiring, and—in keeping with the heritage of the artwork on her walls—French kissed me.

"Supposing I were to fall madly in love with you, as they say?" I conjectured between kisses.

"Supposing you cross that bridge when you get to it?" she answered as she pulled me back onto her bed. "Get it—crossing Ashley Bridges?"

"Funny. Supposing I've already crossed it?" I asked, straddling her.

"Supposing I should charge you a toll!"

"Supposing I cross it and you don't?" I wondered.

"Supposing you live in the moment for once in your life, Stewart Detweiler, or anyway for the next half hour." From under she grabbed my hindquarters and ground herself into me.

"Make it twenty minutes and I'll consider."

"Twenty-five. That's my drop-dead minimum."

"Only if you promise to be gentle with me," I said.

"I'll try not to break any of those brittle old professor bones of yours, Professor."

"It's not my bones I'm worried about."

She rolled out from under me, then stood undressing by her bed as I lay there on my side watching her do so in a state half of wonderment, half of tumescence, and half of...what I'm not sure, exactly. Incredulity? Skepticism? Suspicion? It was as though I were watching her from inside a dream—a nice dream, but a dream nonetheless, from which I would inevitably have to wake up. Meanwhile she slipped out of her ecru camisole under which she wore no bra.

"Are you just going to sit there, or are you planning on joining me one of these days?"

I sat up and began to unbutton my shirt. Note the phrasing: "...*began to* unbutton." When students of mine wrote "so-and-so *began to* such-and-such," I'd point out that the beginning of an action is implied by the action itself, hence no need for the so-called "crank verb." The exception applies when the action is incomplete or interrupted, as was so in this instance, since while unbuttoning my shirt something occurred to me—or rather something *failed to* occur to me, something that *ought to have* occurred to me, according to the laws of attraction and nature. Yet at that moment it pointedly did not occur; it pointedly made itself scarce.

Very well, Dear Reader, if you insist on bald pronouncements: *I couldn't get it up.* Or it didn't get itself up. It sat (reclined? lounged? flopped?) against my inner thigh, where, I sensed, nothing would rouse it. That every day for the past five days I'd swallowed one of Dr. Snyder's capsules didn't help matters, nor did knowing that among the drug's long list of side-effects was the "inability to achieve or maintain an erection"—a prophecy that, self-fulfilling or not, had nonetheless come to pass. Had those pills contained cocaine or confectioner's sugar they would have achieved the same unwanted result.

Seeing my lack of progress in various categories, Ashley, naked now save for a pair of tangerine slouch socks, asked:

"What's wrong, Professor?"

"I was just thinking," I said.

This was so, for in the vacuum occasioned by the absence of certain physiological responses, in that Central Park West bedroom decked out with fin de siècle masterpieces, as—on her knees on her parquet floor—Ashley Bridges took up where I'd left off, unbuttoning my shirt, yanking its tail from my Dockers, my thoughts drifted to none other than Betsy Butterworth. Part of the cause was the part in Ashley's reddish-blonde hair. Seen from above at that angle, it could easily have been Betsy's. The hair was the same color, or close to it, and for all I remembered it had been parted the same way, to where for a moment anyway it was Betsy Butterworth naked on her knees on the parquet floor, or may as well have been; Betsy Butterworth yanking the tails of my shirt from my Dockers; Betsy Butterworth undoing the clasp of my belt, unzipping my fly, tugging down its recalcitrant zipper. As I sat there with my palms pressed flat on her mattress, studying the part of Ashley's hair, I wondered: whatever became of Betsy Butterworth? Had she parlayed those cunning charms of hers into a successful adulthood? Was she married, wealthy, happy? Did she have children, and, if so, had they gone off to college by now and/or had children of their own? Had she become a corporate executive, a fashion consultant, a Marine helicopter pilot, the owner of a brothel, a sex therapist, a breeder of exotic animals? Was she at that moment sunbathing on the fantail of a super yacht docked at Palma de Mallorca or Portofino? Or had she crashed and burned as do so many of youthful promise, gone on to drugs and debauchery, become a Jehovah's Witness or a Republican or a frumpy housewife—or a combination of all of the above? As I entertained these speculations, Ashley kept at it, trying to coax some life out of my unwitting, unwilling dick. Though my mouth was as dry as the

Kalahari, I swallowed hard, aware that her efforts were entirely in vain, that the bounty she sought was not to be found where she sought it; that like Geraldo, she, too, would be disappointed, that the contents of my Fruit of the Looms were as sodden and dismal as those in Al Capone's vault.

"Tsk, tsk! What have we *here*? A lazy pupil asleep in the first row! We can't have that, now, can we, Professor?"

With that she kept on trying. As she labored, I couldn't stop thinking of all kinds of unhelpful things, chief among them how the scene occurring before me would best be translated into prose, how, in order to evoke it faithfully, one could hardly avoid figu rative language. What metaphor(s), I asked myself, would prove most felicitous, most apt? To avoid bathroom humor or bathos ("a descent from the lofty or exalted into the commonplace: comedown; anticlimax"), not to mention a minefield of predictable puns, the rendering of such a scene would require a *stroke* of genius. It would present a *stiff* challenge. I'd have to give it some *very hard* thought. Would I *rise* to the occasion? Or would my talent *let me down*? It would be a shame to *blow it*... I was a one-way passenger on this train of thought when Ashley stopped what she was doing to look forlornly up at me. I shrugged, smiled.

"Is there anything I can do, Professor?" she asked mournfully. *Everything humanly possible has been done.*

"Come here," I said, hoisting her up from her rescue boat onto the deck of my sinking ship. Was it Balzac, I wondered, kissing her, who believed that in order to write a masterpiece one had to be chaste, who, each time he bedded a woman, is said to have whispered to himself ruefully afterwards, "There goes another masterpiece!"? Could I now whisper to myself, "Good show, old boy! Another masterpiece snatched from the jaws of perdition!"

• •

We spent the rest of that afternoon and part of the evening working on Ashley's manuscript. By seven o'clock we had written the first two chapters: thirty-eight pages, sufficient to keep a literary agent's appetite wet. Standing with my coat on by Ashley's opened apartment door, I felt an odd mixture of triumph and defeat.

"Sure you don't want to stay and have dinner with me?" said Ashley. "There's a sweet little bistro on 68th near Columbus. *Le Boite en Bois*. It means—"

"The well in the woods."

"*Exactement!*"

"Sounds lovely, but I really should be going."

"I can't thank you enough," she said.

"*De rien.*"

She kissed my cheek. "My knight in shining armor."

"Since it's complimentary I'll allow the cliché."

With a quick kiss I left her.

Why didn't I have dinner with her? Why be in such a hurry to board a gloomy subway and return to my equally grim Bronx hovel? Call it a premonition, the conviction, acquired from my dread-inclined mother, not that something was wrong, but that something was *about to be* wrong. As I left Ashley's building and walked west toward the subway at Verdi Square, I knew I could no more outrun this premonition than I could evade a nuclear onslaught aboard the uptown Number 1 IRT Broadway Local.

•   •

By now you must be wondering how I, Stewart Detweiler: accomplished, experienced, insightful, a Senior Instructor of Creative Writing—I who preached so steadfastly, so sternly and so passionately against the sin of cliché—could have fallen so hard for one? Was Ashley Bridges not a stereotype, *la belle dame sans merci*? And isn't a stereotype nothing more or less than the human embodiment of a cliché? How much of this was Ashley's fault, and how much mine, her creator's?

To the extent that Ashley is a stereotype, the blame must fall squarely on me, her incompetent author who has failed in his primary duty: to look. And not just to look, but to look *hard* and keep looking, until the object under scrutiny, no matter how seemingly vapid, white paint drying on a wall, reveals its hidden singular wonders. To a vigilant observer there is monumental wonder in the spectacle of white paint drying on a wall.

No, Dear Reader: to the extent that Ashley Bridges is a stereotype, I made her one.

You must also be wondering when if ever the author of this confession will make good on that claim he made several hundred pages back: when will he finally "come to doubt [him]self in every way"; i.e.: hit "rock bottom"? Though I've already filled all six composition notebooks and have been reduced to turning over the last one and writing between its lines in a hand so small it looks like secret code or spiral bacteria, and though I've drained a dozen pens, the ink gone from red to blue to black to red again, still your narrator doesn't appear to be in such dire shape. True, he has yet to publish his novel; true; his estranged twin has become a runaway success; true, thanks to the drug he's been taking for his prodigious prostate he can no longer get it up. Then again, he has gained the good graces of a young, beautiful, talented female pupil on whom he has a considerable crush. So what if she's something of a cliché? So what if she's too patently a symbol for the superficial success that he simultaneously deplores and craves for himself, the kind of success that comes to those who don't try too hard, who aren't in earnest, who care nothing for such things as "art" and "integrity"? So what if acceptance and approval belong to those who least deserve them, to the Betsy Butterworths and Brock Jones, PhDs and Ashley Bridges of the world? Still and all, some would consider Stewart Detweiler lucky. Or anyway not worthy of all that much pity.

Wait, Dear Reader. I promise you things are about to get worse for him.

• •

They did so a few days later on my way to my Wednesday evening class. In the meantime I had made good on my word and spoken to Sally Treadwell. I talked Ashley and her project up to the hilt. She's young, she's talented, she's beautiful. "Most importantly," I said, "she's got a novel with bestseller written all over it." I told my erstwhile agent that Ashley had been all set to offer said novel to Elizabeth "Bitsy" Watson. "But I got her to hold off till I had a chance to tell you about it."

It should go without saying that Sally was interested. Provided it was offered to her on an exclusive basis, she agreed to read the partial as soon as she had it in hand.

"And how are things with you, Stewart?" Sally asked me.

"Fine," I answered. "Just fine."

"Are you working on something new?"

"Of course. Aren't I always?"

No sooner did our phone conversation end than I emailed Ashley with instructions to send the opening chapters of her novel to Sally Treadwell using me as her reference.

Three days later, I was passing Gramercy Park, on my way to the Friends School, when I saw her. She wasn't alone. She and the Ken Doll—Arnold—were sitting together on a park bench. Though the bench faced away from the sidewalk, and though my view was obscured by the six-foot-tall iron fence that protects that pristine private park from riff-raff like yours truly, also by the light snow that fell just then, there was no mistaking the bench's two occupants. He wore a Loden coat; she an Inverness cape. Even from behind they were handsome. At first I made nothing of it. So they wore fancy coats. So they sat together. But then a short while later, as I spread out my documents in preparation for the evening's chamber session, as students filed into the classroom, unbuttoning coats, yanking off scarves and gloves and the other shackles of winter, I noted that Arnold and Ashley weren't among them. When at last Arnold arrived he was alone. This too I shrugged off, assuming Ashley had made a pit stop at the powder room. Only when, sometime later, with all the others including Arnold already having taken their seats, Ashley made her entrance, apologizing again exactly as on that first day of class, saying, in a breathless voice with her white-gloved hand to the base of her scarf-covered throat, "A late-breaking news story! Would you believe a bunch of loose crabs in the cargo hold of a US Airways 727 bound for Charlotte out of LaGuardia delayed its flight this morning? Talk about shell-fish passengers! Or crabby crewmembers. I'm still not sure which headline to use!" did the full extent of her betrayal dawn on me.

Me (smiling, *sotto-voce*): "I thought you'd quit your job?"

Ashley: "What gave you that idea?"

Me (forcing the same smile): "You said so."

Ashley (eyelashes aflutter, stage-whispering): "I told you I was *thinking* about it. You talked me out of it, remember?" With a wink she flounced off to her desk.

Had there been any lingering doubt, that moment should have eradicated it. If not, my doubt should have been eradicated when, after class, rather than wait for me while I put papers in my brief-case, Ashley said, "See you next week, Professor!" and started out the door. I called after her, asking if she didn't want to share a cab with me as usual, per what had become our routine. She mouthed the words "*Other plans*" and was gone.

Soon thereafter, gripping my briefcase in the classroom in which I'd switched off the lights, I stood facing the drafty street-level casement window through which I observed the following tableau: Ashley and Arnold walking arm-in-arm down the snowy sidewalk. It was, I had to admit to myself, a picturesque display. Sketched by Bemelmans or Birnbaum, it would have made a perfect *New Yorker* cover circa 1949. Halfway down the block, she fash-ioned a halfhearted snowball to toss at Arnold's back; he answered in kind. I watched them laugh and chase each other out of sight.

For a while afterwards I remained standing there, gazing out at the now empty (except for the falling snowflakes) sidewalk that, though still burnished pink by the mercury vapor streetlamp, plunged me into my own unique darkness. I doubt that I'd ever felt as empty, as ancient, as obsolete and irrelevant, as pathetically emasculated as I did then, at that moment.

• •

I rode the subway to Grand Central, but instead of going straight home I stopped at the Campbell Apartment and ordered an Armag-nac at the bar, thirteen dollars the glass. The blonde who served it reminded me of Ashley, but then so did everything. There were no other people at the bar. In a rapid series of gulps I swallowed the cognac and had another before boarding the 11:20.

I arrived home to find a package waiting for me in the vestibule of my tenement, a parcel left by the UPS man. By its size I knew what it was: a manuscript box. The moment forces me to relay to you another dream, a short one. In the dream I open such a box to encounter something unexpected: in place of a rejection letter, I find the words GREAT ENOUGH stamped in bright red across the manuscript's title page. Tucked under that page, on publishing house stationary, a letter from the acquisitions editor saying that, however flawed, he or she has found the manuscript to be of sufficient merit to slap between hardcovers. It would be published.

That was a dream.

This wasn't. Elizabeth "Bitsy" Watson had rejected "Duplicity."

• •

That morning, awake at two a.m. (having abandoned my new drug and consequently subject to my no-longer-suppressed incontinence), I found the following in my inbox:

To: *detweiler*

From: *a student in love*

> absolutely positively between just the two of us I really really need your opinion

> If you received a letter such as the attached, what would you think? Might it scare him off completely?

Him?

> I wasn't sure if I should tell you, but yes, my 'other plan' this evening was Arnold, and as of now he and I have an histoire together.

An *histoire?*

> Now I've written this, and I'm not sure I should send it. Mind you, it's not a critique of my deathless prose I'm looking for, though I'm sure it could use that, too. I just want to know your thoughts re: love letters like this one in general.

My thoughts. *In general.* My generic thoughts. She wants.

> For your eyes only, vous comprends? Merci beaucoup, mon charmant professeur.

> ab

Having resisted for all of five seconds, I opened the attachment.

The Boy Two Desks Over

A hazy humid September night in a city where all that surrounds her is strange, the sky over her head smeared with what she at first takes to be the Milky Way, but is in fact New York City smog.

She's late for class. Fiction writing: what she has dreamed of doing now for so many years, and why she's come to New York in the first place, flung far from her lazy hazy Mississippi childhood to this frenzy of swirling ambitions, straight into the noise and whip of the whirlwind, to live and write among fellow ink-stained wretches, to find an outlet for her molasses-rich, Southern fried musings.

She tumbles into the class—so like her, always late, clutching notebook and manuscripts, apologizing fervently as she makes her way across the room to the one still available desk, trying not to draw undo attention to herself as the teacher looks on with disdain...

... The *teacher*??

... As the lecture continues I survey the class, a dozen other students intent on discovering their voices, on telling their stories. Suddenly, to my left, two desks down, I see him: dark brown hair almost to his shoulders hiding most of his face, save a strong proud chin and aristocratically fine nose...

... "Aristocratically fine."

... a face designed to break hearts, and sure enough it's breaking mine already with the notion that I came here to concentrate on the written word and it's just my luck I have to plop myself two desks down from this gorgeous hunk whose eyelids lower dreamily as the teacher drones on...

... The teacher. *Drones on.*

... so I want to kiss them, yes I do; I want to stretch my neck muscles across the desk that separates us and bend forward and lay my lips gently one by one on each of those tired graceful eyelids of his, as soft and delicate as the petals of a blush rose. Discipline, Ashley Bridges, I tell myself, and no sooner think it than I'm dwelling on that crescent moon of flesh behind his left ear, wanting to kiss it, too, and maybe lick it for good measure. Lord, deliver me from supremely sexy men stamped with the Good Housekeeping Seal of Wholesomeness, yet fresh and unbroken....

... "yet fresh and unbroken."

Class over, she gathers her books and makes her way down the four linoleum flights and out into the darkness draped with gray moonlight, trembling with a mélange of conflicting desires...

Ashley's attachment closed with these lines by Apollinaire (the translation hers):

> *My mouth will flame the sulfurs of the Pit*
> *You will find my mouth a hell of sweetness and seduction*
> *My mouth's angels will hold sway in your heart*
> *My mouth's soldiers will take you by storm...*

I closed the attachment and sat there, fingers to mouth, staring at my computer screen. Of course I wouldn't respond. Why would I? I'd ignore her, the only dignified thing to do. Anyway what could I have said? That though she used verbs strikingly (the smog "smeared" across the sky) some of her metaphors ("molasses-rich") felt forced? That there was a comma splice in her first paragraph and what appeared to be an arbitrary point-of-view shift in the fourth? That her rendering of the love object was overripe, while that of "the teacher" (who, after all, was hardly a minor character) felt short-changed; in fact he was barely a character, let alone one well-rendered. Who is this teacher? What does he look like? Does the narrator find *him* attractive? Is he a good or a poor teacher? Does she find him clever? Interesting? Stimulating? Attractive? (You said *attractive* already. Did I? Yes, you did.) Might you exploit further the tension your protagonist must surely feel, torn between her perfunctory puppy love for a callow clothes horse and her far more profound and mature interest in the man who embodies her passion for the written word, the motive that brought her to this "strange" city in the first place? Why (oh why) does your heroine waste herself on some square-jawed flaxen-haired, broad-shouldered, insipid Ken doll when right there before her in that classroom stands a real man, a man of wisdom, talent, experience, substance. Is she fucking *blind*? Might I have said all or some of *that*?

I re-opened my e-mail application, chose Ashley's latest, hit "reply" and typed:

> I confess, I've never been asked to judge a love letter before. Unlike Cyrano, I'm not sure I have the nose for it. Since the first rule of good umpiring is to not be in the game, and as I prefer to think of myself as still being a "player" in the field of love ... well, you see my quandary?

I and the Armagnac still coursing through my circulatory system thought a bit before adding:

> If you're going to have a literary affair in which the bed of words squeaks as loudly as one of stuffing and springs, make sure your Romeo can give as good as he (literally) gets. Otherwise stick to body language — of which you have a more than ample supply.
>
> Yours Professorially,
>
> E. Rostand (writing for S. Detweiler)

I read through my response, fine-tuning it, making it a little more shapely, a little more concise. Then I discarded it.

Hitting "reply" again, I wrote:

> Arnold's a nice fellow and quite handsome I see the logic

I hit "send."

•   •

Perhaps you feel that at last this back-story has arrived at its destination, that Stewart Detweiler has finally touched "rock bottom." But the human spirit is a remarkably resilient organ. Mine survived this double assault—first to my artistic, then to my romantic, ego.

I spent the next very long day walking the streets of the city, from my neighborhood in the Bronx across the Broadway Bridge to Manhattan, then all the way downtown to Battery Park. The day was clear and invigoratingly cold. At the promenade railing across from Castle Clinton while eating a bag of roasted chestnuts I watched seagulls pursue a ferry as it lumbered toward the Statue of Liberty. While it may be true (I told myself while doing so) that I am no longer a young man, I'm not exactly old, either, let alone decrepit or dead.

I shall live to write—and love—another day.

And so, in the ensuing weeks, with stouthearted resolve I took care of business as usual. I critiqued my students' submissions, bought groceries, got a haircut. I brushed and flossed and saw to my other hygienic needs. Not only did I launder my clothes, I washed and ironed my sheets and, for the first time in recorded history, organized my sock drawer. In place of my morning espresso I drank herbal tea for breakfast. Did I draw any parallel with my brother's best-selling epiphany? If so, I wasn't aware; it was unconscious. I was simply going about my existence, with a little more pluck than usual, more *espirit de corps,* in solidarity with none other than myself. I smiled at subway conductors, at the cashier at the corner bodega where I bought groceries, and other service employees. I even smiled at myself in the medicine cabinet mirror while shaving. Happiness, as they say, is the best revenge.

But I wasn't feeling vengeful.

Philosophical? Reconciled? Resigned? There's a perfect word for it, but I can't think of it now. Anyway my life wasn't so bad, it really wasn't. Nor was I such a tawdry human specimen.

• •

One second thought I was a fool, a moron, a coward, a cuckold. Why hadn't I made love to Ashley in her apartment that day? So what if I couldn't get it up? I could have made it up to her by other means. Face it, I told myself (wherever I was, whatever I happened to be doing): you're unworthy, an unworthy lover, an unworthy writer, an unworthy human being.

Really? *Really?*

Buck up, Detweiler. Stop feeling so sorry for yourself. She's one alluring young woman among millions of alluring young women, one gleaming drop of saltwater in a boundless glimmering ocean.

• •

When my next Wednesday class rolled around, the second to last of the term, I treated Ashley Bridges no differently than I treated my other students. I smiled and joked and listened to what she had to say. I was honest, good-humored, respectful. She responded in kind. No one observing us in that classroom that evening would ever have guessed that we had been lovers, if that's what we'd been, much less that it had ended abruptly and un-mutually, with one party's heart (ego?) broken. Class over, I stood behind my desk watching her and Arnold walk out hand-in-hand, making no secret any longer of their newfound love. I smiled and nodded at them as they went by; I may even have given them a friendly cute little wave, you know, with just my fingers, the way old people do. Was my magnanimity merely the form taken by my denial? I like to think that Stewart Detweiler was made of sturdier stuff. I'd like to believe that his spirit extended further, broader, and deeper than envy, than jealousy, than wounded pride. *I am not a bad man!*

But the true—and, it turned out, final—test of Stewart Detweiler's spirit had yet to come.

22. WHAT'S IN A NAME?

WITH THE FBI GONE, BACK IN THE HOUSE, I GRABBED A TOWEL, MY trunks, and my goggles. With them I returned to the dock. When in doubt, swim.

The sky was overcast. In consideration of my neighbors (whom I'd never seen), while changing I covered myself with the towel. Then I thought: to hell with it and let the towel drop. With my goggles on and my swimming trunks playing piggyback on the crest of one of the two Adirondack chairs, feet first and fully naked, I plunged and started swimming.

While swimming, I mulled over the scene described in the second to last chapter. Needless to say it left me with many questions, but mainly one: Who is/was Lester Figes?

To answer that question, it helped to ask another, namely: What's in a name? As a Senior Instructor at the Metropolitan Writing Institute, I preached the values of titles and names: titles, because they help us know what our stories are about, and names because they tell us who our characters are. You can't truly know someone and not know their name. It's one of the first things we learn about people. If people are books, their names are the titles. These and other such thoughts synchronized themselves to the pattern and rhythm of my strokes while swimming to my neighbor's dock and back.

As for how we know when we've given a character the right name, that gets down to the heart of what fiction writers do, to what the uninitiated would see as a contradiction in terms, to the matter of "fictional truth." Yet not only is there such a thing, without it fiction couldn't exist. Name a character Harold whose name should be Horace, and though the reader can't know it, they will experience that character as less true. Call Gertrude Griselda and with respect to the fictional truth you may as well have named her Tom, Dick, or Harry.

So (I asked myself while swimming laps), applying the concept in reverse: to what sort of fictional character would I give the name Lester Figes? For sure it wasn't a name fit for a heroic figure. A character with such a name would have to be a loser, a schlemiel (see: Tommy Wilhelm in Bellow's *Seize the Day*): the timid, well-meaning wimp (Caspar Milquetoast), the henpecked husband (Walter Mitty), the indecisive weakling (Ashley Wilkes), the treacherous sycophant (Iago). Lester as in *lesser* and *jester* (lowly fool), but who also tends to *stir* things up or is a *turd;* Figes as in *figures* (calculates) and a *fig* (what no one gives for him) and *fugue* as in "a fugue state" ("period of loss of awareness of one's identity, often coupled with flight from one's usual environment, associated with certain forms of hysteria and epilepsy"); fugitive: "one who has escaped or is in hiding, a refugee; or (adj.) fleeting transitory, impermanent, faded or fading." Here today gone tomorrow, evanescent. An insignificant human specimen, insect-like, solitary, who preys on other lowly helpless creatures.

Profession? Why, an *exterminator,* of course.

Back from my swim, naked and damp at the computer, I did a little research. Lester: from ancient Anglo-Saxon first found in Cheshire, England, derived from concatenation of Old English tribal "Ligore" and "ceaster," referring to a Roman or Walled City.

Figes: possibly Scandinavian, son of Vig (or Wig or Wigg: change from "V" to "F" as in Venn/Fenn, Vowler/Fowler, Venner/Fenner, etc.); v. Figgin. "Feg" dates to Yorkshire ante 1086, and "Figge" to Kent, 31 (Edw. III). Later period in same county yielded "Figgs," "Faggs," "Foggs," also kindred forms "Fig," "Figgs," "Figes." All the same origin, Old French from the L. "fagus": a beech tree. Lester Figes = a beech tree in a walled Roman city?

None of this was helpful.

A Google search of "Lester Figes" + "Wetumpka" turned up a Facebook page for his extermination services, including address and phone number.

My search for "Melody Jenkins Baker" turned up 62,703 Melody Bakers, 5,384 Melody Jenkins, 4 Melody Bakers, and 2 Jenkins Bakers, none with any connection to Wetumpka or anywhere else in Alabama.

What could Brock Jones, PhD possibly have had to do with an Alabaman exterminator and his niece?

It made no sense, none at all.

While gazing at the computer screen, I heard the patter of raindrops striking the deck behind me. I went out for my towel, which I had draped over the rail. Soon it was pouring again.

• •

I'd hung my towel and swimsuit on the shower rod and settled into one of the wicker chairs in the living room (or the living "area," since it's not really a room; that is, it has no walls other than those it shares with the dining room and the kitchen) to read a book from my father's "Twin" bookcase, a novel. Written by Arthur Hornblow and published in May of 1913 — a little over a year after the *Titanic* sank — *The Mask* is the story of millionaire Kenneth Traynor, the director of a New York mining firm. Summoned to the diamond mines of Africa to investigate a claim, he encounters his long-lost, drunk, dissolute, poverty-stricken identical twin brother "Handsome Jack." Resolved to rescue his twin from a life of destitution, along with the second largest diamond in the world, Kenneth brings Jack with him on the steamer bound for New York. When, in mid-ocean, a fire breaks out aboard the steamship, in the ensuing panic Jack strikes Kenneth, stealing his papers and the diamond and leaving his brother for dead. Back in New York, Jack passes himself off as his presumed-dead twin, fooling not only Kenneth's wife, but everyone else in his circle. Meanwhile the real Kenneth returns to expose and avenge his twin's villainy.

Such a ridiculously implausible plot! Imagine authors getting away with such things! Yet they did; they still do.

Sensationally implausible plot or no, partway through the book I must have dozed off. The next thing I knew, the phone—Brock's phone, Twinkle, which I'd left on the coffee table—woke me with its arpeggio. It was my mother.

"Hi, Mom," I said.

"What are you up to?"

"I was just reading a book."

"Just like your brother. Always with your face in a book."

It had grown dark outside. According to the phone it was half-past-six. I must have dozed for two hours. I switched on the multi-colored hydra lamp next to the wicker chair.

"What's up, Mom?"

"Janet Butterworth. Remember her?"

"Who?"

"Big red hair. Mouth full of fake teeth. Her daughter went to school with you. Betsy. Didn't you used to have a crush on her?"

"What about her?"

"Betsy? How should I know?"

"Not Betsy, her mother! What happened to her?"

"Janet? She's dead. Dropped dead, just like that. Third one this month. I tell you they're dropping like flies. I'll be next, probably."

"Don't say that."

"Why not? It's just a matter of time."

"Well—"

"Patrice Gorman? I don't think you met her. My canasta partner. Lupus. She just found out. A month ago it was Lyme Disease. A few months before that skin cancer. Now Lupus. And all on top of her son dying suddenly of a heart attack. He's taking his morning shower and boom, he drops dead, just like that. His wife found him. The shower was still running. His head was full of shampoo. Can you imagine? Poor thing. I tell you, life can be grim."

I nodded.

"Next week I'm going with the Red Hats to Harrah's."

"Harrah's?"

"The casino. On the Indian reservation. Cherokee, I think it is.

It's two hours by bus from here. I hope they don't give us the same driver. On the way home last time he made us all sick. Or maybe it was something we ate. Who knows? No one should eat shrimp cocktail. Your brother says hello, by the way. Have you spoken with him recently?"

"What?" I said.

"I just got off the phone with him. He said he's got floaters in his eyes. Other than that he sounds all right. He says he's writing again. Working on a new book or something."

"Mom—what are you talking about?"

"Floaters. You know, those little dark things that move around in your eyes."

"I mean...You talked to Greg? I mean—to Stew?"

"Yes."

"When?"

"I told you. A little while ago."

"Mom, that's—you didn't."

"What do you mean, I didn't? Of course I did!"

"I mean...you talked to him—today?"

"Yes: today."

"You're sure it wasn't yesterday?"

"What's wrong with you?"

"I'm just asking."

"I said *I just got off the phone with him.*"

"You called him?"

"Yes. No, wait. He called. What difference does it make?"

"Mom, are you absolutely positive you spoke to Stew today?"

"For goodness sakes."

"I just want to be sure, that's all."

"I'm not senile, you know. Not yet."

"I wasn't saying—"

"There's nothing wrong with my memory."

"I didn't say—"

"Why are you questioning me, then?"

"I'm not!"

"Yes, you are."

"I just wondered, that's all. I'm sorry."

"If I say I spoke with your brother, I spoke with your brother."

"Okay, Mom. Right."

"You might call him yourself once in a while, if you're so concerned, if you're so *curious*."

"Yes, I'll do that."

"They're ringing the gong. Dinner, so-called, is served."

"Bye, Mom."

"Goodbye. And don't read so much. It's doing things to you."

The line went dead.

•   •

I stared at the phone. Of course my mother was mistaken. She couldn't have spoken with my brother. She couldn't have phoned Stewart Detweiler since, had she done so, I would have answered. Nor could he have phoned her, since "he" was I, and I had done no such thing. So—she must have been confused. Yes: that must have been it. When had I—or rather when had Stewart—last spoken with her? It had been three days. Yes, she must have been thinking of that phone call. Had I said anything about floaters? I couldn't recall saying anything about floaters. Why would I have said anything about floaters? True: I had—still have—floaters in my eyes. I've had them for ten years. But it's been years since I've paid any attention to them. Why would I have brought them up? It didn't make any sense. My mother must have imagined the conversation. Or maybe she'd finally gone senile.

Or maybe she'd had a dream. Yes, that was it. You know how she's always dreaming things up. What do you suppose started this whole business? A senile dream. She'd dreamed a non-existent phone conversation with my former self, with Stewart Detweiler. Yes, that explained it, that made the most sense, that was the obvious solution, a logical solution that put the matter to rest for me.

Or was I the one who was dreaming? Had I dreamed the conversation with my mother just then? Was I *still* dreaming?

Or was I losing my mind? Or both?

I shook the thought out of my head.